THE DEATH OF
THE FRONSAC

NEAL ASCHERSON is a journalist
and historian. He reported from Asia,
Africa and Central Europe for the
Observer. He contributes regularly to
the *New York Review* and the *LRB*.
His books include *Stone Voices, Black
Sea, Games with Shadows* and
The Polish August.

NEAL ASCHERSON

THE DEATH OF THE FRONSAC

HEAD of ZEUS

An Apollo Book

This is an Apollo book. First published in the UK in 2017 by Head of Zeus Ltd
This paperback edition first published in 2018 by Head of Zeus Ltd

9 7 5 3 1 2 4 6 8

A catalogue record for this book is available from
the British Library.

ISBN (PB): 9781786694393
ISBN (E): 9781786694362

Typeset by Adrian McLaughlin

Printed and bound in Great Britain by
CPI Group (UK) Ltd, Croydon CRO 4YY

Head of Zeus Ltd
First Floor East
5–8 Hardwick Street
London ECIR 4RG

WWW.HEADOFZEUS.COM

For George Rosie

This story begins in the town of Greenock, in western Scotland, in the first year of the Second World War.

Greenock is an old seaport. It rises in tiers of stone tenements and terraced housing, up a steep hillside along the Clyde estuary. It looks down on the place where the river becomes enormous and turns south towards the ocean.

At its upstream end, Greenock merges into Port Glasgow – 'the Port'. Downstream, it finishes in the tilting town of Gourock – 'all on one side, like Gourock' – under its crown steeple.

Once Greenock was Scotland's door to Ireland and, later, the Atlantic. Then it became Scotland's gateway for emigrants and the hardware of the industrial revolution, pouring out towards every continent. For over a century, the Greenock shipyards built many of the steam-driven navies and merchant fleets on the seas of the planet.

When I was a wartime child in Greenock, the town still seemed to me the centre of the world. The battle fleets of the

Allied nations rode at their moorings under our windows. The great anchorage called 'the Tail of the Bank' displayed the ships of the Atlantic convoys, arriving and departing, discharging tanks and trucks and soldiers. The streets and bars were bright with the uniforms and loud with the voices of Americans, Canadians, Norwegians, Frenchmen, Czechs and Poles.

The Poles fascinated me. Who were they, with their swinging musketeer capes, their rattling language and their merry gallantry? (Scottish women soon discovered that 'they could all dance like Fred Astaire'.)

Less than a year before, in September 1939, their nation had been invaded simultaneously by Germany and Russia, who declared that Poland had been abolished for ever – 'the bastard of Versailles'. Hitler and Stalin partitioned its territories between them. But these soldiers had escaped to France to fight again. When France fell, the survivors reached England, and Churchill sent them to Scotland to recover and retrain.

The Poles had lost their country. Many of them, coming from eastern Polish provinces now annexed and renamed by the Soviet Union, had also lost their homes. But 'home' is an elusive concept in Polish culture. There is no precise translation for it; Joseph Conrad reflected that *ojczyzna* – literally, 'fatherland' – signifies at once less and much more than the English word. The young Polish officer at the centre of this story is exploring what sort of loyalty is denoted by 'home', for himself and for the Scots around him. (I should add that his opinions on politics and religion are his own, not necessarily mine.)

The tale starts in April 1940, in the final days of the 'phoney war'. Nobody – well, almost nobody – imagined that a sudden onrush was about to bring Hitler's tanks to Paris in less than five weeks.

In that last week of calm, a French warship – the heavy destroyer *Maillé-Brézé* – exploded off Greenock, killing most of its crew. Greenock is a mythopoeic town that has always bred novelists and poets, and this disaster touched off a second, imaginative explosion. Some accounts were grisly, some supernatural, some writhing with rumours of foreign spies and traitors. But these stories have haunted me since I first heard them as a boy. And this novel gathers some of them to suggest how the death of that ship, a single terrible but to this day not fully explained event, might have deflected and then stalked the lives of a group of men and women in the years ahead.

As with many other events in this book, I have changed names and some details of the disaster. The oldest Greenockians will notice that. There are stories here that I witnessed, stories that I was told and 'stories I stole'. In that last category is a scene about a Polish general's visit to an East Neuk fishing town, which I have adapted from a wartime sketch by Ksawery Pruszyński. The chapter about wreck salvage took guidance from the expert professional account by Frank Lipscomb and John Davies in their book *Up She Rises* (first published in 1966). The murders at the camp for SS prisoners at 'Abercultie' resemble, not very closely, murders which did take place in the camp at Comrie (Cultybraggan). Margaret and Tadek's love story is true, but their names were different. The French Commandant and his daughter were family friends of ours, and I have changed his name, too.

My gratitude goes to the archivists of the Service Historique de la Défense at the Château de Vincennes, Paris; to the staff of the MacLean Museum in Greenock; to Alan and Mhairi Blair; to Mr Zbigniew Siemaszko, historian and wise veteran of the Polish armed forces in Scotland. And without the happy month spent as a writer-fellow at Hawthornden Castle near Edinburgh, under the care of Hamish Robinson and as the guest of Mrs Drue Heinz, I would never have been able to finish this book.

Once, centuries ago, thousands of Scots lived in Poland as traders, bankers and soldiers. Today, many thousands of young Poles have enriched Scotland by coming to live and work here. I dedicate this book to them, and to the fine, thrawn people of Greenock and Port Glasgow who are fighting their way out of hard times.

… Home. A sort of honour, not a building site,
Wherever we are, when, if we chose, we might
Be somewhere else, but trust that we have chosen right.

— FROM 'IN WAR TIME', BY W. H. AUDEN

O ne day, Jackie came home early from school and blew the world up.

That story should belong to her. So why am I telling it, so many years after it happened? For a strange reason: because nobody can pronounce my name.

I am called Maurycy Szczucki. Yes, Polish, although I have held a British passport for half a century now. When I renewed it in Glasgow last year, the young woman in the passport office was only the latest in the queue of well-meaning meddlers who have suggested that I change that name. 'See, Mister, ehm, Sushi: you could make life easier being, like, Stuart or mebbe Shoesmith.'

I refuse. It's not patriotism. It's not even that, frankly, they could easily pronounce it if they bothered to try. 'Sh-choot– ski': not so hard. No, it's because my name is one of the only two things I have left to stand by, to keep me sure about who I am. The other, less reliable, is memory.

After war and exile, I could have reconstructed what the British call a 'normal' life. But what happened on that day, the midday when Jackie came home early from school, led me off into fogs and mires. In the fog, other people came close to me but then were lost again. Whenever I set out on a paved road, the hard stone under my feet dissolved into marsh.

So many things happened to me – happened senselessly, I used to reckon. But when that girl in Glasgow challenged me, I suddenly thought: my name is a flag. I am still grasping it, even as an old man. If I hold it up and march back through my life, I might make sense of those memories. Not only the tale of a disordered man but a life as a geological core – mud, gravel, then sandstone full of grimacing fossils, then dead granite drilled from earliest times.

That is why I began to write this. For whom? Not for myself – I am finished with myself. Not for a namesake (I have no children) but for the sake of my name. So let us arrive in Scotland, in the year 1940, and start this story again.

One day, Jackie came home early from school and blew the world up.

I remember the day. In some ways, I remember it more sharply than what happened on the day.

It was late April, with May becoming imaginable. Pretty cold still, but handsome. From Greenock, you could see right across the big estuary. The warships and convoy ships anchored off the Tail of the Bank lay in sunlight; the Argyll mountains behind them were black in rain-mist. A northerly breeze kept jumping up and then falling away. It sent dark catspaws racing across the water from Gourock Pier to Princes Pier. The barrage balloon tethered to the Esplanade swayed and glinted.

All this I could watch from my window in the French naval headquarters. This day began as a wartime day: plenty of confident, pointless activity. Two British destroyers were making a mess of coming alongside at Gourock, thrashing up cataracts of foam as they went astern, whooping their sirens. Then a procession of blue naval lorries became stuck in the road outside the torpedo factory at Fort Matilda. Shouting broke out, though I couldn't hear the words. Gulls lined the roof-ridges, jostling and shrieking. A white flying boat passed low overhead, landed almost out of sight by the other shore of the Firth and then, restlessly, took off again.

Everyone else was busy winning the war, but I was not. After all, I had just lost one. As a Polish officer freshly attached to the French navy, that experience gave me authority but also a certain unpopularity. I soon realised that I was losing a friend each time I said to some eager young *enseigne de vaisseau* from Brest or Toulon: 'Your turn will come! Then you will see what they can do when they really mean it!' So these days I sat at my table by the window, smoking Gold Flake and exchanging small talk with French colleagues about the eccentricity of the Scots. I had a telephone, the only one in the office, which was used by everyone else to make assignations with girls. I also took care to have papers spread out on the table, weighed down by the ashtray. These papers were my diary and some draft pages for a novel, but as nobody else could read Polish they gave a diligent impression. I read a lot, library fiction in brown-paper wrappers, to improve my English.

That day, when I came in, Commandant le Gallois told me that I was to wait indoors for the arrival of some personage from Paris. A figure from the Ministry of War wished to inspect the base and meet the foreign liaison officers. Due to the uncertainty of the trains, he might turn up at any hour of the day or night. I was to remain in the building until further orders.

This annoyed me, because there were other things I wanted to do. So, in spite of le Gallois, I did venture out twice. Why not? Who did he think he was? I should explain that all this was happening in the spring of 1940, when the French were free but not yet 'Free French', and nobody had heard of Charles de Gaulle.

This phoney war had, in fact, only ten days to run before Hitler's panzers sprang out of the woods and gave France heart failure. I did not realise that it would be so soon. But of course I knew that it would happen. I had watched it happen to me and to my brave artillerymen and to my country, only seven months before. Where had France been then, with all her promises of a counter-offensive on the Western Front? Where would France be tomorrow, when the Nazi-Soviet dragon had finished digesting my country and came looking for its next meal?

I raised all this with Commandant le Gallois one evening, soon after my arrival in Scotland. He said that I was a pessimist; I said that I was a realist. A defeatist sort of realist, then? I reminded him that one of our great leaders had said that 'to be defeated and not to give in is to be victorious'. We both sensed that it was better not to continue this conversation. Le Gallois smiled at me (he wasn't a bad fellow), and, getting up, remarked: 'After all, many of my colleagues think that we are fighting this war for Poland, for Danzig, but not really for France.' I thought of saying: 'Just wait and see!' But then I decided to say nothing. I decided that I would continue to like le Gallois, who so calmly tolerated my waste of his time and space, but that I would no longer be in awe of him.

So I went out twice. The first time was to walk down to the noisy lorry convoy jammed on the main road at Fort Matilda, and see what it was carrying. Probably the trucks were carrying torpedoes. If they were French ones, strange contraptions with a bad safety reputation, I could accept that they were none of my business. But if they were British torpedoes, then they might be destined for one of our Polish destroyers or submarines based here, and I could make their delay very much my business. I could justify my existence.

While the drivers stared at my exotic uniform, I peered over the tailboards. No torpedoes. The lorries were carrying naval rations in crates. I went back to the office.

The second time I went out was around midday. No, a few minutes after. I meant to cross the main road at the foot of the hill and make for the gate of the torpedo factory. A British naval friend there, a lieutenant commander, had asked me to drop into the officers' mess for lunch and a game of billiards, and I was going to leave a note explaining why I couldn't come.

I do recall going down the headquarters steps and then stopping on the lowest one. Too much smoke in there, too many voices, and I needed to breathe for a moment. The Scottish air was cold, spiced with distant heather and bog-myrtle. Everything seemed to have gone quiet. The lorries had concluded their dispute and gone. The ships were silent; the argumentative gulls had slipped off the roofs and spun away across the water. The soldiers and children of the town behind me had stopped drilling and playing and had gone indoors for their dinner.

Even the little wind had died down. The quiet – and I swear that this is how I remember it – seemed to bulge, to become expectant. As if the universe had exhaled and now, very slowly, was beginning to draw breath again. What word or sign was coming? I thought of our enemy, that double-headed monster with its crooked cross and red star, and imagined it heaving again to its feet, filling its lungs with fire as it prepared to wade across the sea towards us.

I looked up at the sky. In my hand I was loosely holding a small brown envelope, my note to the lieutenant commander. Suddenly the envelope knocked my fingers apart and leaped to freedom. I stared after it, astonished. Then the sound came.

J ackie mounted the steps to the main door and took the key out of her coat pocket. But then she paused and looked around. She was doing a very, very bad thing, and she knew it. Running away home in the middle of the school day. Not asking Mrs Graham could she go, not telling anyone but just slipping out of the gate and off down the steep Campbell Street brae while all the other girls were lining up in the yard to go in and get their dinner – it was just bad.

Why did she go? It was because of her name and the big girls. Every day when they went out to the yard, Ina Ramsay pressed up against her and said: 'O my, it's Jacqueline! O my, and how is Lady Jackie Jackass the day?' And her gang, with their big chests wobbling in their jerseys, would squeal with laughter. Today Jackie had hidden in the toilets for as long she dared. Mother and Uncle Mike, the Polish officer-lodger, always said: 'Remember, you're as good as they are. Just you tell them to get away and mind their manners, and they'll back off.' But being named Jacqueline, and wearing spectacles, and being clumsy and only nine years old, meant that she exactly wasn't as good as they were. So today, when she came out into the yard and saw Ina and the gang over by the tree, and fancied them laughing when they made her say where she'd been, that was it suddenly. She took her gas mask case off its hook, because it must be carried at all times, and ran.

She would get a row from Mother, a bigger row from Mrs Graham, something much bigger than a row, because running away from school was enormous, unforgivable. Even the joy of racing down Campbell Street, feet taking over so she thought she mightn't be able to stop, made it worse. That joy would need paid for, too. Yes, she would get it. Nothing would be the same again.

Union Street, when she got there, was different. At this time of day it had become a place Jackie scarcely knew; the normal shadows were wiped away, the granite setts shone emptily. The Dunrod Dairy was closed for dinner. Nobody was about. But as she approached the house, something pale moved. The huge dirty-white tom cat with red eyes, the cat which belonged to nobody but which was said to kill wee dogs, jumped off a wall and slouched past her. Jackie dreaded this creature. But today she felt a sordid recognition coming from it: another evil-doer.

She slid the key into the lock. It wouldn't go. She pushed it harder until it clicked and then she turned it. The world blew up. Something slugged her body, knocking her sideways down the steps. A sound which began as a deafening crack, the sky splitting, swelled into an insufferable roar which made her clutch her head; she felt the stone house above her heave and dance. Dust filled her mouth, and even with eyes shut, she sensed things flying back and forth, skittering and smashing.

The sound died into echoes rumbling off distant hills. Jackie spat out dust. Then she tried to stand up, but her legs wouldn't hold her and she sat back on the step. A coping stone floated down to the pavement in front of her and silently flew in pieces. She thought vaguely: here's what I should do, and pulled open the cardboard gas mask case, but her fingers were shaking so much that the floppy mask slid out of her hands. She forgot about it. There was a loud singing in her ears. Was this the punishment?

After some while, she managed to get up. Union Street was twinkly with broken glass, the smooth pavements hidden by tree branches, dustbin lids, fragments of wood and stone. Bits of paper were drifting to the ground. People were coming out of their doors, running and calling words she couldn't hear.

She looked up at her house. The main door was wide open, swinging. The downstairs window was smashed, and little darts of glass were still falling from somewhere upstairs. A man in a blue uniform with a brown steel helmet was standing in front of her shouting. She couldn't hear what he was saying, but he looked very angry with her.

When he pointed at the house and grabbed her arm, she tried to say: 'I never meant it, I didn't know.' But perhaps the words didn't come out aloud. The angry man dragged her towards him. She broke away and started to run down Union Street, her good shoes stumbling on the debris. She ran across Ardgowan Square and past the Tontine Hotel, where a crowd of officers in all kinds of uniform had swarmed out of the bar on to the pavement. Several of them shouted at her, but she kept running. Near Nelson Street, she tripped and cut her knee, blood mixing with the dust on her leg.

More and more bewildered people were gathering and standing in her way. An old man came out of a close and said: 'Poor lassie, come in the hoose till I sort your knee.' He put out a hand. She smacked his fingers away and ran on.

What Jackie was doing was what I had always done. I kept running for so many years, starting when I was a child, an only child like Jackie, in Poland. My mother constantly – my father only regularly – used to tell me that you can't run away from difficulty or from bad deeds or half-finished decisions. They will travel with you, they said, and climb through the window to be with you wherever you go. But I believe exactly the opposite. The train begins to move, the abyss between the ship and the quay suddenly gleams, the undercarriage thumps into the wings of the climbing aircraft, and there begins a solo wheels-up party for the escaper. The baggage, unlabelled and unclaimed, remains behind. Somebody will eventually loot it, pressing their face into those beautiful but well-worn shirts. Let them.

So I am an escapologist, and a proselytising one. This Scotland is supposed to be a Protestant country, where people are taught that they can be born anew, sinless, clutching a white stone with a new name writ thereon. And yet it's just these Scots who assume that they aren't on the list for rebirth. Only a few know how to escape without a struggle or a lifetime of guilt.

The others need to be taught. Just go! Don't wait to tie up those loose ends, don't spend years choosing which photograph or budgie cage to take and which to leave behind. Don't waste time buttoning yourself into your conscience; don't brood on how what's coming is only what you deserve. The enemy have reached the bridge; they are just the other side of the wood; in five or ten minutes they will be here. You can still make it. Go!

With me, the skill came early. I ran away from school when I was eleven, because I considered the reverend father-teachers stupid. Home was forty miles away, but I walked through the woods by day and in the evening took a ride on a peasant's cart. Six years later, I ran back to the old city where the school was, because I couldn't stand the hypocrisy – as I saw it then – of my father, pumping out cloudy left-wing opinions while being fed, waited on, dressed and driven by semi-literate servants whose own families lived like animals. In the city, where I consented to live in a small flat owned by my mother, I began to study law.

The next escape was from a pretty, merry girl. I was alarmed to discover that my parents knew Wisia's parents and thought that she would be good for me. But in spite of that, we became engaged. One summer afternoon in my flat, I persuaded her into the bedroom. She smiled a warm, hospitable smile as if I had asked her to cook me one of her special omelettes, and she let me undress her. I got into the bed. Then I saw her kneel down naked at the bedside, cross herself and mouth a little prayer to Mary for forgiveness.

She jumped up, laughing happily and climbed into bed. But no, I had already escaped. No to that future, that closing trap!

All lust had gone. I said that I was suddenly feeling ill. She dressed again, and – full of concern – went out to look for some *cachets Faivres*, the chic imported painkiller in those days. When I heard the main door bang downstairs, I kicked my way into my clothes, dropped some books, my razor and my diary into a bag, ran to the station and took the express train to Kraków.

It was a year or so later that Germany and Russia, the Nazis and the Bolsheviks, together invaded my country. My country! Where is it now? When was it? Nowhere and not now. Of course there is a Poland again today, even a smart successful post-Communist one. But it is not the land I escaped from or, to be more honest, which I fled from and lost.

I was brought up in the east, in a borderland which used to be called Volhynia. To me, a Poland which is nothing but Catholic, Polish-speaking Poles (without Ruthenians and, above all, without Jews) is not my country. That place which I remembered began to vanish when our Jews, in their poverty and prophetic dignity, were driven away to be slaughtered. A Fourth Partition once again tore the 'Poland' page out of the atlas, and my own eastern borderland was seized and swallowed by the Soviet Union. The Polish families in those lands were deported in cattle trains to the east, where some were murdered by Gulag guards and very many more died as slaves. Unknown to me, the deportations began while I sat day-dreaming by my Clydeside window.

My parents were small aristocrats – petty nobility, bonnet lairds – with liberal ideas. They became isolated from their peers because my father became noisily anti-clerical, entertained divorced couples as house guests, had ostentatiously many

Jewish friends and advocated radical land reform. None of that helped my mother and father when the days of doom arrived.

I went to see them in my army uniform a few weeks into the war, in mid-September 1939. They repeated absurdities they had heard on the radio, for instance that six hundred British aircraft had arrived to defend Warsaw. I told them to get out fast, before the Germans arrived. They said there was no petrol. I said that I could go to the nearest army unit and get them enough petrol to reach Kraków. They pretended not to understand me, and fetched up a bottle of French wine in my honour. I became angry, to a degree I find hard to explain, and shouted that they must bury all alcohol, or the soldiers would get drunk and burn the house. They laughed indulgently. Three days after I had gone, the Germans came into the district, stayed for a week and then handed it over to their Soviet allies advancing from the east.

I know my parents left the house then, but I never saw them again. Somebody, a cousin, claimed many years later that he had seen my father standing in a file of convicts, on a Russian railway station close to the Arctic Circle. Apart from me, nobody now alive remembers them.

Perhaps this all suggests more attachment to the past than is appropriate for an escapologist. Don't misunderstand me. The landscape I knew as my own was pre-modern, semi-feudal; round us, a small number of mostly Polish landowners employed Ruthenian-speaking villagers who scarcely knew what to do with a radio set or a bottle of shampoo. Their children were scabby, barefooted. In winter, we ran a porridge kitchen behind the stables, one meal a day, for children under ten.

Often I was made to help, dishing the stuff out with a giant iron ladle or chasing hungry dogs out of the yard. What I dreaded was the women who sometimes snatched my hand holding the ladle and tried to kiss it. But the moment my parents left, between the Germans pulling out and the Russians taking over, the same villagers broke into our house, threw everything out of the windows and set it on fire.

That was the world I escaped from, as a boy. Escaped? No, here again 'fled' is a better word. But in this case, baggage 'unwanted on voyage' has managed to track me down. I haven't ceased to dream. I ride through the forests, or across the open fields of barren, sandy soil. I drive my boot deep into the snow behind the house, hearing the sound it makes which is like a raven's croak. Sometimes I dream of waking in my own bedroom, where a fresh glass of tea is smoking on the table by the window, its saucer leaving a little disc of vapour on the shiny wood.

I also dream of that old city where I was a student. Often I find myself looking down on it from a high hill and about to utter some prophecy, maybe some lamentation for a Jerusalem coveted by all and lost to all. But my father and mother have never returned to me in dreams, never, although I would quite like them to.

Home? I have none. I soon became homeless, and then for a long time stateless. One lives in so many places. But sometimes a hut inhabited for a week with many others is clearer and dearer in memory than an apartment lived in for years.

Long ago, when I first got to know Jackie's mother in Greenock, we used to spend hours facing each other and teasing each other across the kitchen table. Once Helen asked me which word brought tears to my eyes. The game was to shut your eyes, say the word out loud and then repeat it to yourself over and over until something did or did not begin to happen. 'Mother' didn't work. I tried 'Freedom' and then 'Poland' and 'Polska'. No tears.

I tried 'Love': still nothing. Helen put another sugar lump into her tea, and stirred. When I said 'My Country' and to myself *ojczyzna*, something twitched. But when I said the English word 'Home' a few times, my throat suddenly tightened; I saw a child lost in a forest, a fluttering bird whose nest has been taken away. I quickly opened my eyes. She was biting the corner of her lip and watching me. 'But I don't have a home, I don't need one.' I stood up and walked around the kitchen; it was cold in there.

To tell how I came to Scotland, I must return to 1939. No, no account of 'my war'. We did our best. I was with the artillery until we ran out of shells and became infantry. Twice we stopped retreating and counter-attacked. But then the panzers would be behind us again, closing our way out. Their aircraft came at us every day as the sun rose. We had been driven back to the outskirts of my university city when we heard that the Soviets had invaded Poland from the east. By now, the twenty men originally under my command had become six. Three chose to go back to their villages. The other three escaped with me across the Romanian frontier, where we were interned.

Making my way from Romania to Paris, where our government and high command were regrouping, took a little time. My hope was to join the Polish army being formed in France. But headquarters selected me to go to Britain as a liaison officer, to be attached to the French naval forces based in Scotland.

I protested: 'Why me? I am not even in the navy! Most of our navy escaped to Scotland back in September – why can't one of their officers do this?' I was told: 'Because they are too few and much too busy. Because you speak nice French and are wasting it on mam'zelles. Don't question orders!'

When I reached Scotland, which turned out not to be part of England, it was in the middle of the coldest winter in memory. Big snow and ice were nothing new to me. But this was a damp, bitter chill which waterlogged one's very bones. The British, or at least the Scots, seemed not to have heard of central heating.

In Greenock, I was billeted in a tall stone house on Union Street, with an immense view over the Clyde estuary and the anchorage called the Tail of the Bank. There was already a shortage of coal. Nothing burned in the open fireplaces, except a curious gas contraption, made out of fireclay batons, which was ignited only briefly at breakfast time.

I went to bed wearing white seaboot stockings and slept under a British naval greatcoat. In the morning, while it was still dark, I would be woken by the rumble of iron-tyred cartwheels over the granite setts in the street and the hammer-beat of iron-shod hoofs. Then I would get up, wash in a basin of cold water and go downstairs for breakfast. One greenish gaslight burned in the hall and spread a melancholy scent.

The others would be up already. The house belonged to Mrs Melville, a widow, who regulated the breakfast tea and kept the toast within bounds. Her son Johnston, Helen's husband, wore a naval reservist's uniform and spooned up his porridge quickly. Johnston was youngish, my age, with slicked-down red hair. He never spoke to me at breakfast, and left for his office with a muttered word to his mother and a nod to Helen. Jackie, wearing her school clothes, got a spoonful of sugar or sometimes a daud of treacle with her porridge. It was always Helen, never her grandmother, who went for Jackie's sugar from the kitchen. Jackie was the next to leave, sweeping a jotter into her school bag. 'Your gas mask, Jackie!' It was always Mrs M, never Helen, who reminded her.

That left the three of us. As the main door banged shut, Mrs M would turn up the wireless news, quite loud, so that nobody could talk. Helen would rise and take the plates into the kitchen. The plucky Finns were setting about the Russians. The Japs were setting about the Chinese. British destroyers were showing the Jerry navy who ruled the waves, but Poland had sunk without trace. Sometimes I thought that my uniform was its only relic, and I was the only survivor of an Atlantis which had vanished with all its people a thousand years before. Mrs Melville, seated before her final cup of tea, tried not to look at me. She behaved as if my presence, festooned with strange lanyards and badges, was a vulgar prank. There were bad days when I wondered if she was right.

When I first moved in, I was underemployed until the French found a desk for me to occupy at Fort Matilda. So Helen and I began to talk. Her mother-in-law would leave the house after breakfast, to visit a relation or do some messages or other. Helen would make a fresh pot of tea, we would sit down again at the table and I would pull out a packet of duty-free British cigarettes.

At first, it was 'teach me English – correct my accent'. I even wrote words down, offered her a few shillings for an hour of language.

I remember well why I did this. It was a conscious decision, but it sprang from a sudden impulse of caution. Teaching, keeping a table between us. Something to transact, something regular but regulated, which would end with a glance at a watch and a pleasant smile.

We had met the day before, in the afternoon, when she came into the kitchen, swinging a bag. She had been to the fishmonger's. I was standing awkwardly in the middle of the floor, a very foreign figure in my uniform cape and long knee-boots.

'So this is our Pole.'

'So it would seem,' said Mrs M from her chair by the range. My explanation about what sort of Pole I was had failed to charm her.

Helen took out a moist bundle wrapped in newspaper and laid it on the table. Then she looked up at me. I noticed that she had small blue eyes turned down at the outer corners, eyes you might imagine belonging to a sailor who spent time peering into the wind or laughing. Then I noticed something about myself: I was coming alert in a very familiar way. I was searching my small English vocabulary for a phrase to keep her looking at me until I could coax her into conversation. Did I have enough words to be fascinating? Or how about saying nothing, clicking my heels and kissing her hand? That would probably shock a Scottish girl into letting me make the next move as well.

But then I thought abruptly: What are you up to? Where do you think you are? I knew already that she was married, the wife of a fellow officer, a British comrade who was offering me shelter in his house and family in the name of our common struggle. 'Time of war,' I reproached myself, 'is time you learned to treat married women with respect.' So, a fit of virtue. But perhaps I also felt out of my depth, coming from a country where there is no mystery about what other people want or don't want. Here, I had no idea what was behind these calm faces.

I said to her: 'Please, my English is very poor. Is possible you give me lesson, correct speaking, maybe in evenings after work?'

She laughed loudly. 'Ach, a Cartsdyke lassie like me widna learn ye richt!'

'Excuse?'

'Helen, really!' said Mrs M. 'Just spare us that sort of talk here.'

'Okay, all right,' Helen said. 'I'll learn you. I'll teach you. When I've time. Mind, I never taught anyone in ma life.'

'We will have conversation. I need good English accent.'

'Good accent, will you just imagine that?' said Mrs M to her knitting.

So the next night we did begin to have lessons. Mrs M sat there after the tea was cleared, while Helen asked me questions which I was supposed to answer aloud and then in writing.

'What did you get for your dinner at the French canteen today?'

'I may not tell you, it is . . . war confidence.'

'Did you get mince and tatties? For God's sake, Mabel, the face on ye, what's wrong now?'

'Excuse, tatties?'

Helen was war-working at Kincaid's, marine engines, as a typist. Soon she was transferred to the back shift. No more lessons after tea; instead, it was a half-hour after breakfast. Best of all, Mrs M would go out and leave us alone. The lessons dissolved into talking, joking, smoking. My English, its seeds implanted long ago by an Irish governess, grew fast. But the table remained between us. We eyed each other across it.

Sometimes I told her stories which made her laugh uncontrollably, even alarmingly. I am a good story-teller, but her laugh was a dishevelled, unpractised sound, nothing like those 'golden trills' heard in Kraków drawing rooms or on Paris café terraces. Sometimes it was Helen who told me jokes, often too Scottish to understand, or sang me songs from the wireless or the Alhambra in Glasgow – songs which all the girls in the office would sing until the chief stamped in and shouted at them to hold their row. I liked her singing voice. It was straight and confident, like her short yellow hair.

Once Helen tried to show me a card game, but that went nowhere. By now we were absorbed in our words and wanted no silences. Instead, we began to argue. Over the next few days, she tried to make me talk about my life before the war. But she was reluctant to talk to me about hers. This much I gathered: that her father had worked in several shipyards, that she had been hungry as a child, that her mother had died of tuberculosis when she was twelve, that she had met Johnston Melville at a Boys' Brigade picnic at Loch Thom. I learned that Mrs M considered her right common, and no way good enough for her son.

But Helen preferred to talk about issues. She would steer the conversation off herself and towards her views in general. I found her ideas incredible. She told me what she thought about the war ('big business selling guns, nothing in it for the workers'), life at sea ('men wanting free food and away from their wifies'), Communism ('fair shares'), God ('just for old ladies feared of death').

Wasn't she afraid the police would come for her? 'Plenty folk think like me,' she said, surprised. 'It's a free country, you know.'

Sometimes we got vehement. I told her she was ignorant about Russia and Russian Communists. She said I was blinded by privilege. 'Is that no right, all Poles are Roman Catholics who skelp their serfs with big sticks?' 'Quiet, be quiet, you know nothing about this!'

We stared at one another over the tea cups. She ran her hand through her hair, but kept her narrow blue eyes fixed on mine. I realised that in some way I had come quickly close to this woman, and yet I had no idea what was going on in her heart. The rules we seemed to have set up forbade me to ask. But I asked myself if I wanted her, and for the first time in my life found that I wasn't sure of the answer. I dropped my glance. She was wearing a plain blue blouse that showed her neck, strong, with beautiful muscles, very white. How could I be so uncertain of my feelings? What might hers be?

She began to smile. 'How are you so touchy? But then you'll probably be some sort of an aristocrat – baron, count?'

'My father inherited a certain rank, description . . . but to me it's nothing. I never remember or use that. Yes, I have title: I am Major Maurycy Szczucki in the Polish army. Enough!'

'Mike, being a baron or count or whatsoever, that's with you for life, like it or no. Don't they say: once a knight, always a knight but once a night is enough?'

While I was struggling to see the joke, Helen laughed. But when the pun was explained to me, it hurt me in the way her noisy laughter sometimes did: discordant, unworthy. And the stupid joke was wrong, too. Once a count but no longer a count – hadn't I proved that with my own life until now?

She got up to make some more tea. She was away from the table for two or three minutes, and I resented them. When she returned with the pot, I pushed the cigarettes across the table but only halfway, so that she had to reach towards me to take one. Then she showed me how to play the game in which I had to shut my eyes, the game of words for tears.

Commandant le Gallois had never opened a window in his office before. When the explosion came, it took him several minutes struggling with the sash before he discovered that it gave way upwards, not outwards. He squeezed his head and shoulders through the opening. Fresh air blew in, scattering cigarette ash and papers across his desk.

Colleagues stumbled into the office. As I had been standing out of doors, I arrived last.

'It's a bomb,' le Gallois said, backing into the room.

I shook my head. 'No, too big, too far away.'

'Commandant, there was no siren, no alert!' said the French officers.

Le Gallois grabbed his binoculars from a hook behind the door, and went back to the window. A tall mushroom of yellow-brown smoke had appeared beyond distant roofs and cranes. A fire engine began to clang its bells. The Commandant turned round to face his officers and seemed about to speak when the headquarters air raid warning went off. The boots of running men could be felt rather than heard. As the siren finally died down, the telephone turned out to be ringing.

'Ah, no! It's the *Fronsac*? Yes, at once. Move, move!'

Already the streets near the waterfront were cordoned off. British sailors with slung rifles halted the car. Le Gallois waved his pass and screamed at the sentries in French; we lurched onwards, tyres crunching on scattered slates, until we reached a chained and barred dock gate.

A naval officer in a tin hat raised his hand. The Commandant heaved himself out of the car and strode up to him. I went the other way. I walked uphill, pushing through crowds already lining the seaward tiers of streets as if they were the stalls and gallery of a theatre. The stench of burning fuel oil stung my nostrils. After climbing for a few minutes, I turned and looked down.

The smoke from the sea was black, with scarlet slashes. It was flowing from a ship only visible in glimpses, as the breeze rose and relapsed. A din of sirens, close and far. A British destroyer, standing in close to the burning hull. A crowd of small craft alongside, and a fire float blasting plumes of water. Now and then loud cracks and sparks – deck ammunition exploding.

The wind fell away for a moment; the smoke rushed upwards. A slanting, littered stretch of deck appeared. Some of the litter was men, trying to help other men. Moving heads gleamed in the water. From one of the launches alongside, arms were reaching up towards a line of portholes, trying to touch something or pass something.

Then the ship vanished and the stinking cloud poured back over the watchers. There was coughing; women clasped headscarves over their noses. I noticed girls in a group next to me crossing themselves. Looking uphill, over my shoulder, I saw children lining the railings of a school on the terrace above me; their teacher was holding binoculars to her eyes. I could see her lips beneath the binoculars, forming words and then sagging open. The children beside her were silent, staring down.

I made my way back to the dock gate, but the car was no longer there. Instead, there was an ambulance. The gate opened. Four men backed out with a stretcher, carrying a body dark with oil and sea water. They stopped as the ambulance doors were being unfastened, and suddenly the body vaulted off the stretcher and ran with its head down into the crowd. There was shouting, an eddy of caps turning as the man pushed through. But then came more stretchers, this time carrying bandaged shapes with uniformed nurses trotting beside them. The crowd surged against the rope barrier and began to shout questions.

'You, son, whaur ye gaun, son?' I realised that some of the shouts were for me. 'Mister, whit kinna uniform is that?' 'See he's a German, see the wee collar-patches, only fuckan Germans wear that.' I walked, neither too fast nor too slow, across the front of the crowd towards a group of British naval doctors. 'The saboteur, that'll be him,' said a woman's voice. Something hard smacked off the kerb behind me as I reached the doctors. They were standing around a wooden street bench, on which several civilians were hunched over mugs of tea.

Keeping my back to the crowd, I shook hands with a surprised medical lieutenant and went to sit on the bench beside a child with a bandaged leg. Her face was so dirty and her hair such a mess of plaster and twinkles of glass that I took several seconds to recognise her. She looked back at me, quite blankly. Her spectacles were intact.

'You know her? Great. Know where she lives? Great. Get her back to her mum, do us a favour.'

At Union Street, the main door was hanging open, a key still in the lock. I kicked some of the debris off the steps. 'Whose key, Jackie? Whose key?' She had said nothing on the walk home, answering no questions, and had moved her hand away when I tried to hold it. Now she cleared her throat. 'Mine, that'll be mine.' She pulled the key out of the door and dangled it. I followed her into the house and ran the kitchen tap while she filled a glass with water and drank. Then I tried to wipe her face, but she avoided the wet cloth and walked out to the steps again.

There were many people on the street, getting busy with brooms and buckets or riding cycles in swerves among the slates. In the distance a woman was running, her coat flapping. I had never seen Helen running before. She was fast, her knees together and her ankles flying out sideways as she ran.

Jackie began to cry. As her mother came up the steps and grabbed for her, she retreated into the dark hallway. Helen went after her and they sat on the bottom stair together, hugging and sobbing.

Mrs Melville materialised, holding her shopping bag. She looked slowly around and began to nod, as if she had been expecting disaster for a long time. I said: 'Jackie is not hurt, only some scratch, I think.' She took no notice, walked through to the sitting room to inspect the windows there – still intact – and then returned to the hall, where she lifted the telephone.

I heard her begin to instruct a glazier about glass to be put aside for her broken panes.

Helen was wiping Jackie's face as they sat on the stairs. 'Whatever for did you leave the school? There was the bang and all the windows in the office came in, and then it was Mrs Graham ringing for me to say you werena accounted for.'

'I turned the key, I never meant it, I turned the key and it began to happen.'

There was a knocking at the open door. A young naval lieutenant had leaned his cycle against the steps. 'Mrs Melville? Oh, sorry, I mean the younger Mrs Melville. My apologies. Mrs Melville, have you seen your husband today?'

'Johnston went to work after his breakfast. Did he not come to the base?'

'Yes, apparently he reported in, but ... Can we have a word in private, if that's convenient?'

Helen walked out with him, and stood for a few minutes on the pavement while the lieutenant talked. She shook her head, and passed a hand across her eyes. Then she came back alone up the steps and into the house.

'Mabel, it's about Johnston. Mabel ... they think he was on the French ship. There's a list, it's just a provisional list, of who got identified as rescued or as ... He's no on it, dear God, he's no on the list, he's missing.'

Next day, the Commandant let me see the draft of his report to Paris and Toulon. No U-boat, no unseen German dive-bomber. *Fronsac*, an unusually big and modern destroyer of the *Vauquelin* class, had been sunk by one of her own torpedoes, somehow launched along the deck, which had detonated the forward ammunition store under the bridge.

Somehow? 'What am I supposed to say? I mean, torpedoes don't launch themselves. I must report it as an accident, but...'

Twenty-five members of the crew were posted missing so far, presumed dead – twenty-one of them trapped in the burning hull as it sank. The captain too. 'He had many friends here, in the British navy; they want to meet me tonight at the Tontine. I need you there too. You speak better English.'

Had he heard any news about a British officer who might have been on board? Nothing. But he would be getting a more detailed account from his own staff later in the day.

In the Tontine bar, when I got there, le Gallois was sitting uncomfortably on a bench, a row of officers in Royal Navy uniform confronting him. Several civilians peered over their shoulders. A bearded lieutenant commander was talking at the Commandant in a carefully loud voice.

'Look, I'm a submariner and I know! Tubes simply don't fire from the inboard position on a surface ship. And there would have to be a launching charge in the breech, which there never is in port. And then the firing interlock and the safety range interlock would both have to be disabled.'

The barman, who had been listening as he polished glasses, said: 'Aye, that ship had seen a fair bit of fun. Did you know she escorted the French bank gold to Canada, and then put up a grand show in Norway? Just back from shooting up Jerry destroyers at Narvik and Namsos. And next she was due to...'

'I say, you're jolly well informed,' said a small man in a raincoat. 'Wish I was. Who told you all that stuff about Narvik and Namsos? I'd be really interested to know who. Me? Oh, just a civvy who keeps an eye on local gossip.'

The submariner gave him a cold glance. Then he went on: 'So sabotage? German agents in the French navy?'

I hadn't been sure how much of all this le Gallois understood. Now his eyebrows began to jump.

'But of course with French warships, you can't rule out bungling. No offence to the dead and all that, but the lack of training, the junk they serve up as ammunition, the way deck ratings ignore orders and light another Gauloise... No, sit down, sir! Somebody tell the Commandant to sit down. No, nobody is insulting anybody! *Vive la France!*'

I pushed to the front of the group.

'Hello, Major Mike! Just in time, can you take over your French friend? He seems to have lost his sense of humour.'

I followed le Gallois out into Robertson Street and we set off to walk back to Fort Matilda. After a long silence, the Commandant said: 'I forbid myself to be discomposed by people like that.' He took out a pair of dark glasses and fitted them over his eyes, although it was raining. 'Safety devices, launcher charges! I do not exclude sabotage, naturally not. But I do exclude dishonour – which is to talk about good men who died like drowning rats, maybe burning rats, as if they were unskilled idiots incapable of turning the right switch. Yes, somebody is responsible for what happened to *Fronsac* yesterday. I assure you: this somebody was not French.'

We walked on for a few minutes. 'Our intelligence is investigating. You didn't know that we had our own security here? Well, already we have something interesting. When the explosion happened, there was indeed a man in English navy uniform on board, and – you know what? He and a French seaman were doing something with the torpedo tubes. What exactly, none of the survivors seems to be sure. He was blown overboard, or maybe blown to pieces. We have to find out who this was.'

'I know who it was,' I said. 'We have just passed his house.'

The Auchmar Vaults were not far from the elegance of the Tontine lounge bar, at the bottom of a flight of steps off Cathcart Street and within spitting distance of the water.

One of its two gaslights was out of order when I looked in there a few days later. In the half-dark, men were talking loudly over their pints of heavy.

'Did ya hear aboot the bell – the ship's bell? Ach, the sheer damned energy of that blast! It lifted the bell high, high up into the air and it flew clear across the river – jingling away the while, folk could hear it – and it came down at the feet of Highland Mary's statue that's in the cemetery.'

'And the heat of it melted the metal to liquid consistency, I'm telling ya, and when it came doon it was just a perfect sphere of bronze, birling aboot the park, the firemen wis kicking it roon like a fitba.'

'Ye're a pair of idiots, it never happened. That's an auld grannie's tale, ye heard it when ye was weans. It did happen right enough, but fifty years ago when the *Auchmountain* brig blew up off the Tail of the Bank, cram full of blasting powder. And her bell banged down in a field up behind the town, the ship's name on it yet, and the Captain's photie album was lying in the street at Kilmacolm, that's six miles direct flight.'

'It wisny the bell that fell in the cemetery. It was a human heid, I'm telling ya, a French human heid of a sailor still wearing a blue bunnet with a red toorie on.'

There was laughter. A big man in overalls, who hadn't spoken, pulled off his cap and rubbed his hand through his white hair. 'I was there at the French ship maself, boy. Ye shouldnae speak of it that way. I was in the Great War. But no, I never saw the like of this, never.'

He paused. I was standing at the end of the bar, and he gave my uniform a suspicious glance.

'We took a boat, the buoy lighter, and went alongside. There was plenty other boats too. There was sailors leaping down to us, and others swimming and others, casualties, just creeping about. But the hatches on the deck was jammed. The lads below in the mess decks, they couldnae get out. The bridge above was burning, the deck was burning, ye could feel the heat coming off the steel plates as ye came close. And she was going down, listing over and just slowly sinking, ye know? The water was coming up inside around the lads, and the fire was cooking them. They couldnae get out. There was all these portholes and scuttles open, and they could get their arms out and that was all. Oh, God, the crying and screaming of them.'

'Is that right, the men in the boats reached...?'

'Well, aye, first there was a doctor lying on the deck and leaning down to those waving arms; he was jagging them with a morphine syringe. But the deck was getting too hot, he couldnae stay. And then some of the boys with me, they were reaching razor blades up to the hands waving there. Ye know, so the lads could... There was no escape for them, no escape at all. Ach, the hell of a thing.'

Silence fell on the pub. After a while, there was talk of how the injured had been brought ashore and laid in the nearest halls. Women had run out of their closes to comfort them and wash them in clean water, until they could be uplifted by ambulance and taken to the Infirmary. The dead found above deck were taken too. Often, the undertakers were not sure which body parts to put in which coffin.

'There wasn't a soul in the town or the Port that didnae see it all,' said someone. 'Thousands of folk, just staring like at the movies. All the naked men with their clothes burned off. And those arms waving through the portholes. It wisnae fair to let the weans, the school kids, see that.'

'At least they didnae hear it too, what I heard,' said the man in overalls.

So who had done it? Not a lone enemy aircraft, that was certain. Maybe a U-boat which had found a way through the boom which sealed the estuary, down at the Cloch lighthouse? More likely, a German spy. The whole place was full of foreigners; who could keep track of them? Maybe spies who didn't even look like foreigners, wearing impenetrable disguise. In this war, you just never knew who it was standing next to you.

'That's right enough,' said a young man in a duffle coat. 'See, a fella came to me after the explosion looking terrible, drooking wet and all over oil, and I was just fuelling up the post launch. That's the boat that takes the mail to the ships outbye in the Holy Loch and the Gare Loch. He says: "I'm a survivor from the French destroyer, and I'm needing dry clothes?" I says: "Sure, pal, there's trousers and a jersey in the cabin", and he went below for them. But then I thought: he's no a survivor, he's no French, and there's something out of order here. He came back up, in the dry clothes, and I says: "How come ye're no French?"

'He didnae like that, but he says: "I never telt ye I was on the ship, I was out fishing in a wee boat, a wee coggly boat that was knocked over by the explosion, and I got wet..." Anyhow, he stayed with me on the post launch and handled the mailbags hoisted up to the ships, until we got to the pier over at Dunoon.

I went below to check the bilge pump, and when I came back up he was away. The dry clothes, the oily duds he took off, everything gone. And by God he's taken the money oot ma jacket too, and my identity card, and the biscuits and jelly oot the cabin cupboard!'

'I hope you told the police,' said an English voice. Everyone turned to look, and I recognised the small man in the army mackintosh from that night at the Tontine. He was standing at the bar holding a drink, but when had he come in?

He turned to the young ferryman. 'Very interesting story, that. New one on me, too.' When talk around them had resumed, he added: 'Good idea if you didn't go on spreading it, for the moment. But I do suggest you ring this phone number, today or tomorrow latest, and ask for Eric. That's me. We need to talk. Eric, got it?'

The funeral of Lieutenant Johnston Melville was a bleak proceeding; a few uncomfortable people standing in the cemetery above the town and a cold spring wind blowing. They brought the coffin up from the West Kirk, but I didn't go to that part. Maybe there was a bit more ceremony there. But by the time they got to the cemetery, they had run out of ideas.

We crunched up the path past the statues of James Watt and Highland Mary. The grave was just a black slit, without greenery or music or holy water to scatter. There was a wreath of red, white and blue flowers from the brother officers at the base, and a heavy bunch of lilies from Mrs M. The minister began to mutter some words. There were so few men around that I took one of the cords when it came to putting the coffin down. Another cord was held by Peter, the young naval lieutenant who had first told Helen that Johnston was missing. A third was held by an elderly uncle, Mrs M's brother, who had come through from Edinburgh. The fourth was held by Dougie, one of the undertaker's men.

Helen wore a black suit with a skirt – in my view, too short. She held Jackie by the hand. Jackie was holding a china doll, which she had rescued from a cupboard after abandoning it several years before. She had lost weight since the explosion, and she had taken to talking to herself at night and sometimes screaming instead of sleeping. You could read Jackie's sleeplessness in Helen's face as well. The two of them just looked at the grave, tearless. Mrs Melville stood a little apart. Once she moved over to tug Jackie's woollen pixie-hood and straighten it. Then she moved back to where she had been before.

Son, husband, father. Funerals at which women stood to attention like black lamp-posts were something new to me. The other mourners, in contrast, showed signs of feeling. The lieutenant, whom we now knew as Peter, sighed and blew his nose when the coffin was in the ground. Another man present, whom we had also got to know all too well in the last ten days, was in civilian clothes: a fawn trench coat. Eric widened his eyes quite theatrically, and nodded his head as the minister spoke.

The only person who seemed to be behaving naturally was Dougie, from the undertaker's. A gaunt old creature, he gave me a wink as everyone else turned to go. We'd already had dealings. As nobody else seemed able to take the initiative, I had done the funeral arrangements, and Dougie, breathing heavily through a cigarette gripped in his teeth, had helped me to fill out the forms. Now he turned to look back at the grave, which nobody was preparing to fill in.

'Johnston Melville, eh?' he said. 'I widnae bet on it.'

'What do you mean?'

'Ach, we just shoogled all the bits and pieces around and filled up the boxes wi a shovel.'

'I see.'

'Wee secret frae the family. But youse just a fuckan Pole, I can tell youse.'

'Thank you, Dougie. Maybe his soul is in the right place.'

'You cannae believe that shite. Gie yer brain a chance.' He set off down the hill.

The other reason for the bleakness was that the funeral came as an anticlimax. We had spent more than a week with interrogators discussing Johnston and remembering him, and we had nothing left to feel.

The morning after the explosion, with glass and rubble fragments still on the steps, the bell at Union Street had started to ring. The visitors got rapidly through condolences to questioning. Peter, the little naval lieutenant, established himself at the kitchen table with an exercise book. The man we learned to call Eric, who did not explain his position, trotted round twice a day for what he called 'a cuppa and a little chat' with Helen, who loathed him.

A dark, very handsome *capitaine de vaisseau*, Jean-Marie something or other, whom I remembered seeing at Fort Matilda, turned up on the second day. Le Gallois had asked me to help him, as he spoke almost no English. But his first action on entering the house was to order Peter to leave, on the grounds that this was an internal French enquiry. An afternoon of shouting and telephone consultations ended with Peter holding his ground. Jean-Marie took to pacing the pavement outside and waiting for Helen to emerge, so that he could harangue her in French on her way to the Co-op in West Blackhall Street.

He questioned me, too. Was I a Communist? On the other hand, perhaps I was a Nazi sympathiser, an agent of the National Radicals or the Falanga. I took no offence, being almost flattered to find that French naval intelligence knew something about Polish right-wing politics. But most of the interrogations were about poor Johnston. Was his French fluent, and how often had I heard him speaking German (no and never)? Had he shown signs of lunacy or mental breakdown? Did his hands shake at breakfast, and how much did he drink?

In the Tontine bar one evening, Jean-Marie asked me whether Johnston's mistresses tended to be right-wing or left-wing. I thought of Johnston's well-combed red hair and his golfing friends from Greenock Academy, and began to laugh. Jean-Marie scowled and then began to laugh too. '*Mon cher Chouski*, but give me something I can tell the Commandant!'

'Tell him how to pronounce my name! Like this: Szczucki.'

'It sounds like frying, maybe black pudding with bacon. No, be practical.'

We were in amicable mode; I was supposed to be laughing. Suddenly, I didn't want to smile any more. I saw in my head the immense, unprotected late-summer sky of my country, and a car shimmering with fire in a ditch, and women kneeling over a blood-spattered child in the roadside grass.

Why did I see this? I have no idea. Was it a memory? It could have been, because I had passed through many such scenes that September. But it's not, so to speak, a memory I remember. I looked at Captain Jean-Marie, his blue uniform neatly pressed, his gold wedding ring shining from a brown finger. For him, there were still so many inviting ways to the future. His roads were not yet blocked; his hatchways leading up to the deck and into the fresh air were still wide open. But on my people, the hatches had closed. I had escaped, but for them the fire was creeping nearer, the waters were rising.

'My name is not a joke. It is not funny. Don't dare to laugh at my name. Don't dare.'

I went out of the bar, and back to Union Street. It was afternoon, but Helen was hanging a sheet to dry on the back green. It wasn't the first time. Jackie had begun to have accidents in her troubled nights.

'What's wrong wi'you, then?' I said nothing, but went into the kitchen. Peter was writing his notes and supping a mug of tea, his officer's cap on the table beside him. I asked: 'Why are you still here? You make enough notes, enough questions. Why still?'

But I already knew the answer. Peter, impressed by my own uniform, had confided in me. An enquiry into the disaster had been postponed, while two navies and at least two intelligence services were fighting over the blame. At the centre of the fight was whatever remained of Lieutenant Johnston Melville and whatever he had thought he was doing on board *Fronsac*. Peter was simply hanging on at Union Street, making work for himself, in order not to leave us alone with his rivals.

The Royal Navy version was that Johnston was in no way responsible. The explosion was an accident waiting to happen. Its cause, Peter had been told, was almost certainly a defective French torpedo, ill-designed and carelessly produced, coupled with the crew's complete disregard for the safety-lock routines on both the missile and the tube. Lieutenant Melville had been instructed to inspect the equipment, after complaints in the anchorage that *Fronsac*'s insecure torpedo array was a threat to other warships.

The French view, as expressed by Captain Jean-Marie, was that the explosion was demonstrably the result of sabotage. The suggestion of lax weapon discipline was outrageous. Nothing but skilled and deliberate interference could have overridden the locking mechanisms and fired the torpedo. As a British officer was the only stranger on board at the time, and as he had been seen apparently handling the tube's breech, it was obvious that he was responsible for the explosion.

Nobody was sure that his presence had been cleared by, or was even known to, the destroyer's captain. It therefore remained only to establish that the intruder was genuinely British and not a disguised German, and that he had no personal involvement in Communist organisations. If that was confirmed, it would leave only one possibility: that the warship had been blown up by agents of British intelligence.

When Captain Jean-Marie recounted all this to me at a previous Tontine session, I had asked him if he had a logical, Cartesian structure of motives to explain why on earth the British would wish suddenly to deprive themselves of a modern Allied warship. He looked down at the cigarette he was stubbing out. 'In Paris they will know why.'

The third inquisitor was Eric. But in a way he was not an inquisitor at all. The other two asked us questions about Johnston's health, behaviour and opinions. Eric simply talked

– 'chatted'. It was not clear what he was after. He would spend hours sitting with Mrs M, making conversation about the weather or books or the behaviour of the young. She had almost stopped speaking to the rest of us, but one day I saw her talking to Eric and smiling. Another day, she went to the living room and sat with Eric on the sofa to show him family photograph albums: Johnston as child, adolescent and Boys' Brigade marcher, Johnston with relations and friends.

With Helen, he was less successful. His pointless, goofy small talk got on her nerves. Once, as he came indoors, he asked her what had happened to the coat that had been hanging in the hall the day before. 'That's Johnston's coat and it's hanging in the press in my room, it needs a button sewn on it.' Later, she said to me: 'That wee bastard's just watching and waiting. He's got me down for a German spy.'

Eric never chatted to me. 'Keeping well, old chap?' That was about it. One fine morning, a week before the funeral, he said: 'Great day for the race!' I was puzzled. The horses at Ayr, or a sprint somewhere? What race? 'The human race, old man.' He laughed triumphantly. I did not. 'Eric,' I said, 'I have a question. Why the undertakers won't give us Johnston's body? Each day, they are saying: sorry, there is hitch. What is the problem? I think you know these things.'

He pulled that concerned, big-eyed face of his. 'Matter of identification, I expect. Between us, some of the bodies were in quite a mess. You can't rush that sort of thing, but it should be sorted out by now. I'll have a word.'

On the afternoon following the funeral, Commandant le Gallois telephoned me at Union Street. 'I have had a report from *Capitaine de vaisseau* Guennec. Yes, Jean-Marie. He – we – are not satisfied that your position as a witness at the enquiry has been entirely clarified. More preparatory work is required. Be kind enough to present yourself at my office tomorrow at nine tomorrow morning.'

When I got to Fort Matilda the two naval sentries with fixed bayonets surprised me by taking my pass away and examining it in the guardroom. In the headquarters, le Gallois was wandering restlessly up and down the corridor outside his office, smoking. 'Hello, Shoosky, *mon cher Chouski.*' Nothing remained of his stiff manner on the telephone.

'Did you hear the news?' I said yes, I had listened to the BBC at breakfast. 'The Boches are across the Meuse. Well, at least it means that a war of movement can begin now, and we can forget about all that impregnable Maginot nonsense. They are making a big mistake. When they run out of petrol, then our armies slicing behind them from the south, with the British from the north . . .'

I said nothing. That was a morning when I wished badly to be somewhere else, with people who spoke my own language or who had seen what I had seen.

'Shoosky, why are you here? Ah, yes . . . do excuse me. I think we will do this another day; I will let you know. Jean-Marie left a message; he took a travel warrant off my desk and is on his way to Paris. To do what, I cannot imagine. Certainly, there is nothing we can do here. For the moment.' I saluted and turned to go.

'Shoosky!'

'Commandant?'

'You think this will be Poland all over again. It won't! Unlike you, we have been preparing for this for years. We have more tanks, more men than the Boches. And good generals. Well, some.'

'Good day, Commandant.'

After the funeral, everything grew quiet at Union Street. Peter had taken his notebooks and gone, although he telephoned once or twice and asked to speak to Helen. The handsome Captain Guennec was in Paris. Only Eric continued to call, every few days, for his pointless chats. Once he brought a bottle of cherry brandy for Helen. She complained that it was 'exotic', and put it away in a cupboard.

For several weeks, Jackie refused to go back to school. Eventually Mrs Graham came down from Campbell Street with a box of Duncan's best soft centres ('Duncan, The Scots Word for Chocolate') and a letter to Jackie decorated in red, white and blue with a black border, signed by the whole form. Mrs Graham pointed out to Jackie that nobody else's father had been killed in the war so far. Britain was proud of him for making this sacrifice, and proud of his daughter. The school was proud too.

Jackie said nothing, but looked at the floor and put her thumb in her mouth. 'Daddy would wish you to be brave now, like a wee sailor yourself, and to resume your studies with us,' said Mrs Graham. Tears began to run down Jackie's face, but she still said nothing. The next morning, she let Helen take her back up the brae to school.

That day, when Helen came back to the house, we sat down at the table with tea and cigarettes as we used to. That seemed a long time ago. There was a line at the corner of her mouth I hadn't seen before.

'I'm no good with Jackie. There's nothing I can do for her. She's away out of her mind.'

'How?'

'She's saying it's her fault. Whatever I'm telling her, she's just no hearing me. She says she did a wrong thing and she turned the key in the main door and that was it – the big bang, and her daddy dead, that was the punishment for it.'

'She can't believe that. It's crazy.'

'Aye, right, so she's crazy, because she does so believe it. Every night now, the bed soaking again.'

'The doctor?'

'Dr Forsyth, he says she's fine, just needs a while to get over the shock, she's to get radio-malt twice a day.'

'Please?'

Helen brought a huge, dark jar from the cupboard where she had put away the cherry brandy. She hadn't even tried to open the jar. I unscrewed the lid and sniffed the contents: something like the stuff we used to spoon into sick artillery horses.

'I telt Dr Forsyth, she's needing to see a specialist in Glasgow, maybe a mental doctor at Gartnavel. Turned the key, blew up a ship and killed her ain faither? She's no shocked, no, she's dead sure of it. And when I tell her she's daft, that it's against the laws of nature, that she'll get locked up and put away if she carries on this way, she looks aside and it's the thumb back in the mouth. I pull it out, but back in it goes.'

'Jackie's only nine. She probably needs . . .'

'I know there's a war on,' Helen said, 'but I cannae cope wi this. I've not been a good mother to her. We never . . . I never got a right grip of her, know what I mean? She's cold to me. She disnae tell me things, never has. Once I said to her: "D'ye not want me around then?" And she says: "Mum, it's you disnae want me around, that's how you could ask me that."'

There was a silence. Then she went on: 'See, when the big bang came, I thought it was a bomb. I thought: Jackie's killed or under the ruins, that's me punished for a bad mother. I ran to the school; I ran to the house. And when I found her, I thought: God gave me a second chance, I'll be a real mum to her now. And how long did that last? Ach, Mike.'

She blew her nose.

'Did you worry about Johnston, too, when you were running?'

She glanced up at me.

'Mind yer ain biz, cheeky Pole.'

'Why don't you think more about Jackie, and less about you being bad mother?'

'Eh? You fairly make me sick. Fine friend, you!' The kitchen door banged; her cigarette stayed fuming in the ashtray.

After this, we avoided each other for a few days. Instead, to my surprise, Mrs Melville began to speak to me. She too was different. It was not just that her face had grown older in the last few weeks, and her hair greyer. To begin with, she was different with Jackie. Now it was Mrs M who brought Jackie sugar and treacle at breakfast and hung the gas mask case carefully over her shoulder before school. One evening I saw her on the sofa where Eric had been shown the photographs, in the big sitting room. Jackie was beside her, and Mrs M was reading her a book.

This wasn't a room I normally went into. It was cold, but when the blackout curtains were opened its tall bay windows framed a panorama right over the Firth and the shipping. Today Mrs M had put a match to the heating contraption in the empty grate.

I walked in and went to the windows. In the main anchorage at the Tail of the Bank lay a gigantic passenger liner with a single funnel, painted in camouflage zigzags of black, grey and white. I recognised her from photographs: a famous French liner which before the war had broken records on the Cherbourg–New York run. Further out, I identified two British battle cruisers with supply lighters crowded along their sides. Then I looked to the right, eastwards. Princes Pier jutted out into my line of vision. But beyond the pier I could see a mast sticking out of the sea at a strange angle. That was *Fronsac*. A divers' barge was moored to the mast, with a red flag warning of explosives.

I stood and wondered about all those spy-hunters and spies and security men in town. An *Abwehr* agent had no need to go and buy pink gins for officers at the Tontine or at the Bay Hotel in Gourock. All he needed to do, if he wanted to study Allied convoy preparations, was look out of the window.

Eric had asked Helen about the binoculars on the sitting-room window seat. Who did they belong to? 'Mister, every single family on this street has a pair of them. Why for? Because they have spent a hundred years in their armchairs keeking down at other folk doing a job of work on the water for them, that's why.'

I lifted the binoculars and focused on the warships and then on the rainy Argyll hills behind them.

Behind me, Mrs Melville was reading aloud to Jackie. 'For five long months, Prince Charlie wandered in the Highlands and Islands of western Scotland. He suffered hunger, and cold, and wet, but through it all he was cheerful and brave. No house was safe, for the whole country was full of soldiers searching for him.'

She closed the book as I returned from the window. 'Hungry and cold and wet through to his skin; just think how it must have been for him, Jackie.'

I said: 'In this house, I am not hungry and not wet, and I thank you for that. And now not cold, with this . . . hot machine.'

'It's just my gas fire, Major. You can't get anyone to lay a coal fire these days.'

'We don't have in Poland.'

'However do you keep warm, with all your wolves and snow?'

'We have in every room big stoves, covered with tiles.'

'Tiles?' Mrs M shook her head and smiled. It was our first conversation. I tried to broaden my success.

'Jackie, was school nice today?'

Her spectacles glinted, and she put her thumb in her mouth. We exchanged a long look. Sometimes an only child can recognise calculations in another only child which sibling people miss. I know a fake thumb-sucker when I see one.

Telepathy followed. She took her thumb away, and said: 'We got history today from Miss Coutts. She's got golden hair. I really like history.'

'What do you like about it?'

'Because it's before.'

'I see what you mean. Yes.'

'In history, people escape. They put on disguise, so they look poor, and everyone thinks they're dead but they're no. They are escaping.'

Mrs M gave me a warning look. But I said: 'I escaped too.'

'Was that in history?'

'I think so. Not when it was happening. But now, with the big war in France, it does feel like before. You see, I still wear my funny disguise uniform.'

'Do they all think you're dead?'

'I don't know. I think perhaps it's they are all dead.'

'Enough sad thoughts for a tired wee girl,' said Mrs M, getting to her feet. 'I'll make you your tea.'

Jackie hung back, dragging on her granny's hand. 'Poland, where is Poland?'

'Not any more on the map.' I took her fingers, balled them into a fist and thumped it gently on my left breast pocket. 'Poland is here.' She laughed, the first time I had heard her laugh since the explosion.

Helen came back late and weary after the back shift. She went into the bedroom. I heard Jackie wake up and cry. There was argument. Helen came out again, tears in her own eyes, and gestured for a cigarette.

'I'm no good with that child. I say the wrong thing and then she's greeting and wailing, and then I just panic. I just want out, that's what I want.'

'With Johnston gone, you could get leave, be here with her all the time.'

'Aye, right, that's what they tell me at the yard. You could get the compassionate exemption, be at home wi Jackie and the auld creature all day. Some of the girls say they envy me; all they want is to be "hame in the hoose with the wean". You know? Well, I said no. I said: I'm gonnae no dae that. I'm carrying on.'

'Why?'

'Because I'm a brave widow-wifie doing ma bit against Hitler! No. I'll tell you straight, Mike, the way I widnae tell anyone else. It's because I love the fuckan job. I never had a proper job, just setting the shelves in Woolworths one time, temp-typing here and there. You know? But this is different. I'm with a great gang down there at the yard. Kincaid's is paying proper wages, that's money I save which I never ever did in my life, I'm telling you. And I'm good at the work, so it seems, and they could put me up to a night supervisor next year. I'm somebody down there, the girls all know my name, I'm happy, so I am. Husband blown to bits, wee daughter stone mad, and I'm happier than ever I was in my life.'

'No, you are not happy. You cry. Look, now you do it.'

'You'd be crying if you were the world's worst mother. Sure I love her. But I cannae do anything for her, and I feel terrible. She's like me, Jackie, do you know that? She's out for herself. She'll use other people and get all the cuddles she can and then, when she sees a chance, she'll be away on her own. Ach, Mike, have you a hankie? I'm sorry for this.'

I put out my arms, but Helen backed away.

'My father was telling us: "Here's your rule for life. Aye be using them, else they'll be using you. And on your grave they'll write: Here Lies a Utensil." '

She gave me back the handkerchief, sighed and went upstairs to bed. I sat on for a while, the house dark except for the gaslight fizzing softly in the hall. Family problems; parental reproaches and self-reproaches. I had read about them in novels, but until now I had been careful to ignore them in real life. For the first time, I wondered if my pretty and sharp-tempered mother had longed for a quite different existence somewhere else. In a city rather than a village, with a calm, rich employer rather than an opinionated, upstaging husband.

My parents – I didn't even know if they were alive. Some letters were apparently getting through to German-occupied parts of Poland, the 'General-Government'. I had written home too, but my three letters were posted into the abyss, the regions under the Red Star. From there, no words returned.

It was so quiet now, in this stone house in this remote Scotland. I remembered a Mickiewicz sonnet, written far from his own country when – as now – it was under Russian bayonets. 'In such a silence, if I strain my ear / A voice from Lithuania I might hear ... Drive on, none calls!'

Lighting a candle, I tugged the tiny chain that put out the gaslight and went upstairs. I could hear movement; the sound of Jackie crying softly, Helen's voice, and the flap of sheets being changed. Even on an early summer night, it was chill in that house. Back in my own room, I pulled on my woollen stockings and slept without dreams.

The next Sunday, we went for a walk along the Esplanade. Helen had tried to make Jackie come, but she wanted to stay with her granny. 'We'll read the book together, darling, won't we?' said Mrs M. She gave me a smile as she walked past into the big front room and knelt to light the gas fire. Helen she ignored.

It was a blue day, with wind. Waves broke white across the Firth and the merchant ships gathering for convoy nodded at their moorings. Looking over the Esplanade railing, we saw barelegged boys splashing around a ruptured crate of oranges which had drifted ashore. The fruit and the sea around them were black-smeared with oil fuel. One of the smallest boys seemed uncertain what he was holding in his hand. 'Bounce it, and if it disnae bang it's an orange!'

Helen laughed. We walked on. 'Why so serious?'

'Today the German army is in Paris. France is finished.'

'They won't get here though. C'mon, Mike, the navy will never let them across the Channel.'

'I think they come here. Then Britain will burn like France, maybe like my country.'

'Britain wouldnae get beat like Poland!'

'That's what my Commandant said about France. A month ago.'

'The French was all corrupt and against the war, and the French girls will all be walking out down the boulevards with German soldiers in no time. That's what my dad says.'

'And what does Helen say when the very handsome

Oberleutnant smelling nice with cologne asks: "Please do me the honour of walking with me down Rue End Street to the Pavilion to see *Gone with the Wind*, and here's a big poke of sweeties"?'

'Helen says: "Well, I did once know a Polish major, but he never did me the honour of asking me to the Pavilion, and all he offers me is a cigarette. Every so often."'

The cafés and the ice-cream parlour were all shut. When we were tired, we sat on a bench and smoked and looked up at the barrage balloon moored at the end of the Esplanade.

'Mike, you're no like all the other men. So I'll tell you what it's like being a young widow, six weeks into it. I was just amazed, so I was.'

I waited for her to go on.

'They think you want . . . well, ehm, sex. Men you wouldnae believe, they come and say: I know you'll be lonely, and needing a man in that empty bed. You'll be missing it, so . . . how about me? Nae bother, nae long-term love affair stuff, just the bit cuddle while you're starving for it.'

'Who?'

'Well, that wee Peter from the navy. Would you ever think it? You couldnae hold him back. Whiles in the kitchen, I was skelping at him with a dish-clout – get yer dirty wee hauns offa me! – and him looking the model mamma's boy! And in a few minutes he'd be back again: "You know you want it really . . ." And the French captain, of course. Jean-Marie, he was easier. I could see him coming a way off. Brought me soap and perfume from the French canteen, pushed it into my shopping bag when I went to do the messages. His English was about zero, but no mistake about what he meant. And there's another one – a fellow at Kincaid's I work for in the design block. All married men, of course. All Boy Scouts, aye ready to do a good deed for a girl in need.'

'Why didn't you tell me?'

'The trouble is: the more you say "No, I'm no lonely that way, get away with you"... the more you do so begin to feel lonely. I was okay after Johnston died. Now I'm feared of my own shadow. And you know, it's no fair at all to poor Johnston. The way they talk, you'd think he was some kinda sex maniac.'

I took her hand. She didn't move it away, but she didn't look at me. When she started to smile, she seemed to be smiling at the view. We walked back to Union Street.

That night I came into her room and sat on her bed. In the dark, I heard her sit up.

'What's this then? Your turn to do a good deed?'

'No, your turn.'

'Oh. That way round? Now that does make a difference.'

'Come to my room.'

'Okay, okay.'

It was terribly cold there. We clung to each other, standing by the bed. I could scarcely see her outline, but her shoulders were sharp and warm. When I had undressed her and pushed her back on the bed, I tried to light a candle. For a moment I saw her as she rolled on her side and blew the candle out.

'Do it, then.'

'You don't really want this, Helen.'

'It's okay, just do it, it's okay.'

'Not okay for me.'

I slipped in beside her. She turned over to face away from me; I pulled the blankets and the greatcoat up over our heads and held her close until we were warm. I thought she was falling asleep, until she put a hand behind her.

'Whatever could this be? My, are all you Polish fellows this tall?' I began to move.

'No, don't. Mike, no. Stay like that, and I'll just...'

A few moments later, she whispered: 'Noisy beast, you'll wake Mrs M. Kiss me, or am I doing all the work round here?'

Next morning, I woke and found her gone. The greatcoat had slipped to the floor, and when I picked it up I found a button from her nightdress on the lino underneath.

Mabel Melville, who had lost her son and only child, seemed to be discovering new energies.

She bought two second-hand bicycles, one for herself and a small Standard for her granddaughter. She put on a pair of large brown slacks, made sandwiches and rode off with Jackie down to the pier at Gourock, where the ferry was still running across the Firth. On the Argyll shore, they spent a windy afternoon cycling and picnicking round the Holy Loch to Kilmun and back to the boat. From then on, the weekend expeditions became a regular occasion.

Watching her mount the cycle in Union Street, her newly grey hair blowing over her eyes, I was astonished. Perhaps she too was escaping, not only from grief but out of the matronly chrysalis in which I had learned to know her. It had never occurred to me that she could do anything more physical than pour out tea, or engage in the world by anything more than shopping. But a few weeks after the cycle trip, I came home in my uniform to find Mabel in her own uniform: the handsome navy-blue outfit of a Red Cross officer.

New visitors appeared, young women shaking the rain off their mackintoshes as they ran up the steps with bundles of First Aid brochures and wartime recipe books. The big front room had its table cleared for demonstrations of burn-dressing and aircraft recognition.

Jackie's life was now being managed almost exclusively by Mrs M. It seemed to do them both good. The bed-wetting stopped, leaving Helen with even less responsibility for her. At meals, Jackie finished what was on her plate. Every evening, she went eagerly with her grandmother into the front room for more instructive reading, always followed by recapitulation.

'Do you think it was wise for King James to dress up in disguise and go stravaiging about Stirling in the dark?'

'Granny, it was so nobody would know who he was. Maybe in the palace they thought he was dead and gone, but he was only escaping.'

'And what was the funny name he gave himself?'

'The Gudeman ... the Gudeman of ...'

'Ballangeich, Jackie, the Gudeman of Ballangeich.'

'Is that a place?'

'It's in Stirling, but it's a dirty, dark place. We wouldn't go there now.'

Almost every day now Mrs M would get up after the reading

and say: 'It's high time we took your education in hand, young lady.'

'She's doing fine at Campbell Street, what's wrong with it?' Helen would reply.

'It's not such a good neighbourhood. See when Jackie got impetigo all over her face, from swinging on the railings of the Catholic school!'

'For God's sake, Mabel, the Catholic school is nowhere near Campbell Street.'

'Nevertheless.'

Nothing more was said. Helen and Mrs M scarcely exchanged words now. And with me she had returned to her old coolness. Perhaps Mrs M, too, had picked up a nightdress button in my room. Busy as she had become, she was still aware of what was happening in her own house. She did not care for it.

That night in bed, I asked Helen: 'What is impetigo, please?'

'A dirty skin disease.'

'You are so brave, maybe getting dirt disease from this Catholic.'

'It's different, you're Polish.'

'You Lutherans, you don't have dirty disease?'

'What Lutherans? My lot were Church of Scotland atheists. That's clean-living, but no God and no alcohol neither.'

'My lot are very much loving both.'

'How's your God, then?'

'He is away at the moment. Like your Gudeman. He put on a disguise, told nobody where he was going and walked out.'

'He'll be in trouble, then. That King James who was the Gudeman, he got ambushed in the dark by a gang of Stirling keelies who set aboot him. Your God's getting beaten up.'

'We tried that two thousand years ago, but it only made him worse.'

'Ach, ya wee Polish count!' She laughed her raw laugh, but with her hand across her mouth. She had made this joke before. I understood it now, but found it so vulgar and stupid. I felt ashamed for her.

How was it between us, in those few weeks of the first wartime spring? She came to me almost every night. Helen and I seemed to be alone in the world, when we were together. But alone as two people. In a way, my feelings remained exactly the same as they were when we first met – indefinable. She was so important to me; I was obsessed with her; there was something I desperately wanted to do with her. But what? Most men translate that something as sex. But I was always aware that I was getting the translation wrong. I found that Helen was a woman who took delight in the making of love, but didn't take much physical pleasure from it. I was the opposite: a lonely man hungry for the fuck, but almost resentful of the time it took away from talking and laughing with her.

If I still couldn't grasp what I felt about Helen, I had even less idea of what Helen felt about me. It frightened me to be so attached to somebody so unreadable. I wondered occasionally about other men.

Then, one night, she came home from Kincaid's with red eyes. 'That's my job gone!' she said to me. She wouldn't say more; she didn't come to me that night. So I went to her, very early, before Mrs M was up to light the gas, before the first horse-drays rumbled down Union Street, and sat on her bed.

'That bastard down at the yard. The one I telt ye about, offering to give me a wee bit after Johnston was killed. Okay, him. He's still on at me. He got me in his office yesterday, hands going every place, tries to lock the door. He says: "C'mon, just be nice. I'll be nice, nobody will know, anyone can see you're ganting for it." I had this stuff from him before, but this time he backs off and grabs to get the key in the lock. So I knock his hand away, and he takes a skelp at my face and I'm starting a skreich when he sticks a hankie in my mouth – imagine that! All strict movie stuff, Mike. I remember thinking: now's the moment I get the tiny pearl-handled gat out ma reticule, push it in his waistcoat and blam.'

She sobbed, blew her nose, pushed me away when I tried to hold her. 'I get the hankie offa ma face and I say: "This is gonnae get to your wife, ya piece of shite", and he suddenly says in a very loud, different voice: "My mind is made up, Mrs Melville, and blackmail will only make more trouble for you. There is no place at Kincaid's for your sort. Now for the very last time I am telling you to away and get your jotters and off these premises, or do I have to call out the yard wardens from the main gate?"

'So then I notice all these shapes keeking through the frosted glass; these management types must have heard the row I was making. Shapes is right; they were just doubled up with glee. I did one last thing, Mike. I grabbed his tie and wiped my lipstick all over his big white collar. And then I went home.'

Now she began to cry loudly. I heard Mrs M walk past the door, stop, listen and then move on down the stair.

'Did I say "home" then? This is no my home. I've nae job and nae place o ma ain. Mabel hates the sight of me, Jackie doesnae want me as a mother, I get shamed out of ma life every time I see her. And I do miss Johnston, whatever you think; things between us were no sae great, but there were whiles he took my part, stood up for me against the auld bitch. Who do I have now? Okay, Mike, you, or maybe it's you have me. You're a great fellow, somebody's ideal man, so you are.'

I held her hand. Finally, she said: 'Get me out of here, Mike. Outta this dreich old house, outta Johnston's family, outta this town. They say it's never too late to start again. That's a better saying than wishing I'd never been born, when I'm just twenty-eight years old. Get me born again, Mike. In a fine big country with a future.'

We studied one another. Her room didn't look out over the Firth, but we heard the deep grunt and echo of a siren, a passenger ship moving down river.

'I mean it, Mike.'

'Jackie will miss you. If you go, she will think she made you go because you think she is horrible girl, a daughter who is so wicked she blew her own father up.'

'She'll steady down. She'll be better off without me, whatever.'

'Helen, don't go. What about your rent – I mean, war widow pension? What about me? Yes, me. Who do I laugh with? Who do I take to dance, which we never did actually, but I promise we will? Won't you miss your wee Polish count?'

Helen seemed not to be listening. 'The war that's on, and all the foreign people going on and off the boats in the town and the Port. It's see the world for free, and get paid for it.

I know some RAF boys who are off to train in Canada. And the Germans and Austrians and the Eye-talians they rounded up – they're being shipped off too. The Capocci family we used to get fish suppers from: I saw Billy Capocci a few days back. He's in the army now, but his father and uncles are interned. Billy says the word is they are getting sent to Canada any day.'

'Don't go. They are sinking those ships. I know things you don't know.'

'If the Capoccis can go, and them Italian, then I can go. Mike, we have family there too, my own father's brother is married in Halifax. Not just sae close, though. There's no been a word or a parcel outta that bunch for years. Nevertheless . . .'

'Don't go. They will say you run away, you are afraid.'

'I'm no feared of the Jerries and the torpedoes. I'm feared of being trapped in this dump, under the guddle I've made of my life. There's a chance for me yet, if I can get out. And who's talking? Himself, the big Mister Polish runaway.'

I got up off the bed. So did Helen. I thought about slapping her face. 'Don't take the huff with me now. I never meant runaway like that. I'm sorry.'

She came and hugged me. 'Be my friend, Mike. You know people. Help me do this.'

And after another angry, vain day of dissuading, I did. It was easier than I thought. A week later, she was signed up as a children's nurse in a crew pool being gathered by Blue Star, for their ships carrying internees to Canada. They were in a hurry and asked for no job references. I filled in an emergency passport form and signed it as 'Major and Staff Officer, Allied Forces'.

On a rainy morning at the end of June, we – Helen, myself, Mabel and Jackie – stood on the platform at Greenock waiting for the train which would take her south to the Liverpool docks. Mrs M kept one hand for her umbrella and the other on Jackie's wrist. Helen was wearing a new blue jacket and skirt, made of some thick stuff; the perky high shoulders looked wrong on her. In her bag was a shoebox of buttered scones with honey and a wedge of jellied veal, a wartime rarity which Mrs M had contributed for Helen's journey. I had slipped three packs of American cigarettes into the bag, and a half-bottle of whisky from the French mess.

Nobody said anything while we waited. The rain smeared Helen's yellow hair across her forehead. When the whistle blew, she pulled Jackie to her and kissed her cheek and her little ears, and said: 'Be a good girl with your grannie, I'll be back for ye.' As she straightened up and lifted her suitcase, she and Mrs M caught each other's eye. Mrs M nodded slowly. She seemed calm and even satisfied.

Helen didn't kiss me, but as she leaned out of the train window to wave I thought she sent me a wink. I couldn't be sure. The wind was blowing steam and rain everywhere, and I wasn't seeing properly. A Scottish wartime farewell which might well be for ever: three silent, dry-eyed females and one foreigner in uniform sniffing into a khaki handkerchief. Walking down the hill from the station, Mabel and Jackie kept an embarrassed distance from this man crying. I found myself thinking a Helen thought: 'Get me out of this country!'

My life was changing in other ways. At Fort Matilda, the base building was almost empty. After France had surrendered, most of the French naval staff and the crews of their few warships in the Clyde assumed their war was over, and they had chosen to be repatriated to their home country. A ship took them from Britain to neutral Lisbon on their long way back to France. But meanwhile a certain General de Gaulle had escaped to London and raised the banner of a 'Free France' to carry on the war against Germany. At Fort Matilda, where nobody had ever heard of this stork-like army officer, there were arguments.

'Hello, Shoosky!' Commandant le Gallois was still in his office. 'Yes, I am here, last to leave this poor old sinking ship.' There was nobody to make his coffee. The stewards had all opted for Lisbon, and the base's supply of real coffee from France had dried up. We went down to the Bay Hotel and drank in the lounge bar, where there was still whisky for customers in uniform.

'Shoosky, I think I am going to be a traitor. My government has surrendered, and I think I will enjoy disobeying orders. Those individuals in France, who are not any longer my France, sent a telegram that I am dismissed and must return at once. I tore it up. Captain Guennec – you remember him, the handsome one who was interested in your girlfriend? Guennec was shocked. He said: "The government is ignoble and ignorable, but the State remains, and patriotism now, in this hour, is to obey and defend that State."

'I replied: "Dear Jean-Marie, the only State which incarnates France is the Republic, and Marshal Pétain is about to abolish the Republic."

'Next day, this charming Jean-Marie, who I thought was my good comrade, did another of his disappearing tricks without saying goodbye. They tell me he is already back in Paris.'

He sighed. 'I will stay at war – but by getting wet on a handful of Gaullist warships or simply by joining the British navy? I don't know. I am lucky; my family is already here in Scotland. At least I know that the British will respect my choice and protect those who choose to be Free French.'

Things became less simple even for me. Later that day, I received a cable ordering me to call a London telephone number. It was almost a shock to hear a Polish voice again, after months of silence. The voice informed me that in view of the Franco-German Armistice of 22 June, my posting with the French navy was cancelled with immediate effect. I was to report at once to the Supreme Commander's office for reassignment.

'Where is the office?'

'In London, naturally. Where are you?'

'In Scotland. But you knew that.'

'Scotland? I thought you were in Plymouth. One moment, please... Listen, stay where you are. Don't come to London. Off the record, Polish army formations evacuated to Britain are to be regrouped in Scotland. When the Germans invade Scotland, you will be needed there.'

'What do I do now?'

'There is a town called Angus or Fife or something. Proceed there immediately, and establish an advance liaison office with the civil authorities. Identify and list all the Scottish generals who speak Polish.' He hung up.

Less than a week later, I found my way into the base blocked. British marines in full battle gear were standing behind a roll of barbed wire across the street. A Royal Marine officer, speaking fluent French, demanded to see my papers. As I tried to explain who I was, de Gallois came down the steps between two sergeants in steel helmets, one of them gripping his arm.

'What the hell is going on?'

He tried to smile. 'Did I say that the British would defend those who choose to be Free French? Everyone has gone mad. The British have bombarded our fleet at Mers-el-Kébir. They have boarded all our ships here, all the vessels in British ports, and arrested the crews. So now we Free French traitors are also British traitors.'

They thrust him into the back of a blue navy lorry. I ran down to the destroyer base at Gourock, pushed my way into the officers' mess and found the agreeable lieutenant commander from the torpedo factory, the friend I had been going to lunch with on the day of the explosion. I shouted at him, so that the senior officers at the bar could hear: 'In the name of the Polish government-in-exile, I protest against this scandalous act of force against an Allied navy!' That was how I began. As I went on, and as I found how nicely my English was flowing, my voice grew louder.

Admirals and captains put down their glasses. They looked away from this indecency. My poor friend's expression suggested that he had bitten a lemon. He steered me into a corner where his own voice couldn't be heard, and muttered: 'Bit of a dog's breakfast, if you ask me. Wasn't involved myself, but, believe me, nobody liked doing this. Whitehall orders. But, old man, it's just a precautionary measure. Your friends will get their ships back in a day or two.'

Le Gallois came back late that afternoon, driven this time in a shiny admiral's staff car. He sat carefully back in his chair, opened and closed several drawers. I noticed, as clearly as he did, that somebody had removed all the papers from the desk and its drawers while he was out of the office.

'It seems that brave Mr Churchill has killed two thousand French sailors in Algeria. He is very grieved about it. Well, that simplifies my choice. I do not think I will join a navy which sinks my battleships while they are trapped in port and murders thousands of poor boys who only wanted to see their country again. No, if anyone else wants to remain "Free French" after this, it's with them that I'll stand.'

He put a cigarette in his mouth, reached for the lighter on his desk and found it was missing. I struck a match for him.

'Shoosky, once you said to me that you knew what the Germans were really like and that one day we would find out too. Now it is us, the French, who know what the English are really like. And you Poles, one day, will find out too.'

Two days later I was summoned to Edinburgh. A Polish advance party – two elderly colonels – had set up their office in a hotel room. In their French uniforms I did not at first realise who they were. But they recognised who I was; they were enchanted, even amazed, by my appearance. 'Those riding boots! How did you manage to hang on to them? And you still have the whole pre-war outfit: the cape, the lanyards, the *rogatywka* square cap – perfect!'

The senior officer patted my sleeve, appreciating the cloth. Then he recalled himself.

'Obviously you have had it extremely easy, while others were fighting. But there is a war on even for loungers, Major Szczucki, and tomorrow the war begins for you. Report here in the morning with your kit, to act as our interpreter. Later, you will be redeployed to a regular unit. Understood?'

I controlled myself. 'Beg to ask, sir, do either of you speak English?'

'French is sufficient. But here in Scotland, the common people often speak only their own language. We shall need your help.'

I saluted and left. When I reached Greenock that night after a slow train journey, Mrs Melville was waiting for me in the kitchen. There was a newspaper spread out on the table. As I entered, she rose and came up to me and – an act which took me utterly by surprise – reached out both arms to unfasten my cape, a gesture like an embrace. She was very pale.

I took the paper and read that the liner *Selangor Star*, carrying prisoners and interned aliens, had been torpedoed in the Atlantic. There were some survivors. The paper went on to proclaim that the passengers were Nazi thugs and fanatical Italian fascists, who had trampled women and children as the ship went down. Mrs M watched me as I read.

'That'll be Helen's ship, Major.'

'Maybe. Yes, it was a Blue Star boat she was on.'

She began to walk up and down the kitchen. She shook her fists in the air, then pressed them to her eyes.

'Oh, this war, this war. What'll I say to Jackie? Oh, those poor, poor folk – just refugees, the most of them, and the Italians we all knew. Oh, Helen...' She started to shudder and then to weep. I took her in my arms, feeling her body, so thick and hard, shake like a tree in the wind. For many minutes we clung to one another in that kitchen with its blacked-out windows, its sad smell of gas.

When I reached the Edinburgh hotel next morning there was no sign of the two Polish officers. 'Ach, you mean the Rooshians! Or whatever they were. They wouldnae pay the advance, we couldnae make head nor tail of them. Anyhow, they're away. No, they left no message.'

I went back to Greenock and set about telephoning. When we got the first list of survivors, there was no Helen Melville on it. Mrs M spent that day and the next waiting in a crowd of sobbing Italian mothers and children at the Blue Star offices. It was a week until the firm issued a new, longer list. More lifeboats had been found by a Canadian corvette. Their surviving passengers were being taken to Halifax in Nova Scotia.

We read down the column of names. No Melville. I looked for a Houston, Helen's father's name, but there was no Houston.

'Here, see this!' said Mrs M suddenly. She picked up a pencil and carefully underlined a name. Then she took off her spectacles, and leaned back in the kitchen chair. I bent over to read what she was pointing at: 'Miss H. S. MacPhail, Greenock'.

'That was her mother's name. That's her. She's saved.'

'Why give that name, then?'

'I have no idea, none at all.' Mrs M was angry in her relief. 'Maybe her parents weren't rightly married. Her father is some sort of a Communist, I believe.'

I thought: Helen is escaping from us again, yet another stride away into some new life beyond the curve of the earth. More days passed, but we heard nothing from her. A telegram to MacPhail, care of the Canadian Red Cross in Halifax, brought no answer.

That Sunday, Mrs M put on her brown slacks and set to work in the kitchen preparing sandwiches. Once again, she and Jackie were cycling to Gourock and then across the Clyde with the ferry to Dunoon. I had tried before to talk to her about how we should break the news about Helen to Jackie. Now I tried again.

'We could say that she nearly became an orphan, but her mother thought she mustn't die and leave her alone.'

Mabel glanced up at me quickly, and then went back to buttering bread. 'Just don't mention her father to her at all. Not a word, d'you understand? It would set her off again. Orphan, my God. She'll never be that.'

I helped to wheel the cycles out of the yard into Union Street. Mrs M's rucksack was heavy with tins stuffed into the side pockets.

'You'll never eat all that on a picnic, the two of you.'

'Grannie has a poor old friend across there, up the hill. She takes her things to eat and medicines for her cough. She lets me watch the cycles and play on the shore while she goes up.'

'In wartime, it's up to us to see the less fortunate don't get left out,' said Mrs M, bending down to lace up her boot.

When the two of them were ready to mount, Mrs M leaned on her handlebars and told Jackie that her mother had been through a big adventure. The Germans had sunk her ship, but she was rescued in a tiny wee boat, safe and sound, and taken to Canada. Jackie smiled warily. I had expected her to ask a rush of questions. But she only watched our faces and said nothing. 'No need to worry yourself for her,' Mrs M added. Still nothing. As they rode off, I thought: like mother, like daughter.

The days became weeks. I left Union Street and rejoined the Polish army in eastern Scotland. A month or so later, Mrs Melville sent me a postcard to say that a parcel of Canadian chocolate, tinned butter and maple syrup had come for Jackie. There was no note in it, but the parcel had been posted in Winnipeg.

'In such a silence, I strained my ear' for a voice from Canada. None called. After a while, I gave up listening.

At Greenock, in those strange months with the French navy, I had been a solo performer. Nobody else could act my part, for which I was superbly costumed. But now I became a mere extra.

Like the thousands of men around me, I wore dull British battledress with the 'Poland' shoulder flash, black beret and boots and green anklets. Those shiny riding boots, like my officer's tunic and my four-cornered cap, were stowed away in a suitcase under my bunk. They were an outfit for dying in, somewhere on the Masurian plain. They were not an outfit for living in, under the ceaseless Scottish downpour. Moreover, they caused misunderstanding among my new comrades.

Some of the other officers welcomed me, assuming that anyone so proudly kitted out must share their traditionalist, not to say Stone Age opinions. Others drew the opposite conclusion. Our leader, General Sikorski, had only recently taken power from the discredited pre-war clique of colonels. Could a stranger in boots like mine be relied upon to support him?

For the first week after my arrival I simply could not believe that grown-up men in uniform – high-spirited and superbly courageous men who had just emerged from one battle and expected at any moment to enter the next – could waste their time on quarrels about who might or might not have been a Freemason. It reminded me of insufferable conversations with my father's neighbours, and of why he decided to see no more of them.

But I told myself that I had to live with these people, even like them. Perhaps my resentment was out of place. Perhaps I had been away from my country too long. But now I was back in my touchy, disputatious nation, on the proverbial desert island where two Poles would set up three different political parties. I persuaded myself that I was feeling at home, all the more when I was tempted to take personal offence.

How could I have been so patronising? That odious detachment of mine was precisely the proof that I really had been away too long. But it collapsed. One day in the officers' mess, I saw pinned up on the standing-orders board a leaflet about the 'Judaeo-Bolshevik menace' within the army, which should be practising 'cultural self-defence' against the infiltrators in its ranks. Aware that stuff like this was going around, pretending falsely to come with Headquarters approval, I had never actually seen an example. On impulse, I tore it down.

Heads turned. A lieutenant, a boy much younger than I was, strode up and informed me in a shrieking voice that I had no business to change the orders board, which was the exclusive duty of the adjutant's office.

'Have you read this? Are you suggesting that it should stay here?'

'It is a matter of good order and military discipline. You must put it back at once.'

'What do you think this rubbish does to order and discipline? And lieutenants do not give orders to majors!'

'Everyone knows that Major Szczucki is only a captain, pretending to a rank which he was lent for temporary diplomatic reasons.'

By now, I was at the centre of a shouting group. I was shouting too. The Colonel appeared, a calm man who had been a criminal procurator in civilian life. He picked up the leaflet, and glanced at it.

'Which of you put this on the board?'

There was deadly silence.

The Colonel looked round the group. He said in a conversational tone: 'Gentlemen, I have lost my reasons to respect you. There will be consequences. Major, you will come to my office to explain yourself.'

In the office, he kept me standing at attention. 'Are you a Jew?'

'No, sir.'

'Then why did you pull that leaflet down?'

'Because it dishonours the army, sir.'

He looked at me with interest. Then he remarked: 'That bunch have gone too far. They and their friends in London have been using this army as a hunting-field to catch their political enemies. But I have friends too, at the very top, and now it is my turn to go hunting.'

The Colonel smoothed out the crumpled leaflet and put it away in his desk. A week later, I noticed that the young lieutenant and some of his comrades were no longer around. 'Isle of Snakes,' said somebody, with a wink. The officers' mess was suddenly more cheerful.

I knew what he was talking about. One of the first acts of the Polish army in Scotland had been to set up a detention camp for supposed 'unreliables', mostly elderly officers linked to the pre-war regime. The 'Isle of Snakes' was the otherwise tranquil island of Bute, in the Firth of Clyde. Soon there were two or three such camps.

The trouble was that there were too many officers. The ordinary soldiers paid little attention to politics, concentrating on sensible matters like complaining about the awful food and courting Scottish girls. My unit was quartered in a Victorian castle in Fife which had been a teacher training college, a mile or so from a small industrial town. Pitnechtan had a linoleum mill and many pubs. We were soon well known there. Preferring the company of my platoon to that of the officers' mess, I often went into town with them. Why, they asked, do Scottish working men cram themselves into the public bar to drink, while the more comfortable lounge bar next door remained empty? Did they have no self-respect?

Each night, some of our boys would wait outside the mill for the shifts to change and then pursue the laughing and shrieking mill-girls down the street. Others, by kissing women's hands and using their few words of English pathetically, got their knees under Scottish family tables and developed lasting friendships.

Marriage proposals often followed. Our interpreters spent more and more time on grave negotiations between our Catholic chaplain and the town's Presbyterian ministers.

But our first task, in late 1940, was to defend Scotland against invasion. We took it seriously. Lorries took us down to the coast where we built pill-boxes, erected concrete tank traps and mounted guard by day and night. I do not care to remember those nights, facing the sabre slash of the east wind bringing rain or snow off the North Sea. Wearing our steel helmets and long Polish capes, armed in those early months only with a few old rifles, we drank hot tea, took turns to warm our frozen hands at a coal brazier in the pill-box, and waited.

We were waiting for the Germans because we were sure – we knew, indeed – that the Germans would come. It came as a shock to find that Scottish civilians, while appreciating our care for them, thought it less likely that the panzer divisions would start their invasion of Britain by motoring up the beach at Pittenweem.

One day several of us were detailed to escort the Polish sector commander, a general, when he arrived to inspect the defences of a certain ancient East Neuk burgh. The provost was waiting on the quayside, wearing his best blue suit. Behind him, fishing boats bobbed in the harbour and the red pantiles of the old crow-stepped houses glowed in the winter sun. He and his bailies were laughing and joking, rubbing their hands to keep warm. When the general's staff car arrived, with its red and white pennant, the provost himself stepped forward to open the door.

The general wore full Polish uniform. He emerged, came

to attention and gave the provost a salute. He was a short man with enormously wide shoulders; his eyes were small and sharp. He had fought against the Russians in the First World War, against the Ukrainians in 1919, against the Red Army in the Polish–Soviet war of 1920, against the Germans in the September campaign in 1939 and once more in France in 1940. Without waiting for any greeting, he set off at once at a rapid walk up the steep main street.

We followed him to the top of the town, where the houses stopped. A grassy slope led on to the ruins of a medieval abbey, sacked during the Reformation. From here, we could see the whole town below and the fields around it running down to the sea. A small group of men in shabby grey uniforms marked with coloured patches were digging trenches under the eye of a British sentry; they leaned on their spades to stare.

'Who are these?'

'German prisoners, sir,' said the interpreter, after consulting the provost. They were a rarity at this early stage of the war. The general stiffened. He walked towards the group and a tall German, dodging the surprised sentry, strode out to meet him. They spoke for a few moments in German. Then the general removed one of his gloves, used it to slap the prisoner lightly across the face, and walked away.

I caught up with the interpreter. 'What was that about?'

'That German – he said that he was an SS officer, that the abolition of Poland meant that the general was an illegal terrorist, that using prisoners of war for military purposes was forbidden by the Geneva Convention, and that we would all face trial in a few months' time when Germany had won the war.'

'My God!' I glanced back at the group of prisoners. One of them, the man closest to me, had turned his back on us and seemed to be hiding among the others as they tried to gather round the SS officer. The sentry, clumsily waving his rifle with its fixed bayonet, was shouting and pushing them back to work.

The general had gone on ahead. He was standing by the abbey ruin, surveying the landscape.

'They will come from here,' he told the provost. He pointed to a low hill. 'They make first attack down the main road behind us. But it will be trick, a feint. The tanks will mass behind hill, then come suddenly on flank. I know. I have seen it many times.'

He considered. 'Our main anti-tank defence will be here. This must be removed, of course.' He nodded at the abbey.

'The abbey?' The provost was pale.

'Obviously. We need clear field of fire.'

'But... we canny dae that, sir. It's stood for hundreds of years. What would the town be without it? Oh, no, sir. After all, surely the chances of invasion here have, well, just a bittie...'

'Have what?'

'Diminished,' said the provost in a small voice. The general gave him a pitying look, shrugged and continued his inspection. It turned out that the spire of the Episcopal chapel would have to go too, and several of the oldest houses obscuring the approach to the harbour, and all the new council houses out along the Crail road. The herring boats were to be filled with concrete and sunk to block the harbour entrance.

The general saluted again, climbed back into his car and left. The provost, after staring blankly at the rest of us, made his way back into the Town House, tripping on one of the steps. No doubt he began to telephone.

In the end, nothing was done. The Germans dug some more trenches, which filled up with water. The abbey is still there. The general fought in Normandy under that mighty commander Stanisław Maczek, liberated Dutch cities which still have streets named after him, and entered Germany as a conqueror. After the war, he refused to return to an 'unfree' Poland or to accept a pension from the British government, which he considered to have betrayed his country. He came back to Scotland and, like General Maczek, lived quietly and austerely in Edinburgh until his death.

B y now, I was no longer a mere 'extra'. My Colonel, more friendly to me after the quarrel over the poster, had put me in command of the Intelligence Section. Once again, I had an office, a metal table, a window with a view of the rain.

Intelligence, at first, meant listening to the BBC, writing down what seemed important to me, and having it typed up and translated for the camp news board. Less public information about the war avoided me, passing straight from the London office of our Supreme Leader to the Colonel. Occasionally, he would tell me about the latest exile-government intrigue in the Hotel Rubens, or pass on a rumour about executions and deportations in the German-held 'General-Government'. Mostly, he kept the coded telegrams to himself.

Then an intelligence colleague from another unit took pity on me. 'You don't know that wonderful Jew at Ladybank? He is an agitator, but he's informed about everything. Come on, I will introduce you.'

Ladybank was a camp quite close to us, not exactly penal but providing segregation for individuals suspected of Marxism, disloyalty or just indifference to discipline. When we drove up there, I found that the commandant was the same lieutenant who had screamed at me in the mess over the anti-Semitic poster. A few months on the Isle of Snakes had done wonders for him. He smiled at me as if we had been old friends. 'Just don't take my Jew away. He is marvellous, he is organising all the camp education courses, he is running this place for me.'

A small exuberant corporal came in, carrying an English dictionary. 'I let him read it on guard duty,' said the lieutenant fondly. The corporal gave us a benevolent flick of his fingers, more like a professor greeting two promising students than a soldier saluting officers. Then he took off his pince-nez, sat down uninvited in a chair and in twenty minutes told us more about the background and prospects of the war than I had learned since it began. He informed us that Hitler would invade Soviet Russia in the next few months, before the harvest. Stalin – here he pursed his lips – would then become Churchill's favourite ally and defeat Hitler for him. He assured us that both Japan and America would be dragged into the war, sooner or later. If America joined the coming British–Soviet alliance, there would probably be a Second Front invasion of western Europe, across the English Channel.

Much of this seemed outlandish, fantastic. 'How will Poland return to independence?'

He looked at us for a moment in silence. 'As a socialist democracy, allied to a new socialist Germany.' The lieutenant winked at us, and tapped his head. The soldier added: 'I can see you want to ask me: in what frontiers. Well, as the Tsar once said to the Poles, "*Messieurs, pas de rêveries!*" The Soviet Union will hold what it holds. The eastern provinces will never be under Polish control again.'

We all felt that he was becoming insolent. I found myself understanding why this man had been sent to Ladybank. But I gave him a tin of Gold Flake cigarettes which I had brought along as a reward, and we left in silence. As we drove through Fife, my colleague said: 'He is charming, terribly intelligent. But in the end, just another Jewish exaggerator.'

When he dropped me off at my office, he said: 'Tomorrow, something else interesting. The British are going to interrogate an SS officer, and they are letting us in on it. Want to come along?' He got out of the car, and stood beside me for a moment, brooding. 'The Bolsheviks liberating a Red Warsaw? No, it's *koszmarny* – a nightmare.' That evening, I wrote down what I had heard, but put none of it into our camp bulletin.

Next day, we found our way to a police station on the outskirts of Kirkcaldy. The prisoner turned out to be the same tall officer whose face our general had slapped. He sat on a chair facing us, two Poles and two uniformed British captains, and asked for a cigarette. The British refused. One of them, who spoke good German, invited the prisoner to confirm his name, rank and number. He remained silent.

'Don't waste our time. Your paybook says that you are *Obersturmbannführer* Wuttke, Franz, born in Danzig in 1910.'

'Who are these men?' He gestured at me and my companion.

'As you can see, they are officers in the Polish army.'

'There is no such army. Poland was a whore-bastard country,

which no longer exists. You are illegal terrorists, and have no right to question me.'

The British pair glanced at one another. One of them rose and suggested that we should go and have a cup of tea; there was a canteen in the police station.

On the way to the canteen, I noticed the other German prisoners, sitting on the pavement by a lorry some distance down the street. It was raining heavily, and their guards were keeping dry by sitting in the back of the lorry, their legs dangling over the tailboard. Some of the Germans glanced at us, the others kept their heads down. They were very wet.

After half an hour, we went back to the interrogation. Several military policemen were now in the room. The prisoner's hair was disarranged, and there was a bead of dried blood under his nose.

'Let's begin again. Name, rank and number?'

No reply.

'I'll ask you another question. Three weeks ago, when you were being moved here, a civilian saw a man leave the lorry and run away. Yet ten men started the journey and ten men arrived the other end. How do you explain that?'

'How do you explain that you have broken the Geneva Convention three times by using prisoners for military purposes, by torturing a prisoner of war, and by allowing a German officer to be interrogated by terrorists?'

After another hour of this, we left. The British did not hit him again, but decided to try the soft tactic – tea, cigarettes, sympathy. For that, they suggested to us, they needed the 'terrorists' out of the way. We did not think this would work, and disliked the feeling that we were handing victory to an SS man. But, politely, we left.

Outside, our driver came up to me. He saluted nervously. 'Sir, one of the Germans wants to speak to you.'

'To me?'

'He knows your name. I think he was speaking in English, not German, but I don't understand either. Only your name, sir, he kept trying to say it.'

'Where is he?'

'I think he went for a piss, sir, in the police station. He made signs like that.'

At first the dank little room seemed silent and empty. Two urinals with rusty stains, a blackened cold-water tap on the wall, a puddle on the stone floor. Then I noticed that the stall door was shut. At the sound of my feet, the door opened and a man came slowly out.

From time to time in my life, but more often as I grow older, I have met people I know to be dead. It goes like this: the instant of recognition, the recollection that this person is dead, then – naturally – the second glance which shows that this is someone else. What interests me is the moment between the recollection and the second glance. It's a moment of powerful and yet pleasant surprise, not at all a shock of hair-risen horror. So he or she is dead and yet wonderfully present, ready to reconnect where we broke off…

'I went to your funeral,' I said to Johnston Melville. He was in a mess, but not the mess you would expect from a corpse. His thin red hair was plastered to his head with rainwater, and his German tunic with its sewn-in prisoner patches was mud-stained. He had lost a lot of weight, and his face was weathered a coarse carmine. Johnston stared at me wordless, as if staggered to hear about his own obsequies. Even in life, I thought, he hadn't been quick-witted.

'What's going on? Why are you here?'

'Please help me. I need to get away. Those Germans are going to kill me, Mike.'

'Why don't you just walk away? Or stay in this police station?'

Johnston suddenly began to shout. 'You're an idiot! You know fine I can't go to the police. See the situation I'm in!' We both glanced at the door, wondering who might have heard him.

'What situation?' Johnston said nothing. He pulled a lump of cotton waste from his pocket and wiped his nose with it. I saw he had a bad cold. I went outside and told the others to wait; one of the Germans had something important to tell me in private. The remaining prisoners had already been allowed to take shelter in their truck. I told the escort to get them back to their camp, as soon as the British had done with Wuttke's interrogation. I would send the other man on when I had finished with him.

By now, I was making some connections. When Johnston was sitting in a vacant interview room with a mug of tea, I began: 'You were on the *Fronsac*, when it blew up, yes? But you survived, and afterwards, you ran away. Why did you? What had you done?'

'It wisnae me,' he said like a child. His hands on the mug were shaking.

'But you were the officer in charge.'

'Right. I was in charge, so I was. It was my show. Me not

knowing one end of a torpedo from the other. Well, we couldn't open the cover on the firing interlock, to check it out. So I told this French leading seaman fellow to give it a single dunt with the hammer. But he went on and was hammering on the other locks too. I never told him to do that, never. And it went up – the launching charge. It should never have been in the breech, not in port. There was this flash and blast that blew me over the side, then the big bang. I don't rightly mind what happened then, just being pulled out of the water.'

'What happened to the French sailor?'

'God knows. I think he bought it. He wisnae one of our lot, just some French matelot. Never saw him before or since. Never, believe me!' He met my eyes and nodded hard. 'When they put me ashore, I was lying on the quay with the burned sailors. I was seeing what was happening on the ship – smelling it and hearing it too. I thought: I did this. They'll never believe it wisnae my fault. They'll take my life away for this. So when they put me on a stretcher for the ambulance, I ran for it.'

'But what about Helen and Jackie? Your mother? They think you're dead.'

'I got to a post launch; he took me across the water. I went into the hills. Found an empty cottage, up in the forestry.'

He watched me carefully. An idea came to me. 'Mrs Melville knew where you were, didn't she? You must have found a telephone. Your mother was bringing you food and stuff on her bicycle, across the ferry from Gourock. With Jackie. So did Jackie know too?'

No reply. 'Why didn't you tell Helen?' I thought to myself; why didn't Mrs M tell Helen either? Johnston looked sullen.

There was a long silence. One of the British officers opened the door, apologised, took a look at Johnston and went out again. I knew quite well what I should do. I was an Allied officer facing a British deserter who was wanted by the police and the naval authorities. I really had no alternatives.

'Johnston, what the hell are you doing in German uniform?'

Quite unexpectedly, he laughed. 'I got a lift with them.' One morning, he had looked out of his cottage and seen the heads of a naval patrol bobbing above the bracken. (I thought at once of Eric, and his cosy interest in everything that Helen and Mrs M did and everywhere they went.) Johnston took off over the hill. A day later, hungry and midge-bitten, he had thumbed down an army lorry near Arrochar, and found himself in the back of a three-tonner with ten German prisoners of war, on their way to the east coast.

'There was two German officers – aye, that Wuttke bastard was one. He knew me at once for a deserter. They'd hand me over to the escort if I didn't do what he said. See, the other officer was planning to escape. They asked me where there was wee boats, so I had to say Hunters' Quay, Rhu and so on – maybe he was going to make for the Irish Free State. They made me change clothes with this German and get his paybook and that. So the numbers would add up when they were counted the other end.' Somewhere along the twisting Loch Lomond road, the escaper had slipped over the tailboard and rolled into the ditch.

'So now you are a German? For how long?'

'I saw you, Mike, that day the Polish general came to see us digging. But I didnae want you to see me. Now, it's all changed.

Wuttke's bunch, first they reckoned I could be a kinna hostage, but now they're no needing me any more. The word is they are going to a new camp, a real hard place that's being put up at Abercultie for the SS prisoners. No chance I could pass for German there. See, I'm the only one who knows about the escape, so they're wanting to kill me before they get to Abercultie. Help me out, Mike. We cared for you back in Union Street, Helen and I. Okay, maybe you never hit it off with me, but help me for Helen's sake, Jackie's sake!'

I went out, slamming the door and locking it. The British officer was still there, sitting on a bench in the police station lobby and studying a newspaper. He looked up at me. 'Something special about that Jerry?'

It occurred to me that I had not checked the window in the interview room. Why not? I distinctly remembered wondering if it could be closed, as I turned the door key. But for some reason, I had not followed the thought. As soon as I unlocked the door again, I knew that the room would be empty.

The first thing I did in that room changed my life. I went to the open window and closed it. It was a sash window, and I remember noticing how heavy and stiff the lower pane was, clogged with grime and old paint. Tugging it down took a violent effort. Johnston must have struggled desperately to heave it up, and make a space wide enough for his thin, damp body to twist through. When the window was shut again, I turned the snib to secure it. Now I was a criminal, an accomplice.

What possessed me? I was concealing the escape of a prisoner – two prisoners, in fact, counting the German officer who had slipped off the lorry. Worse still, I was complicit in hiding a naval deserter wanted by both the British police and – whatever one called them – the security services. To that I could add my new guilty knowledge, near-certainty, that his mother had for months been helping that man to avoid arrest.

And all this for Johnston Melville? I did not even like him. Who could? All he seemed to have for a character was a caterpillar malignity; the power to poison anyone who bit him – perhaps anyone who tried to rescue him. And his appearance counted against him too. I still felt resentful, even cheated, that my first Scottish acquaintance had been this pallid mother's boy. Book-reading in childhood had given me heroic expectations. But what had Johnston to do with the giants of Ossian or with Ketling, the merry little Scottish warrior in Sienkiewicz's novels?

Every one of those alarms was ringing in my head. And yet I found myself leaving the room, locking it again and making my way to a back door. Our staff car was parked in the police-station yard round the corner; the British intelligence officer was no doubt still pretending to read a newspaper in the front lobby.

I looked down the street. The lorry with Wuttke and the other prisoners had gone. In the distance, I saw a figure dart from one close-mouth to another; even through the rain, his prisoner patches showed their colour. Going back into the police station, I found a black rubber gas cape hanging on a hook.

Stalking Johnston was easy. He gave only a grunt of terror when I grabbed his wrist. 'Put this on. Here's half-a-crown for the bus.' I told him where to get off as the bus passed our camp.

'There's a Catholic chapel down the way on the left. Hide there till I come.'

Looking back on those moments, so many years later, I can't reconstruct my recklessness. But I can recognise the drive which made me act as I did. Not out of pity for a fellow being. Not for Helen, wherever she might be. Not out of any inner bloody-mindedness towards authority, and certainly not through disloyalty to our cause. This war against the two ogre-powers who hated liberty even more than one another, and whose partnership to devour my country seemed so natural – that was still a war I wanted to fight.

None of those feelings moved me. It was the open window. A trapped creature had managed to free the steel hatch-cover jammed above his life, and – dressed as somebody else – to vanish into the future. In the blank rectangle of air between the sill and the sash, air carrying the scent of wet trees and distant frying, I had seen the outline of redemption, rebirth, the mouth of a secret passage open to every man and woman who is allowed to find it. No, I was not – am not – 'religious'. But the open window was to me a sign which I knew that I could not deny.

The Scots sing in their kirk that 'Ev'n as a bird out of the fowler's snare / Escapes away, so is our soul set free'. I had heard those words, a psalm rough-hammered into rhyme, at a Church of Scotland service to which Polish soldiers were invited. It had been a bad idea. Their Catholic instincts were ruffled by the Kirk's grim informality, and they chattered and laughed all through. Embarrassed, I bent over the words in the metrical psalter and saw that, after all, Scots and Poles had something in common:

When cruel men against us furiously
Rose up in wrath to make of us their prey;
Then certainly they had devour'd us all...
And as fierce floods before them all things drown,
So had they brought our soul to death quite down...

That was how things felt to us, as they had once felt to the children of Israel and then to the Scots facing Edward's armies. The psalm went on to give God the praise for slashing a hole in the fowlers' net; he would not give his people 'for a living prey / Unto their teeth and bloody cruelty'. But he had given poor Poland for a living prey. The nets were all about us.

Like fixing Helen's flit to Canada, translating Johnston into yet another existence turned out to be easier than I expected. Easier than it should have been. I gave him some of my own civilian clothes, and parked him in a brick air raid shelter behind the chapel. Then came some telephone calls and a visit to a closely guarded camp with tall radio masts, where we were starting to train what we called in Polish 'silent-shadowy' people – agents to be parachuted back into Poland.

As an intelligence officer, I was known there. Two bottles of Johnny Walker in a gas mask satchel clinked down on the desk of the captain whose shadowy boys produced forged *Wehrmacht* passbooks and movement permits. 'A British identity card? A civilian one? Szczucki, don't fuck this up, whatever it is, or I will get shot too. No, tell me after the war. What name?'

It took a week. Then Alexander Ketling, b. Paisley 1915, certified mentally subnormal and unfit for military service, went sulkily down the road when it was dark enough. I pushed three pound notes into his pocket. 'Stay away from here. Find a job digging holes, caring for sheep, something. Keep out of the war. Keep away from me.'

The dangerous bit, I knew, would be covering his disappearance in Kirkcaldy, the escape of a prisoner of war in my charge. Next day, the British officers who had been in the police station arrived in my office and questioned me. My story was that, after listening to what he had to say, I had let him walk back towards the lorry where Wuttke and the other Germans were waiting.

No, I hadn't waited to see him climb on board. What had he told me? Nothing interesting. He said he was from a part of Germany where there were many people of Polish extraction; his sister had married one of them who had gone back to Poland just before the outbreak of war to join the army. The prisoner wanted to know if his brother-in-law had reached our army in Scotland. I said I didn't see why I should do him a favour. That was all.

The Brits watched me in their calm way. Presumably I had taken a note of his name and number? 'He did tell me, but I don't remember.' Wasn't that amazingly casual of me – an intelligence officer? One of the Brits began to write on a pad.

'Maybe it will come back to me ... it was ... something like ...' A look of resigned disgust passed between the Brits. These Poles! The writing officer glanced up from his notes and said: 'His name was Nuttgen, Hans, an infantry lieutenant. Did he say anything about going to look for this brother-in-law?

No? Doesn't come back to you either? Well, it seems that's as far as we can take it today.'

I foresaw very bad trouble indeed. But days passed, and I heard nothing more. Then, a couple of weeks after I had sent Johnston off to become Alexander Ketling, there was a telephone call. 'Major, er... Shoosky? I thought you'd like to know. We've caught him.'

'You caught him?' I looked round my familiar office, mentally saying goodbye. I had made myself comfortable here. Would they let me take a book with me? Were Scottish prisons heated in winter?

'Absolutely! Should have told you before. Pretty enterprising chap – he seems to have walked across to the west coast, nicked a dinghy and rowed himself all the way to Ireland.'

'Oh, you mean... Nuttgen did.'

'Yes, of course. Is this a bad line? He got to Ireland – but the wrong one! The Royal Ulster Constabulary picked him off the shore in County Antrim. Good try, one has to say.'

'Did he tell you anything more? Who helped?'

'Well, some things still don't add up. How he got civvy clothes. How he got from Kirkcaldy across to Argyllshire. That SS sod Wuttke probably knows more than he's saying. We've got him in a punishment cell. By the way, Nuttgen keeps saying he never talked to any Polish officer, and doesn't have a brother-in-law anywhere. Bizarre!'

When he hung up, I sat for a long moment in silence. Then I went to the office safe, and brought out a bottle of whisky. Beside it in the safe was a small brown envelope. I took that out too, and as I drank to my own escape I spread out the German

Wehrpass in the name of Nuttgen, Hans, which Johnston had been given with the escaper's tunic. Not something I wanted to be found with. Next day, I gave it to the 'silent-shadowy' people up the road. They and their parachutists would find a use for it.

The war came closer. Although London and the English cities were being blitzed, I had assumed that Scotland was more or less beyond the Luftwaffe's reach. Then, on two nights in the middle of March 1941, the German bomber fleets came for Clydebank. One of our destroyers, *Piorun*, was in John Brown's yard for repairs at the time. She cheered the town's survivors with the banging of her guns, but hit nothing.

Greenock was only a few miles away downriver. I thought uneasily about Union Street and Mrs Melville and Jackie. Mrs M was on my conscience. She knew nothing about Johnston's second escape, but I was certain that persistent Eric knew what she had been doing in the Argyll hills. Sooner or later, he would be ready to pounce. It seemed to me that there was little I could do to stop him. To visit Union Street would only set Eric wondering whether I too had something to hide. Anyway, the less Mrs M knew about Johnston, the better.

I sat quietly at my typewriter, drinking tea and editing little bulletins. Polish troops had been in action far away in Syria, and perhaps would soon be fighting in Greece or North Africa. Speeches by Churchill, speeches by our Supreme Commander. Weeks passed. Then, at breakfast in the mess one day, somebody said: 'They hit Greenock last night. Isn't that where you were, Szczucki?'

Back in my office, the external telephone rang. I knew who it would be. 'Mr Ketling? Yes, I heard. No, don't talk now. At St Monans, at six, outside the harbour gate? Fine, Mr Ketling.'

I hardly recognised this figure in fisherman's yellow oilskins, over a dirty white jersey. It wasn't just that Johnston had put on weight. There was something newly self-assured about him, even insolent. I had to ask him twice what he was doing until, reluctantly, he explained that he had got a job with an East Neuk drifter going after haddock. 'The other lads? They're no bothering me. They just ignore me now, when we're ashore. Coarse types, you know; off the boats there's only beer for them and getting the wee bit with the women. They get their pay and it's away in an evening.' Johnston was healthier, but no more likeable than before.

'There's no way I can go through there myself. But you could go. See if the house is standing yet. See if my mother's fine, and Jackie. And Helen.'

'I never told you. Helen's gone away, last year after you – after the funeral. She's in Canada.'

'Canada? What for Canada? She never telt me she was going.'

'How could she? You were dead.'

'Aye, right.' He stared me down. 'If you're through to Union Street, there's things I need. My father's watch, it's gold. And my passbook from the Union Bank. I'm putting my money away here, a fair sum now, and I'm wanting it safe in the bank.'

'Johnston, are you mad? If you use that passbook, they'll catch you.'

'Aye, right,' he said again. He thought for a moment. 'Just the watch, then. And my suit – the good suit, that's in the press in my mother's room. That'll be enough for now.'

'Will I tell your mother where you are?'

'Ach, just tell her I'm fine. That and no more. That'll be plenty for her.' He turned to go.

I called after him: 'Don't telephone me again!' But he took no notice, and marched on down the steep harbour street. Gulls with yellow bills snarled at him as they hopped out of his way.

The operator said that she couldn't connect me. The lines in Greenock were down. That night, the bombers came again, with more squadrons. The town burned, and then the peat-covered hillside above caught fire. People watching from Helensburgh, on the north side of the Firth, looked across the water into a trembling open furnace three miles long.

It was three days later that I was able to take leave and go to Greenock. The trains to the town had stopped; rumour said there were parachute mines the size of laundry boilers lying across the rails. But some buses were running as far as the outskirts. The inner streets of Greenock and Port Glasgow looked like my own last sight of Warsaw: blackened gables, smoke still rising, tangled hoses flushing the roadway with rippling fans of water.

I stopped to question an elderly air raid warden, as he watched a fire brigade team digging into a hill of rubble. He guessed the dead must number hundreds, maybe thousands. Many families were still hiding in the moors up by Loch Thom. He peered at me over his spectacles. 'It puts me in mind of Pompeii. But it was no the volcano we got. It was the barbarians.'

I walked on. As in the London blitz, the Germans had used their curious instinct for class discrimination. The working-class part of town had been devastated, while the west end of Greenock, with its broad, straight avenues, was almost untouched. As I came up Union Street, everything seemed normal except for the smell: a thick marzipan reek of burned plaster mixed with the scent of peat smoke from the hill.

Mrs Melville was sitting in the kitchen. Her smart Red Cross uniform was creased and stained. Beside her, at the table where Helen and I used to share cigarettes and eye one another, there was a pale young woman staring at me fearfully, clasping an equally pale small boy on her knee. 'Goodness, see who's here,' said Mrs M weakly. She tried to get up, but fell back into her chair. 'I was up all the night. There's no gas. I'll just make tea on the wee Primus.'

'Don't . . .' But she struggled to her feet and lit the methylated spirit under the little burner perched on the table. I wondered how to get her alone for a talk. Everyone seemed too stunned to speak.

When the tea came, the small boy grabbed the spoons and pulled them into his lap. When a plate of biscuits came, he grabbed them all too. Next he snatched a box of matches which I brought out to light a cigarette, and I saw that his pockets were bulging with small objects. Mrs Melville reached out to take back one of the spoons from his fist, but he clutched it tighter and began to scream. 'That's mine, that's Mammy's.' His mother tried softly to unlock his fingers, but the screaming went on.

I took my cup of tea and beckoned Mrs M into the next room. We closed the door. 'That's Stella and that's wee Francis,' she said. 'Bombed out from Clydebank, you know. They've been here for a month. They lost everything, just every single thing. Did you ever know anyone who had nothing – not a roof, not a change of shoes, not a toy?'

'Mabel, I know where Johnston is.'

She sat down on the sofa. She did not look at me, but took off her spectacles and began to polish them alertly with her silk scarf.

'Mabel, he's fine. He's changed his name, got a job, a new identity card. The empty cottage at Kilmun – I think I know all about that.'

'What are you going to do about it, then?'

'About him? About you? There is nothing I can do about him – not now. The *Fronsac* – the explosion – I think it was not his fault. But I helped him hide and become somebody else. So if he is caught, I am also falling in the, in the... how you say?'

'I would say: in the soup. But wouldn't soldiers and sailors say something else?'

She suddenly yawned. A strand of grey hair fell over her face, but she seemed too tired to brush it away. It was if she had forgotten what we had been talking about. There was a silence.

'And how is Jackie?'

'You are risking something on my son's account. Risking a great deal. I realise that, and I wouldn't have you thinking I do not.'

'Yes, but Jackie?'

Mrs Melville sighed, then suddenly shook her head as if she were waking from a doze.

'Ach, I took her out of that wretched school. She goes to St Columba's in Kilmacolm now. The girls have to wear white gloves there. If they aren't wearing their gloves when they get off the train from Greenock, they get a row. Oh, it's right perjink, is St Columba's. And their motto is "Variety Without Disorder". It's my view that at Campbell Street it was all "Disorder Without Variety".'

'Is she happy?'

'That one keeps her feelings to herself. She does very well in the new school, just excellent marks. But she's wanting privacy in her own house. She'll not be sorry when Stella and Francis are away back to their own folk.'

'Helen?'

'Isn't it me should be asking you that? Not a word to me or to Jackie. Not since that parcel. And it's the best part of a year now. That young lady has all the butter and eggs she can eat over there, and no blackout, and no bombs to wake her in the night. And the bright lights and the big cars. She'll have found better things to do than remember her own child.'

I got up and went to the big window. It was the same view that I remembered. There were warships out there at anchor, and freighters flying barrage balloons, and an Atlantic liner painted grey. A dispatch launch was cutting an important line of spray. It was sea business as usual, unconcerned by what had happened to the town behind.

'Did they hit any ships?'

'Not one. It's a mercy; that big one was fairly packed with Canadian soldiers. But the noise of their guns was terrible, worse than the bombs.'

'Worse?'

Mrs M looked down into her cup of tea, gone cold. Without a spoon to stir it, she swirled the tea around for a few moments.

'Aye, well. Worse? I was down in Cathcart Street the second night. We had an aid post... I thought it was clear and I could make a dash for it across the way. Then I heard this one coming. This skreiching whistle, louder and louder. It seemed to go on for ever, the big one saying he was coming for me, just for me. I lay down on the street with my helmet on, and I gripped my handbag as tight as tight. I mind thinking: how will they tell Jackie? She's alone in the shelter in the garden with Stella and the wee boy. Who'll care for her? Please, God, don't do this.'

I said nothing. Knowing her well enough, I knew she would wish she hadn't spoken this way. Already she was frowning.

'There's always others worse off. Like my father used to say, worse things happened at Culloden. Well, it went into the houses by Station Avenue. Quite a mess. There were families sheltering under the stair. Quite a mess. We were at it there with the wardens and the firemen all night. A "night to remember"? No, thank you.'

'Mabel, we need to talk about you, what happens to you about Johnston. Do you see Eric?'

'It's been a while now. He used to come by once in a few months and blether about Johnston. Still those nice manners and that, but persistent. He had some idea that Johnston wasn't dead; once he asked me, quite suddenly, if I had heard from him. That was after I found the cottage empty. It was a shock, that question, but I told him nothing. I believe he will have given up now.'

'No, Mabel, I think he has been watching you all the time. Johnston left when he saw a shore patrol coming to search the cottage. Eric must have sent them.'

'That was more than a year ago, Mike. There's more important things to worry about these days. I'll not ask you where Johnston is, but I'm sure there are things he asked you to bring from the house. Is he keeping warm?'

'Does Jackie know he's still alive?'

'She certainly does not! Well... but I think she makes up stories for herself. She likes reading about people hiding in the hills, Prince Charlie, the Bruce and all that. She's reading *Kidnapped* just now.'

I left, promising to come back the next morning. Mrs M would make up a suitcase with the watch and the clothes and maybe a cake. My problem would be to find a room, if there was a hotel left standing.

The Tontine, a few hundred yards away, was full. Maybe there would be somewhere in Gourock or Fort Matilda, where

I had begun my Franco-Scottish life with Commandant le Gallois. I set out to walk.

Gourock seemed almost untouched. But the grey streets I remembered had become a coloured parade of uniforms. Most were British: Royal Navy or RAF. A platoon of Australians in wide-awake hats tramped by. I passed several Free French naval officers, but recognised none of them. A man and a woman in neatly pressed Canadian Air Force battledress strode out of the Bay Hotel as I approached.

No room there either. A Polish sergeant – what was he doing here? – saluted me in the lobby as I turned to leave. He was staying with a family in a tenement up the hill; there was a spare bed in the kitchen.

'The daughter is nice, but no chance – *niema mowy!*' I took down the address with some difficulty. 'Mathie Crescent' doesn't trip easily off the Polish tongue. Then I went out of the hotel and stood on the pavement, wondering how to spend the rest of the day.

In front of me was the harbour railway station, where troops coming off the big ships 'entrained' for unknown destinations. The two Canadians were standing outside the booking hall, evidently saying goodbye. They kissed, and the man vanished into the station. The woman looked up towards the hotel, and began to walk quickly in my direction. I moved aside to let her pass as she came up to me. But she didn't pass.

'Mike!'

Who was this elegant, laughing airwoman, with her yellow hair in a bun under an officer's cap? For two seconds, I didn't know.

'I saw you there going into the Bay. Looking so serious. Couldn't believe it.'

'Your hair. It's grown so long. You have lipstick!'

Helen stood in front of me, still laughing. I took both her hands and held them tightly.

'What are you doing here? How did you get here?'

'I flew, that's how. That's what I do. See these wings? I'm a flyer.'

'What are you talking about?'

'I'm a pilot, Mike. Six months' training, and I'm passed for a co-pilot on bombers. Ferry duty! The Yanks build them and we fly them over the Atlantic.'

'Your voice, you talk like an American.'

'Canadian, okay? Maybe, but on the base they still call me Scottie.'

We went inside, and found somewhere to sit in the lounge among a pack of convoy seamen. They stared at Helen in her neat pale-blue tunic. There was a table between us. Suddenly, we were not sure what to say.

'The *Selangor Star*. We all thought you had drowned. But you were in a lifeboat. What happened to you then?'

'I don't talk about that. I can't think about it.' She pulled out a pack of Camels and lit mine with a gleaming silver lighter. The taste was new to me, sweetish. 'Now I've to go back by sea, on that big liner out there with the next convoy. See, we flew the planes into Prestwick, and came up here to embark. That'll be ten days and nights on the Atlantic zigzagging back west. Looking down on the water from up high, I can take that. But I've been too close to it once already, Mike.'

'Bad dreams?'

'You guessed it.'

There was another silence. The things I hadn't said, the things she hadn't asked, were becoming monstrous.

'Let's go for a walk.'

We went through the streets near the Free French base, and up to the top of the Lyle Hill. It was steep; we didn't talk much on the way.

'Are the trains running?'

'After the blitz? Not yet. Why?'

'Craig thought he would go through to Glasgow for the day. If there's no train, he'll be waiting on me down there. I'll need to go back and find him. Britain's still a bit of a mystery to him.'

'Craig?'

'My husband. Met him in Winnipeg, when we were training. He's a farmer in peacetime, somewhere in Ontario. Good guy. Good flyer too. Boy, I hope he stays on the ferry job and doesn't go bombing Germany.'

'You are married?'

We had reached the summit. The whole panorama of the estuary lay below us: the tiny ships in rows at the Tail of the Bank, the stone houses clinging to the hillside, the Argyll mountain ranges clear in the background. A destroyer's siren whooped and echoed. To the east, a yellowish smoke haze lay over Greenock.

Beyond the ships, on the distant side of the Firth, I noticed the hulk of a vessel on its side, bows tilted below the surface. I didn't need to count the funnels to recognise her. The *Fronsac* had been towed into the shallows and beached, along with the dead men under her deck.

I didn't feel like pointing that out to Helen. She was smiling to herself, taking deep breaths, at ease. She might have been appreciating a vast, familiar painting. 'My father used to take me up here. He said it was the mountain where the Devil took Jesus to tempt him. He showed him all the kingdoms of the world and their glory, and he could have them if he bowed down to Satan.'

'Helen . . .'

'I'm not Helen any more. Well, to you, okay. But my name's Mary now. Craig married Mary Helen MacPhail.'

I shouted at her. 'What are you doing? Jackie could be dead in the blitz, and we have been together for an hour, and you didn't even ask after her. You cried once because you were a bad mother. What are you now? Your father, Mabel, they could all be in the hospital dying. Butter, eggs, maple syrup, Canada, pretty uniform? This is your country, you bitch! What have you become?'

She sat down on a bench, and looked at me calmly. Her eyes tightened at the corners in the old way.

'This Craig – you are not married to this Craig. I give you the news: Johnston is still alive. The funeral – it was all a fake. I tell you the whole story. But no, you are not interested.'

Helen shook her head and turned away. She seemed to be consulting the wind, the Firth.

'Well, I'm asking a question now. Tell me about Jackie.'

'She is fine. She is still at Union Street with her grandmother. At a new school. Will you go to see her?'

'Well, I don't know. They won't tell us when the convoy goes, but the word is we need to get on board tomorrow. Johnston . . . my God! I'm glad, but it's so long since I thought of him. I can't rightly picture his face, even. He's not at Union Street . . . no? That's one mercy.'

'How can you say that? He is your husband. You have to tell Craig.'

'You're daft. He wouldn't understand. I'll need to sort this, some way, but it's wartime. In wartime, there's nothing can't be sorted. See your long face! Ach, Mike, you's just a wee Polish prig. I liked you better as my wee Polish count!'

She was sounding less Canadian now. And that jarring laugh was the same. It hurt me and it moved me.

'Let's go down, Mike.'

At the edge of the Lyle Hill, with the view before her, she stopped again and stood looking down. Then she turned to face me, crossing her arms over her breasts in a movement – sure, imperious – that I didn't remember in her.

'I want you to get this, Mike, once and for all. This is no my country now. It's just the place where I was a wean. Bens and glens, sure, that's fine. Maybe I'll get Jackie away to Canada after the war, and then she and I and Craig and our kids will come one summer and drive around and see the sights. But there's nothing for me in Scotland.'

She swept an arm across the view, as if she were throwing away stale crumbs. 'I cannae believe I belonged here. See all those worn-oot folk in their worn-oot houses down there. And they knowing no better. I could never go back to that . . . dump. Never!'

A sigh. She folded her arms again, more tightly. 'I'll tell you. When we were on the approach, coming in for Prestwick, it was right misty. We were just at a couple of hundred feet when I saw that grey old coast coming up towards me. And you know – I felt sick at my stomach. And it wisna the big Hudson shoogling about in the wind. It was me thinking: Oh no! I got away from this land, and here I'm back.'

I was lurching into angry words – you do belong here, you can't just – when her violent stare made me stop. Of all people, was I going to lecture her about loyalty to a place, to people? Me, foreign Mike, who used to boast to her in that kitchen that he needed no home? But then I imagined myself in a swaying aircraft suddenly breaking through clouds to see the Polish countryside – those straight white roads, those Sunday-best little fields striped green, gold and brown – streaming past below me. I felt my throat tighten, here on this Scottish hilltop, but not with dread.

Helen, I saw, was the true escaper. I was evading something else, something closer than a country. The game of words for tears . . . it occurred to me, for the first time, that it had always been Helen playing it on me. I had never taken my turn to pitch words back at her. Somehow, for some purpose, she had kept the game one-sided.

Now Helen advanced on me. She hadn't finished. But at first the words wouldn't come. Frowning, she stabbed a finger on to my breast-pocket button, over and over as if she were ringing the bell of an empty house. Then she said: 'When they lifted me out of the boat, I was no seeing much at all. And no hearing much. There was damn-all to hear by then, anyhow. We pulled four children from the water after the ship went down. But six days and nights in that boat; the voices went quiet, and . . . well . . . I wasna seeing properly but I was thinking yet, I was still thinking. And the thought when I felt those Canadian sailors gripping and raising me up was: never again, no way back. If it's life I am being given, then it's a new life.'

She was shaking. I put out my arms to her. But on the instant a thud of wind came from nowhere and blew her smart cap off. We ran after it, as it wheeled under the hilltop bench and on to the roadway. By the time I caught it (an envious glimpse at the red waterproof lining and the burnished patent-leather strap), Helen was laughing. We began to walk down the hill arm in arm.

'Leave Jackie to me,' she said, as we came to the first houses. 'Don't tell her I was here. I'll maybe see her next time we're over. No, Mike, worry about yourself.'

'Me? I am in no danger.'

'Ach, Mike! It's not bombs and that. It's what's going on inside of you. I never knew, and I don't know now. Do you know it yourself? All the time we were together, you never asked me what I felt about you, and I was feared of putting questions. You were that charming, aye, and sensitive – I could tell you things I never thought I could tell a man. But then I would think: there's a door closed here. He's away taking a walk, he's daundering through life, and I'm just an interesting piece of scenery. You're a sarcastic man, Mike. Everyone's just a bit of a joke to you, right?'

'So what did you feel about me?'

'Trust a man to miss the point! It's you we're talking about, you. What's it you care about? Get a grip, Mike, or the wind will blow you away like my hat.'

When we reached the Bay Hotel, Helen took the cap off to give me a sharp kiss. Her cheek was cold. She gave me a long, critical look, not smiling. I thought that if I were a pilot I would feel safer with this young woman beside me, her small blue eyes fixed on the altimeter and the airspeed dial. Then she walked off down the slope to the station. I could see the Canadian officer standing outside the station gate, glancing at his wristwatch and then at passers-by. Before he found her, I turned away.

I made my way to Mathie Crescent, where the 'nice daughter' fried egg and chips for me and my Polish fellow lodger. She had black curly hair and seemed shy. Her mother stood in the kitchen watching us while we ate. After a few minutes, she remarked that Mary-Margaret was engaged to a fine young man in the bank where she worked as a clerkess. 'Liam lives a clean life; he's one of us. This is a Catholic house. You being Polish, you'll feel at home here.'

I glanced at the shelf sagging under a procession of devotional china, the swags of beads casting their shadow on the wall, the crucifix over the hearth, the portrait of the Holy Father smiling thinly through his spectacles. 'Why do they exaggerate so?' muttered the sergeant, in our own language. 'It's like being in a pilgrimage shop at Góra Kalwaria.' We sniggered together, as if we were schoolboys.

Mary-Margaret took our empty plates. She said, apparently to her mother: 'Now that Liam's getting called up, I'll not see him for ever so long.' She turned slightly pink. The sergeant sighed.

It was warm in the kitchen that night. The range, damped down under a shovelful of slack, made feathery sounds and the wind tapped against the blackout board on the window. I was comfortable in my narrow bed, but for the first hours I could not sleep.

I had let Helen off so easily. Sentences I hadn't spoken paraded past me. I wanted to have told her that she was the first truly immoral, totally egotistic person I had ever met. Paris whores, Kraków con men, all had some grimy loyalty to someone, to something. But you, Helen . . . you are like a damned Russian Bolshevik: you don't live by any fixed standards at all. You respect nothing. You think: today I will have this country and no more that country, I will have this man and no more that yesterday man. A child? I will wave at her from my aeroplane. Bye-bye, look at me, see how your clever mama can fly away.

I cursed her. In the dimness, I could make out the outstretched arms of the crucifix on the wall, the sombre rosary festoons beside it. Last night, in the glare of the electric light hanging from the ceiling, they had seemed risible. Now their vague shapes seemed grave and familiar, childhood anchors which I had cast loose so long ago.

They had no power over me; I would never be a believer again. But suddenly, half asleep, I desired Helen to be here in this kitchen with me. I would force her to look at these things! With one hand, I would hold her arms behind her back; with the other I would cruelly grip the nape of her neck and twist her face towards that wall.

She must not say a word. Minutes would pass. Then I would feel her slacken in my grasp, and I would say: 'You see? This was here centuries before you were born, watching over a million families whose children can imagine other lives but put a common good before their own fancies. It will be here centuries after you are dead. Something outside has to tell you how to live; you aren't meant to make up your own rules. Submit! Learn how to respect!'

Now I was fully awake. I pushed back the blanket and sat on the edge of the bed, finding that I was damp with sweat. My fantasy disgusted me. In the Bay Hotel, Helen would be sleeping tranquilly beside her Craig, embarkation order and identity papers clipped together on the bedside table, uniform hanging clean and newly pressed in the cupboard. Soon the alarm clock would ring, and she would set off into another complicated, well-organised day. How could I say that her life was lawless? Whose rule did I observe in mine?

I trudged back to Union Street in bright May sunshine. The French headquarters was on my way, now flying a Cross of Lorraine as well as the tricolour, but I didn't feel like calling on Commandant le Gallois. All I wanted to do was shoulder a bag with Johnston's belongings and hurry back through to my own people, to easy companions and petty routines.

The stove in the company office would be hot, there would be the rhythmic tramp of men marching back from morning drill. The phone would ring to announce some tiny crisis. We had a joke that it would always be an anxious voice saying: '*o sprawie tych koców* – about those blankets . . .' I would go to see the adjutant and begin: 'About those blankets . . . is it true the Brits are going to give us a real tank for training?' We would both laugh. Meaningless and unfunny when remembered afterwards, but these things dropped a sweetness into military life, a sugar lump in a bitter mug.

Mrs M had cleaned her uniform and was waiting to go back to her Red Cross post. In the hall beside her there was a brown suitcase. 'There was a label with Johnston's name on. I snipped that off, no bother.'

I lifted the case to try its weight, and at that moment heard someone coming up the steps from the street. We looked at one another. The bell jangled. Mrs M took the case out of my grasp and swiftly stowed it in a cupboard under the stair.

'My word!' said Eric. 'Just the chap I needed to talk to. Great day for the race, isn't it. Can we all sit down somewhere?'

'Why, Eric, how are you keeping? I was beginning to think we had lost you.' She spoke brightly, but Eric ignored her. He was watching me and nodding. His old air of vagueness had gone. I noticed that he was carrying a briefcase, and had grown a small, ugly moustache.

We went into the kitchen and sat down. Mrs M did not offer to make tea. Eric pulled an army foolscap jotter out of his briefcase and spread it on the table.

'I'm afraid this is not a friendly visit. Not a chat. Nobody is to leave this house until you have answered my questions. There is a police car outside. So let's get started.'

He turned to me. 'I'll begin with you, Major. Mrs Melville, I want you to leave the room until I call you back. No phoning. Thank you.'

Eric pulled a pair of gold-rimmed spectacles out of his breast pocket and put them on. They changed his face. He looked unexpectedly wise.

'Now, Major, we know that you have been in contact with two German prisoners. Wuttke and Nuttgen. Is that right?'

'Yes, I took part in their interrogation.'

'Oh, but that's not quite true, is it? The second man you spoke to wasn't Nuttgen. And I think you knew it wasn't. You see, Lieutenant Nuttgen has turned out to be a most cooperative bloke. He hates Wuttke. In fact, he hates the Nazis. But very patriotic, doesn't want to be disloyal to Germany. That's why he tried to escape – to get home, but also to get away from the SS crew he was locked up with. He's a pious type. Belonged to some Catholic youth group in the Rhineland which didn't approve of Hitler. Anyway, he has agreed to help us. He tells us what the other prisoners are up to in the camp at Abercultie.'

I said nothing.

'Wuttke suspects something. That's why we had him in a punishment cell for a bit. He threatened Nuttgen with some sort of Nazi honour court. But of course that's not all Nuttgen has been telling us. We know a bit about how he escaped from that truck, and the deserter they picked up on the road. And I am ninety per cent sure I know who that was.'

Eric paused. 'Now look, Major. The fact is that officially there's nothing I can do to you. You are not under our jurisdiction, and it will be up to the Polish army to deal with you. I wouldn't like to be in your shoes when that happens. But they don't have to find out. If you help me.'

'What do you mean?'

'I want you to help me with Nuttgen. Major, can't you see that Wuttke is getting ready to prang our whole eavesdrop operation in the camp? What I need, fast, is evidence hard enough to put him away in a proper jail – and keep our source in place. And you will be present, Major, when we try to get that evidence out of Nuttgen. You have to testify in front of him that you never saw him before. You have to confirm that Wuttke – and you – both knew that the man you talked to in the police station in Kirkcaldy was somebody else.'

He wagged a finger at me, shook his head very slowly. 'My word, Major, I really do wonder who that man was. Don't you? Old chap, it would be such a help if you really told us everything you know about Johnston Melville.'

I thought fast, but could see no way through this. 'I could arrange to be at Abercultie when you are there. As an Allied intelligence officer.'

'So far, so good. Where is Johnston Melville?'

'I don't know.'

'Are you really going to stick to that? Does Mrs Melville know where he is?'

'I cannot say.'

Eric, I noticed, had written nothing in his big exercise book. Now he took out a pencil and tested its point on his finger. He rose and walked over to open the kitchen door. 'Mrs Melville?' I noticed what a small, frail man he was. Maybe I could find somebody to kill him.

Mabel Melville came in and sat down on a wooden chair, across the table from Eric.

'Where is Johnston?'

'I really can't say. I don't know.'

'Well, at least you aren't pretending he's dead. That's a start.' He wrote something down, then leaned back.

'Now listen to me very carefully. I want you to understand just what a mess you have got yourself into. When we arrest your son, we are going to charge him with treason. Not just with desertion, but with assisting the enemy in time of war. And possibly with sabotage as well. Is that clear to you so far?'

Mrs M looked levelly back at him. She kept silent.

'Your own situation isn't much better. I could take you down to the police station this minute and have you charged with conspiring to conceal a deserter, with deliberately obstructing the police and security in the exercise of their duties. We would make an example of you. It will be in all the papers – we can see to that. The prison sentence for that offence in wartime would be a long one.'

I said: 'Are we in Nazi Germany? All this lady did was natural, not a crime. She was a mother, she helped her son. She is a good woman, who works for others in the Red Cross, who has bombed-out families in her house. And what would happen to her grandchild, to Jackie?'

'Ah, Jackie. I was coming to her. It's a pity that none of you spared a thought for that child, when you started lying and deceiving. Her father, assuming now that he's alive and not dead, has abandoned her. So did her mother, although she lost her life running away. Scarcely what decent people would call a loving family.'

I saw Mabel Melville lick her dry lips. She said with difficulty: 'Go on. Go on with what you are going to say.'

'Well, Jackie won't be left on her own. Of course not. She will be taken into care and sent to an orphanage, or a home for children from criminal families in the slums. The Quarrier Homes at Kilmacolm take in orphans, though they'll be pretty full just now after the big raids. But the best solution is Australia. Yes, the Aussies are taking hundreds of children shipped out from bad homes. They get put out to foster families. Change their names, get a new life down there. Yes, in my judgement Australia is where Jackie will probably end up.'

'No,' I was saying. 'Mabel, no!' I was gripping her shoulders, pushing her back into her chair. Eric watched calmly, as if he had been through scenes like this before. Mrs M let out a long, harsh breath and became still again.

'Now then. Let's be clear, Mrs Melville. None of these things has to happen. It's entirely up to you. And I'll let you into a little secret: I haven't told my colleagues, my bosses, about this case. Not yet. Well, they know the rough outlines – tracking down a deserter – but not the names or the places. If they knew just how big it's getting, all the juicy details like a Polish involvement, then they would barge in and take it off me. But I'm rather an ambitious type. I'll only put them in the picture when I have everything wrapped up – in a parcel with my name on it.'

'Why did you tell us that? Something we didn't have to know?'

'Well spotted, Major. But then you are a sort of intelligence officer yourself, aren't you? You see, I want you to trust me, so I am taking a little risk and showing I trust you. All I need from Mrs Melville is where to find her son. Then we can forget this chat. No prison, no headlines in newspapers, and Jackie goes on living with her granny in Union Street.'

'But she doesn't know where Johnston is. She told you.'

'Then perhaps you can help her. I'm not making any suggestions about what you may know, Major. I'm just floating a thought.'

'I will come with you to the camp – yes. But about Johnston, Mrs Melville and I will have to talk. Can you give us time for that?'

'No rush, Major. A day or so. But no more. As for Abercultie, I have arranged to be there tomorrow afternoon. Is that convenient?'

Mrs M rose from her chair and went slowly towards the door. She was pressing a handkerchief to her mouth. Eric made no move to stop her, but called out: 'My men will search the house now, Mrs Melville. I'll want you to be present, and show us Johnston's room.'

I said: 'I must return to duty. You know where our unit is. Pick me up there tomorrow.'

'Righty-o, Major. That's the ticket.' He slid his notes into the briefcase and went out into the hall. The two policemen came in, nodding awkwardly to Mrs Melville. She and I exchanged a glance before they all went upstairs together. When they had gone, I took the suitcase out of the stair cupboard and stepped quietly out into the street. The police car was empty — no driver to notice what I was carrying. Only the big white tom cat, the one who was supposed to kill dogs, glared at me from a wall and bristled its dirty fur.

Next day Eric's car, an old blue Rover, was parked in a corner of the parade ground. As we walked over to it, I said: 'I heard you asking for me in the Orderly Room. How did you learn to pronounce my name? You are the first Englishman who could.'

'Well, I speak German. Some of the same funny noises. I hope you have enough German for today's job.'

'I can understand. Speaking is not so good. You have my name, but you never told us yours.'

'Kent, as in the county. Eric Kent.' We drove north towards Perth. The roads were narrow, often blocked by crawling convoys of army lorries. It was spring, and on the slopes there were whin bushes in golden flower. Lochs and ancient castles, green mountains hunched over sparkling rivers, peaks silver with snow along the horizon. I had never seen this Highland Scotland. For a time I forgot my anxieties, my anger, and thought about climbing holidays in the Carpathians, about forested gorges beneath towers tipped with red-white flags.

Near Perth, we stopped for petrol next to a draughty café. While Eric negotiated his petrol coupons, I ordered tea and toast. He came back and sat down, warming his hands on the cracked white cup.

To break the silence, I asked: 'Where did you learn German?'

'In Germany, old chap. I was brought up there.'

'English people living in Germany? Was that normal?'

'Well, actually we were German. Were, so to speak. Moved to London before the war. Before Hitler, in fact. My dad saw it coming, so he decided it was better to become English. He wanted America really, but we couldn't get the papers. So we got naturalised here.'

'So Eric Kent is refugee? Not English? How do you speak it so perfectly?'

'If you weren't Polish, you'd pick up a touch of an accent. Other people do.'

'Your father had wrong politics? You aren't Jew – you don't seem like a Jew.'

'Oh, yes. At least other Germans thought so. Family name was Kantor. Kantor, Kent, get it?' I began to laugh, and tapped with my spoon on his cup, so that he had to look up at me. 'And you, Kantor-Kent, will send Jackie to a foreign country, and make her change her name and become a different person? You?'

'Well, at least the Aussies speak English. Up to a point.'

I must have looked dangerous, for he got to his feet and went over to the counter to pay. 'Time to hit the road again, Major.'

The camp, with its wire fences and ranks of Nissen huts, lay on the floor of a broad, beautiful valley. The air smelled good. I stood and smoked a cigarette while Eric went to report to the guards at the gate office. He came back in a fury.

'The camp commandant won't let us take Nuttgen out. I was going to take him to a safe house – well, the village police station over there. Some nonsense about me being a civilian, should have had a special military permit from Edinburgh. Well, we'll have to do it inside the camp. There's a library hut we can clear everyone out of.'

The camp guards turned out to be Polish. 'Put it like this,' said Eric, 'we can rely on them not to do German prisoners any favours.' We went through two gates heavy with barbed wire. Inside, there were prisoners in groups doing callisthenic exercises, prisoners walking about reading books, prisoners just leaning against the huts and watching us.

A Polish sentry brought Nuttgen into the library hut. He was young and thin, with black hair and striking dark blue eyes. He looked terrified. Eric stepped over and pulled the curtain across the hut window, but not before I had seen several prisoners outside strolling casually past. They seemed to take care not to glance in our direction.

The interrogation began. I was resigned to what Nuttgen would say. No, he had never seen me in his life. He had no brother-in-law. He had escaped from a lorry somewhere in the hills near their previous camp in Argyll, not from a police station in Fife. They had picked up a dirty, exhausted British man, a deserter, and Wuttke had made the man give Nuttgen his clothes.

He answered more questions about where he had found the rowing boat, and what he had intended to do when he got to southern Ireland. I noticed that he was sitting on his hands to stop them trembling.

Eric said: 'You are perfectly safe in here, my friend. The guard is outside the door and his rifle is loaded. Now tell us what is really going on in this place. What is Wuttke up to?'

Nuttgen drew a shaky breath. I offered him a cigarette, but he stared at the floor and muttered, '*Ich bin Nichtraucher* – I don't smoke.'

Then he went on, almost whispering: 'There is an SS group. I told you all this already. Wuttke runs it. They meet every night, and have lectures – the history of the Movement, racial hygiene, the ways to solve the Jewish problem, how Germany will deal with the Polish area after victory. They take oaths. More and more people are joining them.'

'Because they are afraid of Wuttke?'

'Yes, he orders punishments. For defeatist talk, for stealing – everything. But not only fear. Many people believe him now. They see that Hitler is winning the war.'

'And do you think he will win the war?'

Nuttgen looked at the floor again and murmured something. 'What?'

'I think he is saying something from the Bible. That God will spare the city, for the sake of a few just men.'

Eric shrugged. He began to write in his notebook. After a few minutes of silence, Nuttgen asked if he could go to the lavatory. 'Guard!' shouted Eric, without looking up. 'Don't take too long,' he added to Nuttgen as he was led out. I noticed that the soldier had fixed the bayonet on his rifle. He looked worried.

'That wasn't much good to me,' Eric said. 'I need more details to get Wuttke put away. Maybe I'll get what I want when he comes back. Not too good for you either, Major. But we'll come to that later.'

I turned away. There was a British daily newspaper on a stand near me, and some British propaganda leaflets in German. I began to read the newspaper, but there was little I hadn't heard on the BBC. Eric was still completing his notes. I wandered up to the window, and pulled back the curtain.

On the other side of the camp road there was a knot of four or five men. Unexpectedly, as I watched they lurched together and began to fight. There were screams and shouts and a prisoner fell to the ground, kicking his legs dramatically. From the left of my view a Polish soldier came running towards the brawl, the same guard who had taken Nuttgen to the latrines.

Eric, standing behind me, suddenly howled in English: 'Fuck! Oh, fuck!' He burst past me and raced out across the camp, ignoring the struggling men and heading for the long shed of the latrine block.

Nuttgen was dangling from the roof pole. He was naked below the waist, and his trousers trailed down from his feet. His hands had been tied behind his back and, as well as the wire under his chin, there was another wire sunk tightly into his neck. I had time to glimpse blood as well as shit on the concrete. Eric was shouting: 'Get a medic! A fucking ladder, a wire-cutter!'

I ran out. Eric began to follow me, then impulsively turned back and tore open the door of a broom cupboard by the latrine entrance. I was outside by now, maybe ten yards away, as Wuttke stepped in a quite leisurely manner out of the cupboard. He seemed to bump into Eric by accident, putting out a hand to the other man's shoulder as if to steady himself. Eric lowered himself to his knees. A geyser of blood jumped towards the ceiling, then subsided into small gouts and pulses. Wuttke pulled the weapon out of the base of Eric's neck, raised his eyes and noticed me.

I was close enough to see that he was holding one of those fancy SS daggers – had nobody searched him? He came towards me on tiptoe, almost dancing rather than running. How slowly he moves, I was thinking, when the soldier with the rifle crashed into me from behind, knocked me over, spun his weapon round and struck Wuttke full in the face with the butt.

The trial took place in Perth, a few weeks later. I was a witness, the star witness in fact, for I had seen the murders, or, to be accurate, one of them. Eric was quite dead, his carotid artery professionally severed. Poor Hans Nuttgen was still technically alive when they cut him down, but died that night without regaining consciousness. It turned out that Wuttke had not quite finished with Nuttgen when we appeared. In his tunic they found a sheet of paper which Wuttke apparently intended to fix to the hanging body: 'I betrayed my comrades and my Führer. Loyalty is our honour.'

Wuttke was hanged by the British. So were four of his fellow prisoners, on the slender evidence of an informer who named them as the other members of an SS *Femgericht*, a Teutonic vengeance tribunal. I went to Nuttgen's funeral, which was attended by only three other people. The camp chaplain was there, and a priest from Perth, and a small, brave man – a German Jew, like Eric – who had just been posted to the camp with the task of persuading the prisoners to renounce Hitler and embrace democracy. They let him live, I heard after the war, but I don't believe he made many converts.

The funeral, like the trial, had been done with a bleak rapidity – cut to the bare essentials in a very British way which left me uneasy. When I woke in the mornings, I kept remembering the tight smile on Wuttke's black-bruised face as he stood to attention to hear his death sentence. I remembered the way Nuttgen's dark hair had fallen over his face as he leaned forward and murmured words from the Bible.

Everyone else had spoken of retribution and justice. Nobody but Nuttgen had spoken words of mercy or pity, the words which ghosts need if they are to cease their restless walking to and fro. When I heard the news of the executions, I found my way to a Catholic chapel in Kirkcaldy and arranged a requiem Mass 'for the intention' of Hans Nuttgen's soul. I told nobody else about that. It was done as much for me as for him.

The telephones had been repaired in Greenock, but for several days there was no answer from Union Street. Finally, somebody lifted the receiver. There was a silence, but in the background I could hear little Francis crying.

'Hello? Is that Jackie? It's Mike, Uncle Mike.'

'Granny says I'm not to talk to anyone on the phone just now.'

'Is she there? It's okay to talk to me. Tell her I have some good news.'

'Are you coming to see us again?'

'No, Jackie, but I want you to give Granny a message. Tell her that the man she was worried about, the man who was talking to her and me the other day, has gone away. In fact, he's suddenly died. She doesn't need to worry about him any more.'

'Is that good news? How, was he killed in the war?'

'Yes. Yes, he was. Just tell her that, and say I will ring again tomorrow morning before she goes out. And how are you, Jackie?'

'Fine. I got top in history yesterday. Fine.' She hung up.

Next day, I telephoned again and talked to Mrs M. When I had finished the story (careful about what I said, for who else might be listening in?), she sighed.

'Jackie gave me your message last night. What did I do? Well, I felt like a walk by myself would be the right thing. I walked along the Esplanade and up the Lyle Hill to the top, and sat for a while. It's a long time since I did that. You can get your ideas back into shape up there.'

She paused, then went on: 'You'll get a shock when I say this. But there was good in that wee man as well as bad. Last year, after Johnston – after the funeral – we got to talking a lot when he came round. He had a dirty job to do, but at first I didn't know that I was going to be part of his dirty job. He wanted to see my old photograph albums, talk about Johnston as a boy. So he comforted me. He was kind of warm, in a way folk here don't know about. I didn't know Germans could be like that.'

'You knew he was German?'

'He told me, when I asked. He talked that chatterbox perfect English, like a comic off the Light Programme, but I picked up just that bittie of foreign in his voice. You know, before he started setting those traps for me like "had I heard from anyone?" and all that, we had real conversations. We used to talk about books, music, things I hadn't bothered with since I was a girl. There was a while I looked forward to him calling.'

'It was pretending, Mabel. To make you trust him – an act.'

'An act? Well, all refugees need to be actors. But what he was saying to us the other day, what he'd do to me and Jackie, that was no act. That was his duty, and he was enjoying it right enough. Some folk, you never get to the true end of them. Nevertheless, to die that way – I'm sorry for it.'

I wanted to ask her if the big Atlantic liner was still in the river. But that was not for the telephone. 'Careless Talk Costs Lives.' Careless talk – questions, confidences, words overheard or suspected or betrayed - had already cost three lives under my eyes. And now Helen was about to set off among the U-boats again, was probably at sea already. 'Time for me to ring off and do my own duty, Mabel. I think we are three very lucky people. I'll call when I have any news for you.'

I took the brown suitcase with Johnston's possessions – the best suit, the gold watch – back to Pitnechtan House. It was conspicuous in the corner of my office, so after a few days I stowed it under the bunk in my sleeping quarters. But Johnston did not ring. Several weeks passed. Once I went down to St Monans and walked up and down the quay of the fishing harbour, a futile proceeding as I had forgotten to ask him the name of his boat.

Men were busy unloading boxes of haddock and herring, and the pubs were full. But I avoided them. An officer in Polish uniform asking after Alex Ketling – that would be too intriguing to be forgotten. There was no sign of Johnston around the harbour, and I went away without speaking to anyone.

I was vexed and puzzled. I had hoped that handing over the suitcase to Johnston would break the circuit of my complicity with him, switch off his presence in my life. But that circuit still lay there live. From time to time, in the next days, his sullen face and flat red hair came uninvited to mind. What was he waiting for?

On a clear Sunday morning in late June, I switched on the nine o'clock news ('... and this is Alvar Liddell reading it'). Nazi Germany had invaded the Soviet Union.

I hurried over to the mess, and ran into our British liaison officer coming out of the door. He grinned at me and made a thumbs-up sign. But I gave him a chill stare. Yes, that little corporal at Ladybank had tried to warn us. But I had paid no attention and clung to my altar-boy faith that this would remain the Armageddon war – the hosts of the just against the hosts of evil. What an idiot! I hated – still hate – being so wrong; I fancied that the British officer knew my mind and was laughing at me. For him, Stalin was just another foreigner. And now, all of a sudden, an ally – why not? But for me there was only shock, then foreboding.

Inside the mess, the Polish mood was excited, almost merry. 'The Russians can't fight. The *Wehrmacht* will just drive over them. They will be in Moscow in a few weeks, wait and see.'

Round the wireless, a group was shouting for silence. Don't imagine for a moment that we supported the Nazis. But almost all of us came from the Borderlands, the regions into which the Germans were advancing. We listened, hoping to hear the names of Polish towns freed from Bolshevik occupation.

I found myself standing next to our Colonel, the shrewd ex-procurator.

'So what do you make of it, Szczucki?'

I thought again of the corporal at Ladybank, adjusting his pince-nez in order to prophesy.

'Perhaps, sir, it won't be so easy for the Germans. Think of Napoleon, sir. Didn't we think that he would restore a free Poland for us by invading Russia? Excuse me, but what will happen to Poland this time if the Russians win?'

'Major, you are supposed to be an intelligence officer! Look at the facts. This Red Army is an untrained rabble; in Finland they let themselves be slaughtered. This is not the old Russia, Major. Believe me, I knew that Russia; I was born in Petersburg and my father, a university professor there, taught military law to cadets in the old army.'

He lit a cigarette, and smiled at me as he made a show of smoking it in the 'Russian' way: holding it upright between finger and thumb. 'These are not real soldiers, Major. They are no more than starving peasants terrorised by commissars. As Hitler advances, they will throw their rifles away. And the Ukrainians will rise and join the Nazis – you can expect that. As for the rest . . . when they have the choice, they won't die to defend Bolshevism.'

'But, Colonel, perhaps they will die to defend Russia.'

The Colonel considered for a moment. He nodded slightly. 'The Russian people . . . who knows? They have never been our enemy, only their leaders. A Russian can never be quite foreign to us, in the way that the Germans are. Yes, like you, Major, I am not sure of my feelings today. Mostly I rejoice, because now Stalin will be sent to burn in hell with all the Bolshevik comrades he murdered. And yet when I think of what the Nazis will do to that people who have already suffered so much, who will be buried under the ruins of Bolshevism – when I think of that . . .'

He shook his head. He allowed two ribbons of smoke to drift from his nostrils towards the floor and form a dissolving wreath around his boots. Then he turned away.

The German tank armies drove eastward, and a moving sea of Soviet prisoners flowed westward. For many weeks, it seemed that the Colonel had been right. But for us, the game of the advancing arrows on newspaper maps was not just 'war news'. Our families, the families of most of the officers I knew, were among the million and a half Polish civilians deported to the Soviet Union in 1940.

The Germans might liberate them. Or their Soviet guards might 'liquidate' their captives as the front approached. Nobody doubted that they were capable of that. Already, enough stories had reached us about the casual shooting of deportees, about dead children flung out of the trains, about mothers and grandfathers dying in the snow as they hauled logs. As for the officers taken prisoner by the Soviets in 1939, most of them reservists, nothing but particles of rumour had reached us for over a year.

A thick, nameless depression settled on me. I felt out of line, stranded at an angle to what was happening around me. In the Pitnechtan pubs, cheerful Scotsmen unnerved me by patting my shoulder and assuring me that 'you'll be right glad that your pals are back on our side!' Many, all too clearly, still assumed that Poles were a sub-species of Russian.

Some of the older men were Communist Party members, relieved to be allowed to support the war effort now that it had changed from 'an imperialist struggle irrelevant to the working class' to 'proletarians of the world against Fascism'. They were hurt and puzzled when, having been bought a beer, I refused to raise the glass to Comrade Stalin. Puzzled partly because they knew I enjoyed drinking. I had begun to drink noticeably too much. Most nights now, I was unsteady on my feet on the long walk back to Pitnechtan House.

A month later, we were informed that General Sikorski, our Supreme Commander, had signed an agreement which made the Soviet Union formally our ally. The Polish deportees and prisoners of war in the USSR were to be 'amnestied', and a Polish army would be formed on Soviet territory. The Nazi–Soviet Pact of 1939, under which Hitler and Stalin had abolished and partitioned my country, was cancelled. But there was only murky generality about where the frontiers of a free Poland would lie after the war.

In our mess there was angry confusion. Above all, the word 'amnesty' was so outrageous – as if over a million men, women and children had been guilty of crime, rather than their kidnappers. And Sikorski had failed to extract any assurance that the Russians would give up the Polish territories they had seized in 1939.

We heard from London that our government-in-exile had split over the agreement. Some of us urged the Colonel to hold an open meeting, a free debate.

'Are you crazy? You are in an army, not a student society. This is a moment for unity, whatever our feelings. Anyway, the Supreme Commander is coming to Scotland to address us.'

He looked us over, as we stood in his office, and shook his head. 'Do you suppose Poland is in a position to dictate terms to Stalin? The prisoners liberated, a free Polish army allowed to form over there – we are lucky to have won that much. Children, this is nasty medicine. So swallow it!'

General Sikorski came and spoke to us in the rain. I had not seen him before and his bearing impressed me: stiff, bleakly determined. A few people had muttered that they would not salute him, or would interrupt his speech. In the event, we all behaved proudly and properly as he strode along our ranks. But his speech made me uneasy. He went on too long about his own heroic experiences in eastern Poland. 'Would I therefore give up those territories, or overlook their importance?'

Rhetorical questions like that were imprudent, I thought. And it was about now, as I remember, that a sort of schizophrenia began to affect us which was to last to the end of the war. As long as one thought about fighting the Germans – in North Africa and later Italy and France, in the air and at sea – it was easy to feel the required emotions: purpose, urgency, hatred. But if one allowed oneself to think about our 'gallant allies' in the east, those simple feelings became hard to summon.

So we tried not to think about it, to hold it in a separate mental compartment. For a time, that worked. But later, as we began to meet some of the Polish survivors ('amnestied') who had left the Soviet Union, and later still as mass graves were opened, the bulkhead of that separate compartment began to leak. If we let ourselves think, the thoughts were bitter.

A Saturday dance and concert had been arranged by 'friends of Poland' in Kirkton of Lochend, a small town not far away.

A three-tonner picked up about twenty of us, private soldiers and non-commissioned officers. I went along with them: to make sure matters didn't get out of hand, but also to keep myself away from the Pitnechtan pubs.

I had been to several such parties already. This one started like all the others. There was a platform at one end of the hall, with Lady Somebody in hat and tweed suit sitting on a chair and waiting to say a few words. In a corner the band was sorting out its music – accordion, fiddle – and a fair-haired girl was waiting to sing a few songs.

A gramophone was already playing a foxtrot, but nobody was dancing. The young women were all perched on benches along one wall, whispering to one another. The red-faced country boys were huddled along the opposite wall in their tackety boots, glancing furtively at the girls. This was a 'temperance' hall – no strong drink. But a half-bottle of whisky was slipping from hand to hand.

Our lads burst in, a khaki surge of men, and stopped for a second to take in the situation. Then they went straight to the girls, bowed, stunned them by kissing their hands and swept them off on to the dance floor. Boy, what dancers they were then! I watched their partners' faces grow pink and blissful as they were spun and swung. I watched the faces of the Scots boys along the wall darken as they looked on. Their bottle circulated more boldly.

Private Jaciubek whirled past me, his arms full of amazed beauty with its mouth open. In Kirkton of Lochend, all the dreams of the movies had arrived at last. I remembered Helen in that Greenock kitchen, ironing a blouse and winking at me as she sang 'Someday, my Prince will come...!' Private Jaciubek, a coal miner from Silesia, would soon be telling his partner: 'In Poland, I am Count, big castle, you come and we ride sledge together in my forests...' Corporal Godzik, whose family mended tyres in a Praga backyard, would offer that sweet freckly Land Girl a tour of the Tatras in his Rolls-Royce, a ski holiday in one of his father's luxury hotels.

Why not? Mrs M had said that all refugees needed to be actors. Foreign soldiers too, especially those whose homes and old lives had gone for ever, had a duty to invent new realities. The Germans had shot Private Jaciubek's father as a hostage, and his town had been annexed and renamed by the Reich. He was about as much a Count as he was a Polish miner now. And what and who was I? Unlike these men, I had not used my imagination. If my parents were still alive, which did not seem likely, they would have had no chance to become actors. All they could imagine would be staying alive until the next day. I should use my own freedom while it lasted.

Well, I could dance too, as well or better than my soldiers. My men had given Lady Somebody no pause to make her speech of welcome, so I took her off for a waltz to console her. I put on a bit of a show, whipped her about more than I needed to. But she threw her head back and enjoyed herself. When the music stopped, I walked her to the trestle table bearing cream soda and sausage rolls, and she took a glass of lemonade.

'Thank you, Major.'

'You haven't danced like that for a long time, have you?' I watched her eyebrows go up; she wanted to ask 'How do you know that?' but stopped herself. I could read her thoughts. I was in a strange mood, reckless, a bit manic, drunk without alcohol. When she had finished her lemonade, I asked her to dance again but this time she was wary in my arms, keeping me at a polite distance.

We sat down, and talked a little. Lady Somebody was called Margaret. She was slender, in early middle age. I liked her snow-white hair, red cheeks and sapphire eyes. Would I bring a few friends to lunch one Sunday at 'our place' near Forfar?

'And your husband?'

'He was at St Valéry. With the 51st.'

'A prisoner?'

'I'm afraid not.'

'I am so sorry.'

We were quiet for a moment.

'You must all be very homesick. For your poor country.'

'Yes. Yes, we are. Thank you.'

I looked at the dance floor. My lads did not look homesick at all; the accordion band had struck up, and the girls were shrieking with laughter as they showed the Poles how to do the Gay Gordons. My feeling of manic restlessness returned. I excused myself, and went over to talk to the young singer at the far corner of the platform.

She was sorting through sheets of music, arranging them on her stand.

'Ach, no, I'm no a professional. Just a local nightingale, ken?'

'So what do you sing?'

'Old favourites. Burns songs – have you heard of Robert Burns? That's fine, then. I sing them straight, ma ain fashion.

No that BBC way, warbling like German Lieder, that fairly scunners me.'

She selected a song sheet, studied it and then looked up at me.

'There's one song here... maybe it's the wrong thing, but then maybe it would be saying something for you folk. D'ye know what was the Jacobites, the Forty-Five?'

'Bonny Prince Charlie?'

'Huh, so you do so know! Well, Burns wrote this song, "It was a' for our Rightful King". About the Jacobites leaving Scotland for ever, going into exile in Ireland. About farewell.'

'Show me. Let me read it.'

In those days, the language of Burns was usually closed to me. When Scots friends recited, I would nod and pretend. But these words were not closed:

> Now all is done that men can do,
> And all is done in vain;
> My Love and Native Land fareweel,
> For I maun cross the main, my dear,
> For I maun cross the main...

I read on, to the song's end, and then read it again. I glanced up and met the singer's worried stare.

'Maybe it's no the right thing for the night. A wee bit too...'

I cleared my throat. 'No. No, you sing it.'

'I'll keep it to near last – last before "Auld Lang Syne". It's a fine air forbye.' She whistled a few bars, but it was hard to hear her over the din of the band. I gave her a friendly smile and moved away.

The evening went on. Some of the Scots boys tried to repossess their women, and there were tricky moments. I followed two huffy rivals out of the hall and pulled them apart before serious damage was done, and the Scot, after spitting on a comb and carefully rearranging his hair, gave me a pull from his bottle. It didn't help. The wild feeling was turning physical, a crawling on my skin, a hurt in my chest.

The singer did a couple of songs, with the fiddler accompanying. She had a clear, pretty voice with a tang to it, like the voices of mountain girls in my own country. There was polite applause, then more dancing. Near the end of the evening, I called for silence and thanked Lady Margaret, the band, the singer and the organisers on behalf of the First Corps of the Polish army. More applause. Someone tapped me on the shoulder, and pointed across the hall to where the singer was waiting. She gave me a nod, and then began:

> ... The sodger frae the wars returns,
> The sailor frae the main;
> But I hae parted frae my Love,
> Never to meet again, my dear;
> Never to meet again ...

She was right about the tune: simple and sharp as an arrow. Before she finished, I was making my way towards the door. 'Corporal Godzik, you'll be responsible for getting the men to the lorry and back to camp. I have to wait and come later on my own.' With his arm round the Land Girl, he winked. The major gets off with Lady Somebody; it's the way the world is.

Outside, it was a warm summer night. I walked rapidly away, without thinking where I was going. Down the street to a square with a war memorial. Down a side street until I came to a bridge over a small river. There was nobody about. I leaned on the parapet and studied the braided currents shining at me in the dark, the passing clots of foam. After a long while, I heard 'Auld Lang Syne' in the distance and the sound of motors starting.

I walked back. The singer was coming out of a side door, calling something over her shoulder and buttoning up a long woollen coat. When I took her by the arm, she seemed not to be surprised and let me walk her slowly as far as the town square. We didn't say anything. I let her go and stood aimlessly, until she put her arm round my waist and pulled me gently away and along until we reached the river. There I began to tremble and shudder, and she guided us off the roadway and into the darkness under the bridge.

Even now, I remember the softness of her coat as I clutched her, and the feel of its big, smooth buttons. I started to weep as I have never wept before or since. At first loud sobs, so loud that she pressed my face into her shoulder. Then tears, streaming minute after minute so heavily that I thought, for a muddled second, that I was going to empty my whole body and soul through my eyes. She said nothing, but from time to time ran her fingers through my hair. Her coat collar grew soaked with tears, her neck was wet. But she stood with me for many, many minutes, maybe half an hour, until I slowly remembered her existence, pushed myself shakily back against the stones of the bridge pier and stared into her face. Her expression was serious, investigative rather than inquiring.

I thought about the feel of her neck. Maybe she had been expecting something else from me under the bridge. But she pulled out a handkerchief and made to wipe my face. I pushed the handkerchief away.

'You look a right ticket,' she said softly.

'A what?'

'A mess, son, a mess.'

'Son? I'm older than you are.'

'So where's your mother, then? Is it her you're wanting?'

'No. Not a mother, not a woman. I don't know.'

'It was the song. I could just see you were in trouble when you were reading it. I'm sorry for that.'

'You are a good person.'

She laughed and we kissed, a tight hug and kiss like brother and sister after a long parting.

'Are ye right, then?' I said I was fine. We set off back to the town square, swinging our linked hands. On the way, she sang for me, a cheery song about a tailor who fell through the bed, thimble and all. The small town was silent and asleep.

In the square, we faced each other. There were no street lights allowed in wartime Kirkton, but the moon had risen, casting a gleam across her features that made her look older. I could see just what she would be like at forty: handsome, sure, broad-shouldered from years spent carrying the trust of men and children.

She asked: 'How will you get back?' Then, hesitating, she said: 'I'm staying with my auntie just down the way. There's a couch you could...'

'I'll be fine. I'll hitchhike back.' I needed very much to be alone. She nodded. 'Ships that pass in the night, huh?'

'I'll never forget you,' I said, wanting to mean it. We kissed again and she turned away, waving once before she walked round the corner. When she had gone, I set off to walk back to Pitnechtan.

It was a friendly night, rich with country smells, and on the road I met an owl, a pair of whirling bats, two half-seen beasts plunging in the hedge which I thought were deer. Once I heard the rumble of many aircraft passing overhead until their sound died away towards the North Sea. As I tramped, I felt emptied and even happy, thinking of nothing but the noise of my boots as the miles went by.

The sun was well risen by the time I arrived back at the camp gates. Tired and pleased with my aching legs, I made my way to the door of the officers' mess to seek a cup of hot tea. It was Sunday morning and a few colleagues were already standing round the urn, waiting for a truck to take them to early Mass. It was only when one of them spoke to me – 'How was the grand ball last night, Major?' – that I realised that I couldn't remember the singer's name. Had I even asked her what her name was? I couldn't remember that either.

Not long after the dance at Kirkton, the Colonel sent for me. I stood to attention before his desk. He did not tell me to stand easy. The Colonel was not a professional soldier, but he had metamorphosed himself into the old-fashioned kind of Polish commander, with traditions of discipline drawn from the Tsarist and Prussian armies. In other words, he treated his officers coldly, sometimes harshly, but to ordinary soldiers he was fatherly and intimate, using their first names as if they were children. The British did exactly the opposite, relying on their own easy-going, unquestioned class system. Their officers were a band of brothers, often old schoolmates, whose commanding officers addressed them by their Christian names, while 'other ranks' were kept strictly at a distance.

'I am not satisfied with your performance, Major. You have become casual. You are drinking too much, with civilians in the town. The other night, you went absent when your duty was to escort your men back to camp after a dance. And your intelligence reports are not contributing anything. Nicely written, but I am not training journalists.'

He tapped a finger on a movement order lying on his desk. 'Szczucki, you are in the wrong job. The talents you have – languages, foreign experience, an independent mind – are being wasted here. For some reason, you have lost energy. I don't ask why, it is not my concern; every Polish soldier receives bad news or no news. So, Major, I am having you transferred for parachute and radio training.'

'The silent-shadowy ones, sir?'

'Obviously. Assuming you survive the course, you will find yourself back in Poland long before the rest of us. Among the Germans. That prospect should restore your energy.'

This news did not come as a complete surprise. The adjutant had privately warned me of the Colonel's plan a few days earlier. And what the Colonel thought about me coincided with what I had come to think about myself, since the night under the bridge at Kirkton.

I could see now that for nearly two years I had been tormented by this sense of loss. Escapology had been no use to me; one can dart free of a person, a duty, a place, but not of an absence, a hole. It was as if I had been abandoned by something, or had abandoned it, but I could not give that something a name. Certainly, I had lost captaincy of my own feelings. What had I wanted from Helen, or why had I let myself become entangled with Johnston?

Supposing it would still be possible to go back to Poland after this war, how much did I really want to? And how could I bear to sit so tranquilly, so contentedly, in my warm office in this Scottish backwater while tanks blazed on African sands and battleships sank? And while – in my own land – men and women were put up against walls with their mouths crammed with plaster of Paris, to silence their screams as they were machine-gunned?

I had no answer to any of these questions except the last. No, I could not bear it. It was time to escape into a world where the problems would be reading my compass at night, jumping from an aircraft without fouling its tail with my parachute, hitting the ground without breaking my leg.

But as often happens in wartime, high suspense deflated into anticlimax. For no particular reason, my transfer was postponed, then postponed without a date. With little to do at Pitnechtan – my replacement as intelligence officer had already taken over my desk – I set myself to learning German properly, and spent the weekends in Edinburgh with an old Austrian lady who gave private language tuition. Her idea of conversation practice was to take turns reading Schiller's *Die Räuber* aloud. I wondered what Gestapo interrogators would make of my Romantic choice of idioms. At least I was acquiring a fine, querulous Viennese accent.

One day, my successor told me that a civilian had rung me on the office telephone, and would call again in an hour. He pretended not to be listening when the call came, and I pretended to be discussing camp supplies – 'about those blankets'. But Johnston sounded unusually calm and civil. We arranged to meet next Saturday morning on the station platform at Inverkeithing, on my way to Edinburgh.

Once again, I did not at first recognise him. A stocky,

formidable man in a blue suit, white shirt and stripy tie stood grinning at me. A short ginger moustache, setting off his white teeth, made him look voracious.

'Your suitcase, Mr Ketling.'

'Very good of you to look after it, Mike. I should have come through and uplifted it a while back, but...'

'But what?'

'But work comes first, am I no right? Specially with a war on. We need to set an example to the lads and not walk away from the desk when we feel like it. An example to the lassies too. Else they'd aye be off in the toilet blethering about the film stars.'

'What the hell are you talking about? Desk? Lassies? Have you left your boat?'

'The fishing? Ach, that was just my seaside adventure, what they call a brief encounter. I'm with Lang & Wilson's now, down the way at Rosyth, in the engineering wing. Quite a well-managed old firm, in my opinion, but not venturesome at all.'

I thought of several things to say, but was too astonished to try any of them. 'Lang & Wilson's?'

'The shipbreakers. Breaking dead ships for scrap. They call us the navy's undertakers. I say: salvage merchants by appointment to Mister Churchill. Oh, gosh, this war sure keeps our books full.'

The whistle blew. As I climbed back into the compartment, he followed me and asked through the window: 'The gold watch? Did you mind and bring it?'

'It's in your suitcase – Johnston Melville!' He said nothing, but his grin vanished. Sharply, he raised his head to look me directly in the eyes and for the first time, I felt that he was dangerous to me, a fugitive no longer. Steam poured up and the train lurched off towards the Forth Bridge.

Another winter, more of a six-month autumn of downpours, drizzle and soaking mists, crawled across the tens of thousands of foreign servicemen – Poles, Canadians, Americans, French, Free Danes and Norwegians – who waited in Scotland to be called into battle. Every morning, they wiped the rust off their virgin weapons and marched out to salute the hoisting of their soggy flags.

The Allies landed in North Africa, and Stalingrad burned. But it all seemed far away. English words on a sputtery wireless, Polish words on grey-typed bulletins pinned to a board, reached us as dry news, drained of fresh hopes and fears. Nothing evoked that June morning when Hitler attacked the Soviet Union, when we had crowded round the radio gasping, shouting, sometimes even laughing. That electric sense of erupting history had long left us.

So we sought distractions. Football championships gave our men a chance to meet other soldiers, and often to fight them. Several officers bought a racehorse on credit, and we all had to put money on Kaszanka until she broke a leg at Musselburgh. The chaplain's art classes on Polish Madonna paintings were instantly popular: his hut was well heated and dim enough to allow undisturbed sleep.

And I took up distilling. I knew nothing about chemistry, but my casual remark one evening – 'What we need is vodka!'

– enchanted several comrades who claimed that they did know. The battalion storeman had worked for a French pharmaceutical company before the war and instructed me what to look for in Edinburgh on my language-learning visits. In a Boy Scout shop I found a pre-war chemistry set complete with glass retorts and worm – 'Made in Germany', as it happened.

The old man behind the counter considered me. 'Mister, is this you telling me you're a Boy Scout?'

'Once a Scout, always a Scout. The pass, I forgot to bring it.'

'Who d'ye think I am – an eejit? Take a look at yourself.'

There was a long mirror on the wall beside the counter. How many years since I saw my own reflection in civilian clothes? The light in there was odd: weak and yet searching. I saw a small, broad-shouldered man wearing a suit too tight for him. There were new furrows on that face around its wary, greenish eyes. Brown hair cropped so short that the cheekbones jutted. Skin a bit olive, 'foreign-looking'. Where did this fellow belong?

'Ach, take it then. You're the third Pole that's been in for such-like kit, and it's the last set in the store. And watch the hooch disnae leave ye blind.'

Back at Pitnechtan, the vodka team set to work in a shed next to the coal bunkers. But after weeks of trial and error, fermenting potatoes with yeast and beet sugar and distilling the liquor, we only produced clouds of giddily scented steam and a few jars of oily rotgut. We pretended that it was authentic Polish homebrew – 'bimber' – and drank some to rescue our self-respect. The rest I poured away. What remained with me was the dark stare of that man in the mirror. For a moment I had not recognised him. Had he recognised me, and what did he think of me now?

One heavy morning, as I promised myself never to touch that stuff again, a travel-worn envelope reached me. Addressed only to 'M. le commandant Chousky, Maurice, auprès forces polonaises libres', it had travelled round Britain for many weeks, accumulating in-tray stamps, sealing wax and scribbles. At one point it had reached our Supreme Commander in London, whose minions had redirected it to Fife.

It contained a typed letter, a handwritten note from Commandant le Gallois, and a travel warrant from Edinburgh to Gourock. The letter summoned me to give supplementary evidence to a reconvened enquiry into the loss of the destroyer *Fronsac*, off Greenock on 30 April, 1940. The note said: '*Mon cher Chousky!* This is a big bore, but something new has come up which indirectly concerns you. It could become a nuisance if you don't clear it up. It would be good to see you, if you get this letter. But perhaps you are far away in Tunisia, charging M. le général Rommel's panzers on horseback at the head of your Uhlans! *Amitiés.*'

I got off the train at Fort Matilda, and set off to walk the few hundred yards up to the Free French base. Rounding the corner, I found my way blocked by a bus, more of a dilapidated charabanc, slewed across the roadway. Inside, through grimy windows, I could see Scottish policemen packed into the narrow seats, some sleeping, some smoking.

I walked past. 'Hey, youse in the black beret, get back there! Naebody gets through here, naebody, back wi'ye now!' I showed the excited inspector my typed letter in French, and my military pass. He scanned my papers, and then, baffled, stood back. Beyond him was an extraordinary, carnival sight. A roll of barbed wire blocked the street from one side to another, decorated with a row of tricolour flags, and behind the wire stood a rank of French marines in full battle order with glittering bayonets.

'Where is the Commandant? I have to see him. What is going on?'

'This is French territory. It is closed. Go away!' I thrust my letter across the wire to the marine officer, a tough-looking Polynesian with a face scarred by smallpox. Presently le Gallois appeared. He was wearing a helmet, and apparently bursting with high spirits. 'Shoosky, *bon Dieu*, so you got my letter, but what a moment to choose!'

Round the corner, the guards dragged the wire aside and le Gallois led me into his office. A coloured portrait of General de Gaulle on one wall, flanked by a copy of the General's proclamation of 18 June 1940 – these were new. Otherwise, nothing much had changed in the dim, shabby room. The ashtray was still overflowing, but the stolen table-lighter had been replaced with a larger silver one.

The Commandant hung his helmet on the back of the door. He had grown heavier since I had last seen him.

'What...?'

'We are in a state of siege. Let me explain. Six seamen, from the French merchant ships out there which have been rotting at anchor for two years, come to me. They declare that they wish to fight, to join the naval forces of Free France. But the ships' masters demand their return. And lamentably, yes lamentably, the British insist that the masters are correct in international maritime law. Of course, I refuse. So they send the police to arrest the seamen. I refuse again. And now, can you imagine – *les Anglais* – they inform me that they intend to use military force to take these men!'

I had never seen le Gallois so blithe. He offered me a glass of cognac, which I declined, and poured himself one. 'I have responded decisively, correctly. I have declared this base to be sovereign French territory, an overseas department or dependency which foreigners may enter only with French permission. As its military governor, I have proclaimed a state of emergency, *état de siège*, in this territory and taken steps to defend it. The surrounding streets – I have provisionally annexed them and closed them with barricades, as integral to the defence of France. If they violate our frontiers, we will open fire.'

He paused, and began to laugh. 'I know what you are thinking, Shoosky. You think: my God, Commandant le Gallois has turned into a Pole!'

I was thinking exactly that. Our own recent history wasn't free of theatrical confrontations, but some of them had ended in bloodshed, the blood of poor peasant soldiers and of civilians caught in cross-fire.

'Commandant, this could become a tragedy. I can't believe you would order French troops to fire on British troops.'

'Why not? We killed each other just the other day in Syria, in Lebanon.' But he looked uneasy. 'No, there is a way out. I am up against stupid civil functionaries, against stupid soldiers. But, Shoosky, there is such a thing as the fraternity of the sea. The Admiral here is a decent old Scot. I have appealed to him. I wrote to him: "Admiral, let us understand one another as seamen. You know that to give these men up would be a crime against the unwritten laws of naval brotherhood, the trust between comrades which holds men at sea to their duty. Send me your men, your Royal Marines! Send them to stand beside us at the barricades and prevent this disaster."'

'That's a fantasy!'

'Not at all. It worked. Listen, the Admiral received my letter, and this morning he presented himself. He stood at the wire – wouldn't come inside – and we talked. He kept laughing. "My home is up this street. Do I have to show a passport to cross French territory and go to bed with my own wife?" He said: "There are some bloody fools involved in this who can't see further than their own shiny army boots. But I know how to go over their heads. I think I can get you a guarantee that your six seamen can stay and join your navy. If I do – it could take a day or so – would you promise to take down the barbed wire and give Gourock back its streets?"'

'You accepted?'

'I think I must accept,' said le Gallois. He seemed suddenly tired and melancholy. 'For the sake of the Admiral, for two good navies. For the fraternity of the sea.'

'What does General de Gaulle think about what you have done?'

'Officially, he has said nothing. Unofficially, I have heard that he is not at all displeased. Anyway, his visit to us next month is still being organised. My little daughter Françoise will give him a bouquet; he will embrace me ... He doesn't forget people who stand up for our dignity, Shoosky. Especially those who stand up against *les Anglais*.'

He brooded, pushing his empty glass back and forth across his desk. 'Remember the last time we met? When I was being arrested, after Mers-el-Kébir? I told you then that you Poles, too, would one day pay a price for trusting the British. They are so nice, so generous, such noble words. Then one day – when their national interests are at stake – you wake up to find a noose round your neck.'

The Commandant stared at me, his eyes dilated. I looked away. This was a thought I didn't feel like pursuing. Instead, I asked him: 'There's something new about the *Fronsac*? I don't see how it can concern me. But of course I will help if I can.'

'Yes, well. Something disturbing, a bit mad. Our intelligence people think they have found a Nazi agent. He was one of the *Fronsac* survivors, who has been working on a depot ship with our submarines. There is a Vichy spy here in Greenock – but yes, it's normal, what do you expect? They know perfectly well who he is, not dangerous, a self-dramatising imbecile who doesn't even know how to operate his radio properly. So they leave him alone, listen to his telephone, watch his contacts. But a month ago they picked up this sailor lurking outside the spy's house in the blackout – a policeman had taken him for a burglar. He was carrying a list of the shipping in the river, the list of the next convoy to leave.'

Le Gallois got up, grunting a little over his belly, and unlocked a filing cabinet. From a green cardboard folder, he pulled a sheet of paper, a smeared carbon copy.

'Have a look. I mean, it's a confession but it's daft. I suppose he said this to make them stop hitting him.'

I read. 'My name is Kellerman, Albert,... born in Alsace... blah, blah...'. Then: 'In 1937, I joined a secret youth cell within the Parti Populaire Français, in touch with the *Sicherheitsdienst* in the German Embassy in Paris. On a visit to Germany, several of us were recruited to join a cycling tour of western Scotland, a cover for intelligence-gathering about naval bases. In Greenock, in the summer of 1938, I was introduced to a certain Melville, Johnston, a probationary youth member of the British Union of Fascists, an admirer of the new Germany and a militant against the growing Jewish–Bolshevik threat to Scotland. In 1939 I was conscripted into the navy. I served on *Fronsac* in the Norwegian campaign. I met Melville again in April 1940, when *Fronsac* arrived at Greenock.

'We agreed to carry out a symbolic act of sabotage. I was under training as a torpedo rating, while Melville, now a reserve officer in the British navy, had an excuse to board the ship. The agreement was that we should disable the safety and firing locks on all the torpedo tubes. Before this action, we wrote an account of our motives and put it in a steel cashbox, which we hid in a cabinet in the chartroom under the bridge. Our intention was to confess when the damage was discovered. We would come forward and appeal to the British nation: end this absurd war, make peace with Germany! Then we would face our punishment together. Unfortunately, for reasons I cannot understand, disconnecting the first group of locks led to the torpedo launch with the well-known consequences.

'I suspect now that Melville deceived me. Recalling his repeated instructions to use more force on all the locks, I believe that he was aware that there was a firing charge in the tube and that he intended the torpedo to be launched. I cannot exclude that he was a double agent, working for the British Secret Service. Although he was posted missing and presumed dead after the explosion, this is not true. I saw him alive on the quay and, later, making his escape into the town. I have had no contact with him since. I have heard a rumour that he was seen in another part of Scotland in the company of a Polish officer, but I do not know the source of this rumour.'

At the foot of the sheet, under the signature, someone had written in pencil: 'A Major M. Szczucki was lodging in Melville's house, Union Street, at the time of the explosion. Present whereabouts not known.'

Gently, le Gallois pulled the sheet of paper out of my fingers and laid it face down on the desk. 'You are not supposed to have seen that. But I mean, it's like the Moscow Trials. I confess to meeting Trotsky on a tricycle in Monte Carlo and promising to blow up the Dnieper dam. That sort of thing.'

'But why didn't Kellerman take his chance to escape, to return to France after the Armistice? If he was a fascist, why did he stay here and join the Free French?'

'Evidently he wanted to go on spying. They are still interrogating him in prison. But it still doesn't quite add up. This confession is comedy, senseless.'

'None the less, they are going to reopen the enquiry.'

There was a silence. The Commandant seemed to be waiting for me to say something more. Then he shook his head, and glanced sharply at me.

'Shoosky, old friend, be very careful. Fine, fine, you know nothing about it, it's all nonsense. Yes, but it's poisonous nonsense. Get your name off it. Go abroad, find a nice war, but get your name off it.'

On the train, I decided that I must take time off to find Johnston at Rosyth and bully the truth out him. But when I arrived at Pitnechtan I found my kit piled in the hall, my books and papers spilling out of an open orange crate.

'Where the fuck have you been? The truck from the signals school waited all afternoon for you. Now we will have to borrow the Colonel's staff car. Where is your movement order – still lying on your office table? Shameless!'

In the army, you learn not to say: 'But nobody told me...' By nightfall I was unpacking my stuff in a draughty girls' school at Polmont, near Falkirk. Men were running about, orders were yelled, heavy boxes of equipment screeched along the stone floors of corridors. My life jerked into high gear as one strenuous course followed another: signals and clandestine radio operation at Auchtertool and Polmont, parachute training at Largo, tradecraft at the 'spy school' in Glasgow. Conditions were often grim, the food was often terrible, but the other trainees were good company. I let Johnston Melville and the *Fronsac* slide to the back of my mind, and if the French sent me another summons to testify, it never reached me. I became very fit.

The house was still. Jackie had it to herself. The vibrations from the main door closing, the chatter of Granny's heels going down the steps, had passed into silence.

Jackie became a bat. She rose from her chair and flew noiselessly about the house, arms outstretched, back and forth from one room to the next. When her arms grew tired, she steered herself through the kitchen door and alighted on the window ledge. With a little gasp of breath, she broke the quiet. The bat was thirsty.

Her tea was out on the table. Corned beef, some lettuce and tomato, the bottle of salad cream. Two slices of bread and butter: Mrs M always kept her own butter ration for her granddaughter. A glass of milk. But Jackie didn't feel like eating just now, did not even like drinking the milk. Bats didn't drink milk, which was disgusting anyway, even if you could forget about it spleetering out of a cow. Eech! Sliding off the ledge, she went to the sink and filled a glass of water.

She carried the glass back to the front room, where her

drawing book was spread out on the table facing the big window. The view was full of ships, but before she sat down, Jackie took up the binoculars and trained them on the far side of the estuary, where she could pick out three black dots in a neat row. High tide! When the tide was really in, that was all you could see of the *Fronsac*: the tips of her remaining funnels just breaking the surface. When it was out, specially at low-water springs, then the whole scorched hull could be seen, and the stumps of the masts. Everyone in Greenock and Gourock and Port Glasgow had learned to glance out to the *Fronsac* when they needed to know the state of the tide.

Jackie sat down, selected an HB pencil and turned the closely written pages of the drawing book until she reached a blank sheet. 'High water, Saturday, 1943.' The date could come later. She looked up and out of the window, pausing every few moments to consult the tome of *Jane's Fighting Ships* borrowed from the library. She wrote: 'Battleships: King George V class: ? *Duke of York*?, *Ramillies*. Battle cruiser: *Renown*. US battleship (v. big): *Iowa* or *New Jersey*? Heavy cruisers: 2 County class, *Dido*, 1 City class (HMS *Glasgow*), USS *Pensacola*. Light cruisers: *Curlew*, *Coventry*, *Hawkins*. Sloop: *de Brazza* (France). Destroyers: *Blyskawica* (Poland)... Aircraft carriers:' When she had finished listing the warships she could see, she drew a line in red pencil and began to write again under it: 'Liners. *Queen Mary* (black and grey camouflage)...' Jackie sucked her pencil briefly, then added: 'NB: bows mended after accident.' Last year, the *Queen Mary* had anchored out there with a huge buckle in her stem, as if a sea monster had taken a bite out of it. This was because, after crossing the Atlantic carrying fifteen thousand American soldiers, she had sliced straight through a British cruiser off Northern Ireland.

The *Queen Mary* did not stop to look for survivors, but steamed on to Greenock: live soldiers mattered more than drowning sailors. Jackie knew all that from Françoise le Gallois, who was at St Columba's with her. Françoise, who was exciting and French but not always to be trusted, had got it from her father.

Next, Jackie took out of her pencil case a mapping pen, uncorked a small bottle of specially black ink and drew a sketch of the Tail of the Bank with the positions of the important ships marked in. The pen was narrow and had a disagreeable sputtery nib, but Jackie had been adding a plan to each entry she had made over the past two years and had learned how to prevent blots. Sometimes, if she felt like it, she made a pencil drawing of a ship – the *Queen Mary* with the bite out of the bow, for instance – but drawing wasn't her strong point, as Miss Coutts had told her right out, in front of the class.

On the cover of the drawing book she had pasted a square of white paper, with STRENG GEHEIM in red – this was definitely the German for Top Secret. Now she took the book upstairs, into the cold, empty room which had once been her mother's bedroom and later the place for Stella and wee Francis after the Clydebank blitz. In the corner there was a loose board which Jackie now howked free. She laid the drawing book on top of the four others already filled up with spy notes and sketches, and fitted the board back over them.

By the time she walked softly downstairs, she was not a bat but a cat. She mewed silently as she crossed the hall and sat down at the table in the kitchen, gnawing delicately at the corned beef with her head cattishly tilted to one side. She was no cuddly kitten. But neither, she thought with a flinch, was she that terrible white tom cat on Union Street who slashed dogs open with a scuff of his grimy paw. No, she was a thin black cat who knew how to keep secrets, who saw everything she wasn't meant to see, whose power might one day undermine the whole world.

She finished her tea and thought about her secrets. Apart from STRENG GEHEIM, the main secret was Dad being alive. At first, and she was only a stupid wee thing then, she had thought that she had killed him when she turned the key and the ship blew up. She knew better now, but she could tell everybody blamed her for it, whatever they all said. And again, the death of the other sailors remained; that had been somehow to do with her turning the key. Not that she had intended the explosion. So who had intended it – God? That was too hard, because it meant trying to imagine God doing real things, not creating whales and clouds but coming quietly up the steps behind her to do something in Greenock.

Soon after the funeral, however, another story began to tell itself. Books turned out to be full of lurking men who were not really dead but in disguise or hiding. Coffins had been dug up empty, or packed with stones or treasure. Jackie had begun to wonder: would all the folk who kept coming to the house and asking questions about Dad, would they be asking after him if they really thought he was dead? He could be alive in a hospital somewhere, maybe not knowing who he was because of getting knocked out. Or escaping in the heather across the hills, sleeping in a cave, catching trout with his hands.

So it hadn't been difficult to suspect what Granny was about, when the cycle trips to Kilmun began. One day, Jackie waited until Granny had set off up the steep path through the birch wood. Then, leaving the cycles unguarded by the loch shore, she raced up the side of the hill until she could look down on the cottage and who came to the door. It was such a shock to see him again, after so long. Even from far off, she saw how feared of everything he was, keeking this and that way into the trees and the bracken to see who might have followed Granny. But one day he and he alone would tell them that she didn't know what was going to happen when she turned the key. He would call everyone into the front room and put his arm round her shoulders, and he would tell them.

A harder fankle was the puzzle of who knew what. Jackie had no intention of telling Granny what she had found out. What way should she tell her? Granny had been treating her like an idiot, putting her son ahead of her granddaughter although Dad belonged to Jackie more than to her. Jackie grew scornful of her silence. If Granny had now come and told her the truth about Dad, she would have almost felt disappointed. On the other hand, she needed to know why Granny had long ago stopped going over the water. Was Dad not there any more? She had left herself no way to ask.

Then there was Mother, and what she knew. Last year, about the time that she saw the bite out of the *Queen Mary*'s bow, Jackie had come home from St Columba's and heard voices from the kitchen. This dazzling, merry woman with an

American accent looked up and said: 'Hi, baby mine!' Her blue uniform tunic was unbuttoned, and the table was piled with gaudy packets and cans. There were bananas and sweeties and chocolate, which Mother called 'candy', and biscuits which she called 'cookies'. Granny, with a new silk scarf round her shoulders, gave Jackie a tight smile but said nothing. 'Now try this,' said Mother, pouring something green out of a bottle into a glass, 'but wait till I put some water to it.' The way she jumped up, leaned over the tap and flicked it open was the same as it always used to be; it was Mother sure enough.

'Lime juice! Straight from the West Indies, and it keeps you healthy. Like it?'

Jackie sipped. 'It's awful sour.'

Helen laughed a lot, and said Jackie was just the same except for growing so big. Then she and Granny talked for a long time about the war, and about her job as a ferry pilot. Jackie was astonished, then proud. Who else had a mother that flew bombers, Flying Fortresses, over the Atlantic? Mother had changed, she thought. Easy-going, chatty like somebody on the wireless, no longer so girny about everything.

'I have to go now. Want to walk along with me?'

It was autumn, already chilly on the dark street. Helen turned downhill to the Esplanade, and they walked beside the sea, the ships invisible behind a chain of red and green riding-lights.

'When the war's over, you know you could come and stay with me in Canada. Stay, live, make your life over there. There's a home waiting for you. Think you'll come?'

'What about Granny?'

'Ach, she'd maybe come over on visits. There's people here in Scotland would take care of her when she's old.'

'Mother?'

'What, big beautiful daughter?'

Jackie meant to say something else, but courage failed. 'Will you take me in your plane one day?'

'Maybe. Want to be a stowaway in a Flying Fortress?' They stopped on the deserted pavement, and mother and daughter stared at one another. 'That's not what's on your mind, Jackie. I can still tell. Spit it out, kid.'

'Like Granny says: tell the truth and shame the Devil?'

They laughed together suddenly. Helen put her arm round Jackie, who leaned into her and said: 'There's something you need to know. Dad's alive yet. He's hiding somewhere but he's no dead. You could find him and rescue him.'

Helen sighed, then shivered. She moved forward, and the two walked along arm in arm.

'I knew that, Jackie. I heard it a while ago. I thought it was you didn't know.'

'Who told you?'

'Well, it was Mike told me. Does it matter?'

'Uncle Mike? How did he know?'

'Who cares? Give us a break. Listen, Jackie, Dad will always be your dad, if he ever turns up again. But the time he and I were together, that's over. Don't you grieve about it, there's no hating between us. But I've changed. There's been the war, Canada, the flying, all that... I couldn't go back to Union Street. But you, I'll always be there for you.'

'Always' means a couple of hours every six months or so,

thought Jackie. But she felt calm. Her mother had said: 'I've changed!' In some ways she had, but in other ways she hadn't. Jackie smiled to think of it. Mother still suited herself, put herself first, just as she always had.

When she got back, there was a cardboard box waiting on her bed. Inside lay an amazing sort of quilted winter coat in red tartan, with an outsize zip fastener and a hood with royal-blue lining. A note said: 'This is called a parka. You'll need it in Canada among the grizzly bears! Luv and xxx, Mother.' She tried the parka on. It had a funny, different shop smell and the pockets were enormous. Would people not stare after her in these bright colours?

She sat down on the bed, forgot about the coat and thought about her new discovery. Uncle Mike knew. That meant he probably knew a lot more than she did, maybe more than Granny did. Such as: which cave Dad was hiding in now, sleeping on dry bracken and roasting trout from the burn.

Granny was surprised. 'Uncle Mike? I'll give you his old army postbox address, if I can find it. But that's a while back, he'll maybe have been moved somewhere else. A letter? Why do you not just postcard him?'

Jackie wrote the letter and her granny, sighing with vexation, showed her how to spell Uncle Mike's name on the envelope. She licked it shut and put 'Forces Mail' on it. In the letter, she said she had seen Mother, who brought her a parka from Canada and American chocolate. Would Uncle Mike be coming through to Greenock soon? There was a very important matter to discuss. Extra private. She hoped he was well.

A long time passed. A winter came and went. The warships

of all the Allied nations and the liners and freighters kept gathering at the Tail of the Bank, often so many that you couldn't see across to the *Fronsac* to tell the tide. And then one morning the estuary would be empty again, the convoy gone until the next gathering.

The American soldiers, the Yanks, came off the ships to the landing stages at Gourock. Their troop trains moved very slowly through the first station at Fort Matilda, so slowly that you could walk alongside and talk to the soldiers as they leaned out of the windows yelling and cheering: 'Hey, kid, you really English?' When they first started coming, Jackie thought they must be hungry after that long journey across the sea, and took her sweetie ration along to throw up to them. But there was a roar of laughter from the Yanks, and then it began to rain all sorts of things on the platform around her: chewing gum, Hershey bars, packs of Lucky Strike and Camel, a doughnut with a hole through it, even a fountain pen. Soon mobs of children were racing to the station to wave and beg as the troop trains moved through. Jackie did not go back there.

No answer came from Uncle Mike. Six months later the letter found its way back to Union Street, with 'This Officer Across Posted' written on it in spiky foreign handwriting. 'He'll be away on invasion training,' said Granny.

That summer, Granny and her friends organised a treat for Jackie and a few other girls from St Columba's. They all went down by train to Wemyss Bay, and took a steamer to Tarbert in Kintyre. There was an old castle and heather and a herring fleet at the pier, a scent of old seaweed and peat fires, and the girls were allowed to eat fish suppers and pokes of chips in the street. Even though they had just been given a full tea at the boarding house run by Mrs MacQuarrie, a cousin of Granny's, where they stayed for three nights at special rates.

Françoise le Gallois complained about the midges, and didn't like the dressing on her haddock. Jackie finished it for her. She was watching Granny carefully, in case the cave was near here and she was planning to slip out at night with a bag of food. But Granny shared a bedroom with one of her friends, the granny of one of the other St Columba girls, and each night Jackie heard them both snoring so comfortably that she soon fell asleep herself.

On the journey back, Jackie stood on deck and hung over the rail so long that the sun scorched her nose and forehead. Presently the ship began to roll and heave, beam-on to the open sea as she rounded Ardlamont Point. Françoise was sick into the wind and had to be taken below and cleaned up. Jackie stayed staring at the sharp-toothed waves and things like little black sails between the waves.

'See that, it's the fins of the basking sharks, each one the size of a fish lorry!' said a sailor. He added: 'No worry, wee girl, they'll no eat ye.' But Jackie was not worried. She was trembling, but with excitement: the greatness of the indifferent sea, the mystery of the places far below her where wrecks lay in the dark, the monsters poking their heads out of rusting funnels.

One of the St Columba gang was English; her father was an important naval officer who could get petrol for his car. A few weeks later, he drove the girls up to Arrochar on Loch Long, a fjord used for the test-firing of torpedoes. They were allowed to sit on one of the distance-rafts, set every half-mile along the range, and fish for whiting. Alongside the rafts were jaunty little steam pinnaces with brass funnels, which hurried out to retrieve the practice torpedoes as they bobbed to the surface at the end of their run. There was one rule, said the large, grim seaman in charge of the raft. When the red flag went up, you took your line in – fast.

Jackie wore her new parka. It was already cold out on the sunless loch, and its waters were so deep that the fishing lines ran out for many minutes before they slackened as the weight touched bottom. But the fish down there were awake. The pinnace crew helped Jackie to unhook a thrashing, dripping whiting and drop it into a basket, just as the distant red flag went up over the firing sheds. Frantically, the other lines were wound in. A whistle blast echoed over the loch. Then a long silence fell.

She felt the tremor before she could hear it, a deep humming which grew until her bones whirred. Then a gleaming red and silver monster that seemed as big as a subway train flashed under her, deep in the transparent green water; it was gone long before its wake of bubbles tore up to the surface and made the raft sway. Jackie felt rapture once more, as if she were riding the missile into the darkness down there, far down there, where one day she must go.

A year is declared to be a long time in a young man's life. Some of my junior comrades at the radio school and on the parachute courses certainly thought so. They were loudly indignant about the loss of each month, counting it out like misers snarling at a tax collector.

'I am only going to be twenty-two once, and I have to waste it polishing boots and belt, standing about in the rain in this fucking Scotland where nothing happens, not even a German to shoot at. In Kraków, I would be finishing my law degree by now. I would be painting the apartment for Kasia and me when we get married. Where the fuck is she now? Am I supposed to do what some of the others do, and visit that frightful ten-bob hag out there in the bushes? This is my youth I am losing here. Youth? I might as well be forty, what's the difference?'

'Easy, Jacek, easy! Soon enough you'll be on the end of a parachute, wondering who's waiting for you down there. Then you'll be wishing you were back at Polmont, queuing up for a nice piece of spam with baked beans and chips.'

'Soon enough? Make it bloody sooner still!'

I couldn't stand this avarice of the young about their youth. It seemed to me obscene. Weren't we supposed to be careless, generous with our lives and time? 'We'? I realised that I had forgotten what being young felt like. Thirty-six is already old age in wartime.

The training was hard, often harsh. I was still fit: I could run five miles in full battle order, keeping up with the squad, but it hurt. I couldn't be like young Jacek and the others, who flung themselves gasping and cursing on the grass, lit a cigarette, and five minutes later were ready to sling their rifles and run on.

All the same, that was a good year in which to lack time to think. There was just enough space for anger at what was happening, but not enough for proper grief and mourning. The last Poles to be released by Stalin had emerged through Persia and a few of them, women as well as men, were sent on to us in Scotland. While they were telling their stories, the Germans opened the mass grave at Katyń.

As I remember, we were not really surprised. The three-year silence from our officer prisoners – those thousands captured by the Red Army whose letters had stopped so abruptly in April 1940 – had already been filled by terrible rumours. What did surprise us was the silence of the British. They knew as well as we did who was guilty, but they pretended that there was some doubt. So when General Sikorski was killed a few months later, in an air crash at Gibraltar which the British called an 'accident', it was our turn to doubt.

I recalled, not for the first time, what Commandant le Gallois had said about the ruthlessness of *les Anglais* when their national interest was at stake. No, I don't believe they directly murdered the Supreme Commander. But perhaps it was like this: if Soviet agents crept towards the plane on the airstrip at Gibraltar and cut its control cables, someone had orders to look the other way. For a day or so after the disaster we all argued among ourselves, at times shouting, occasionally with tears.

That was the only occasion when bad news brought training to a halt. And it frightened us. Not just the shock and anger over Sikorski's death, but the discovery of how vulnerable we were. We looked tough, we talked tough, but underneath we were all living on our nerves. What kept us going was a continuous act of will, the daily effort to concentrate on the job of war against the Germans and not to think about what would happen when the job was done. But of course the effort often broke down. Sometimes it was news on the wireless which made us sit on our bunks at night and talk in low voices. Sometimes it was the stories we heard from fresh arrivals; men and women who now began to reach us from the Soviet immensity, refugees from the future.

My best friend at Polmont was a tall, gloomy-looking captain called Tadeusz Ostrowski – 'Tadek'. He was the man who, for two bottles of whisky, had provided me with a British identity card in the name of Alexander Ketling. Now he was an instructor on the radio course and I was his pupil. We were much of an age, and he came from the same part of Poland as I did, but Tadek looked more Scandinavian: a bony, beaky nose, fair hair already receding. A lot of Swedish soldiers had been around his district three centuries before. Maybe Tadek was the echo of some thigh-booted scuffle in the hay. He certainly liked to think so.

One day, he said to me: 'Tomorrow, there is a canteen revolution. No more army cooks. But instead real women – Scottish ones, even Polish ones!'

'Polish women?'

'Yes, fresh from Siberia. Well, from Egypt or Palestine; after Siberia, that's where they landed up.'

Next day, we spent a silly morning laying out green-painted wireless aerials supposed to be invisible in the grass. They showed up brilliantly on the Scottish turf, leading the *Abwehr* or the Gestapo straight to the concealed transmitter. The class began to snigger. Tadek said: 'If you laugh, you will have to paint the grass darker green after lunch. Fall out!'

The canteen floor had been swept and washed; the tables had been scrubbed and laid with white cloths. Behind a new serving counter stood a line of women in aprons and headscarves. They were wide-eyed, expectant, a touch nervous.

I took a bowl and went up to the steel vat containing soup. Behind it stood a thin, sad woman who seemed to be terrified by the sight of me; she flinched away and her mouth opened, showing missing teeth. She was a bit clumsy ladling out the soup: oxtail or something, but an improvement on turnip. 'Thank you,' I said in Polish. 'You are very welcome here.' She said nothing; something about me still alarmed her. Maybe she wasn't Polish after all, but one of the Scottish ladies.

A voice said in English: 'Major? We meet again!' I looked

along the counter, and met the eyes of Lady Somebody as she shovelled out sausages, bacon and fried bread. Working clothes suited her; she seemed younger and more free. I noticed that she was wearing her engagement ring – a pretty blue stone mounted in gold, that went with her eyes – at the same moment she did. She twisted it off her finger. 'Damn, I forgot! Will you hang on to this till afterwards?' I dropped the ring into the tunic pocket of my battledress.

When the men had all been served, she came over with a mug of tea and sat down with Tadek and me.

'It seems so long ago now, the dance at Kirkton. I was going to ask you and some of the others to Sunday lunch, but you left early. Remember? You rushed off. The corporal had quite a job getting the lads into the truck without you.'

'I remember. We danced.'

'I hope you'll call me Margaret. And you are ... Maurycy.' She pronounced it properly. I looked hard at Tadek, whose long horse-face had assumed an idiotic expression.

'Tadek is teaching me Polish. Well, we are quite old friends, aren't we. We met at headquarters in Leven, when we volunteers took over the kitchen in the officers' mess. But now I'm here. With all you secret agents, in the hush-hush department!' She laughed merrily.

Men at other tables were looking round at us. Margaret's voice was as sharp as an oboe, the voice of someone who had never understood why other women whispered. I wondered how much the soldiers had understood. Tadek still sat in a daze of love.

'That singer at the dance,' I asked, 'what was her name? I don't recall.'

'Oh, that was Isabella Fowler, Tibbie – quite a character. And such a sweet voice. Yes, her mother was with us at the castle for years till the war broke out.'

'With you?'

'Well, yes, she did the beds and the floors at Balbrudie, kept the drawing room nice, helped Cook – you know. And we let Tibbie use the library, little bookworm. Sitting cross-legged on the carpet, reading all the old poems in Scots. She'll go to university if this war ever ends.'

'Where's Tibbie now?'

'You'll never believe, she's a policewoman in Edinburgh. Big Tibs, the terror of couthy Liberton. She's been at it for over a year now. I'm surprised you didn't know. They say you made quite a hit with her that evening.'

'Ships that pass in the night.'

'How sad. Well, I must ship myself off now. *Do widzenia*, both of you.'

She jumped up, took her mug through to the scullery and vanished into the gardens. That night, as I undressed, I felt the ring in my pocket.

Tadek said: 'I'll give it to her tomorrow.'

'Why you? I'll be seeing her, too, and she asked me to look after it.'

'Sod off, will you?' We both laughed.

Next day, the row of women waiting for us behind the counter were smiling and joking as if we had all been together for months. This time, a different woman stood at the soup vat and she was definitely Polish. Small and sturdy, she chattered away about the fresh fruit and vegetables – bananas, oranges, asparagus – they had enjoyed in Palestine. It was so strange to hear again a woman speaking my language: in a way delicious, in another way almost shocking. How could she blether on as if she were in her own farm kitchen? Hadn't she noticed that she had landed on another planet where the skies were dark, where nobody picked the wild mushrooms in the wood and Mary Queen of Heaven didn't stand at each crossroads?

Tadek gave the ring to his lady, who laughed and nodded her silver head towards me. I sat with them for a few moments after the meal, but Margaret soon excused herself. 'I have to help clear. We're so shorthanded; half the Polish women who came yesterday are off sick. Their state of health ... God, I had no idea. They should all be in hospital really.'

Walking across the gardens towards my hut, I passed the sickbay. It was sunny, and a woman in a headscarf was sitting on a bench outside the door smoking a cigarette. Her legs were bare, and I noticed dark, coin-shaped scars, ulcer marks, on her shins. It was the gaunt woman who had served me soup the day before. She was obviously one of ours. Why had I thought she might be a Scot? I sat down beside her.

'Let me introduce myself. I am Maurycy Szczucki and I come from a place not far from Lwów. And can I ask madame for her name?'

She said nothing, but raised her head and began to stare at me. She was looking straight into my eyes, but it was the stare of somebody trying to make out a distant landmark, perhaps a broken tower on the horizon. The cigarette went on burning between her fingers. Then the corner of her mouth twitched, but no smile followed.

I tried again. 'They say that your group is still in bad health. Were you in the sickbay to get medicine?'

She put her hand on mine, as if to steady me. Then at last she smiled, and said: 'I am afraid that in Scotland they don't run to *cachets Faivres*. Not like that pharmacy downstairs on Czarnecki Street.'

I sat bolt upright. As I have written, meeting dead people is not so very surprising. But this was utterly surprising. There was a moment of silence. I expect my mouth fell open. I remember taking up her hand and squeezing the bones of her fingers, as if I were counting them.

'I don't believe this. This is not possible, I don't believe this.'

Now the smile widened; and it was tender and, in spite of the missing teeth, familiar. She trod out her cigarette, pulled off the headscarf and shook out her short, greying hair. Wisia had been nineteen then, when we were together, and that had been seven years ago. So this worn, yellow-faced woman must be all of twenty-six years old. We clung to one another and wept, and I felt the bony knobs along her spine.

That evening, after duty, we met again and sat on the same bench. On her knees Wisia balanced a brown-paper bag containing two real oranges.

'Let's share. They give them to me for my vitamins. In Palestine, we had fresh oranges all the time.'

'But before Palestine. Tell me everything, starting in that September. And your family? You were the oldest, the big sister.'

So she told me. Now, as I look back on what she said, I see her cropped head bowed as she talked, looking down at the orange she was slowly unpeeling in her lap. At one point in her wanderings Wisia had worked in a Persian carpet factory in Ispahan, and I remember her story as one thread in an enormous tapestry, a kilim made out of countless individual stories which I imagine in dark reds and blacks and bright green. That is the narrative of the Poles driven back and forth across the world, a journey through captivity and war and famine and plague, across forests and winter steppes, across oceans and deserts and – for brief moments of joy – into green Paradise gardens of fruit and flowers.

Don't talk to me about a 'pilgrimage'. I hate that sort of pious-patriotic syrup. Don't talk to me about an Odyssey or an Aeneid. Like us, Odysseus and Aeneas left a burning city to sail through every kind of suffering and peril, but one came home to his wife in his own house and the other reached the destined shore and founded a better Troy. For the Poles, there was no homecoming, and nothing was founded. One by one, we slipped overboard and swam ashore to a hundred different beaches, and the empty ship drifted over the horizon.

I remembered Wisia's family well, though I had never felt close to them. She had a noisy ten-year-old brother, Władek, and a younger sister, Hania ('Haneczka'), with dark hair, and an energetic, restless mother. Her father, a reserve officer, had been captured after 17 September and she had no news of him. I imagine we both thought about the sodden bundles packed layer on layer in those pits in Katyń Forest, and there was no need for words.

In April 1940, her mother and the three children were crammed into cattle trucks on a train which took three weeks to reach central Asia. They survived the journey, which many did not. In Kazakhstan, mother and children dug ditches or stacked railway sleepers, and Haneczka died of dysentery a few weeks before they heard of the 'amnesty' in the summer of 1941.

Hitching lifts on lorries, they set off to seek the new Polish army being formed in Russia. But after a month on the road they were intercepted, and put in a desolate transit camp with thousands of other ragged fugitives. Everyone had lice; typhus broke out.

'Mama was ill; we took off our coats to cover her. I thought if I could find milk, at least, she could get well. So I walked for a night and a day, and with a gold earring I bought a tin can full of sheep's milk in an Uzbek village. But when I got back, Mama was dead.'

Wisia and young Władek set out again, this time on foot. They lived by scavenging, begging. Once Wisia found a crate of matches in the back of an overturned lorry, and they kept alive by selling the matches at the side of the road. Meanwhile, the Polish base had been moved even further away, to near Tashkent. By the time they got there, in the spring of 1942, both of them were skeletal and weak with scurvy. Army nurses, themselves starving, did what they could for them, but the children of the incoming Polish survivors were dying by dozens every week.

One day Wisia woke in her tent to find Władek gone. He had told a friend that he was setting out to look for his father. In the next few weeks, she searched for him in the streets of Tashkent and in all the hospitals and cemeteries she could reach on foot. But she never saw him again.

That summer, Stalin was at last persuaded to let the Polish army leave the Soviet Union and join the British in the Middle East; the soldiers and their ragged civilian retinue were brought down to the Caspian Sea. Wisia, who wanted to stay and wait for Władek, cried and screamed; she kicked the soldiers who thrust her back into the lorry. When they came to Krasnovodsk, rusty steamers were alongside the dock, ready to carry them across the sea to Iran.

The crossing took two days. The sick and dying lay on the deck under a black cloud of flies. Everyone else had to stand, packed shoulder to shoulder. Wisia remembered the soft splashes as the dead were heaved over the rail into the sea.

On the Persian shore, British doctors in uniform and Red Cross ambulances were waiting for them along the beach at Pahlevi. Wisia unbuttoned her filthy clothes and waded into the cool water, indifferent to her nakedness and to the fuel oil floating on the surface. Then she came out and lay on the sand and slept for three days and nights. On the second day, an army squad collecting corpses along the shore noticed that she was still alive. When she woke, she was wearing a clean nightdress and smelled of soap; her head had been shaved and she was lying under white sheets in a hospital ward.

Wisia stayed in Persia for many months. Soon she was well enough to help in a Polish orphanage, and later to stand and work at the looms with other women in the Ispahan carpet factory. Then she joined the army as a nurse. This meant that she could stay with the troops as they went on to Baghdad and then Palestine, while the civilian families were sent off to Egypt and then to wait the war out in India or Southern Rhodesia.

But in Palestine Wisia fell ill again. 'Respiratory problems, also a nervous crisis,' she said dismissively. Instead of following her field hospital into battle in North Africa or Italy, she was put on a white cruise liner which went down the Red Sea to South Africa and then up the Atlantic to Scotland. 'Cadet nurse Kaczmarek, Wisława: transferred to Polish First Corps for health reasons, light duties to be assigned by appropriate supply company.'

She recited this formula with a grave expression. Once I could have told from her voice if she was being satirical. Now I could not be sure. When you are old, as now I am, it often happens that you meet somebody you haven't seen for twenty years – but he's plump and bald, but she's become an old lady with puckers round her mouth! And yet, after only a day or so, you have moved back into this well-known house with its changed furniture. You soon forget that curly head on the young giant swerving towards the goal-posts, the lips which shone when they parted to kiss – all these memories fade into brown snapshots in a mislaid album. It takes more time to realise that the house itself is no longer in the same place.

Wisia's different face had again become Wisia to me, by the time that we met on the same bench on a third afternoon. But it was as if she was speaking with a new grammar whose rules I didn't know. She spoke evenly, sometimes smiled. But was there agony or anger under the level surface, or mockery behind the gentle smile?

This time, she rolled her orange up and down her knee, but for a long while didn't peel it.

'What did I do?'

'When? What do you mean?'

'You know. When I came back to your room, and you had gone. What did I do wrong?'

I was silent.

'I thought for a long time: it must have been because I was so easy. I didn't try to stop what you were doing. So you thought: after all, she's just another little whore.'

'No, Wisia, no, never! Listen: that never entered my head; in fact, it was exactly the opposite...' So I told her. Well, I told her that I was unnerved when she knelt down to pray beside the bed. That much. Not about feeling that I was being trapped. Not about escapology. I told her something about how marvellous she had looked naked, and how the contrast between hands raised to Mary and what we were about to do in the bed had been... suddenly unbearable to me.

To my surprise, she began to laugh.

'Maurycy, you are such a complete idiot. Just for that? I don't believe you – unless all that pompous atheism of yours suddenly vanished.'

She laughed again, putting up her hand to hide the gaps

in her teeth. Through her fingers, she said: 'The Miracle on Czarnecki Street! Pious maiden prays to Our Lady to save her virginity, and her prayer is heard.'

I thought: she never talked like that in the old days. Better if she had.

Wisia said, 'Your family – you think they were so sophisticated and modern. But they brought you up as a total innocent. Only child, with no brothers or sisters. Anti-clerical household, with no prayers, no holy pictures. Didn't you know that nice girls are always meant to cross themselves and say a prayer before they get into bed? After brushing their teeth, of course.'

Once again, I couldn't read her mood. I muttered: 'What I did to you was unforgivable. When I think of what you have had to suffer . . .'

'Quiet, quiet!' She stuck a segment of orange into my mouth, and kissed me on the cheek. But that was something she used to do, the old Wisia, when we were walking in the park and I was in the middle of some speech about the absurdities of clerical fascism. Sometimes it was a piece of the apple she was eating, sometimes a chocolate plum. Always with the same light kiss. I felt a prickling in my eyes.

'Listen, Maurycy. What you did to me and what happened afterwards to me – to our family – have nothing to do with each other. But, well, you gave me my first loss. I was lucky. I grew up with people who adored me and protected me. I was nineteen, I was in love with you, I trusted you. Nothing had prepared me for what you did. It was like the earth's crust suddenly giving way and dropping me into a darkness which had always been waiting underneath.'

She was silent for a moment. 'First love and first loss. Nothing which comes afterwards is like them. Still, that feeling that we walk on a thin crust, that we can at any time fall through it... I had learned that through you, which is why I wasn't broken, not mentally, by what happened to us later. I already knew there was a pit beneath us all.'

'You make me feel like a hangman, who lured you on to his trapdoor, wound the pretty rope gently round your neck and pulled the lever.'

'My dear, you should have been a writer. I thought so then. Maybe you still could be. Maurycy, it's such a blessing that we never married. Not just because you are a charming monster who ruins other people because he doesn't know what he wants. But because of history. Here we are, breathing this Scottish air. If we had married and stayed where we were, you would be in the earth beside my father at Katyń, and I would have died in Siberia trying to keep our baby alive.'

Wisia carefully brushed together the orange peel on her lap, and wrapped it in her handkerchief. 'For the kitchen. For nice cakes.' She got to her feet and faced me.

'I'm away tomorrow to hospital, a place near Glasgow. My trouble is tuberculosis. Well, it's not surprising after Russia. Some of the other girls are bad with it, too, but mine seems to need the specialists.'

I said: 'I can't lose you.'

She laughed. 'Wisia is tough. It's not about losing me, it's about finding yourself. Walk delicately, my dear. Remember how thin the crust is. Even in this stony Scotland.'

O ver Greenock, that was an autumn of deep war and wet streets. Men and women pulled cloth bunnets down over their noses or unfurled black umbrellas as they flowed in and out of the yards. The soft rain made the granite setts gleam under their feet. The angry 'Second Front Now!' slogans were beginning to wash off the walls.

There was no end in sight to rain or war. From the Lyle Hill, there were many days when you could barely see the Argyll mountains. The misty rain came from there, out of the north-west, drawing across the estuary in long, sleepy curtains before it made the slates of Gourock shine.

It tasted sour, this water picked up by clouds from the ocean or the inner seas. This rain had taken flavour as it trailed across distant green islands, across rocks and strands piled with debris from the Atlantic war: red buoys and yellow smoke bombs, white-painted fragments of lifeboats, grey pods of rubber latex, shapeless black bundles which had once been seamen.

The battleships still came and went with their convoys.

The great Firth would be crowded for a few days, then suddenly empty. The troop trains still cantered slowly through Fort Matilda, but the children no longer ran to beg from them. Some trains now carried lorries as well as men, Dodges and Studebakers and jeeps painted with the white star of the Invasion. Soon, it'll be soon now. 'Aye, right,' said the men in the Auchmar Vaults as they settled to their pints. They had heard that before.

Jackie was in trouble that autumn, and causing trouble. It began one afternoon at Union Street, when she made a big mistake.

Françoise had come to tea. It wasn't the first time; if they travelled back together on the train from St Columba's, it was an easy walk from the station. Granny would sometimes make pancakes for them on the girdle, if she had eggs. Françoise didn't drink tea, and didn't much like milk either. So Granny kept a bottle of orangeade for her.

Then the girls would take a plate of biscuits up to Jackie's bedroom. Since the summer trips to Tarbert and Arrochar, Jackie had been reading books about 'the wonders of the deep'. She wanted to talk about sharks, whales, giant squids, but Françoise found this boring. She preferred to talk in her funny accent about film stars, lisle stockings and the blouse she had worn when she gave General de Gaulle a bouquet.

Her chest was already making bulges under her jersey. Sometimes, when weddings or babies came up in their talk, she would screw up her eyes and nod at Jackie with a special fat-lipped smile which Jackie found quite provoking. What was so secret or special? Husbands and wives kissed after the wedding, then a baby came out of the wife's tummy. But that didn't seem to be the exciting thing Françoise knew and she did not.

Two could play at that secrets game. 'C'mon, I'll show you something,' said Jackie, and led the way to the spare room upstairs. It was almost a year since she had grown bored with STRENG GEHEIM, but now she pulled up the floorboard and pointed to the stack of drawing books. Françoise picked one up, turned over its pages and shrugged. 'What is this? Who wrote it – you?'

Jackie hesitated. Then she said: 'No, it was a German spy. He stayed here once and left them behind. See, it's all the battleships in the river, the convoys, lists he was going to send to Germany by wireless. But nobody else knows about this. Nobody but me. And you.'

She took the book, dropped it into the hole and replaced the floorboard. Françoise said nothing at all, which was unlike her. Her black eyes were unreadable, and she didn't smile. Jackie's feeling of triumph began to drain away, and she felt uneasy. Why had she told that daft lie?

A French staff car came to pick up Françoise and take her home. This time, for some reason, she didn't thank Granny for the tea.

Next day was a Saturday: no school. At breakfast-time the bell rang, at once followed by banging on the front door. 'Whatever...?' Mrs Melville opened the door and found three men standing in the rain: two with bristly foreign haircuts and a Greenock police sergeant. They pushed her and Jackie back into the kitchen, as the policeman began to recite a formula about a search warrant. 'Ach, for heaven's sake. Not again?'

The bristly hair of one of the French agents was grey; he seemed to be in charge. The other, younger man spoke English. They ran upstairs, and within five minutes were down again holding the five drawing books. They spread them out on the kitchen table. Mrs Melville put on her glasses and began to turn some pages. Slowly, she shook her head. 'For pity's sake...'

The younger Frenchman asked: 'Who was living in that room? Who hid all this under the floor? Who wrote this?'

'I did,' said Jackie. 'It was... just a game.'

Mrs M said: 'It's in her handwriting right enough. Anyone can see it's a child's handwriting.'

'I ask again. You must say: who lived in that room?'

'Well, there was a bombed-out family from Clydebank. And before that, my son and his wife – they stayed there.'

The greying *en brosse* man jerked his companion's sleeve and whispered something.

'Your son? Named Johnston Melville? Officer of English marine?'

'A British naval officer, yes.'

'Where is he now?'

'My son was killed when the *Fronsac* blew up. It's more than three years back now. But you'll know that very well.' Jackie began to cry loudly. Mrs Melville gave her a sharp glance.

More French whispering. 'Nobody will leave this house. Telephone: not allowed. Do you understand? You are detained. The police watches the door. Later we return for full search, full interrogation. And I advise you to pack a bag for several weeks.' They left, with the drawing books in a briefcase. The policeman sat down on a chair in the hall. He sighed and slowly put his big hands on his knees.

Mrs Melville closed the kitchen door.

'You stupid, stupid girl! Did you not think what a wicked, stupid thing you were doing – and in wartime? Whatever will happen to us now?'

Jackie abruptly stopped crying. 'I know about my dad. How did you not tell me all that time? I know he's alive.'

'Do you indeed! And who the devil told you? I can guess: that daft Pole. Well, there it's out between us at last. Your father was in bad enough trouble already, but he's in a worse mess now. Thanks to you.'

They sat in silence, grandmother and granddaughter, avoiding each other's eyes.

'Why are they after him? What did he do?'

'Oh, so there's something Miss kens-it-all doesn't know. Nothing. He did nothing. Well, they think he had something to do with the explosion on the ship. Which he never did. That wee horror Eric, he that's dead now, got it into his head that your father was some sort of enemy agent. My God, it's you that was the enemy agent, playing the spy and hiding it all away. Suppose a real German had walked in and found it?'

Jackie went off into the chilly front room, stood at the window and pretended to study the ships. Hadn't she nearly killed her father once? Now she was sending another torpedo after him.

Her wickedness! She hated Granny for saying that she

was just stupid, stupid, when it was dead wicked that she was. Destroyer of ships, father murderer, spy. Not stupid but evil. It was Françoise who was stupid – feared of a game she didn't understand and then clyping to her father. Some friend, and her with her fat chest too.

In books, people who knew they were evil wished they were dead. Maybe she should be wishing that. Jackie thought of how sorry Granny would be when she found her hanging up with her feet shoogling in the air, or lying pale on the floor with a disinfectant bottle beside her. Granny would be greeting and telephoning for the doctor and wishing she'd never said those things about stupid. Too late!

She lingered over that scene. But then she admitted to herself that she didn't really want to be dead. What she wanted was to escape from everyone and live in a deep, clear elsewhere with her real friends: the mackerel and the porbeagles, the ugly angler fish and the thresher sharks, the halibut wafting after their own wide shadows on the sand. She would get a diving suit with a big helmet and walk on the sea floor. She would gather queenie-scallops and brittle-stars and explore the dark corridors of wrecks. Nobody would find her there.

In the afternoon, the bell rang again. The policeman struggled off his chair and opened the door to a heavily built officer in blue uniform.

Jackie had met Françoise's father before. Commandant le Gallois gave her a sharp, twinkly look as he folded his umbrella. 'Who is this other lady? Good; your grandmother. We have to talk – quickly, quickly.'

He tossed his cap to the policeman, who muttered but hung

it on a hook. Then they went into the front room. Le Gallois walked to the window and glanced at the fleets below. He rubbed his hands together: 'Ah, *bon Dieu*, it's cold in here!' He seemed ill at ease.

'Listen, you have nothing to worry about. You say in English: a misunderstanding? Yes, exactly. You see, my daughter is very loyal, patriotic. Françoise has a sense of duty – very developed sense, one can say. Normally, one admires. But this time, well – I am sorry. My people had to investigate the report, you must understand that. But as soon as I saw the notes, the drawings, the handwriting, I thought: *ouf*, no dangerous spy, but a child. Maybe a little girl, lonely, who wants to have secrets.'

He advanced on Jackie, smiling, and reached out a broad brown hand. She backed away, but found her way blocked by a sofa. Le Gallois ruffled her hair and then ran his hand gently up and down her neck.

'Why did you tell Françoise that a German spy had been living in that room? Instead of saying that it was you who wrote it all? You know, that could have had very, very bad consequences for several people. Maybe even for somebody you know.'

He looked at his watch. 'I have to go. I bring an apology for the shock you suffered today, but also an invitation. In a few months, it will be four years since the *Fronsac* ... accident. So I am arranging a small ceremony. A boat will go to the wreck, an official party with wreaths, but also with some families of those who died. Alas! most of the families are in France, occupied France, so naturally they cannot come. But for example you, who lost a father, a son ... Free France would be honoured if you wished to be present.'

The Commandant bowed to Mrs Melville. He turned suddenly to Jackie. 'Do you miss your father very much?'

Eyebrows raised, he waited for an answer. Jackie returned his direct stare, but said nothing. She could still feel his fingers on her neck, a confusing feeling.

'Well, then perhaps I will see you both again. Next April.'

He nodded again to Mrs Melville, and went to look for his uniform cap in the hall. The policeman stood to attention. 'My friend,' said le Gallois, 'you are not required any more. No crime here, after all: no suspects. You and I, we can go and win the war somewhere else.' The front door thumped behind them.

I went to see Wisia a few weeks later. The hospital was out in the countryside near Glasgow; a long wait for a bus, then a long tramp down a wintry road. Early snow had turned to slush. I was in civilian clothes, and my flimsy shoes let in water. By the time I arrived, I was wishing I had never come.

I had expected a big old building, but this hospital turned out to be a fleet of barrack huts parked in a field, connected by a 'spider' maze of covered walkways. Finding Wisia's ward – 'Kaczmarek, Wisława' – 'Eh? Is that somebody foreign you're wanting?' – took another half-hour.

'What's the matter? You don't look happy.'

'My feet are wet.'

'What a tragedy! When the nurses here jag a needle in me and I flinch, they say: "Worse things happened at Culloden." A bad Scottish battle, apparently. Shameless – we have so many more bad battles than they do.'

'Worse things happened in our September. And our January. And our November. And...'

'Exactly. So take off your socks and dry them on the stove.'

At least it was blissfully hot in Wisia's hut. It had a rich smell of coal-flame, floor polish, medical gauze. When I had arranged my shoes and socks by the stove, I padded barefooted to the bed and opened the damp paper bag in which I had brought a chocolate bar, a tiny scent bottle, an English novel (*Captain Hornblower*), a sealed tin of cigarettes.

'Not allowed,' she said sadly. I laid it on her table anyway, and she hid it in the drawer. There was a rosary looped round the knob of the bedstead, and she had pinned a postcard of the Black Madonna to the wall above her head. A small red and white flag, made of paper coloured in crayon, peeped out from behind the postcard.

I pointed to this display. 'Making yourself at home?'

I had half expected to find Wisia coughing dramatically, 'unnaturally flushed'. Nothing like that. Her hair had grown longer, so that she looked younger. Otherwise, she seemed unchanged. But I saw how weak she had become when she struggled to lift herself up on her pillows.

'What are you smiling at? That's what I have left, that's who I am.' She was angry, but in a tired, dry way I had never seen in her. 'You know, when I was a girl at home, I sometimes felt how fine it would be to become a gypsy, to be a voyaging bird which owns nothing but its wings! But now – it's so strange – the dream has come true, and I really do own nothing.

'Listen, this is the list of everything I possess. One fountain pen. One notebook. An American ten-dollar note, a wristwatch I bought in Ispahan. One white cotton blouse. A hairbrush, a comb and, yes, a wicked red lipstick – I got that in Haifa.

A penknife. One book, a tiny one: it's a miniature Mickiewicz, *Wiersze*, the short poems. An old Jew in Haifa who liked talking Polish gave it to me. And from my old life, I still have a gold earring. I told you what happened to the other one.'

She took a drink of water, and shrugged her shoulders. 'That's it. What else? A rucksack, but the rest of my things don't even fill it. Uniform, cap, two shirts, underwear, shoes, even toothbrush – those all belong to the army. Family? None: lost. House and property? None: lost.'

'Country? None: lost.'

'Don't dare to say that!' Wisia was suddenly shouting. Other patients in the ward looked up. The strange language seemed to startle them as much as her passion. 'Don't you understand anything? Do you laugh at everything?'

She was thumping her fist on her thin chest. 'Poland is here. As long as I am alive. And in you, too. Listen, you will sneer at this. But I have three more possessions I didn't tell you about, three jewels which I found in Bolshevik Asia and brought out wrapped in a silly slogan. God, Honour, Fatherland!'

I must have looked astounded. Wisia went on: 'God's mother, Queen of Heaven, Star of the Sea, also lost those she loved, but she promises that she will never lose me – whatever happens, wherever I am when I meet my end.' Tears began to run down her cheeks. 'Honour: whatever I do now must be pure, because I offer it up to the memory of all those men, women and children I saw die. And our poor country, our *ojczyzna* ... don't you remember the poem you learned at school? "I and my country are one / My name is Million / because I love and suffer torture for those millions ..."'

She was crying quietly now. I went to sit on the side of the bed, and she moved her legs under the blanket to make room for me. A nurse came up to see what was wrong; I waved her away.

'Wisia! Listen, I have lost almost as much as you, and many of the same things. Maybe my list of possessions is a bit longer. More books, and I paid for my own sword. We are both orphans now, but we don't need that old three-word slogan. Let's leave it to bishops and headmasters and generals on parade. After the war, I'll see if I can find God hiding with false papers in some refugee camp, and ask him what he meant by it. As for honour, it means to me simply fighting the Germans, anywhere on earth, and not letting down my comrades. And my country? Maybe it's not a Poland-place any more, but any place in the world where I am still behaving with honour.'

'Maurycy, stop it, you're raving!'

'It's hard to explain. Look: soon, in the middle of some night, I will be dropped out of an aircraft and fall towards what they say is my country. Yes, I have memories of a familiar land in my head. But what's down there now? Maybe nothing.'

'How nothing? Don't modern parachutists carry secret maps printed on silk?'

'I don't mean landing in the wrong place. No, of course you jump with every sort of baggage: the radio is heaviest, but pistol, compass, torch ... And yet I have this feeling; there's fear in it, but more a sort of longing: physical, sensual. How would it be if there were no meadows and trees down there in the darkness, no anything, and I just went on quietly falling for ever, deeper and deeper, into a hole where once there was Poland? And as I fell, and as I realised the fall would be endless, I might become free and happy.'

'Happy, Maurycy?'

'Do you remember one day in summer – your name-day, I think – when we went with some friends and a bottle of wine into the meadow by the university? We lay on the grass on our backs. And you said: "Suppose we could switch gravity into reverse. Suppose we began to fall upwards, faster and faster, into that beautiful blue sky until nobody could see us, until the world was just a little globe. Wouldn't that be lovely?" Well, that's what I mean.'

Wisia began to smile. 'You haven't grown up much, have you? Anyone who didn't know you and listened to your nonsense would say: this man has a death wish. But to me you are really saying: There's no darkness I wouldn't jump into to escape being tied to other people.'

She lay back in the pillows and patted me on the leg. 'Yes, I do remember that day. And I also remember one of the boys saying: "Wisia, can I hold your hand while we fall? And then I can steer us to land on the moon and have you all to myself." But that boy wasn't you.'

The nurse, who had been hovering, came up to me and said in a carefully loud voice: 'Your friend is wanting her temperature taken. She's no a well lady, ken? And that's visiting hours over now.' She thrust a thermometer into Wisia's mouth. Then she picked up the bar of chocolate I had brought and began to crack it into squares, which she dropped into the front pocket of her apron. I put a hand out to stop her. But the nurse said: 'In ma ward, all sweeties and cookies and biscuits get shared out. That goes for foreigners tae. There's a war on, did ye know?'

Her mouth full of thermometer, Wisia nodded earnestly. I could see she was trying not to laugh. My socks and shoes were fairly dry now, so I put them on again. The nurse whipped the thermometer out of Wisia's lips, glanced at it, shook it, and went off muttering to herself.

'Come and see me again, before you go. If you can't, I'll ask some saints to take care of you where you are going. Someone I talk to a lot these days is St Thérèse of Lisieux. Very quiet little person, not your type at all. Dear Maurycy, I know what you are doing is dangerous. But when you hit our Polish earth and feel it under your feet, you'll become normal again. No more death wishes, no diving into space. After the war, you can put all that into the book you must write.'

Outside, darkness had fallen and the slush in the road was beginning to freeze. Wisia had annoyed me. It wasn't just her lapse into God-Fatherland national cliché, dismaying as I had found it. It was that she seemed to have joined the ring of people, mostly women, who reproached me for being a drifter who didn't know what he wanted. Perhaps that had once been true. But now, surely, I had changed. I had given up my selfish detachment, thrown out my illusions about cause and country, narrowed my focus. All I wanted to be was a soldier in a war with an enemy and a job to finish. No space for other entanglements.

Was that so hard to grasp? When the Glasgow bus came, I sat in the back and brooded with a cigarette. Wisia, for one, clearly hadn't grasped it. Helen, if I ever saw her again, would be sceptical; she didn't think people changed. That singer at the dance – Tibbie – she obviously thought I needed salving. Commandant le Gallois, Johnston Melville and probably several different intelligence services all had plans to ensnare me in their own schemes.

Le Gallois, though, had been right when he told me to find a good war far away from Scotland. How long till the night when that Liberator burdened with extra fuel tanks would begin its long take-off run? Then, heaving itself over the tree tops at the end of the runway, it would bank away eastwards, carrying me towards Polish stars. I was impatient for that night.

In the middle of that winter, Tadek and I limped in from a five-mile speed march to find two pale-blue envelopes waiting for us. We threw off our muddy denims, took a shower and sat on our bunks in our underclothes to open the letters. They contained invitation cards. Lady Margaret Beaton-Campbell was asking us to lunch at Balbrudie Castle. The words 'Sir James and...' had been carefully scored out.

The invitation came at the right moment. Tadek and I were packing our kit for yet another course, this time at Ringway airfield near Manchester. This was to be our final test before we were dropped into Poland, and we had reason to dread it.

At Ringway, squads of ten men learned to jump together. Not all of them were fully trained. And not all the British dispatchers in the aircraft checked the safety gear or dropped our boys in the right place. Two friends of ours had already died: one when his parachute failed to open, another when he fell into a mud-pond and drowned. Others had broken legs or crushed vertebrae. After Ringway, we told each other, we had nothing to fear from the Germans.

Seeing Margaret in her castle would take our minds off it. An army lorry going north to Montrose carried us up to Forfar and then to the end of her drive. As we walked up between snow-loaded rhododendrons, I expected to see one of those grim Scottish tower-houses, another black keep with arrow slits and crow steps. But then, rounding a bend, we faced a palace in miniature. Balbrudie reminded me of some of our own petty manors at home, a tiny classical mansion which from a distance looked elegant. Only as we approached the outside staircase did I notice the uncut, knee-high grass, the stains on the walls left by choked rone-pipes, the broken slates on the ground under boarded-up windows.

The front door opened to a push. 'Come on down to the kitchen!' shouted Margaret from somewhere in the dimness. 'It's the only place it's half warm.'

She jumped up from the kitchen table and gave Tadek a quick, loud kiss on each cheek. When she turned to me, I clapped my heels together and kissed her hand. After all, I was in uniform. And she was an odd sight herself. She was wearing a rust-brown boiler suit, over a blue cardigan and a string of pearls. Two dogs, golden retrievers, slapped hopeful tails against our legs. Margaret gestured around her. 'Do forgive. We're pigging it, don't you know.'

There was a reek of hot meat and frying onions, and a rattle of running water from the sink where a young woman in a headscarf was scouring a basin. When she turned round, wiping her hands on her apron, I saw it was the singer from Kirkton.

'You remember the Major, Tibbie.'

'Aye, I mind him.' She studied me. Tibbie was bigger than I had remembered. She held herself very straight, but when she walked across the kitchen towards me, her body swayed as if she were moving to music. A slight smile, warm as a pie. 'God,' I thought, 'why don't I marry a woman like this?'

'Is that right, you're a policewoman now?'

'Well, aye, but it's no the real polis stuff. The chiefie in Liberton says thief-catching's no for girls. So I sit in the back office and I type and I put on weight and I read books.'

'Which books, Tibbie?'

'Whiles I feel like skeerie stuff – Dennis Wheatley, Yankee murder stories. Whiles it's poetry, for what I'm to study in college after the war. Hear this!'

She held out her hands before her like a priestess, cleared her throat and began to chant:

> Like the Idalian Queen,
> Her hair about her eyne,
> With neck and breast's ripe apples to be seen . . .

'Good heavens, Tibbie, should you really be learning that sort of thing?' Margaret sounded severe, but I saw that her hand was on Tadek's shoulder. Tibbie laughed. 'It's no coorse. It's Drummond of Hawthornden wrote that.' She went on:

> In Cyprus' gardens gathering those fair flow'rs
> Which of her blood were born,

> I saw, but fainting saw, my paramours.
>
> The Graces naked danc'd about the place . . .

'Tibbie, that's enough, stop it! Whatever's happening to you? It's time we had something to eat or it'll get cold.' But I could see that she was delighted, even proud, as if this broad-shouldered Tib had been her own daughter. And as we sat down and started on a huge pan of venison stew, I was aware that social frontiers, the fine dividing lines drawn on that British caste chart which I would never be able to read, had rearranged themselves.

Tibbie, it turned out, had been on weekend leave with her mother when Margaret asked her to come over and help with the meal and the washing-up. A call from the Lady in the Big House. And she would do some cleaning next day – and be paid something for it. But here she was sitting at the Lady's lunch party, even if it was at the kitchen table, placid in her right to be there. Was it because I was a guest, and the Lady had a private scheme to converge Tibbie and me? Or because of the war? Or because Scotland had never been like what I knew about top-hatted, upstairs-downstairs England – or thought I knew from reading P. G. Wodehouse?

'Hey, Margaret, whit did ye have to dae to get yon?' She pointed at the steaming roe-deer venison.

'Curiosity killed the cat, Tibbie. And cat meat's not rationed.'

I didn't think the joke was so great. But they all laughed wildly. Even Tadek, though I suspected he hadn't really understood it.

After lunch, we all had to go for a walk. Tadek, who was in civilian clothes, protested that his shoes would leak in the snow.

'Gumboots! No shortage of gumboots here,' said Margaret. She took us to an alcove by the main door, where a pair of black, man-sized Wellington boots stood empty. Tadek picked them up. Out of each boot he pulled a thick woollen stocking, with a name-tape in red. He glanced at me, but I was too far off to read the name. Margaret had turned her back and was selecting a walking-stick.

We went through an overgrown orchard and then out on to the hill and up a track to the crest of a ridge. There were two standing stones on the skyline, leaning a little towards each other.

I was walking with Tibbie, and put my arm through hers. She was wearing the same coat with the big buttons and a blue beret. At the stones, she pulled me away from the track so that she could touch them.

'Did you ever read *Sunset Song*?'

'Another book, Tibbie?'

'There's standing stones in it. Like the dead watching over the living, ken? And for once the story's no about high-heid folk like you and herself. It's about normal people, a book about me and Mother. About ma grannie, that hired herself out as a bondager to the big farmers every season. About lairds that flung my two uncles off their ain land, out their ain homes. That's how it's aye been for us. And I doubt it's no better in Poland.'

'Why are you telling me all this? A political speech?'

'I heard you once. Now you can hear me. There's a new world coming, son, when this war is over and away. Wait till you see.'

'They say you are a bookworm. In the new world, will you change into a book-butterfly?'

She laughed and tucked her arm back under mine. We walked on, and it began to snow.

The short day was ending when we got back to the house, and Margaret brought out whisky. We talked and told jokes and stories. Tadek went out to the shed and came back with more coal to stoke the range, his hair white with the falling snow. Tea was made, and then it was more whisky for Tadek and me, and more still. 'You two had better stay the night.'

'Sing, Tibbie, sing!' So she gave us a sad one, Mary Queen of Scots' lament, and then the merry song I remembered from that night at Kirkton – the tailor who fell through the bed. How I longed to possess Tibbie – not just her wide, smooth body and her bold soul, but the brown hills and stubborn land which seemed to me to be part of her! I wanted Tibbie and Scotland to be part of me. I wanted to devour them, as a savage devours a lion's heart, to take their strength.

'Dance with me, Tibbie!'

'Major Mike, sir, you're three parts blootered. And it's time I was away to my mother doonby.'

But Margaret had jumped up and gone to a table at the other end of the kitchen, where a sheaf of bills and letters lay weighted down by a wedge of old Christmas cake.

'Dance,' she said. 'Yes!'

From the stack, she pulled out a letter of several pages, with diagrams inked in between the handwriting. She brought it across the room. I thought at first it was a set of chemical formulae.

'All the way from Germany!' She frowned. 'You see, James's friends... well, after he died, the others at St Valéry were all taken prisoner. All the officers and men of the 51st. And they have been in the camps for nearly four years now. And d'you know what they have invented to keep themselves warm, to keep themselves sane? They've invented a dance.'

'You mean, a Scottish dance?'

'It's a reel. Quite complicated. They sent it home to their wives, but the diagram's a bit different in each letter that got through. Anyway, Kirsty Caithness lent me hers, such a kind, kind thought. Let's try it.'

We followed her upstairs, into a big hall with drawn curtains. Our breath condensed into steam clouds on first puff. Margaret seemed not to notice the cold; she switched on a light and began to roll back the carpet.

'Tibbie, give us a hand! Tadek, Tadzio, you know how to wind up the gramophone, be a love.'

The floorboards revealed under the carpet were stained and uneven. In one place, someone had drawn a rough double circle in chalk. 'Don't tread there, it's dry rot or wet rot or something. No, Tadek, I know where the records are.'

She squinted at the diagram. 'God, we need six people for a set! No, never mind. I know.' She ran to the mantelpiece and lifted down a large stuffed wildcat. Tadek went downstairs and returned with a wooden statue of a Highland soldier, which had once stood guard outside an Inverness tobacconist's. We faced each other in line: three soldiers, one scowling; three Scottish females, one snarling.

The cold was making me drunker. We walked through the

movements, not unfamiliar to Tadek and me after a few village hall dances, but – I thought – too much bowing and pacing before one got to the turning and whooping. Those poor lonely males, in their huts under Teutonic pines, had too much time on their hands, no bright-eyed girls waiting impatiently to be whirled and spun.

The music suddenly roared up from the gramophone. Off we went, Tadek and Margaret first, then me and Tibbie, and in no time the wild cat was on her back and the wooden sergeant was on his nose. We didn't care. We improvised. We turned the reel into a rapid, heavenly pattern of four human beings weaving an interlace of physical trust, every step the happy answer to a question, every partner-spin a proof of union.

So it seemed to me. Could this be what I had been looking for? I was setting to Margaret, then to Tibbie, and they were smiling as if they had been only waiting for me to understand. Soon I'd drop through the night and land among those pines – if only I could take Tibbie, Big Tibs, down with me instead of the heavy radio. If only I could find those lonely men in their huts behind the cruel wire, and tell them: You don't have to grieve, you are home already – for home isn't Scotland or Poland, home is a dance.

I was swinging Tibbie a bit clumsily, bumping into Tadek. So I danced her out across the room, then flung her round and round with our arms locked back to back. Now I'll kiss her. Now . . .

Margaret's face was above me, spinning like a wheel. As the wheel slowed, I saw that she looked worried. Why was I on my back? Somebody was lugging at my shoulders. 'Don't pull, wait till I free his foot!' I tried to get up, but my right leg was caught in something, in a black rent among rotten planks and splinters. I tried again, and the jag of pain up my ankle made me swear.

'Sorry for the language!'

'Don't worry, it was our language,' said Tadek's voice from behind me. They manoeuvred my foot out of the hole, and helped me, my arms round the shoulders of Tadek and Tibbie, to hop to a sofa. The reel music blared on and then died into scratchy hissing until somebody lifted the needle off.

'That bloody floor. I did warn you, but...'

Tibbie sat down next to me. 'It's yer ain fault, Major. See the way ye was stottin and skriechin like a daft cave-man! And now see!' She leaned down to unlace my shoe, then roll down the sock.

'He'll have raxed his ankle.'

'Worse than that,' said Margaret, inspecting. And it was worse, already bloated and dirty crimson. Tibbie gently moved my foot. 'Is that sore?' I said more words in Polish.

'Do we need a doctor?'

I said it was okay, the medics at Polmont would see to it the next day. Maybe it would be better in the morning. I started to apologise, but Margaret cut me off. 'There's beds made up for you both. Meanwhile, whisky is what you need – we all need.'

Down in the kitchen again, we sat round the table and Margaret poured out what was left in the bottle. Tibbie politely refused, and pulled on her coat to go. She borrowed a torch for the road, and leaned over to give me a kiss. I fingered the big coat buttons. My leg was hurting like hell now.

'Take care, Major. You'll never get home if you carry on treating yourself this way. But that'll be you excused boots for a wee while now!'

When she had gone, Margaret lit a cigarette, which I hadn't seen her do before. 'Nevertheless,' she said, 'that's a fine reel. I do think it will catch on. When the boys come home. We can't really do it without the boys.'

Upstairs, Tadek helped me into a frosty spare bedroom and took off my shoes. I guessed his own bedroom wouldn't be a spare one, and he wouldn't lie alone in it. The thought cheered me. Tadek was a fine fellow, the finest of fellows, who deserved happiness.

He stood looking down at me. 'You lucky sod. You won't have to go to Ringway now. And that's the last course for our group. So they'll have to find another posting for you. Lucky sod! Mind, you were always meant to do something better than parachuting. I wish I had your brains.'

Tadek paused. I was sliding away into coma. He added: 'I'll give your love to Poland.'

'Happy landings, Tadzio.' How fatuous! But it was all my vanishing mind could find to say to him.

Next day, the truck from Montrose took us back to Polmont. My ankle turned out to be broken, in a way not easy to set. I was taken off the 'silent-shadowy' course and transferred to a military hospital near Edinburgh.

In a few days I was up to hobbling with a stick. But my future now looked different. An officer from General Maczek's staff came down to the hospital and told me that I would be assigned to intelligence, at the headquarters of his new First Armoured

Division. He told me what I already assumed: that the Allied landing in France was only months away. Meanwhile, I could take two weeks' sick leave.

Tadek left Polmont the day after we returned. He handed me a leather satchel containing letters, papers, some British money, a ring, a spare watch, 'in case things go wrong'. I didn't see him again after that. He passed the Ringway ordeal. Then he went south to an airfield in the English Midlands, and from there he was flown across the North Sea and the Baltic and dropped somewhere in eastern Poland.

Much later, in the autumn, I heard that Tadek was missing. He had sent one radio message reporting a safe landing, somewhere near the Lithuanian border, but then there was silence. It was an area which had already been occupied by Soviet troops. Polish partisans emerging from the forests had expected to join them as they drove back the Nazis, but instead they were faced with the choice of joining the Red Army or arrest. The NKVD were treating the parachutists from London as imperialist agents; those they caught were shot as spies or sent eastwards to the Gulag.

I lost contact with Margaret after I left Polmont. Later, a friend told me that she had been summoned to London to work with British intelligence, in liaison with the Polish government-in-exile.

She was right about the reel. After the war, the Scottish Country Dance Association – with some reluctance, for they disapproved of new inventions and found some of the steps incorrect – accepted it into the canon.

If I find myself at a party when the accordion sounds the

first chords of the Reel of the 51st and the dancers cheer, I stay in my seat against the wall. Not just because I am so old – I can still get round the floor. But because, after all those years, something in my ankle still hurts.

It was spring in the hospital grounds, and birds whistled at me from dripping trees. I limped along the paths, stabbing my stick into the gravel. Water welled up and filled the line of little holes behind me, one by one.

Where were the others now? I missed them terribly. I imagined them in a forest clearing, showing partisans how to strip down the new American carbine. I pictured them looking at their watches in the tense quiet of a safe house, fitting on their headphones and then coaxing the frequency dial, millimetre by millimetre, towards a sputter of Morse from London. Didn't I know how to do all that, too? And hadn't I been impatient – at the end of those months of intricate training, of hardening fitness – to dive away with them through the hatch of a British bomber and fall through the night into a different planet?

I had been so ready to jump. This new idea that I might soon be in action somewhere else, in France, seemed perfectly unreal. Back to that world of a divisional mess: adjutants, daily 'sitrep' meetings, red and green circles on maps covered with talc?

I had seen enough of it in Poland, in 1939. Now, in France, I would probably revert to acting the sardonic bystander I had played so often. Once again, war had done its dirty trick and dropped me in the wrong place – alone in front of a stained, familiar mirror. Perhaps Wisia had been right to say that I would find myself only when my boots drove down into Polish soil.

The knots I had hoped to cut still chafed: Johnston, the *Fronsac*, that grotesque confession le Gallois had let me see. Johnston was still out there somewhere, and he could do me harm. But how could the French story about pre-war fascism be anything but fantasy? Johnston was malignant but surely too wary to have ventured into anything like that. And yet I had dreams. They were never about him or Greenock people, but about the burning ship itself. I beheld it monstrous and in agony, twisting and turning as smoke gushed out of its hull across the sea like blood spreading from a dying animal. The *Fronsac* asked: Who did this to me? In my dream, it was the ship and not the human beings I wanted to help.

In the daytime, hitching myself along those gravel paths, I brooded on the three women who didn't believe I could escape myself. Thinking of Helen excited me but made me angry. Did she really care for anyone but herself? For me? So what about Tibbie Fowler? I groaned aloud. Yes, but I could see now that my drunken passion at the castle was no better than cannibal lust, to devour all that she stood for. And I remembered her under the bridge asking if it was my mother I was missing.

Then there was Wisia. One morning, with rain rapping on the hospital windows, I sat down and on impulse wrote a letter. Marry me! 'I know you said how glad you were that we never did get married. But the world has changed so much since then. Me, too. And I am all you have left from your past, and you are all that I have left from mine. Who remembers my father and mother, who remembers your parents and Haneczka and Władek, except you and I? To share what we have lost in a way nobody else will ever understand – that's love, isn't it? Let's finish what we began long ago. After all, we never officially broke off our engagement! Maybe a wartime wedding in your hospital chapel, if you aren't well enough to come into town. And when I get back, after the war, we'll make babies and rebuild that new Poland they talk about...'

It went on like that for another page. I posted the letter, but instantly regretted it. Wisia didn't answer. I could understand why not; the vulgarity of what I had said made me shudder. Her silence came as a relief.

But finally I rang her hospital. 'Who's that you're wanting? Ach, right, that'll be the Polish lady? "Madam Fisher" we call her. Wee minute, now...'

A male voice came on the line. 'Doctor Lynch speaking. Are you related to this patient?... I see. No, I'm afraid she's not up to visits just now. There was a haemorrhage – did you not know? We operated on the lung, and I was able to complete the procedure, but she isn't responding too well. Not at the moment.'

'I am an army officer, Doctor. So is Lieutenant Kaczmarek. Tell me.'

There was a pause. 'You'd do well to come through at once. Ask for me when you get here.'

It was nearly midnight when I came hobbling up that long track. But Dr Lynch – burly, middle-aged – was still on duty. He walked towards the reception desk in his surgeon's gown, a small rucksack in one hand.

'I'm very sorry, but I have bad news. Your friend passed away this afternoon.'

We sat down on two chairs in the lobby, side by side. He blew a long, tired breath.

'We did our best. Patients her age usually get through. But it was like operating on somebody in their eighties: nothing left to fight with. Shockingly underweight, no blood pressure, the other lung nothing to boast about. You take a chance, but... If I had known how bad her heart was, I would have put the whole thing off.'

He frowned. 'I couldn't believe it when they showed me her paybook afterwards and I saw her date of birth. Still in her twenties – a girl, in fact. Who'd have known it? Had she been in prison or something?'

I found nothing to say.

'You Poles seem to be having quite a rough time in this war.'

He handed me the rucksack. 'She didn't regain consciousness. Wouldn't have suffered. It's no comfort, I suppose, but she couldn't have lived long anyway. Condition much too advanced.'

I touched the bag, which felt light, almost empty. Dr Lynch said: 'She did get extreme unction. This morning, when I realised she was going, I got Father McGilligan to her. I saw to that. I'm a Catholic, too. Like yourself, I imagine. So we have to believe she's in a state of grace, safe in somebody's arms. That's what they tell us, isn't it?'

When I stood up to go, Dr Lynch added: 'I'm sorry, but we'll need an idea about what to do with her. Cremation? The Vatican doesn't approve, but in wartime… anyway, it's something we could help to arrange.'

'Can I see her?'

A shrunken, austere woman lay on a bed. She could have been a distant relation of my Wisia, perhaps an aunt. Her eyes were closed, and somebody had wound a rosary around her fingers. I kissed her forehead, which was hard and cold, and left the room as quietly as I could.

It was mid-morning the next day before I got back to Edinburgh. Sitting on my own hospital bed, I opened the rucksack. There was the postcard of the Black Madonna of Częstochowa, a medallion of St Thérèse of Lisieux, a wristwatch and a pen, Wisia's army paybook, the poems from Haifa, my tin of cigarettes still unopened. Carefully and separately wrapped in tissue paper, I found a red lipstick and a single gold earring.

My own letter to her was there, too, replaced in its envelope. There was no sign of an answer. But there was a short note, written in English and not addressed to me. 'In case of Death. Corpse to be buried in a free Poland, when such is possible. If possible in City of Lwów, after Bolsheviks removed. My watch and valuable things must take Major M. Szczucki, First Polish Armoured Division. I bless him.'

It was silent in the room. I shared it with two other patients, but they were out. When I put Wisia's possessions back in the rucksack and shook it, they rattled loudly. I kept shaking them, to cover the sound of my angry, painful sobs.

The cremation was done in Glasgow. I slipped the tiny book of poems into the coffin before it was closed, and the lipstick. The undertakers were kindly; they agreed to store the ashes for me 'until this is all over'. The golden earring I buttoned into the breast pocket of my uniform.

Walking away from the crematorium, I tried to visualise Wisia's face, her smile as she pushed a cherry into my mouth. But all I could see was the black asphalt under my feet. All I felt was pity for myself: robbed.

In my hospital, there was nobody I wanted to talk to. But neither did I want to be alone or in silence. So, with my leg almost recovered, I used the last week of my leave to telephone Greenock and ask Mrs Melville if I could stay for a few days.

'Would you not prefer to be down in London with your pals, having a fling in all those Piccadilly blackout parties?' But when I came through the door at Union Street, she conceded a small smile. In a kitbag, I had brought her a length of parachute silk, even more precious than the legendary nylons. 'That was *not* necessary, Major. But we'll find a good use for it.'

I gave Jackie a wooden statuette of a bear, whittled by German prisoners out of an old chair leg. 'Thank you very much, Uncle Mike.' It was impossible to know whether she liked it. She was much taller now, and her manner warier. Her hands had grown long and capable, protruding far beyond the cuffs of her blouse. The book she had been reading lay on the table: *The Sea-Shore: Ecology of Intertidal Zones*, Volume II.

'So you are staying in Union Street again? But that young lady you and Captain Guennec used to admire, the merry widow, I heard she was drowned.' The Commandant shook his head, then coughed. The cigarettes, once Gauloises, had long ago become Pall Mall from the US Navy PX, but smoking had done nothing to reduce his weight.

'Did they tell you, there was a comedy with her little girl, the one who is at school with my Françoise? So ironic! She was writing down details of all the convoys, just like Kellerman – you remember all that? Our security even raided the house. I had to call them off, it was just *enfantillage*. Little girls, even my own daughter, they want to feel important, invent secrets to keep. Big girls, too, of course.'

He smiled. 'Shoosky, I have to tell you, you look terrible. Not the leg. The face: such sadness. Who is she? Tell me everything – *tu es ici en confessionnal!*'

The cognac bottle came out of the cupboard. I took one of his cigarettes, and the rich smells and tastes in that office – overheated, untidy, un-British – became comforting. I told him about the parachute course – he knew what that implied without asking for details – and then about breaking my ankle.

He laughed so much that I thought he would choke. 'Dancing? With a policewoman? Fell through the floor? Shoosky, you are telling me a Charlot silent film, a Charlie Chaplin! It's too good. And this policewoman, now she has broken your heart as well as your leg?' He began to heave and turn crimson again.

'No, not her. Somebody – something else.' Le Gallois glanced at me, and filled my glass again. Then I told him about Wisia. I talked for longer, and told him more of her story, of our story, than I had meant to. But I had forgotten what it felt like to talk about myself, about my life and feelings, to another man. When I finished, I looked up at le Gallois and saw that his eyes were wet.

After a long moment, he got up and walked up and down the office. He pulled out a big handkerchief, very white in that shabby room, and carefully blew his nose.

'My dear, I will tell you my philosophy. I could say, like the English: "This fucking war". But instead I say this: a wind came from the sea.'

He sat down again. 'We grow up, we count up our little choices, we learn how to move safely between who we think we are and what we think we want. But then the wind comes from the sea, and we are blown into the night, like little birds, like leaves. A revolution, a "fucking war", a deportation which drives a million families from their homes. A time when good girls who said their prayers starve in Asian deserts, when a ship you trust torpedoes herself and locks you in to burn or drown. The wind comes, Shoosky, and before the lights go out you see your mountains crumpling, your changeless landscape tattering into flying pieces of paper. Just stage scenery! And when light returns, you are lying naked on the beach of an unknown continent. Soon people will come and shout at you in a language you don't know, put you in an itchy foreign uniform, give you a mug of tea – ugh!'

This speech astonished me. Considering my friend, as he lay back in his chair and reached for another cigarette, I couldn't picture the Commandant struggling ashore naked on an alien strand. His uniform was worn and faded, but still the uniform of his own country. Hardly a leaf flying before the tempest, he had been sitting comfortably in the same office for the last four years and – almost unique among Free French officers – he had his family with him.

All the same, even if it had scarcely rattled the Commandant's windows, he was right about the sea wind. A verse of our own poetry came to mind, lines to a falcon clinging to a ship's rigging:

> You too, on life's sea – you saw monsters,
> And the gale drove me astray; the rain drenched my wings...

I said: 'The wind does not only destroy. It can transform as well. Yes, I have lost almost everything – everybody. But I have also seen in this war how the wind makes some people grow wings, lets them discover that they can fly. For them – maybe only a few who can see their chance – the war means that they can drop an old life. They can be reborn as somebody quite different. It's as if they jump through the holes torn by your wind, and escape. Like birds flying through a hole in a hunter's net.'

'How strange! My Polish friend is talking like a Scottish pastor. Perhaps Catholics in your country are Calvinists without knowing it. Rebirth? Who wants to be reborn? The point is precisely the opposite: when you are blown away to a strange place, you must become even more yourself. You have nothing familiar to prompt you, so you must become your own prompter. You must look in the mirror – if you can find one in the wreckage – and ask: Old boy, which line of conduct is mine, and which is not mine? Like an art collector, you know? So you have to develop an instinctive taste for yourself. This proposal is a Rembrandt, the real thing – me. But that one is not genuine Rembrandt – not me.'

'You can be so sure?'

'Of course. After the Armistice in 1940, I looked at the Marshal and all the little monarchists and holy perverts and Jew-baiters running towards him, and I said: that is not me. Then I looked at de Gaulle: alone, a bit mad, not even a reliable Republican ... but, yes, that's me. When I go back after the war he will probably offer me a government job, like deputy consul in Manchester or Oslo or somewhere ... not me. Or I could take over my father's old business in the Midi, wholesaler of herbs and seeds ... yes, that's me.'

'Commandant, it's you who are the Protestant here! Listening for the inner voice, claiming the right of private judgement? Soon you will tell me to follow my conscience.'

'Why do you want to jump through a hole and become somebody else? I look at you and I see the same dreamy fellow I met four years ago: a fine Shoosky of the early mature period, torn out of its frame but definitely authentic.'

'You don't understand. Yes, your France is authentic, indestructible whoever wipes their boots on it. But my country keeps changing its shape and its name. I was born in the Habsburg Empire. My mother went to school in the Russian Empire. My birthplace had four different names – five, counting "Leopolis" – before I could talk, and was told that I lived in Poland. My father ...'

'That's enough, Shoosky: I can imagine how much more, but it's lunchtime. The mess – you'll see changes; we have arranged our supplies quite acceptably.'

It was true. Fresh eggs in mayonnaise, veal, new potatoes with garlic, bottles of rich red wine from Algeria. At the end, there was real coffee.

'Did Madame Melville tell you about the anniversary? We are making a boat trip, day after tomorrow, to lay a wreath at the *Fronsac*. You'll come too, naturally.'

'What are you going to do with the wreck? I mean, it's a French vessel; the Royal Navy can't touch it without your permission.'

'Yes, well, we should talk about that. You remember our last conversation . . . that crazy letter and so on? The wreck is several big problems. First of all, it still contains the bodies of the crew. France must recover and honour them. Secondly, the hull is full of unstable munitions – shells, torpedoes, but depth charges above all. The Brits have been making a big fuss about this. They are right; but they are the only people who know how to remove that stuff safely. Thirdly, and – Shoosky – this is between you and me . . . the box. Yes, the box in Kellerman's letter, where he and Lieutenant Melville put their manifesto. Probably it never existed. But I would like to make sure.'

'How can you find it?'

'Ah, that's arranged. A man came to see me from a firm which cuts up wrecks for the British Admiralty. He was here only last week. We discussed a contract to raise the *Fronsac* – technically, that could be complicated – and tow her out to a shipbreaker's yard. He said he would get on board in the next few days and make an estimate.'

The Commandant smiled. 'I put off telling him about the depth charges. But I did mention the box. I said that in a certain place, in the chartroom, there might still be a steel box containing highly secret French material, naval code books and such-like, which must be secured before any other work began. Could he look out for the box? I warned him not to attempt to open it; I said the lock was fitted with an armed explosive device. He seemed to understand the problem very well.'

'What was his name?'

'I don't remember – why does it matter? Yes, I do – he was called Mr Ketling.'

The officers' mess was in a different building, the other side of a parade yard. After lunch, we walked back to the Commandant's office. The fresh wind cooled my head after the bottle of Rabelais Rouge, while I thought carefully. Then I asked: 'While we're on the subject, what's the news about Kellerman?'

'I'm not supposed to know. And certainly you are not. Well, he is in London. Free! Sort of free. He sat in a cell here for a long time, and then our people said to him: "Enough of this comedy. Prepare yourself, because tomorrow morning we are taking you to the rifle range on the top of the hill, and there will be an accident. No trial for little cunt-crabs like you."

'So he began to weep and beg, and they said: "Don't worry, nobody will recognise your body. I'm afraid we use rather large, soft-nosed bullets, which take most of your face away." That did it. A proposition: go to London for us, and mingle with certain officers our colleagues have doubts about. "You will be a soldier-servant: make their coffee, iron their trousers, read their letters. Perhaps you can let your own Vichy sympathies show, so that they confide in you. If you have no results after three months, we will see you again on the rifle range." But it seems that he is producing very nice results. So I suppose our people no longer need his *Fronsac* confession.'

'But it still exists.'

'Somewhere, yes. But it's without interest; they won't follow it up now. So tell me something really secret: when is your mad Polish cavalry going to gallop across the Channel and invade my country, and will there be anything left afterwards? *Pauvre France!*'

When the invitation arrived, delivered by a French sailor on a motorbike, Mabel Melville decided to turn it down. But it was impressive right enough. That's to say pretentious, typed on thick pre-war paper – the waste!

Capitaine de vaisseau Luc le Gallois, Free French Naval Forces (Clyde), invited Mme M. Melville and Mlle J. Melville to participate... the fourth anniversary of the tragic events concerning the *contre-torpilleur Fronsac*... weather conditions permitting, the launch conveying the delegation would leave Princes Pier at 11 a.m. on 30 April 1944.

Mrs Melville sighed. Unexpectedly, she missed her long-dead husband. Not that Charlie would have had any useful advice. A timid man, he would have second-guessed what she might want. Still, even mocking his suggestions ('Och, Charlie, for heaven's sake!') would have steadied her.

Searching out her last pad of Basildon Bond, she composed a polite note to the Commandant. She excused herself on the grounds that such a ceremony would put too great a strain on Jacqueline, whose nerves were easily upset. She was sure the Commandant would understand. She was grateful for his considerate offer.

Mrs Melville did not tell Jackie about either the letter or her reply. So when the phone rang and Jackie answered it – 'Hello, my little spy!' – it took her some moments to recognise the voice of Françoise's father.

'Why don't you want to come with us on the boat next week? Your grandmother, she didn't tell you? But I have kept two special places for you on the boat, I have ordered a special wreath. You only have to decide what to write on the card...'

Jackie dropped the telephone from her ear and glanced over her shoulder. Mrs Melville, standing behind her, took up the receiver. The Commandant, it seemed, did most of the talking. When she was finally allowed to hang up, she walked over to where Jackie was sitting.

'Are you a sensible, big girl now? Can I trust you to behave?'

'Och, Granny!'

'You're to keep your mouth shut about what you and I know. D'you understand that? We'll be going on this boat trip, this expedition, after all. He just keeps on about it, and, well... it would look strange not to go now. Strange and rude. I don't want that big fellow in his uniform getting ideas.'

'But, Granny...'

'You can think of it this way. If it's not your daddy you're grieving for, then think of all those poor French sailors who are dead and gone, sure enough. So the wreath and such-like is for them. Have you got that in your head, young lady?'

'Okay, Granny.'

'Don't you "okay" me! A plain English yes is what I'm wanting out of you.'

'Yes, Granny.'

Uncle Mike came too. Jackie thought he had changed. It wasn't just that he was wearing a British sort of battledress now, with a black beret and a POLAND shoulder flash. His face was redder, more weathered-looking. He had a leg that was sore from an accident. And he seemed quieter altogether, less of his daft remarks and jokes.

'Any news from your mother?'

'Aye, she was through from Canada for my birthday. That's fifth of March. I was thirteen. She was bringing in a B-17, I think it was, a Flying Fortress...'

'How's she keeping?'

'Fine, fine. She gave me an American book about sea life. Big colour pictures of giant squid and such. Wee bit childish, you know. Not about science and tidal zones. I like reading about tidal zones.'

'Did she ask after me?'

'No, not at all. She's very sad about a friend of hers who got killed. A Canadian man who used to fly with her. But, Uncle Mike...'

'Remember the man's name?'

'No, sorry. See, Uncle Mike, I need to ask you something. It was you told mother my dad wisna dead, that right? How did you find out?'

'As you say here, curiosity killed the cat. I tell you another time.' His English was amazing now. But still that funny rat-tat way of pronouncing.

The boat was quite large, a peacetime pleasure launch with a long windowed saloon. A dozen or so people had gathered on Princes Pier, coat collars up against the snell north-wester coming in across the water. Mrs Melville wore black and a small, surprising black hat with lacy trimmings; Jackie was not allowed to wear her parka but was fastened into a navy-blue woollen coat with horn buttons. There was a Catholic naval chaplain, a photographer from the *Greenock Telegraph* and three or four silent French women in foreign raincoats. As the Commandant reminded everyone, most of the bereaved families had returned to France four years ago, after the Armistice. Françoise was not there, either. Perhaps she was feared of sea-sickness.

Le Gallois himself, flanked by four French marines in parade uniforms, was already standing on the launch, welcoming the guests as they made their way down the gangplank.

'Shoosky! Come and talk to me when we get going.'

In the wheelhouse, as the engines began to vibrate, le Gallois said: 'The salvage men have just started work on her. Preliminary survey. They have a lighter alongside and ladders. So we keep well clear, and put the wreaths down in open water where she first sank. Then, afterwards, you and I will go across and see what's happening on board.'

He pulled a business card out of his pocket. 'That supervisor who came to see me left me his very grand *carte de visite*: Lang & Wilson's, shipbreakers, operations engineer Mr Alexander Ketling. Shoosky, you are making a funny face, do you know him?'

'I met him. Two times – three times. But it was a year or so back.'

'Not my type. A reptile. All dockyards in the world have them, waiting with contracts when you come in for refit. Not your best pal, I hope?'

The launch cast off and headed out into the Firth. The Commandant ordered the helmsman to take a big circle out into the anchorage so that the passengers could see the vessels mustering for convoy: rusty American 'Liberty' ships with goal-post gantries for unloading tanks; a two-funnelled liner discharging a file of soldiers into a ferry; a flat-topped aircraft carrier; a long British battleship dazzle-painted black and grey.

Further out, masking the hulk of *Fronsac*, lay a cruiser whose flanks showed red-leaded scars of damage. 'Back from the Arctic convoys,' explained le Gallois. The man from the *Telegraph* and one of the French women began to take photographs. Le Gallois frowned, then shrugged.

A buoy with a tricolour pennant was bobbing in the dredged channel off the Greenock waterfront. The launch slowed, frothed for a moment astern, then switched off engines. In the silence, the Commandant saluted, then removed his cap and with one gloved hand slipped a wreath into the water. A French lady in a veil threw some flowers. Jackie threw the wreath provided for her and Mrs Melville. She had written the word

'Love' on the label, but couldn't think how to go on before it was time to throw.

As the priest opened his book, Jackie's wreath began to sail briskly away. Alarmed, she looked up and saw that Greenock itself, the tier upon tier of grey stone tenements ranged up the hillside above them, was rushing past her towards Argyll and the distant Atlantic. For a moment she felt sick; a vertigo, but also a terror. Then the launch trembled as the engines growled back to life, spilled a pile of foam from the stern and drove against the incoming tide-stream. Greenock hesitated and came to rest again.

The priest read from his book. The Commandant made a long speech in French. The Marines blew their bugles. The Commandant saluted several more times and so did Major Szczucki. Jackie noticed how Uncle Mike did a funny salute with two fingers squeezed together. Polish, huh? More like what the Boy Scouts did, if you asked her.

When the launch returned to the pier there was a lunch on board, served by the Marines wearing white gloves. The bread was not loaves but long, crisp sticks made in the French naval bakery, and something sharp and liquid had been added to the lettuce instead of salad cream. There was wine, which some of the ladies drank. Jackie thought that was very unsuitable.

Afterwards, the guests went ashore. Major Mike explained to Mrs Melville that he was staying on board and would be back at Union Street in the evening.

'Why don't we take your little friend along?' suggested le Gallois. 'An adventure for her. Not so little, anyway. She is growing tall now.'

'No, I think not. No.'

'Why not? You could keep an eye on her.'

Mike said in French: 'The dead – they are still on board. I mean, it's not for a child. A girl who has lost her father on that ship.'

Le Gallois gave him a long, considering look. Then he said: 'Well, yes, the crew, the poor creatures. Whatever may be left of them now. It's the first problem I must discuss with Ketling today. Bad to think about.' He turned to Jackie and suddenly smiled at her. 'Still, what a pity not to give a treat to this one. *Elle sera belle, tu verras.*'

'What's he saying?'

'That you will be a great beauty one day. Even better than your mother.'

'But I've got spectacles,' said Jackie, aghast. The two men began to laugh loudly at her. Why, what was so funny? What had she done wrong? Behind the spectacles, tears pricked her eyes.

'I have, then, three things to do this afternoon,' the Commandant told me. 'One: my dead sailors. Bones, I suppose. The salvage men must be reminded to take proper care of anything they find.'

The wind had risen. Wedged in the wheelhouse as our launch bumped and pitched across the Firth towards the wreck, le Gallois lit a king-size Pall Mall. 'Two: to tell these guys about the explosives. The big bang – that was only one magazine and some of the fuel. Down aft, she is still crammed with live depth charges. I didn't want to alarm Ketling before, but I have to tell him about them now. I have the list: sixteen of these fat brutes, still in their launching chutes. Cut into one of those with a burner flame and – pouf! – Mister Ketling and his boys are fish food. Well, and then the matter of the box. That's three.'

The launch slowed and turned sharply into the wind. An overhanging steel cliff leaned out of the sea a few yards from us, a long, rusty wall banded with brown and green tide marks. Frayed lengths of rope hung down from above, swinging and slapping against the side. The launch edged along towards the stern and came to a pontoon with ladders; men in worn overalls caught and steadied us both as we leaped to the raft.

I jumped, landed, straightened up and found myself looking into Johnston's face. 'Mr Ketling, hello! Didn't we last meet in your office, in Rosyth...?' But Johnston, after a moment's expressionless stare, had turned away to greet the Commandant.

We scrambled up the ladders to what had been the deck, now tilted so steeply that we had to cling to a web of ropes run up by the salvage crew. The stench of a dead ship hit us, an overwhelming reek of rotting seaweed, fuel oil, burnt paint-work and putrid deck-head wadding. Overhead, a few gulls balanced and a red danger flag cracked in the wind.

The *Fronsac* in death seemed gigantic. Above the slanted deck towered the three surviving funnels, stained and spattered by birds and weather. The fourth, an unrecognisable crumple, lay on its side; a blue spark showed where a worker was starting to cut it away. *Fronsac* was not only listing but was steeply down by the head, so that her bows and forward deck were submerged.

The tide was still rising as we watched. Sea water with rainbow gleams of oil was already slopping in and out of the doorway leading up to the bridge.

Johnston was wearing the gear of a Clydeside gaffer: a brown gabardine raincoat buttoned from chin to ankle, a pork-pie hat, heavy black shoes. As he talked to the Commandant, he kept his back turned to me.

'No, sir, no chance we could get into the forward accommodation. Where the, ehm, the remains might be. Not till the ship's upright and the silt pumped out of her. Meanwhile, anything of that type we came across, we'd show respect, you know. After all, it's an Admiralty contract we're on.'

The Commandant's English was awkward but loud. 'Keep me informed. Mister Ketling, this ship is also our business. I mean this is Free France, not only British Admiralty. They can raise it, but that's all. Now, Mr Ketling, here's a list of the munitions. Probably there is more. *Fronsac* was ready for action when the explosion took place.'

'The *tragic* explosion, sir. A tragedy we all of us here feel, sir, because . . .' His eyes were on the list. 'Oh, Jesus! Oh, no!' He swung towards the man cutting into the funnel. 'Dowse that fuckan torch: now, right now!'

Le Gallois caught my eye and his mouth twitched. Johnston said furiously: 'Naebody telt us we was cutting into a volcano. I'll need to phone the office and report this. We cannae proceed till the depth charges are removed. I mean, my lads are no qualified to do that. See, that's a Royal Navy job, it's for bomb disposal folk. How's it they didn't do it already? That's scandalous, so it is.'

'Easy, Mr Ketling. Nobody asks Lang & Wilson's to blow themselves up. Obviously, the British navy will remove all that – I will see to it. But tell me something more fascinating. How will you raise my poor *Fronsac*, how will you float her to a scrapyard? You are the true expert, Mr Ketling. Tell us.'

Johnston Melville had pulled off his hat, letting the wind toy unkindly with his flat red hair. But the Commandant's words seemed to calm him. He began to nod importantly. It was a reassured Mr Ketling who put his hat on again.

'I'll not be discreet with you, sir, I'm telling you openly: we at Lang & Wilson's have a big, big problem here. We thought of cutting her into sections. But they wouldnae float safely; her shape is wrong. So she's needing lifted – all three thousand tons, all in one piece. That means lifting craft alongside. And the silt from inside her wants shifted, and the superstructure needs cut away to bring the weight down.'

He glanced at the man with the acetylene burner, whose gear was clanging and dragging on the deck as he made his way towards us. 'You need to grasp this, Commandant: this would be pretty certainly – pretty definitely – the heaviest vessel ever lifted this way. She's settled eight or nine foot into the mud here. So it means divers going down to tunnel in the dark, working by feel. Black as midnight down there: ye cannae see your hand before you, even with lights.'

'All that, just to tow a wreck to a scrapyard?'

'Ach, months of work in it, sir. And it could all go wrong on us forbye. See, if she's corroded bad, the lift cables could just saw through the hull like wire through a skelf of cheese. And the tunnelling underneath. There's boulders down there in the silt. If the tunnelling weakens them, any one of them could fracture. Then the hull would fall back deeper.'

'On top of the divers. In the dark.'

'Right enough, sir. On the divers.'

Le Gallois reached into his pocket for his cigarettes, but met a look of horror – ah, of course, the depth charges – and stowed the pack away again. 'And now, Ketling. I want you to show me the chartroom.'

'Chartroom?

'Yes, but we discussed this, how you don't remember? A code book. In a *caisse* – how do you say it?'

'A briefcase? What like of case? What are you talking about?'

'He means a cashbox, a little steel cashbox.' The interruption was mine.

There was a silence. Once again, an expressionless gaze met my eyes for a few seconds, then dropped.

'Well, precisely, that's what I mean. Did you find that steel box in the chartroom? Or anywhere?'

'There is no chartroom, sir. Come on till I show you.'

Holding on to ropes and rails, we stumbled forward to the door leading into the lower bridge. This was now the tide's edge, the sea lapping over the door-coaming. Looking towards the bows, we could see only a twisted gun platform and the stub of a crane rising above the water.

'The chartroom was under here. See, it's high water now; it's flooded. But even when the tide's down, there's nothing left – took the main force of the explosion, ye with me? Bust-up steel furniture, lagging from the ventilation trunking, every kinna wreckage – just a damned mess.'

'So you have been in there?'

'Aye, right, I climbed in. But didny get far. None of your case, your box, anyhow. Never saw anything of that kind.'

He paused, then added: 'I'll need to warn the lads about the depth charges now. And then ashore to the phone.' He walked away to where his crew were waiting, clapping their gauntlets to keep warm.

Commandant le Gallois nodded. He was staring forward, at the cold, scummy expanse of water over the *Fronsac*'s bows.

'Take a look, Shoosky. That's where the forward accommodation was. Under there. The mess deck, where the hatches jammed. All those lads who drowned before they burned, or burned before they drowned. They are still there, Shoosky.'

'Four years ago, Commandant. You can't help them now.'

'The morphine jags? The razor blades given to them? Those bare arms reaching out of scuttles too small to squeeze a body through? Is all that true?'

'Yes, it's all true. But I think now it was not an act of war, and not murder. Even if Kellerman's confession is true, it was some sort of accident.'

'No accident, never! No. Maybe not Kellerman, but somebody... well! We shall know one day. When France has been liberated by Americans and Poles and Scots and English and even by a few Frenchwomen and Frenchmen. When I have watched these poor bones go home. Then we shall settle accounts, Shoosky.'

'Is that all home means to you? The place where one settles accounts?'

'And if nobody in the family house pays their bills and everybody is afraid to enter the cellar – is that a home?'

'We Poles have paid our bills. Unfortunately, we no longer have a house and the cellar is all that's left of it. Very dark, full of the bones of good people who were sold to their enemies. We can't hope to make anyone else settle those accounts. That is why that place is still our home.'

We were silent. Le Gallois gently patted my shoulder several times, as if he were soothing a trembling horse. Then he said in English: 'Fuck Mister Ketling, I smoke anyway. You?'

'Thank you, no. But I have to speak to him.'

I took 'Ketling' aside. 'We have to talk. Something looks bad for you, also for me. In the next few days.'

'Get your voice down! Can you find the way to Helensburgh? A couple of miles along this shore? The Clyde Café there, the Saturday morning that's coming.'

Helensburgh is opposite Greenock, on the northern side of the Firth. When I was staying at Union Street, I used to look across the water to where, in the distance, I thought that I could make out rows of shining mansions, tall churches, the glint of unbroken windows reflecting the afternoon sun.

On my shore was the half-ruined town leaking smoke through the din of the yards, where shabby crowds hurried to work and where it seemed always to be raining. On the other shore, a place of wealth and peace. A place often in sunshine, which looked to me like a home.

So when I came to Helensburgh that morning I went to the pier and looked back across the miles of water to Greenock. It was a clear blue day. The wind had blown the smoke away, and not a sound reached me from the other side. But over there, tiny in its details, there sparkled another blessed, distant place.

I seemed to see a serene Grecian city set out on the margin where the hills met the sea. I saw a grove of elegant spires, a proud municipal tower, a lattice of shipyard cranes in a frieze along the waterfront. Of the bomb damage, the jostling people, nothing could be seen.

I had arrived early. Now I walked slowly about this town which had tricked me, which after all seemed to be composed only of dull and wealthy stone houses, and I felt despair.

Long ago, in the Union Street kitchen, I had told Helen that I didn't need a home. Now, suddenly, the lack caught me by the throat. No door would open on faces happy to see me. My spirits wouldn't jump as I came to a familiar birch tree at the last turn in the track. No room with a warm tiled stove waited for me, no salon in which I could finger my stack of unopened letters, yawn while that glass of tea cooled, reflect on how to settle my accounts.

No house at the end of this journey. But along it, I had met so many comrades, both men and women, who still carried a bunch of keys with them – keys to a manor house now lost in the Soviet Union, to a Warsaw flat long bombed to dust.

When I was young, I never felt this longing for the place I always thought of as 'my parents' house'. Now I was sharing a grief I had sensed in other people, but never before in myself.

I envied them, with their orphaned keys. They had something to imagine and to mourn, even if it was only a bricked-up gateway with nothing but a charred gable beyond it. All I had was a mirage, glimmering across deep water.

Self-pity! To pull myself together, I began to march rapidly along the seafront. Left, right! I repeated bracing things to myself in English as I marched. Helensburgh folk glanced at this daft Polish soldier tramping along the pavement, muttering to himself: 'Pack up yer troubles in yer old kitbag and smile...' Singing helped. 'Hitler's only got one ball...' How did it go on? It ended 'And Goebbels has no balls at all.' But what came in between?

'That's you needing a doctor, son,' said a milkman, glancing up from feeding the horse on his wagon. I stopped, realising that I had been chanting aloud. Behind the wagon, on the other side of the street, was the Clyde Café.

In there, a bunch of British sailors had dumped their kitbags against the wall and were settling to play pontoon. 'Twist!' There was a shout of laughter and a clink of coins. The proprietress burst out from behind the counter. 'Whit ye daein? Gambling! Away with thae cards, or I'll get the polis, so I will.' A man coming through the door stopped very still.

I went over to Johnston and made a show of shaking him warmly by the hand. The sailors were arguing loudly with the proprietress. We sat down.

'How did you no tell me you were coming to the ship?

How did you know I would be there? What have you told yon French officer? What's he after?'

'He doesn't know who you really are. But Johnston, do you know – did you know – Albert Kellerman?'

He didn't look frightened when I spoke the name, merely cross. Cross, vexed, as if I had spilled my cup of tea on his big black shoes.

'It's none of your business. But I'll tell you. Now you mention it, I think that was maybe the name of the French fellow supposed to help me on the . . . ehm, the torpedoes, right? The fellow who gave the safety levers a big dunt and got blown overboard and drowned. Just an idiot, that man.'

'Don't fool around with me! Kellerman is alive. And he knows you are too – but not where. And he has made a statement. About what happened on *Fronsac*, and about you and him before the war. Is it true?'

'Is what true?'

'That you joined something? That you were a wee Fascist?'

He made no reply. Instead, he pulled a small notebook out of his pocket and slowly, carefully, tore out a leaf. I noticed that it was an accounts notebook, the pages ruled for pounds, shillings and pence. On the leaf, he drew two circles in purple indelible pencil. 'That's me. That's you. Ye with me?'

Then he drew a fierce arrow from the Me circle to the You circle, and another in the opposite direction. 'Any time, Mike, I can smash you for what I know you did. And any time, you can smash me. So let's be showing respect. Discretion – that's the word. Discretion.'

'But were you a Fascist?'

'I was a daft kid. Well, when I was at the Academy, some of us boys were talking about Scotland. About nations. And there was this Captain Ramsay, going round the halls blethering about Hitler's folk-community and how Scotland was threatened by inferior breeds. So, aye, I was fifteen, I joined. Mind, I was in the Boys' Brigade too.'

He grinned at me. He was powerfully at ease with himself, as he had been on the platform at Inverkeithing. What had transformed him from that shivering supplicator in wet denims? Shame and hatred, perhaps. 'Any time you can smash me,' he had said. Could I? It felt more like a warning than an admission.

'Your turn to talk, Mike. Is it the police have Kellerman's statement now? What's to happen about it?'

'He was in jail, Johnston. Not the British, a Free French jail. Worse! But now he is doing secret work for them. They don't follow up his statement about *Fronsac* and you. Not unless he tries to cheat them. But he won't. They'd shoot him, anyway.'

'There's no Johnston any more, Mike. Will you get it into your thick Polish heid? Johnston's away, gone. See and remember that.'

'Did you and Kellerman really make a plan when you met again? And the steel box. Where is it?'

'Ach, that nonsense. I've made enough confessions the day. But, Mike, about the wee girl. Jackie, ma ain daughter. I'd truly like to see her. Does she ...?'

'Sure, she knows. That you are alive, but not where you are or what you call yourself. And she doesn't know that she could just about see you from Union Street through the binoculars.'

'Maybe it's better she disnae see me. No yet. But you could

bring her across to the ship – I can fix a launch and a permit – and I could get a keek at her. Or what do you say, Mike? How if I did just walk up and "Hello there" and a wee chat, is she old enough to keep that secret too?'

I hadn't expected all this. Suddenly now, fatherly feelings? 'I wouldn't count on it. She's only thirteen. But I could maybe bring her across. If all you want is a sight of her.'

We paid and stood up to go. I put on my beret. 'That'll be you away to France any day now, with the invasion?'

I was about to nod. But a wary second thought made me say: 'No, no, it's Canada for special forces training . . .'

'You'll maybe be seeing Helen there?'

I didn't reply.

Yes, I would be seeing Helen, and very soon. But I didn't know that when I left the Clyde Café. It was the next morning at Union Street, after Sunday breakfast, that the main door thumped and she walked into the kitchen, dragging a heavy leather suitcase behind her.

'Could you not think to ring us up first?' But Mrs Melville did not sound as put out as she would once have been.

When Helen and Jackie had hugged, the pair of them began to push the big suitcase into a corner. I took over, did it for them. But there was more: a fat blue shoulder bag Helen had dumped in the hall.

This arrival wasn't like her. I had never seen her impeded, struggling under burdens. Usually Helen strode, travelling light. If there was more she needed, her style said, there would be somebody else to provide it. Now she sat down slowly, and only nodded when Jackie brought her a tea cup.

In the shoulder bag there were gifts. For Jackie, a rubber diving mask with a glass window: 'you can look your porpoise in the eye, the way they do in California'. On the kitchen table, familiar offerings piled up: another flask of maple syrup, a block of maple sugar, cans of orange juice, peaches, butter and ham, more lime juice.

'Is there anyone biding in upstairs?'

'Are you wanting your old room, then?'

'Aye, well, Mabel, could I maybe stay a while longer this time?' The ferrying of aircraft from Gander to Prestwick was winding up, she said. The new planes had longer range, bigger tanks. Now American crews could fly them direct from the factory in the States, across the Atlantic to the bomber fields in East Anglia.

'So they'll no be needing us any more. The hop yesterday, with a B-17: that was my last crossing seemingly. So it's leave for me – I've two weeks' leave. And then? No more flying, I guess. If I go back to Canada now it'll be a job as a clerkess on some dreich airbase in Manitoba. Or maybe I could get myself a discharge, family grounds – something of that.'

She undid her top tunic button, and sighed. 'No thanks, Mike. I'm off the smokes just now. Queer, eh? Can't fancy them.'

When Mrs M and Jackie went off to church, I lit one myself. Helen got up, wandered about the kitchen and then put the kettle back for more tea. She picked up a waxed carton.

'Are you still eating this dried-egg shite? Is that all the hens in Scotland called up for war work?'

'What's the news with Craig?'

'I thought you were no interested in Craig.'

'Tell me.'

'He's dead. That's his news. Okay?'

'Helen! Don't talk like this. How – what happened?'

'He got killed. Why are you on at me this way?'

I saw that she was not so much in grief as embarrassed. Did she think this death was also her failure to keep her own life in the air?

'How?'

'Accident. He was flying a Mitchell, training a British guy, and it went into the Gulf of St Lawrence. Both engines failed. Some smart fellow put fuel filters back the wrong way round. So Craig bought it. So I'm a widow-woman, and no pig farm in Ontario for Mrs Mary Helen Douglas MacPhail.'

'Douglas? Was that Craig's name?' I put my arms round her but she stood slack, indifferent.

'Don't get the idea I'm biding here in Scotland. Craig's folks took against me even before he died, so I'm better off here with Mrs M for a while. But it's Canada for me and Jackie when everything settles down. When the war's over.'

She glanced up. 'Mike, that could be soon, right? The invasion's coming any time. And you – are you going with it?'

'Could you keep a wee Polish count away from a fight?'

She smiled, but it was just a fond smile. There was something altogether unfocused about her today. I suddenly thought: she's pregnant. Why did the thought anger me?

'Mike, I need to talk to you. D'ye know where Johnston is?'

'He's on a ship.'

'Will he be back soon? See: without Craig, and the end of the war coming, and me wanting citizenship over there ... and I've to think of Jackie's future, I need to get things straight.

With him. Cut through the fankle, so I can forget about all that time. And him too.'

'You can forget without seeing him. Helen, don't you remember you're both officially dead? The widow Douglas, born MacPhail, has nothing to do with the widow Melville, born Houston, who went missing at sea. And nothing whatever to do with the new name he's got now. So just keep clear of it all. Stay dead, the pair of you!'

'No, Mike. That'd be no fair. Ye think I'm a hard bitch – that's the way you liked thinking of me. But there's another side to everyone.'

If there was another side to Helen today, I wasn't in the mood to explore it.

'I tell you he's on a ship. I don't know when it comes home – maybe never. He thinks you are settled in Canada. He won't want to see you anyway; he doesn't need trouble. Helen, why don't you just go back to Manitoba or wherever and find... well, a new life? Like you did before. The way Johnston's done.'

She sat quietly. The sun was out; I could hear a bell tolling from the West Kirk. Two women were passing down Union Street and laughing.

'Scotland's looking quite good today. Quite good.' Helen sounded surprised at herself. 'Are the boats running to Bute and the Kyles yet? I could maybe take Jackie "doon the watter".'

There was a long silence. Helen poured herself more tea; she didn't look up at me.

I stood up and reached for my beret. 'Helen, my leave is over – embarkation leave. So this is big goodbye, you and me.

Listen, if something happens to me, if you're still here – can I give your Mrs Douglas name? For stuff that I leave in Scotland, any money – you know.'

'Sure you can. So it's any day now, is it? See and keep your poor wee head down.'

Our embrace was muscular, hard, like two old comrades. I kissed her cold cheeks in the way of my country, three times.

I had given Helen my advice. If she didn't take it, there was nothing more I could do for her. So I told myself. Then I went to the war.

It was early June; school term just about to end. Jackie was making her way up to the station for the Kilmacolm train when Miss Coutts came whirling round the corner. Jackie was disconcerted. The lofty goddess who used to bestow history at Campbell Street was giggling and jouking about as if she was trying to be a girl. The sun shone through her golden hair as she cried: 'Isn't it just wonderful? Isn't it great news?'

'No, I mean hello Miss Coutts. What news?'

'They've landed, they've landed! It's the Invasion, Jackie. Did you not hear the bulletin?'

Jackie thought: What's gone wrong with Miss Coutts is that she's history. Over, and out of date. So if I said something to her about biology, or larval flatfish eyes migrating, or *Zostera marina*, or even said 'Ecology' to her, she'd go daft.

'That's fine, Miss Coutts. I'll tell the others on the train.' The teacher swooped on downhill, waving a hand over her shoulder.

Later that day, with everyone at St Columba's blethering on about the Second Front, Jackie remembered that Uncle Mike was going to be part of the Invasion too. Lucky him, he'd be right famous. But how would Mother take it? Better leave her to bring it up first.

The peacetime paddle steamers, taking Glasgow families down the Clyde for day trips with music and booze, were only a memory now. But the MacBrayne's mail boats were still running to the Argyll coast, carrying civilian passengers, seamen with kitbags and terrified calves swaddled in sacking.

Helen and Jackie took the steamer through the Kyles of Bute to Tarbert, where Jackie had been a few years before with her grannie and Françoise. They stayed the night with the same Mrs MacQuarrie, and then took a bus down the Kintyre shore until they came to sandy beaches. There was a chapel looking out over the sea, huge boulders of black basalt and an arc of empty white sand.

The sun came out. Helen stood on a rock to see if she could catch sight of Ireland. Jackie had already put on her swimsuit under her dress; now she wasted time trying to put on the diving mask with one hand while unbuttoning her dress with the other. She perched her spectacles on a slab of driftwood.

'Are you not coming in?'

'No, kid. The sea and me have seen enough of each other. In the air or on dry land, that's where I belong.'

Jackie was already a good swimmer, even very good. She had a certificate of proficiency for swimming and another for life-saving, written on thin 'economy' paper, but she hadn't been in the proper sea since she was paddling. As Jackie waded in deeper, the cold bit into her legs with a pain she hadn't expected. She frowned and kept going until the water was up to her armpits.

'Baby, you okay?'

Jackie replied with a loud groan. Then she settled the mask over her face, thrust her whole head and body under the water and began to swim.

The tide was low. She was gliding over zones of sand and tangle never dried out or exposed to the sun. Small fish; scallop shells lying on a clearing in the weed. The trails of hermit crabs across the seabed. A flounder, nestling down into the sand until only its gleaming eyes were visible. Jackie swam to the surface to draw breath, then dived again.

Now the seabed abruptly shelved down. She saw, deep and dim below, an open plain of sand, and on it a live queenie-scallop, its half-open shells fringed with diamond eyes. As Jackie watched, it suddenly flew upwards, its shells batting like a butterfly's wings, sank away and landed a few yards further off.

Another rise for breath. Then down. She couldn't find the sand plain with the scallop again; the current was drifting her along the shore. But a pale shape was twisting among the huge brown fronds of the *Laminaria*; a dogfish. Such a big one; was it a nursehound, like in her book of fishes?

She rose and she dived. Once she went too deep, hunting across an underwater boulder gaudy with sponges and red starfish to see if lobsters were hiding under its overhang. It was darker and the surface was far above, as she suddenly knew she couldn't hold her breath any longer and struggled upwards. In the air, she gasped and waited.

'Jackie, come in now, that's too much.'

The vice of cold biting into her legs, which had relaxed, was gripping her again. But she shook the water out of her mask and dived for the last time, aiming back towards the sponge-littered boulder. There at last was a blue-black lobster, backing into the weeds of a wide crevice in the rock, and, on the sand at the foot of the crevice, a man's empty boot. Waving her thin legs, Jackie went down closer: not much breath left. But where the lobster had gone, there was a cluster of crabs and starfish on top of something bulky and yellowish. Part of the something protruded like a stick, with one of its white twigs wedged through a gold ring.

Jackie kicked away with all her strength. She thought she was going to die, because she only just reached the surface in time and because she knew what she had seen. She tried to scream but water poured into her mouth, and when she finally scrambled through to the shore she fell forward and couldn't stand up. As she lay flat on the sand, coughing out sea and hearing her own sobbing, she saw the *Fronsac* and what was still inside the *Fronsac* and she felt her child-hand turning a key.

She tried to raise herself on all fours and fell back again, as Helen ran to her. The sun had gone in. A chill north-west breeze was driving white flecks across the sea towards them.

In the weeks that followed, after the body had been worked out of the crevice and driven away by the funeral-parlour folk and the police, Helen and Jackie tried to find out who the man had been. Forget all about it, they were told, this is wartime and they had no need to know. Eventually, many months later, Mrs Melville asked an old friend on Argyllshire County Council to ask an old friend of his who was senior in the police at Campbeltown to find out. Yes, the remains had been identified almost at once: a young South African pilot officer who had gone missing after an accident on board an aircraft carrier. What accident? Never you mind.

Jackie told her mother that she wanted to go on diving, in spite of what she had found. Helen said: 'Are you morbid? You'll get more bad dreams. Girl, it's time you started thinking about a proper training. Look at yourself; you're a big lassie now. I'm your mother, and I can see your lady equipment is being delivered up front – you with me? So we need to talk about a few things. Men, undies. Wait and I'll take you up to Daly's, Saturday in Glasgow, and we'll get a proper bra and knickers.'

'Mother, I'm after being a scientist. A marine biologist. Know what that is?'

Helen studied her daughter. She nodded slowly. 'That'll be you getting paid money for diving under the sea? Well, great. If you go for what you want, I'm right pleased with it. You're taking after me, you know that? So see and get good Highers in biology.'

Jackie felt it was all flowing too easily. She said sharply: 'How do you say it's morbid? The sea's full of dead things; if there werena any dead things, there'd no be any living ones either. It's the law of nature. See now, the lifecycle of the hermit crab . . .'

'Whiles you really vex me, Jackie. You think because I don't have the blazer and tie education, I'm dead ignorant of science. Well, speaking as a ferry pilot, the Survival of the Fittest is me. And I do so know about the hermit crab. When it's scunnered at how it lives, it flits to somebody else's old shell. There's a few wee crabs like that around this family, I'm telling ye!'

So Jackie did science and biology, and when she was fifteen she went by herself down to Largs and across the ferry to Millport in Cumbrae and rang the bell on the Marine Biological Station. 'My name is Jacqueline Melville, aged fifteen, I stay in Greenock but I'm at St Columba's, Kilmacolm, I'm studying science for Highers and I want to be a marine biologist.'

'Well, well, young lady.'

'I have the certificates for swimming, diving and life-saving.'

'Does your mammy and your daddy know you're here?'

'My mother does so know, and I think this is a fine place, a fine establishment, and I would like to come and work here.'

'Young lady, you know this is not really the sort of work for girls. It's cold and wet, and there's a lot of complex analysis with chemicals and maths.'

'Girls make tanks. Girls make rockets and my mother flies bombers. Look, mister, just give me that piece of paper over there.'

'My goodness, you're awful forward. I think you should be getting home for your tea.'

'Mister, just kindly see us that sheet of paper. Right, thanks. Now this is going to be a diagram of how the intertidal zone ecology in the Firth of Clyde varies with seasonal temperatures. Okay? Just stay where you are. Oh, I'll be needing a red pencil, too. And d'ye keep graph paper?'

The assistant director went home to his wife in Millport that evening. He said: 'Elspeth, I just met a phenomenon. She's fifteen years old and she's just dead brilliant. A real grasp of what we do. And she's wanting a job.'

'Well, so give her a job.'

'Ach, I don't know. I more or less did. I told her: come back before you go to university, and if you're still keen, we'll maybe see about it. But a young woman on the research staff? We've girls sterilising glass in the lab and that, but the offshore fieldwork, the recovery diving out at sea and at depth – is it really for females? She's quite attractive too, unfortunately. You know, she said her mother flew bombers: what am I supposed to make of that?'

'Andrew, will you get off your big fat bahookie and move with the times?'

So Jackie went back to Millport when she left school, and again when she had done the science honours degree at Glasgow, first class, and was taken on as a junior.

Lab work, then shallow-sea fieldwork and diving. The big lads on the boats were surly at first, not sharing the rum they added to their navy 'kye' cocoa or, when she needed the toilet, telling her the heads below was out of order when it wasn't. But Jackie barely noticed.

'Cauld as yesterday's fish supper, that high-heid lassie.' But even when she was back ashore, her hair drying as she wrote up reports soon noted for their neatness and exactness, her soul was underwater with the living organisms and the dead.

The war; I don't want to talk about it. Many of us say that, but only some of us mean it. I don't quite mean it.

But for a good many of my friends, silence has been a positive decision. I'm thinking of those who were in Siberia or in our country during the German occupation, and especially those 'of Jewish origin'. Their children complain: why won't they tell us? Surely it's healthier to tell, to pour it all out and 'come to terms with it', to reach 'closure'? They say: Surely we have a right to know?

And yet I have come to understand that decision for silence. Admittedly, I don't quite understand why it's usually men, rather than women, who take it. Women are better at keeping secrets than men, and yet Wisia wanted me to know what had happened to her and to her family. Maybe men feel they have the patriarchal right to edit and redact the narrative of history before it is passed down the generations. More likely, men are simply more pessimistic, less resilient, less able to see beyond their own disabling experience than women.

Such men say to themselves: I have seen things done by human beings which no human being should see, or even know about, or imagine to be possible. To know what I know has damaged me, taken something from me that can't be put back. I can never be quite like other people.

And yet there remains a sort of remedy. I can make sure that this bad seed, this virus of terrible knowledge, does not reach my children and the generation of their friends. I can make sure that it stops right here with me, and dies with me. I will be silent.

Why am I explaining all this? My own case is nothing like so bad. I am not going to write much about this part of my war, not because it shouldn't be remembered but because it would not mean a lot to readers. I saw foul and terrifying things, but when I occasionally meet old comrades who were in the Division, we talk about the in-jokes: the grotesque orders from on high, the obsessions of adjutants, the folly of allies. We talk about what happened to a Him and sometimes to a Her (women began to enter our lives again as we liberated Belgian and Dutch cities). We have no need to remind ourselves of horror.

And speaking of suppression, I came to appreciate the English art of understatement at bad moments – and I mean English, not Scottish. Infuriating at the time, treasured for style later. Take this scene in a command post near our forward positions in Normandy, after the Royal Air Force had bombed our tanks for the second day running. A Polish colonel who had made a furious protest the first time had just stamped out after an even longer and louder outburst. When he had gone, I heard one of the young RAF liaison officers on the phone to his head-quarters: 'Yes, well, I'm afraid they do go on about it rather.'

Normandy wasn't like what I remembered of the September campaign in Poland. For one thing, I was five years older. For another, we had far better weapons and armour, though never near German quality. In Normandy I was part of a highly organised headquarters as an intelligence officer; in 1939 I had soon been reduced to a straggler with the survivors of my battery.

And this time it wasn't a simple war to defend our country. Was our advance supposed to take us all the way to Warsaw, to liberate Poland before the Soviets got there? Would there be a Poland left to liberate? Or were we killing Germans in France just to take our minds off these questions?

General Maczek's First Armoured Division crossed the Channel well after the first wave of landings, and was at once embroiled in the horrible fighting before Caen. As I have said, we were repeatedly bombed by our own side. This fate earned *les Polonais* the warm sympathy of French civilians, generally cool towards the other 'liberators' who had left their villages in rubble.

About a month after we had landed I was driving a jeep along a long, straight Norman road, well behind our forward positions, when an American fighter-bomber skimmed low overhead. It was heading for the German lines. But when I saw it bank, roll and start back towards us, I slammed on the brakes, yelled for the radio operator to take cover and bolted for the ditch.

The cannon shells bounced the jeep across the road in an eruption of smoke and dust. I tripped and fell as my leg jerked, and realised that I had been hit. For some reason, as I lay there, I felt for Wisia's earring in my tunic pocket. Still there.

The plane had vanished. In the silence, the jeep suddenly gushed flames. I limped over the road, but the young radio operator was very dead in the other ditch. A quiet boy from Lithuania, whose parents wanted him to train for the priesthood.

I had the sense to pull two jerrycans of petrol off the back of the jeep before the fire reached them, and then lay down on the grass verge. I saw blood on my boot and felt a throbbing, but it seemed a good time to have a sleep.

Such was my ignominious war wound: 'friendly fire'. But it was truly friendly in one sense, because while bits of metal were being tweezered out of my leg in a field hospital, I missed Falaise.

This was the Division's worst or, if you like, finest battle. General Maczek was sent to close the 'Falaise Gap' against the escaping German army, and the full strength of many desperate panzer divisions was hurled against the Poles. My replacement as an intelligence officer was killed trying to fight off tanks with a rifle, the day after he reached the Division. I lost good friends there.

Some of the prisoners who put their hands up at Falaise were shouting in Polish: men from western Poland who had been forcibly drafted into the *Wehrmacht*. I acquired a new wireless operator, a fat, merry fellow from near Danzig who had German university degrees in radio technology. He was a Kaszub, from the small Slavic people who over centuries have learned to adapt towards whichever masterful nation happens to be hoisting its flag over their landscape. He told me: 'Home is Mum, the farm, a good funeral wake with the neighbours. Oh, and a deep cellar to hide our women until the next army has passed.'

In Belgium and then the Netherlands, we became heroes. Old cities fell to us. Crowds cheered and threw flowers, girls clambered on to our Sherman tanks with bottles of wine and kissed us. Streets were renamed after General Maczek and city fathers wiped away tears as they made speeches of welcome. Several officers were standing with me on the roadside in Breda, watching this carnival as the Division came through the town, when a passing tankman shouted down to us: 'This is how it'll be in Poznań, in Warsaw – only better!' On the pavement, we looked warily at each other. There was nothing anyone wanted to say.

The Warsaw Rising had begun that August. Our Parachute Brigade, formed for the purpose, was ready to jump into the outskirts. But the British forbade it because they wanted the Brigade for their own purposes. When Warsaw finally surrendered to the Germans, nearly a quarter of a million people were dead.

It was winter as we approached the borders of the Reich. By now, Liberation euphoria was only a memory. The bad news and worse guesses about Poland's future were on everyone's mind and in every conversation. Would the Allies keep faith with their promises to Poland? Meanwhile, the Division halted on the Dutch side of the Rhine, and for many snowy weeks waited for orders to advance again.

Our General alone seemed unmoved by rumours. He was imperturbable, often sharp with officers betraying signs of depression, never uncertain about what was next to be done. We loved him. And yet he had his own reasons to be sardonic about our allies. When Britain's Field Marshal Montgomery met him for the first time, Monty said: 'Now then, Maczek, you can answer something I've always wondered about. You Poles – which language do you speak when you are in Poland? Is it German or Russian?'

I like to think our General counted up to twenty before he allowed himself to reply. Another time, near the end of the war and following the news from Yalta that Churchill and Roosevelt had abandoned Poland to the fate of a Soviet protectorate, Monty heard that there was unrest in the Division. He sent for our General. 'I don't see why you are upset about all this. Buck up, Maczek! After all, here you are only a General. When you get home, they'll make you a Marshal in the Red Army!'

The truth about Yalta broke around the time that the Division was moving forward again, in February 1945. They say that some of the armoured units halted and that men climbed out of their tanks and began to debate. They asked why they should go on fighting one enemy, when their allies had sold their country to the other one. General Maczek – so the legend continues – immediately came to these soldiers and spoke to them 'like a father'. I find it hard to imagine what he can have said. But after a while, the ground shook again as the Shermans' engines let out their bison-bellow of ignition, expelled a thundercloud of blue smoke and lurched back on the road to Germany.

I can't be sure what happened, because I wasn't there. The shrapnel remaining in my leg – the same leg ravaged by dancing with Tibbie – made me hobble and swear. So just before Christmas I found myself on a fortnight's leave, an outpatient in a London hospital.

I had hardly seen the city before, and knew nobody. It was

black, ominously quiet, gap-toothed by bombs. The gutters of what had once been fashionable streets brimmed and sparkled with broken glass.

How she found me, in a small Pimlico hotel requisitioned by Polish armed forces, I don't know. It was afternoon, but I was in bed fully clothed except for my boots, trying to keep warm and reading a Graham Greene thriller, when there was a loud triple rapping. Margaret burst into the room without waiting for me to open the door.

She was wearing a British army overcoat which came down to her ankles, over a smart black suit and that familiar string of pearls. 'Mike, darling! God, it's freezing in here. No, get back in bed; I'll perch on the edge.'

Margaret was 'stationed in London now', working for a government department. When I asked her which department, she was evasive.

'My Polish comes in useful, smattery as it is.' We talked about Normandy and my leg, and then she gave me a little packet done up with a red-white ribbon. It held something purely extraordinary.

'But these are Polish! I mean, these are pre-war Wedel chocolates, from Warsaw. Where on earth did you find them?'

'Oh, one of our chaps brought them back for me. I shouldn't have said that, should I?'

'No. No, you shouldn't. Let's agree you didn't.'

She rubbed her cold hands together. 'Heard anything about my poor Tadek?'

'Well, I have been in the wrong place to get that sort of news. I have a feeling I should be asking you.'

'They nabbed him – you must know that. Dropped in a place already swarming with Russian soldiers: the Home Army guys he was supposed to meet had been mostly rounded up. Wandered about for a few days, trying to contact. Then they got him. Maybe somebody gave him away, maybe they just tracked down his radio.'

I remembered Tadek's wireless aerial at Polmont, too green to look like grass. 'Anything more?'

'Well, actually... there is a notion about where he's being held. Of course they could ship him off at any moment, to Moscow if he's lucky and Siberia if he's not.'

'I think I would put it the other way round.'

'Yes, well, those interrogations in the Lubianka. I can't let myself think about all that, not about Tadek. But there's apparently some outfit – not ours, if you get what I mean, let's say locals – who want to try and get him out. They say they need an airdrop with lots of money – only gold will do, needless to say – and masses of plastic explosive.'

'Airdrop? Are the British still doing that in Poland?'

'Well, not officially. Not any more. If Tadek was a Brit, one of their precious officers in Special Ops, maybe they would.'

She frowned, then stood up from the bed.

'Tadek's chances are pretty awful, really. No use pretending.'

'I see that,' I said. 'Let's go out and find a drink somewhere.'

'Mike, I really really didn't say anything to you today. All we talked about was Scotland or dancing with Tibbie Fowler or the weather or something. All right? You do have to promise.'

I promised. I pulled on my boots and we went out into a darkening street. A search for alcohol seemed to threaten a long, limping trudge through the blackout. But Margaret took me to a club belonging to the Brigade of Guards, where several tall officers shouted 'Good God! It's Meg Beaton-Campbell!' and kissed her. There was gin in abundance, and dinner was roast pheasant shot on somebody's estate.

'Meg, come over and sit with us, and bring your Polish pal.'

'Lovely, in just a minute. Mike, can I ask you something?'

'What?'

'Is there something wrong with me?'

'No, but why do women always ask me that?'

'I've lost the two men I loved most, one after another. Of course it's not my fault, it's the war, I know that. Obviously. And yet I can't stop feeling there must have been something about me that I did or I said and now nobody will ever tell me what it was. Can you understand that?'

'No. No, I don't. How could you say such daft things?' I thought: Margaret should meet Jackie Melville, who believed that a ship had blown up because she ran home in school time and turned a key.

'Poor darling Mike, I shouldn't have made you listen to that. I suppose I must just pull myself together.' Margaret picked up our two glasses of pink gin and led me across to the other table.

The day before my leave ended, I reported to our army headquarters. There was a return travel warrant to collect, and messages might have been left there for me or for friends in the Division. High Command was in a small hotel on

Knightsbridge, once probably luxurious but now shabby and dark. A double breastwork of sandbags and a yawning Polish sentry blocked the front door.

There was one letter for me, with French postage stamps. It had evidently been waiting a long time.

Paris had been liberated six months before. This letter came from an office in the Ministry of War and informed me that the naval enquiry into the loss of *Fronsac* was resuming in Paris. My failure to attend the previous session in London four years before had been noted as a refusal to comply with an order. If I again failed to appear at the reconvened enquiry, a request would be issued to the Polish military authorities for my immediate arrest and delivery to French custody. My status had changed from that of a simple witness to that of a hostile source of evidence, against whom criminal proceedings might eventually be taken.

The letter ended by summoning me to appear in Paris before a closed hearing in the Hotel Wagram, on a date in November 1944. I was reading it in January 1945. I looked at the two signatures. One was illegible: some admiral who was president of the board of enquiry. The other read: 'Guennec, Jean-Marie, Capitaine de Frégate'.

My first thought was in my own language, and would not translate nicely. 'Who do these little fuckers think they are?' is a sort of equivalent. I was too angry to make sense, so I sat down in one of the scarred leather armchairs in the foyer and read the letter again. Splendid letterhead; wretched wartime paper flecked with what looked like particles of oatmeal.

My second, more coherent thought was: how can I find le

Gallois? He could explain what's going on. After all, it was the Commandant who had told me four years ago that Guennec had bolted back to France to join the Vichy regime of Marshal Pétain. If I had thought about him at all since the Liberation, I had assumed he would be in jail as a collaborator. Or even shot at dawn.

On the other hand, it was two months since the order for my arrest should have gone out and I was still free. Perhaps it never went out at all. Perhaps the French had decided not to bother with me. Or perhaps our High Command had shrugged and thrown the request into the waste-paper basket. With a Soviet-sponsored 'Committee of National Liberation' now established in Lublin, asserting that it was the legitimate government of Poland, our leaders had bigger things to worry about.

There was still time to telephone the French military attaché in their Embassy. I pretended that I was an officer on our naval staff, and, after enduring some haughty cross-questioning, established that le Gallois was still in Scotland, although his warships had returned to Toulon or Brest. Then I bought a bottle of black-market whisky from a friend of one of Margaret's friends and set out for Dover.

The war was ending as our tanks crossed the Rhine and drove into Germany. From every direction, desperate people came towards us for rescue, food and a return to humanity. *Wehrmacht* deserters were followed by thousands of Polish men and women, some from the concentration camps, some escaping from slave labour in Nazi industry and on north German farms, some who had survived the Warsaw Rising or the 1939 campaign as prisoners of war. A group of Polish Jews reached us with their last strength from the camp at Bergen-Belsen, after they had been liberated by the British. But many of them soon died in our field hospitals.

My best memory comes from the day we drove to a prison camp for Polish women. The guards had fled, and the women had somehow heard that we were coming; they had tried to make themselves 'look nice' in spite of their shaven heads and stick-thin legs.

They were crowded up to the wire, shouting to us in Polish as we jumped out of the vehicles, and they were laughing and smiling. Yes, they acted as if we were boys late in coming to take them to the movies, rather than soldiers rescuing them from death by typhus or starvation. Only a few of the older ones were weeping. I can see those women's faces now. I still think that everything was worth it for that moment.

The numbers grew, and soon there were more 'displaced persons' than soldiers; the Division looked more like a nomad encampment than an alert fighting unit. In the end, we simply took over a small German town and threw out all its inhabitants. Our horde of camp followers moved in and we declared it 'a Polish town', renamed 'Maczków' in honour of our General. I remembered how Commandant le Gallois had annexed part of Gourock as a French town. Home can be just a proclamation.

Hitler died: the Third Reich surrendered. The British held an Allied victory parade in London, but they did not invite the Poles. This was because Churchill was preparing to recognise the Communist-dominated 'Provisional Government' as the legitimate rulers of Poland. Accordingly, Britain would withdraw recognition from our exile government in London.

British friends said privately that they felt rather sad about this, but reality was reality. The 'Provisional Government' was in command of Poland now, with Stalin behind it, and one had to accept that. Again, I remembered le Gallois and what he had said about *les Anglais*: 'so nice, so noble – then one day you wake up to find a noose around your neck'.

What about us, the soldiers? If many of the men in our original First Corps came from the lost eastern regions of Poland, the same was true – even more so – of the Second Corps which had ended up in Italy. They no longer had homes to go back to, and the survivors of the Polish population in those provinces were being expelled.

Some of the ordinary soldiers hoped that, as humble 'workers and peasants', the new regime would value them. A fifth of Poland's population had been killed; its cities and factories had been shattered or deliberately razed to the ground. So sheer patriotism could urge men and women to return and rebuild their country, whatever they thought about Communists in the government.

But for most officers, return to a 'People's Republic' under Russian hegemony was unthinkable. In the forests there was civil war, as boys and girls of the Home Army resistance movement were hunted down by the 'internal security forces' of the new regime. I heard several comrades on the Divisional staff say that this new Poland was not the country they had fought for. They would only return to that soil, alive or even in an urn of ashes, when Poland was free again and when 'atheist Bolshevism' had been driven from the land.

There was no mystery about what the British wanted. They wanted to get rid of us. They urged us to lay down our arms, demobilise and go back to Poland as soon as possible. I thought this disgraceful, and yet my own feelings were mixed.

I had no illusions about the brutality of Soviet power. I had no problem in believing that Russia would always be, as it had always been, the enemy of a truly independent Poland. But I was also convinced that the pre-war regime in Poland – super-patriotic, super-conservative, blind – had been responsible for our national tragedy. Was there a slim chance to build a new nation which would be both democratic and strong? Would the Polish Communists and their Soviet masters agree to share power in the long term? In our officers' mess nobody believed that. I wanted to believe it, but the evidence was against me. So I held my tongue.

We sat around for sterile months. Exile or return? The British soon had to accept that most of the troops would choose exile. As a sort of apology to these men and women who had stood by them from the first day of the war to the last, they set up an elaborate system of transit camps in England and Scotland, with a Resettlement Corps to teach English and ease the way into civilian jobs.

I was among those from eastern Poland who could be called homeless. Why not wait out the future in Scotland, where I at least had friends and connections? So, through the Division, I reluctantly put my name in for resettlement, and almost at once received a message from the army's legal department. I was to report to an address in Hamburg. There was, it seemed, a problem connected with my request.

Most of Hamburg had been obliterated by the RAF. But the jeep driver jolted his way to a handsome white villa at Blankenese, on the Elbe shore. In the hall, somebody had pinned a Polish flag on one of the doors. I knocked and found myself facing somebody I knew very well.

My old Colonel, the same severe gentleman who had been my commander at Pitnechtan, was sitting behind a trestle table stacked with buff-coloured folders. A single folder, a blue one, lay open in front of him. I could see the 'Ministère de la Guerre' heading on the top letter inside it.

I reminded myself that the Colonel had been a public prosecutor in civilian life. Today he was in uniform, but had acquired an unmilitary pair of gold spectacles. They gleamed austerely in the pale light reflected from the Elbe.

I saluted. 'At ease! You may sit down, Szczucki.' Behind his head, a white rectangle on the wall showed where some departing Nazi had removed the inevitable portrait. He came round from behind the table, and we settled opposite one another in two uncomfortable Teutonic chairs, carved out of black oak with protruding heads of wolves and eagles.

'Well, Major, you have come through the war pretty well. I heard about the leg. But you are alive. Not all the men we both knew in Scotland are alive. And your Division seems to be satisfied with your performance. By the way, what happened to your career as a silent-shadowy parachutist?'

I explained that I had broken my ankle, during a weekend's leave. He raised his eyebrows, then heaved himself off the chair to fetch the open folder.

'Major, I thought you were a reasonable man. A bit lazy, a bit too inclined to dreaming and drinking. But reasonable. That affair over the absurd leaflet on the orders board – remember? You made a sound impression on me then.'

'Sir.'

'So what the hell is this? Read it. I await your explanation.'

The letter repeated much of the letter I had opened in London. But it ended by stating that the naval enquiry, meeting in November last year, had indeed issued a request for my detention, pending transfer to the custody of the judicial branch of the French navy. The same signatures. The Admiral, again illegible, and Guennec, Jean-Marie.

'Colonel, I have done nothing to be ashamed of. There is a misunderstanding, but somebody seems to be trying to invent...'

'I don't want your opinions, Szczucki. Facts! What is all this about?'

I told him about the sinking of the *Fronsac*. I told him that the French – as opposed to the British – stuck to the view that it was a case of sabotage. I said that it was a fact, but also a coincidence, that I had lodged in the house of the British officer whom the French suspected of causing the explosion, or at least of complicity. He had died when the torpedo detonated.

'How do you know he is dead?'

'Did I say dead? Excuse me, Colonel, I should have said missing, but of course presumed dead.'

The old procurator looked at me evenly. 'How well did you know him?'

'We hardly spoke. He didn't like having me in his house.'

'Was he married?'

'Yes.'

'Was she young? Where is she now?'

'I think she may be in Canada. She had a daughter.'

'You think. Why don't you know?'

I didn't like the way this was going. What was he after? I told him about Captain Guennec and his defection from Free France to join the Vichy government. 'For some reason I don't understand, he is trying to frame me.'

The Colonel nodded and stood up. I remembered his taste for delivering rapid verdicts.

'Two things are clear to me, Major. One: you are not telling me all that you know. Two: whatever the truth of your story, the French are up to dirty tricks. You are probably just a banana skin, which one crew of Paris scoundrels is using to trip another crew.'

He took a cigarette from a box on his desk, snapped a lighter and began to smoke it in that 'Russian' way I remembered.

'Dismiss, Major. Come back here at four. I take it you have transport.'

I made the jeep drive me around for a few hours. I had hardly looked at the ruins. Now I saw that everywhere, less than a year after the war had ended, the Germans were making broken houses habitable: walls were rising, and piles of salvaged bricks and roof timbers were neatly arrayed on cleared pavements. I could hear hammers and saws. While I wasted my life in army camps, this must also be happening in what was left of Warsaw.

Back at the villa in Blankenese, the Colonel kept me standing before his table.

'In making my decision I have regard to the following considerations. The first and second, I have already made clear. One, you are not telling me the full truth for some reason; two, the French request is dishonest, unconvincing. But, third, I cannot refuse indefinitely to comply with it. Fourth? Well, you are a Polish officer who has served decently through this war. And you have been one of my own officers.'

He took up another sheet of paper. 'You have applied for resettlement in Great Britain. That is your choice. But I should point out that you will not be safe there, if the British security people cooperate with the French. You are in very serious trouble, and ultimately I cannot help you.

'Major Szczucki, my decision is this. I do not intend to arrest you immediately, here and now. So I will find reasons to wait for a month, but after that I must order your detention. I suggest that you use that time to think again about your future. That young lady in Canada? A big country which is not very inquisitive. Dismiss.'

He smiled for the first time. I went back to the Division and asked for leave. It turned out that a Polish frigate was leaving Kiel for Rosyth, and I was taken comfortably back to Scotland in time for a hard-drinking Hogmanay evening with several Polish seamen in the Edinburgh pubs. Later, when the sailors had left me and headed off to visit a famous madame in Danube Street, I found a telephone box in working order.

The bell rang and rang vainly in distant Fort Matilda. But just when I was about to press Button B and regain my heavy, clattering British pennies, a cross janitor voice answered.

'D'ye not know whit day it is? Ach, for God's sake! No, nae Frenchmen here any more.'

How didn't I know the base had closed? 'I've no got the right to disclose this. But seeing it's Hogmanay, I'll release information tae ye: the Commandant is in the Central Hotel, Glasgow, waiting to be away to France. Have a good New Year yourself.'

Built over Central Station, the hotel's dim, enormous lounges were swarming. Many of the men and women were still in uniform, keeping their greatcoats on against the chill of unheated saloons. It was noisy in the hungover aftermath of Hogmanay, and dwarfish pageboys in pill-box hats sauntered through the crowds, shouting: 'Mister MacDonald... Please! Telephone for Mister MacDonald... Please!'

The lift was out of order, in this disjointed transition between war and peace. As I started up the staircase, two English officers came trotting down past me. One was saying to the other: 'No, Timothy's having a jammy life since demob. Saw him last week with an opulent-looking popsy in Quaglino's...'

Le Gallois had a suite to himself. The main room held a huge unmade double bed and many tiny tables with ashtrays; there was a smell of railway smoke and brown sauce. The heavy curtains were drawn, but I could hear wind and rain shaking the panes as the Commandant jumped up to embrace me with a bristly kiss. He hadn't shaved, and was wearing a blue silk dressing gown with white polka dots. I had never seen him out of uniform before.

The bathroom door opened and a young woman came out, tugging sharply at the corners of a creased jacket. She gave me a disagreeable glance as she retrieved a pair of shoes from under the bed.

'Martine, I present my Polish friend Major Shoosky. Now you must leave us alone to talk. Yes, off you go. Listen, come back at seven and I'll take you to the Malmaison downstairs and feed you properly.'

Martine took two threatening steps towards him. She shouted: '*J'en ai assez, tu entends! Assez, assez, assez!*' The door slammed behind her.

The Commandant pulled a face. He didn't seem much discomposed. He ordered coffee on the room telephone, and, while we waited, we caught up on my war, his war.

'No, the base is closed of course. My only ship on the Clyde now is *Fronsac*. That's why I am here, in this hotel full of drunken Brits and their girls, eating the lamentable food of the London, Midland and Scottish Railway.'

He and the French consul were waiting to perform a final, doleful act. This was to take formal possession of the remains of *Fronsac*'s crew. The wreck's forward accommodation was being opened up, and whatever was found would be delivered to French care. Meanwhile, caskets had been ordered. A small ceremony would follow when they were brought ashore and handed over to the Consul as the representative of France.

'Ketling will call me when they are ready. You remember

him, naturally. Me, I can't like him; there's something...
snake-like there. But, as everybody is saying, he has turned out
outstanding at this job, exceptional even. Did you know that he
is planning to lift the whole wreck in one piece? Ketling goes
around saying that if he brings it off, he will be famous.'

It was half an hour before the coffee appeared. The silver
jug was splendid, but the coffee was lukewarm and tasted of
chicory. While le Gallois spat and grumbled, I took the first
Paris letter out of my briefcase.

Le Gallois read it. He lay back in his armchair and gave me
that strange stare, with dilated pupils, which I had seen before.

'Shoosky, my dear, this is a letter for me as well as you. Thank
you for showing it to me. But I should have foreseen it.'

'What do you mean?'

'Let me tell you about Jean-Marie Guennec. He went back
to France and joined Vichy; he rallied to that pathetic old
shipwreck, our Marshal Pétain. You remember all that. And in
the Vichy Navy's legal branch, he even helped to draw up the
indictment of General de Gaulle as a traitor.'

I must have looked shocked. The Commandant laughed at
my expression. 'I mean, you must understand, Jean-Marie is not
pro-German, not a Nazi. No, he is just an ambitious imbecile,
brought up in a Catholic-Royalist family in some mucky
backwoods. Anyway, soon the wind changed. The Americans
were in Algeria; Germany was going to lose the war. Oh-oh,
Jean-Marie! It's time to invent a new past, in case the Gaullists
and Communists are unkind to you after the Liberation!'

'He turned his coat again?'

'Not exactly. But as the Allies landed in 1944, he made

discreet contact with the Resistance, sacked one or two real Fascists in his office. And after Vichy collapsed, he denounced many of his own colleagues to de Gaulle's security men. Before they could denounce him!'

The Commandant laughed again. 'But here comes the really shameless bit. You remember how the French fleet at Toulon scuttled itself, when the Germans occupied southern France in 1942? Well, Guennec is claiming now that he helped to organise it all from his navy office. It was he who sent secret messages encouraging the ships' captains. It was he who guaranteed that they would not be arrested. It was he who had the German naval mission's telephone disconnected. But no, sorry, it absolutely wasn't him. Several of those Toulon officers are old friends of mine. The truth is that Guennec didn't even know the scuttling was going to happen.'

'So this letter...'

'But exactly! Captain Guennec steps forward as the backroom Resistance hero, and then as the righteous avenger hunting down collaborators in the navy. But, Shoosky, I am one of the people who knows his true story very well. He has obviously got hold of the crazy Kellerman confession I once showed you. And that tells me he is going to suggest that – because I knew you and that Melville family – I was implicated somehow in a plot to sink the *Fronsac* and then cover up the conspiracy. So you, poor Shoosky, must be destroyed too. But only as a way of getting to his real target. Which is me.'

'Are you worried?'

'No. It's disgusting but not serious. There's a lot of this shit flying round in France, and Guennec – well, in reality he has his back to the wall. Too many people know his 'patriot' story is a fabrication. Sooner or later, he's doomed.'

Le Gallois slowly shook his head. 'The only thing that worries me is the Kellerman paper, that so-called confession. Evidently, Guennec has read it. But that means that somebody in our intelligence services is helping him; otherwise he would never have known it existed. That's bad news. Well, bad for you. Me, I can deal with them. But if the French spooks get interested in Shoosky again and pass the file on to *les Anglais* – their famous secret service – then who would protect you?'

I told him that I had applied for resettlement in Britain.

'Not wise! Seems I am always telling you to run away, escape. But you'd be safer in Canada. Or, better still, your Poland? Surely it can't be so bad there.'

In the train to Greenock, I wondered what I would find. For nearly eighteen months, I had heard nothing from Helen. Christmas cards had reached me from Union Street twice, in Holland and then, only ten days ago, in Germany.

Mrs Melville's cards hoped I was safe and warm; in Scotland there were shortages but victory was on the way. Was there anything they could send me? Jackie's last card said she was planning to ask for a job after university in a fishery research station. She said that she was studying hard but the house was awful noisy. It ended: 'Mother sends love'. So not in Canada?

Helen opened the door with one hand. The other was holding the baby against her shoulder. 'Meet Major Mike,' she said to him, and to me, 'Meet Mister Hugh Douglas.' A big, heavy baby, amazed to see me. 'Well, he's a wee bit over a year old now. Aren't ye?' She kissed him and then me. Her hair had grown long and her cheeks had hollowed; she was thinner, but she gave me a huge, pleasant smile. I thought resentfully: like the smile you give to a favourite uncle.

Helen followed me into the kitchen, as Mrs Melville put her arms round me. No kiss, but a sharp, measured squeeze. I studied Jackie as she stood up from her jotters and books and came round the table. Almost as tall as Helen, a face less angular, breasts... I would not have recognised her on the street. Still wearing glasses, which she now took off. Large, sceptical grey eyes, black brows.

Her kiss and embrace were passionate. 'I've missed you, Uncle Mike, so I have. I was that feared the Germans would get you; I was cutting out the war maps in the papers to see where you were. Was I not?'

'Aye, she was!' said the others in chorus. They all looked at me in fond surprise, as if I were a purse left on the bus and unexpectedly returned by Lost Property.

Tea was herring fillets grilled in oatmeal. I had never quite forgotten that taste and ate slowly. But by the time we had finished, Helen's baby had grown tired and began to girn. 'I'll just put him down. Don't start without me.' Start what? I looked at the three women. Mrs M was expressionless. Jackie grinned at me and poured tea.

When Helen came back, it was Jackie who sat very upright in her chair and said: 'There's some things want straightened out here. When we knew you were coming, we thought:

this is the moment. Mike is the missing piece. We've to talk about my dad.'

'No need for this,' Mrs Melville said. 'It can end in tears.'

'Who knows what? We are none of us saying. You two, Mum and Mike, know some things, but I've no way to tell how much. It's just… ridiculous.'

A pause. 'Okay,' said Jackie, 'I'll begin. I'm in touch with my dad now. Did you know that? He was waiting for me at the station one morning, a few months back. "D'ye no ken yer ain faither? I'm no deid, Jackie." I says: "Father, I know that fine. How are you keeping?" So he tells me he's working just across the water from us, on the wreck of the French ship. He's chief salvage engineer. Seen him three more times since; he comes through to the station and waits on me. He's saying: "I'll send a boat for ye, come and watch what we do."'

Mrs Melville set her tea cup down and pursed her lips.

'Young lady, your trouble is you collect secrets and then can't keep them. Don't think I didn't know all about that. Your father and I have been in contact for a long while. On and off, that is. He sent me a letter from Rosyth in wartime, and then I agreed to meet him in Glasgow when this job on the wreck began. That's when he told me he was going to find you, Jackie. I said to him that was about the worst idea possible, dangerous and upsetting, too. But he wouldn't be told.'

Helen said: 'I'm hearing stuff I never knew, and I don't want to know. You all lied to me. Who d'ye think I am, some sort of daft evacuee woman with a baby and a mind the size of a peanut? Mike, you lied to me, telling me Johnston was away at sea. And, ach, Jackie, how could you be with your mother all these months and seeing your dad and no telling me, not a word? Yer ain mother? Ye're just dead selfish and cold, nae normal feelings, so ye are.'

Mother and daughter were both crying now. Mrs M started to say that she had warned us it would end in tears, but I interrupted her. I said: 'Listen! Helen, Jackie. It's not over. Now we all know where Johnston is, but nobody must give him away. Which of you has learned his new name?'

There was no answer. Three stubborn women looked back at me. Helen wiped her eyes with her sleeve. Jackie wiped her nose with the back of her hand. Mrs M stirred her tea.

'Johnston has to stay dead, understand. The salvage man has to be somebody you never met before. All right, I tell you his name: he is Mr Ketling.'

'Alex Ketling! And he's grown a wee red beard.' Jackie sounded defiant. Her grandmother looked at her and looked away again.

'Now I explain why it has to stay a secret.'

I didn't go into all the details and names. But I described how the police and French intelligence were still looking for Nazi agents who they thought had blown up *Fronsac*. They were after me, for no good reason, and I might have to disappear. But if they thought Johnston – their first suspect – was still alive, then they would come after everyone else who might have helped or hidden him.

'That means every one of you. Well, maybe not Helen so much; she was in Canada. But now, as from today, we are all in this together, hiding a wanted man. So we have to keep the secret, for our own sakes.'

'What about my son's sake? You speak about him as if he were guilty. But there's no a scrap of evidence that he would ever do such a dreadful thing. You have no right even to hint that he could. So you can just leave this house!'

I kept silent. Helen went round the table and took the older woman's hand: 'No, Mabel, give us all a break. He's only saying what others are saying; he's never saying he believes it. I'm not in the know about what went on after the sinking. But I'd guess that if it weren't for Mike, Johnston wouldnae even be in the land of the living. Am I no right?'

I stayed in the spare room upstairs, where I had slept before. It was convenient: le Gallois had invited me to the handing over of the crew's remains, down at Princes Pier two days later.

It was January, but the house seemed warmer than I remembered. On the second night, Helen slipped into the room while I still had the light on, leaving the door slightly ajar. 'In case wee Shuggie wakes.' She sat on the edge of the bed. I wasn't sure what she wanted. She seemed not to be sure either.

'Got a ciggie?'

'Started again?'

'Nobody's smoking in this house now. But it's the sight of you puts me in the mood.'

She fetched a soap dish for an ashtray, and we lit up and quietly talked.

'You'll be going home soon. When are ye away?'

'Maybe not.'

'But everyone else, the Yanks, the Free French, even the Italian prisoners is going home. What's wrong with Poland?'

'The Russians are there.'

'So what's so bad about that? They'll be wanting home to Russia soon, just like you want home to Poland.'

'Not so easy, Helen. Talk about something else.'

'Okay, tell me about Johnston. Was I right, you saved his life and hid him? Why did you do that?'

'I don't know why. Don't even like him . . . perhaps because he was on the run, he was alone.'

'Was it for me?'

I put my hands gently round her strong neck. 'No. I think about you so often, but not then. Like I said before I went to the Invasion, don't try to see him again.'

'I never thought about you for a whole year. But here you are back, the only person round here I'm not feared of. Wouldn't say I trusted you, though. Huh, did you not tell me Johnston was at sea? Liar!'

She lay down beside me, and I kissed her. I could smell the baby on her skin, but when she pulled her nightdress off, I forgot about it.

Before she went back to her room, she leaned over me and whispered 'Old times, eh?' But it had been different. She was softer, less playful. And at one moment she suddenly pulled up her knees, covered her eyes and made a sound: the despairing groan of a woman cornered by an enemy. Never before, with me. Was it Craig who had shown her how to get there?

———

The ceremony was not grand. A picket boat came across from the Tail of the Bank to where we stood, lined up on the quay. Le Gallois was back in uniform, and I noticed that his heavy chest had acquired more medal ribbons.

French naval ratings with black armbands shouldered two coffins up the weed-slippery steps and laid them before the Consul. Only two caskets, for twenty-eight dead men?

A woman officer marched up and presented the Consul with two folded tricolours, which he spread over the coffins. As she saluted, I recognised the Martine who had recently had more than enough in the Central Hotel. She gave no sign of recognising me.

Mr Alexander Ketling had followed the escort up the steps. He was wearing a black tie, and a blue suit which went strikingly with his new red beard. Bugles rang out. He took his hat off, showing pale scalp through thinning ginger hair. I kept behind the rank of French officials and edged away from him, but it was impossible not to glance at his face as the sailors gently handled the coffins into the hearse.

I thought: 'Here, passing you, are the bones of men whose death you must have brought about, whether by criminal negligence or on purpose.' But this Mr Ketling was clenching his jaw, simulating Churchillian sorrow. 'We have to endure our grievous losses with courage and renewed resolve...' that would have been the caption to his photograph.

As the hearse bumped slowly towards the dock gates, I turned away to seek the Commandant. I suggested a drink at the Bay over in Gourock, after the Consul's party had left. As he nodded, somebody else nudged me from behind.

'You'll be away back to your own country now.' I couldn't tell whether Ketling meant it as a question or a suggestion. Walking away from him, I headed after the hearse.

The Commandant slapped the mahogany bar with affection. 'Our last time. I mean goodbye time, Shoosky. Day after tomorrow, I will be in Paris.'

He looked around. Once seething with men from half a dozen navies, the Bay Hotel lounge was almost empty. A few civilians sat at the tables with beer, but le Gallois and I were alone at the bar. I saw the vacant armchairs where Helen – trim in her blue tunic – had once offered me a Camel. No sign in the bar of Martine, or of any other woman. Scotland was reverting to normal.

'Only two caskets?'

'Well, they tell me there was nothing much there. Don't forget how bad the fire was before she sank, my God. I imagine they just filled the coffins with whatever they could.'

I thought of Dougie the undertakers' man, at Johnston's 'funeral'.

'Anyway, Shoosky, I'm tired of half-mast flags, coffins, writing letters to widows. I'm tired of the sea. Lovely men I knew, strong, funny men. One, ten, a hundred of them, all dissolved into the ocean like pinches of salt.'

He looked down into his whisky. 'You don't know how many ships of our little Greenock navy we lost out there in the Atlantic. The submarines, the brave little corvettes. *Alysse*,

Mimosa, *Aconit*. Well, *Aconit* survived. She sank two U-boats in twelve hours. Even *les Anglais* said it was a record.'

'The town will miss you.'

'Ha! Certainly not! The mothers of Greenock will be dancing. They no longer have to go looking for their daughters in those cosy little train compartments, in the railway carriages parked for repair behind the station. Yes, I knew where to find the boys when a ship had to put to sea in a hurry.'

Before we left, he wrote an address on the page of a notebook. 'My wife and Françoise are there already. Some day you must come. You must sample the life of a lazy Provençal seed merchant who sits in the sun, reading the Fables of la Fontaine because they tell me more about our politics than the newspapers.'

The scrap of paper was thrust into my tunic pocket. 'And you, when are you going home? I see everyone is asking you Poles the same question. But evidently there's no easy answer.'

'I am thinking about it.'

'Stop thinking. Do something before it's too late, before Guennec and the other silly bloodhounds catch up with you. Start a farm in Australia. Get married. Shoosky, you are such a loner, so passive, always waiting for that wind from the sea to make up your mind for you. But these times are deadly dangerous for a *promeneur solitaire*. Join something – somebody.'

We paid and went to the door.

'Such a pity that she drowned, that handsome woman of yours that Guennec used to fancy. Do you still miss her? Where I come from, the old men in the café say: "Young widows are best!"'

It was true that everyone was asking me – asking us – when we were going home. The mood in Scotland had changed. Once heroic guests when we stood alone with Britain against Hitler, we had become guests who had overstayed their welcome. In Edinburgh and in Glasgow, I had seen 'Poles Go Home' painted on walls over the fading 'Second Front Now' slogans. Painted by the same people, I suspected.

At Union Street, I read the papers carefully. There had been a packed-out rally in the Usher Hall in Edinburgh, where a Church minister had been cheered as he abused the Poles as scroungers and Papists. They were hanging on in Scotland to take the jobs in mining and steelmaking which belonged to our men coming back from the war. Didn't the Poles have their own country to go to? They should be rounded up and sent home.

He was contemptible. But I was tired of dodging that question. 'I am thinking about it...' The truth was that my own decision to stay in Britain was fast dissolving, and I had to admit it. Many reasons: those warnings from the Colonel and the Commandant, this sudden hostility in Scotland, that hope of Wisia's that Polish ground under my feet would bring me to myself. And Helen.

In these weeks with her, in the old stone house, we had become close again. Well, close? I helped with Hughie; she came several times to my bed when she thought the other folk in the house were asleep; we could still make each other laugh. I mustn't lose her again. But the only way I could think of to keep her was ungainly, conventional: to marry her. And then take her back to Poland.

Lose her? Helen had never belonged to me. 'Another marriage, are you daft?' She pulled the sheet back over me, as she stood up. 'And in Poland would I not just be your Scottish souvenir?' But I saw that she was listening, reflecting.

I read that in Paisley there was to be a public meeting on 'Rebuilding Europe: Progress, Peace and Socialism'. The speakers came from the National Union of Mineworkers, the Labour Party, the Transport & General Workers... Then I came to the last name on the list. 'Councillor Isabella Fowler, Cowdenbeath, Communist Party of Great Britain'.

It seemed wiser to go in civilian clothes. A light snow was falling on the town; there had been a power cut, and oil lamps stood on brackets round the school hall. But more than a hundred men and women, huddled in overcoats, had turned up on this winter night to sit on the narrow school chairs.

I saw Tibbie at once. Looking down from the platform into the smoky gloom, it took her some time to see me. But just as a speaker was asking: 'Comrades, rise for a moment's silence in honour of the Red Army men and women who died for our freedom!', she noticed me and went quite scarlet with delight. While the audience hauled themselves to their feet with a great scrape of chairs, trod out their Woodbines on the floor and stood, Tibbie kept smiling at me.

Her speech was about the new National Coal Board, about

the end of the cruel dynasties of colliery owners, about the way
workers were taking over production from the bosses in France,
Italy, Czechoslovakia and the new People's Democracies. At the
end, the convener asked 'Comrade Isabella, as a noted voice in
the revival of working-class music', to give us a song.

She stood up and, unaccompanied, began 'A Man's a Man
for a'that'. I heard again that sweet, tangy voice, which seemed
to give Burns' words a flavour of remembered joy rather than of
future struggle. The hall loved her and joined in, more loudly
than in singing 'The Red Flag' which followed.

As the hall began to empty, she came down and hugged me.
'Ach, Major Mike, for God's sake! I was feared for you. And is
the foot sore yet? Ach, it's so great to see ye.'

The pubs had closed, and a coach was coming to take her
and some of the comrades back to Kirkcaldy. But we talked in
the corner of the hall until the janitor threw us out. I told her
about Normandy and Germany.

'Are you really in the Communist Party, Tibbie?'

'Sure I am. Where else? I mind a talking to I gave ye, about
the new world coming after the war, power to the people and
that. But ye widnae listen. Ye'd no be tellt.'

She told me about how she and a group of comrades were
trying to spread Scotland's treasure of popular song and bothie
ballads. 'The folk need them back. They're songs of protest
forbye. I'm learning the guitar, Mike, and setting the old songs
to it, and we go round the pubs with them. No round the halls
yet. But that'll come.'

Later, the inevitable question arrived. 'How come ye're still
here? When are ye away back to Poland?'

'I'm thinking about it. Maybe soon.'

'Thinking? They're needing ye there for the reconstruction. Rebuilding Warsaw. I saw such a grand film, about the Polish railways getting moving again, getting steam up after the Nazis tried to wreck all the locomotives. And the music to it: Khachaturian's Sabre Dance as the pistons get thumping again. What are ye waiting on, with Poland liberated a year and more?'

'Liberation? It looks more like a new Russian occupation.'

Tibbie stepped back and stared at me. 'What are ye saying? It's Polish working folk that's in charge now, with the Red Army to guard them from the old landowners and the foreign spies. I never thought to hear you talk that way, of all people.'

A horn tooted. Men and women were lining up to board a coach. Somebody was waving impatiently at Tibbie.

'Ye should come and see what we're doing in Fife, Mike. The coal mines, the railways, next the foundries, maybe then the lairds who fancy they own the land of Scotland. The Labour government's awful timid, but the miners will no be held back. And it's what we see in the Soviet Union that's guiding us, Mike.'

She turned to go. She didn't kiss me. 'You're a dear man at heart, Major Mike, so ye are. But that's you drifting into shocking bad company. The world's on the move, so don't you be left behind.'

Tibbie went across the snow to her bus. She had grown more stately – broader round the shoulders. But her walk was as proud and graceful as before.

A few weeks later a man came to Glasgow from the new Polish Embassy in London, to talk to the 'ex-combatants'. Most of us ignored the meeting. A dozen or so turned up and told him what they thought about Katyń, the loss of the eastern provinces, the lies of Communist leaders. He tried to answer above the uproar, but fell silent.

When the others had gone, I went up to the platform and asked the speaker about repatriation to Poland. I thought he would be surprised, even gratified. But he merely glanced at me over steel spectacles and – unsmiling – handed me typed application forms from his briefcase.

'Will it be possible?'

'I cannot answer such questions. I have a train to catch.'

The war was long over, but the carcase of *Fronsac* still lay rusting across the tidal stream. Twice in a lunar day, the sea rose until only three black funnels could be seen across the estuary. Twice the tide washed slowly down to uncover the stub of the bridge and a gleaming length of deck. The gulls, slanting high above the wreck, disdained its broken steel.

'High time to put her out of her misery,' said the naval officer from the Salvage Service, leaning back against the tilted forecastle to keep his balance.

'How d'ye mean, misery? It's just metal that's here.'

'Yes, Mr Ketling. Yes, I'm aware of that. A flight of fancy.'

There was nowhere on board to sit or shelter. Rain was blowing in from the west as the officer lowered himself carefully down the ladder to his launch. Ketling followed him. They settled in the cramped cabin.

'You're in charge, Mr Ketling. I've read your contract with the Admiralty and the Ministry of Transport. But I gather you have been telling people that you anticipate no problems lifting this vessel. Even though she's bedded in well over a fathom of mud? Even though a lift on this scale has never been attempted, let alone achieved? Forgive me, Mr Ketling, but your experience at marine salvage seems to me pretty limited. Do you really know what you're taking on?'

He flipped open a stapled set of papers: the latest survey from the Boom Defence and Marine Salvage authority. *Fronsac* displaced 3,600 tons, almost the weight of a light cruiser. She had settled herself nearly nine feet into the sludge and gravel of the seabed, and there was some six fathoms of water over her submerged section even at low water. She was lying at a steep seventeen-degree list to starboard. On top of that, the gaping rent in her side caused by the explosion had allowed hundreds of tons of sand and silt to slide into the hull. Below decks, in ammunition lockers and passageways, there remained an unknown quantity of shells, some probably rusted. Under the stern decking, covered chutes held the depth charges.

'No way I'm starting work before you get those damned things removed.'

'I can see why you worry, Mr Ketling. Depth charges do look nasty. But these ones are probably not even primed for depth. You could chuck them over the side like dustbins and nothing much would happen.'

'I want them away, nevertheless.'

'I'll talk to somebody. But I'm a salvage chap, not a bomb chap. And it's your "lift her in one piece" plan I'm worried about. Look at the state of her hull! With that damage and that weight inside her, she'd simply break in two. And then, apart from everything else, the five hundred tons of fuel oil inside her would be all over the anchorage.'

He stabbed a pencil at the plan of the ship, spread on the table in front of them. 'No, forget your big lift. Just cut her up into sections, here and here and maybe up at the bows, too. It'll take longer, but it's the hell of a lot safer.'

'I'll be doing this my way. And I'm telling you for why. First, because cutting through the bilges would release that oil anyhow. Second, because you maybe didnae notice the flared bows on her, French-style. Cut the bow off and it would never stay upright. There's no way you could tow that to the breaker's yard.'

Back in Greenock, the officer said: 'Typical Scotch, might as well have been talking to the backside of a Highland bullock. Takes everything personally. Well, he's only got himself to blame for what happens.'

'Who's taking it personally, Peter? He's probably right about the bow section, and he's got a point about not cutting into the bilges.'

'Funny thing, he reminds me vaguely of that Scotch "Wavy Navy" chap who was killed when *Fronsac* blew up. Never actually met him, but saw a photo in his house. Went to his funeral all those years ago. God, whatever was his name? Had a rather scrumptious wife.'

Ketling knew people who knew people. From now on, he avoided crossing the water to Greenock and took a room in a hotel at Dumbuck, on the other side of the Firth and only a few miles from the wreck. In the dark lounge, men from the shipyards, the Clyde Port Authority, the boom defence flotilla and the Admiralty salvage teams came to talk to him.

Day after day he sat there, a humped, half-seen figure with a sharp red beard who kept his hat on while he drove question after question, scribbling notes with his indelible pencil. He never smiled. But on occasion, he would clap a man's shoulder as he walked him to the door. 'No bother, pal. The boss at your place will never hear you was through here and talking to me.'

He learned fast. The day came when he confronted the masters of the two dredgers which lay alongside *Fronsac*, working to clear the banks of silt which had built up against her sides.

'You're wasting ma time. At this rate, ye'll still be here when there's a man on the moon. So the Admiralty said ye to carry on? I'm no interested. Away back and moan to the Port Authority. There's a proper job needing done here.'

'C'mon, Alex, dinna take the huff that way. If the silt's no cleared, how will ye run the cables underneath her?'

'Tunnels. Divers with pressure hoses. They'll drive tunnels under the keel for the messenger wires.'

'Are youse fuckin crazy? Tunnels? It's black as the deil's erse down there, and rocks and metal wreckage to howk oot the way. Ye'll never get divers to look at that job, never.'

A month later, in early summer, Ketling stood on a pontoon and listened to the rattle of the divers' air pumps, the whine of the generator powering the undersea lights. Three support vessels lay along the ship's sides.

Two divers stood in front of him. The support team had lifted off their helmets, but they still wore muddy insulation suits and the monstrous, clogged boots of their trade. Blackish water was running off them to form pools by their feet.

'What's the progress?'

'It's the most bloody 'orrible job I ever let meself in for. I did clearing the inner basin at Devonport after the blitz, I thought Scotland would be a doddle after that. More fool me.'

The other diver, a younger man with untidy black hair, said nothing. He shuffled to the edge of the pontoon, held on to a rail and began to vomit.

'Aye, but how's the tunnel?'

'It's inch by inch. Can't see two foot in front of our noses, even with the lights. The tools are bloody useless; much of the time we're using our hands. Big stones, jaggy bits of metal. Yeah, a new pair of these sodding gauntlets doesn't last an hour, often as not. You should see the state of the lads' hands – see mine!'

'Aye, right, but how's the tunnel?'

'Given time, we'll probably get there. That's if loosening the muck down there doesn't dislodge the whole bloody ship and bring it down on top of us. *Frogface*, that's what we call 'er. Digging our own graves we are, in a manner of speaking.'

When Ketling had gone, the diver said to his mate: 'I really hate that bloke. He don't give a fuck about us. Oh, why ain't I back on Margate Sands with me little bucket and spade?'

The first tunnel to be finished reached under the ship to the port side. When a pair of four-inch messenger wires had been passed through, the support ships delicately harmonised their winches to 'saw' the wires forward towards the centre point of the hull. But an attempt to do the same with the wires in a second tunnel, near the bows, came to a standstill against massive sandstone boulders.

There was a meeting on board a support vessel. Peter, the naval officer from the Salvage Service, said: 'Look at it this way. You could never have lifted her with just two sets of cables anyway. And she's getting heavier every day with the sand drifting into her.'

Ketling said: 'I know that fine. Did I ever say two would be enough? I'm needing more wires, more tunnels.'

'How many more? Look at the cost of them.'

'Sixteen more. That's on top of the two we have already.'

'Good God, Ketling! For a start, you'd never find enough divers.'

'I'll find them.'

'And you'll have to reduce the weight. That means getting the silt out of the interior of the hull, where it's submerged. So you'll never be able to do that till you raise her. But you can't raise her till you get the silt out. Sort of checkmate, wouldn't you say?'

There was a pause. Ketling carefully took off his hat and laid it on the table. 'If ye think the only road to lighten a boat is to pump it clean, then you are ignorant. It needs said to your face, Lieutenant Commander. Ignorant! I'll be getting near a thousand tons off her in the next three weeks, all according to my plan. See, I've a job to finish here. And I won't be doing with obstruction, I'm telling you, no from the like of youse nor anyone.'

Afterwards, the retired naval surgeon who looked after the divers came and stood by Ketling. They watched the visitors' launch lift up its bow and foam off across the Firth.

'You shouldn't have been so hard on that little Peter fellow. Didn't you know he was mixed up with *Fronsac* before, back at the time of the sinking? When that Lieutenant Melville was lost overboard, naval intelligence sent him to question the family for weeks. Pointlessly, in my view.'

'Is that the case? Well, now.'

Back in Greenock, the Lieutenant Commander said: 'Get me off this job, can you? That fat bugger insulted me to my face today – said I was ignorant. If it was still wartime, I could have had him charged.'

'Well, I suppose I can see to it. But, Peter, why do you get on so many people's wicks? That's probably why you never made it to Commander.'

From Paris, two French officers arrived in Glasgow and were driven down to Dumbuck in an Admiralty staff car. One carried a briefcase with detailed design drawings of their ship. His English wasn't up to much. But Ketling pushed his thick finger back and forth across the drawings as he explained to him that the 'centre of buoyancy' – the focus of the lift – would have to be well forward of the ship's centre of gravity. This was because the wreck's bows needed to leave the bottom first, to ease her out of the trench she had dug for himself. 'Are ye with me?'

The Frenchman listened intently but made no reply. He looked again at the elevation plan of the hull. Then he went back to his briefcase and pulled out a tiny, exquisite model of a destroyer in white balsawood. He placed it on the bar. Very delicately, he raised the bow a quarter-inch and then slid the model forward and upwards until it was dangling free between his finger and thumb.

'Aye, that's right. Ye've got it! That's just the very way we'll lift her.'

The other Frenchman was more difficult. He seemed to be a naval lawyer, not an engineer. In English, he explained that he had been a member of the Court of Enquiry into the *Fronsac*'s sinking in 1940, and he had some questions.

Did Ketling know Commandant Luc le Gallois? Yes, he did, but only met him a year ago. Had two or three short conversations, about the salvage and the human remains. Did he know anything of a certain Kellerman, a French naval rating stationed on the Clyde during the war? Never heard of him.

'Now I ask you about a Polish officer, a certain Major... ehm... Chouski, Shoosky? Who lived for a time in Greenock? Here is a photograph, an old passport from Polish wartime authorities.'

'Well, I think... wee minute till I remember... I never knew his name but this looks awful like a Polish officer that came across to the wreck one day with your French Commandant. That was back in the war, before the Invasion – would have been early in 1944.'

Who else did he see with le Gallois? Nobody he could recall. Meetings were in the Fort Matilda base or on board the wreck. Why was the Polish officer with le Gallois that day, and where is he now? No idea. Maybe he was away to the war in Normandy and never made it back. 'Ye'll be wanting to see the wreck now, Captain. I'll fix a launch to take you out there so you can see how she lies.'

More divers gathered. It was a booming season for their profession. All over Europe, ports were choked with wrecks and harbour floors were sown with drowned vehicles and unexploded bombs.

Off Greenock, down in the blinding murk, the new teams of divers bored their sixteen extra tunnels under the ship. Above deck, a squad from Ketling's shipyard at Rosyth worked with oxyacetylene burners to cut away what was left of the superstructure: funnels, forecastle, gun platforms and any other projections. One salvage hand, spraying sea water to keep the metal cool, very gingerly burned open the steel plates under which the depth charges still lay in their chutes. They were shipped off down the Firth beyond Ailsa Craig and detonated. It was over thirty miles away, but the sound reached the men on *Fronsac* and rolled around the Argyll hills.

With the superstructure gone, the divers excavated the two six-ton phosphor-bronze propellers from the mud, cut them off their shafts with torches and hoisted them on to a raft. Ketling sat in his Dumbuck hotel and made fresh calculations.

The weight was now well down. But his salvage manuals required a margin of 25 per cent more lifting capacity than the weight of the wreck. With *Fronsac* still wedged deep in her underwater trench, and with an unknown load of sand and gravel inside her, that margin could be too fine for comfort.

September, month of equinoctial tides, was approaching. The pace grew desperate. The salvage crew cutting into the compartments below deck were hit by concentrations of stench and chemical fumes; several men collapsed and were carried ashore to an ambulance. But the tunnels were completed on time; the messenger wires were passed through; the pairs of giant nine-inch cables followed them and some of their slack was very delicately taken up by winches on the lifting vessels.

Jackie found the letter when she came home from school. Her name and address were in anonymous capital letters.

My Dearest Girl,
This is to invite you to the Big Lift. All is Ready. I think your Sea Studies make it one for you to remember. And maybe it will make you Proud of One who is Proud of You.

The note gave a day and a time – six in the evening – to be uplifted at Princes Pier. 'Warm clothing Advisable. Tell your grannie you will be away till morning, and not to worry herself.' Not a word about Mother. That was awkward.

Helen didn't care for the idea. But Mrs M said: 'He'll see she's safe out there, Helen. And sailors just love spoiling children.'

'She's fifteen years old, Mabel, for God's sake.'

'Well, I dare say she'll take better care of herself than you did at her age. From what I heard.'

Jackie would have liked to wear the old red tartan parka, the Canadian one. It was still almost big enough, but not quite. Her wrists stuck out foolishly, beyond the sleeves. So it was the woolly coat with horn buttons that Mother used to wear before the war. Into her pockets she put a comb, her reading spectacles and a notebook.

The launch was waiting at the pier. 'I was telt to look out for a wee girl, no a great big lassie,' said the seaman helping her to jump in. He sounded indignant, but Jackie thought he might be teasing. Why did people not say what they meant?

Out at the wreck, she was lifted up to a much larger boat alongside, with many important-looking men on board. Her father introduced her to a pair of friendly fellows in donkey jackets: 'This is Jacqueline, my oldest niece. I was hearing she studied marine science, so I told her dad she should see this. I've to take charge now, so just keep an eye on the lassie.' To Jackie, he muttered: 'Watch what ye say now. Well, ye're no stupid, so. And this'll be a long night, I'm fearing. Ta-ta for now!'

The friendly fellows were foremen from the Rosyth breaker's yard. They brought her a mug of cocoa, and found her a seat on the bench by the deckhouse window. 'See, we're waiting on the low tide – the spring tide, as low as she goes. A few minutes after eight, it turns. And then – see all the winches down here and there's a line of them on the port side too – then we draw the cables in taut. And then, just right gently, handsomely, we set to taking up the strain. And the rising tide and the lifting cables together will bring her off the ground.'

'Here's hoping,' said the older man. 'You're in luck, young lady. Nobody ever tried a lift this big before. They raised that submarine *Truculent* in one piece, but she was a bairn's bath-toy compared to this.'

'Could it go wrong?'

They both laughed. 'Your uncle's a terror for getting what he wants. But, aye, his job's on the line the day. That's if he's no done his sums right.'

'Aye, the things he's up against. See, the rise and fall of the tide at springs is nae mair'n ten foot: mebbe enough to lift her, mebbe no. And if she does rise, she could just bust in half; down where the stuff exploded, there's a nine-foot rent through the structure. And it could cheese. D'ye ken cheesing? If the hull's right weak, the lifting wires could just slice up through her. Oh aye, your uncle's a hard man, gey good at chasing the lads to get going. But, boy, he'll be sweatan blood the night.'

They sat and waited. A ferocious sunset, scarlet, gold and royal-blue, burned over the Argyll peaks to the west. The sea was flat calm, almost oily. As the light began to fade, the older man said: 'Wait and it'll get going any minute. But there's a long night in it. One, two in the morn before we know she's risen. If she's risen.'

He took out a pipe and began to stuff it from a pouch. Jackie noticed the pipe had an interesting metal lid, with perforations, and she was just about to ask about it when she heard shouting. Men were striding about the pontoons and waving a lamp from the bridge of a lifting vessel. She saw her father run across the vessel's deck and vanish down a lit-up hatchway. An enormous iron clattering rose from the winches, growing unbearably loud and then suddenly cut off into silence. Another burst of clattering, then more silence.

'That's them taking up the slack.'

Hours passed. Over and over again, the winches made their brief clamour and went quiet. Jackie fell asleep.

When she woke up, it was dark. Dirty water was pulsing out of the wreck's side but the floodlit hull didn't seem to have shifted at all. The two men from Rosyth had moved away, and a tall, thin young man with black hair was sitting beside her.

'What's your name? Okay, Jackie, I'm Malcolm and I'm a naval diver. What's your thing?'

'I'm at school yet. Studying science. Were you diving here? I like sea diving, I'm going to be a marine biologist.'

'I'm a student. Well, I will be a student. I was at Edinburgh University and had to break off. Called up to the navy, and went for the diving course; you're more independent and there's bonus money. And one day I'll get back to my Honours degree.'

'Student what like?'

'Philosophy.'

'Wow! But tell me about the diving here. Was it good?'

The young man ran his palms back and forth over his knees, and looked at his feet. She noticed the deep, half-healed scratches on the back of his hands. 'It's dark, black down there. Most times, you're just feeling forward with your hands, groping, and no hard ground to stop you losing balance. It's not so deep, but when the dive's over I get sick to my stomach, needing to boak – excuse me. And the gaffer, him with the wee red beard, no sympathy from that swine of a slave-driver, I'm telling you. Right bastard, he is – sorry for the language.'

Jackie said nothing for a while. Malcolm's hair was nice but he didn't look well at all, grey in the face, red around the eyes. Then she asked: 'What was your best time diving, Malcolm?'

'There's no best times. But I had wild times with the big bonuses last year. I was still in the navy, and we were on clearing the harbour at Kiel, in Germany. Big naval base, bombed to pieces. Great money. But I nearly lost my mind there.'

He gave her a sizing-up look. 'See, I went down to the harbour floor. And then I'm surprised: there's another diver over there already. And another, and another further off. What for did nobody tell me? So I went over to one of them. It was a dead man, a German sailor. They were all dead men, standing on the bottom with the weight of their boots, a whole crowd of them. If you took a step, they swayed towards you. Jesus! I heard that another diver went up to one of them and it put its arms round him. He went off his head after that. Aff his heid altogether.'

'O God! That's so . . . Malcolm, d'ye not get nightmares?'

'You say you like sea diving? I'll tell you something good then. The Germans at Kiel were working on something amazing – a lightweight diving gear. You just wear a mask, connected to miniature oxygen cylinders on your back, and rubber flippers on your feet. We found a set in a marine lab there.'

'So you're on your own? No airline, no lifeline, but you can stay under. How long for?'

'It near killed me. Two pals and I took it up the coast where there was depth. The cylinder seemed to be half full, by the gauge on it, so I went first – right deep, so it gets to be the same dimness all round you. Ever been that far down?'

'No, never. Not yet.'

'Lost my sense of time; it was so great feeling free under water that way. But suddenly that tight feeling. I look at the dial: Oh God, air's almost done. So up – but which way's up? I was disoriented. Every way around me was the same dark. So I do the diver thing: loosen the cylinder valve a turn. And the wee silver bubbles come rushing out – but rushing downwards.'

'Downwards?'

'Aye, I told you – I was disoriented. I looked at the bubbles and saw the air was done and thought: this is death. The mind tells you down is up: those bubbles have to be going to the surface. But your whole body's screaming: don't do it. Don't follow the bubbles down into that blackness when the light and the fresh air are behind you. Jesus, no! But you have to. So I went down, away from life into death. And in a minute there I was up again, back under the blue sky.'

Jackie said: 'That's some courage you had. I think I would have swum upwards and died.'

'My father's a minister, United Free. I told him all that and he said: "Son, that's the Conversion experience. To reach the light, you need to force yourself down into your own darkness. What looks like death is life. For our Lord God, down is up."'

'Are you believing in God?'

'He could have said just: "Son, I'm glad ye're no deid." But he never did. I do so believe in God, and I hate him.'

Malcolm turned his thin face towards Jackie. He gripped her hand painfully.

'D'ye have a boyfriend, Jackie?'

She tried to free her arm, but he wouldn't let go.

'Is there a fella you're going out with, regular, you know?'

'Shucks, Malcolm, I'm only fifteen.'

He grinned in a sad way that frightened her. Maybe he too had been driven aff his heid like the diver in Kiel. Maybe . . . she saw her father coming towards her across the cabin and managed not to shout 'Dad!'

Malcolm dropped her hand and walked away without looking back. 'That laddie's a wee nyaff,' said Ketling. 'Aye blethering and girning. Does a fair good shift, though.'

Jackie hadn't seen him smiling before. Or not broadly, as if he meant it.

'She's coming up out of it! She's rising just the way I said she would. Give it another hour, when the tide's full, and she'll be there.' He was going to say more, but the winches roared out and drowned his voice.

Dawn came. A clear, sunny morning began. But the chill night air was still in the cabin as Jackie woke from under a navy blanket; even with the blanket and Helen's coat, she was shivering.

A mug of tea was on the table for her, next to her father's clipboard.He sat beside her on the bench, spooning sugar into the mug and pushing it towards her. This seemed odd to Jackie, still half asleep. Had she ever in her life seen him proffering tea instead of accepting it? She took a searing sip and winced.

'Come out on deck, my girl. And see this.'

The dripping hulk towered above them. Now upright in the water, the creature which had been *Fronsac* had become a huge blind platform, stripped of all the funnels and features which had made it a ship. In the early morning light, raw surfaces glittered where superstructure had been burned away. The sides were shaggy with green and black seaweed. Now Jackie could see the dark rent near the bows which ran down to the waterline.

Ketling went off to the pontoons. His hat was on again, and she could see him checking his clipboard and pointing to the men around him. Two of them were wanting to shake his hand, but he shouldered past them.

She pressed the mug to her belly, feeling its warmth through the coat.

'That'll be you wanting back to Princes Pier now,' said the older Rosyth man, leaning on the rail beside her.

'Is it over now? Is it done?'

'Aye, it's done. She's in a couple of foot of sand, no more. We'll get a patch on her side now she's above water, hose out a bittie more silt, and then she'll float. Take her in tow and away to the breakers.'

'What happens then?'

'Sky's the limit for your uncle now. Boy, they said the big man coudny dae it and he done it. What happens then? Knock her apart for scrap, that's what happens. Could be across the way at Smith and Houstons. Could be round in the Gare Loch, at the Faslane yard.'

'And then?'

'Then it's into the railway trucks with the metal and away to Lanarkshire to the steel mills. Why, are you wanting a souvenir?'

He reached into a pocket. 'See, here's a French navy button. Out of the crew accommodation where the fire was; some poor bugger's no needing it. Wee minding of your uncle's big day, eh?'

From the launch, she looked back across the Firth as Greenock grew larger ahead. *Fronsac* shrank in the distance, from a ship's hull to a dark coffin lifted from the grave. Jackie dropped the button over the side.

When I switched on the hall light, to get a better look at the men at the door, they both stepped back a pace.

One was stubby and sullen-looking, with an untidy moustache. The other was elongated and officer-like; he smiled at me. A black car waited.

'You do speak English? Well done! Major Szczucki, we want to ask you some questions.'

I noticed that he could pronounce my name. I was meant to notice.

'Who are you? Police?'

'No, no, we're on the legal side of the military, so to speak.'

Did he expect me to believe him?

'Come in, then.'

'We'd prefer you to come with us. Goodness, you don't need to pack a bag. Not like that at all.'

I thought the car would take us to Glasgow, maybe even to London. But instead it wove round the back of town to a bungalow on the Inverkip Road. Perfectly clean, perfectly empty. But somebody had turned on an electric fire in the front room. It was still daylight, but the chintz curtains were drawn.

It was the stubby man who took charge. I watched him adjust his expression from 'sullen' to 'concerned'. As he spoke, he leaned his head to one side, miming sympathy.

A check on my name, rank, age, service record.

'You applied for repatriation to Poland. Right. You must be one of the very few officers who did. Something you don't like over here?'

'No.'

'Some trouble you might want to get away from?'

I said nothing.

'The French authorities want to talk to you, don't they. Badly. About your wartime friend Albert Kellerman.'

'I know all about that. Friend? I never even met him. That statement is lies, fairy story.'

'How do you know there was a statement? Who showed it to you?'

'A French officer told me about it.' The long man was scribbling.

'Kellerman only wrote that because they said they would shoot him if he didn't cooperate.'

'But Major, he wasn't the only person who said there was something fishy about the loss of the *Fronsac*. And about how Lieutenant Melville disappeared. By the way, when did you last see Eric Kent?'

'Who? Eric? But I saw his murder. I was chief witness at the trial. You know that perfectly well.'

'He left a lot of interesting notes behind. Nothing completed, but we are working on them. What do you think really happened to Lieutenant Melville? And where is he now? A little hint? I promise you it'll go no further.'

'He's dead. I went to his funeral and he's dead.'

'Well, he doesn't seem to be in his coffin. Bits of other people are. Wonder where he went.'

The stubby man considered me. 'Feel like a cigarette? Want a break?'

'No!'

'Funny that you were on the spot at Abercultie when Eric was killed. But of course you had already been in contact with Wuttke, the chap who stabbed him, for quite a time. True?'

'I interrogated him once. With British officers. That's all.'

'When Eric was dead, did you feel a tiny bit relieved?'

'Why should I? How can you ask?'

The questions went on, or, rather, went round and round, repeated with changing emphasis. The early winter night came, and the tall man rose and switched on a standard lamp.

At about six, they made a pause. Both men stood up. The small one went out, and we could hear the banging of a raised toilet seat. The lean, lengthy man lit a cigarette and offered one to me. This time I took it.

'*Słuchaj, Panie Majorze* ...' He was speaking Polish, with a very English inflection. His father had emigrated before the war, he said, to work as an art restorer for some English earl with a country palace.

'Listen, Major ... you can see how things are building up. Obviously we know more than we have shown you today. More than the French do, in fact. You aren't being cooperative, and I don't blame you. But ask yourself: do you have a future here? Either we or the Poles will have to hand you over to the French. And even if you come out of the French justice system in one piece, it will be our turn to hold you while we consider charges.'

'Charges? You can't be serious. You can't really believe that I had anything to do with Eric Kent's death. Or with Kellerman's fantasy about amateur Fascists?'

He was standing and looking down on me. I jumped to my feet and faced him.

'You have applied to go back to Poland. I don't quite know why, but that's for your own conscience. Obviously, we can stop you leaving, and we will. But on the other hand... Major, would you just calm yourself and stand away from me? Thank you.'

He went on: 'But that doesn't quite have to be the end of the story. You never know: some reason for us to stall the French could turn up. So you could find yourself on that boat after all. And to be honest, that might suit us much better. It really does depend on you.'

I heard a chain rattle and a flush. The other man came back into the room. The two nodded at one another. Slowly, we all sat down again.

When he had pulled out a pipe and lit it – that maddening British silence between tamping down tobacco and finally waving a dying match in the air – the small man leaned back.

'We could talk about a sort of gentlemen's agreement. D'you have any idea of what I'm driving at?'

I did.

'But he can't divorce me,' Helen said. 'Not if he's dead.' Heads down in the rain, we were walking along the Esplanade. Hugh lay in the pram which Mabel had once used to wheel the infant Johnston.

'Helen Melville doesn't need a divorce. Why can't you remember she's dead too? … And we can say Helen Douglas's birth certificate got burned in the blitz. Then we could marry in the registry.'

'Third time lucky, huh? How could I pass for a wee Polish countess? I'd be better off with Craig's godly folk in Ontario, even though I scunner them. And you'd be better off staying here than howking big stanes out the rubble in Warsaw.'

'Helen, I've explained all that. I'm not staying to rot in a cell for some spy-novel shite left behind by Eric. Or because I helped Johnston to walk free. It's him should be getting chased, not me.'

'Okay, okay. If I said yes, I'd become stateless same as you, right?'

'No, Helen, listen! Once we register over there, you become Polish citizen married to another Polish citizen. Yes, you lose British passport as wife of a foreigner: it's British law. But you'd never be stateless.'

'Are there any houses left in Poland? Was it all not flattened in the war?'

'We'll be in a different part. They call it the Recovered Territories, where the Germans were. We'll be getting a fine, warm German house for free, with maybe a garden. More modern than other regions: better roads, more electricity, and there's state aid for the settlers coming in. Schools for Hughie when he's older . . .'

'It's all daft. Why am I even thinking on it? How would it be with you out all day and me no speaking a word of the language?'

'Neighbours are so friendly in Poland. They'll help you to manage. You'll soon learn how to ask for things.'

'Aye, that'll be right – just perfect! I wonder. And that's you who said he never needed a home.'

'I never meant it that way.'

'Ya did so.'

'I did not!'

'Ya did sot!' We both started to laugh. She pushed wet hair off her cheek.

'There's us talking like we was five-year-old weans. See now, Mike, I'll think about it. If it wasn't you, I'd be dumping this whole scheme of yours away in a second. Me and Hughie in Poland, for God's sake! Just tell me this: if I didna like it, I could come back here, right?'

'And walk out on me? Of course. But please don't.'

That night, I went wandering. The Tontine didn't fit my mood; I walked on until I found myself outside the Auchmar Vaults.

In a dark corner, I stared into my pint of heavy until a man came to sit beside me.

'They was asking after ye. The men from London, that wanted the coffin lifted.'

I recognised Dougie, the undertakers' man at Johnston's 'funeral' all those years ago.

'I telt them: "Ye'll no find him in there, just bits of other poor bastards." I said: "See, we filled up the box, gave it weight, for the family's sake." Mister, are you going with Helen the widow now? I heard ye were.'

I said that I was. I hoped to take her back to Poland with me.

'I kent her as a lassie, Helen Houston. They came frae Cartsdyke and stayed in the next close to us up in Hope Street. Most days I saw her, and she was aye laughing, that's before her mother died. Boy, a big coarse laugh she had. The wife would be telling me: "Get that Helen to hold her row or I'll go crazy."'

I wished he would leave me alone. But he said: 'Youse Poles is all away hame now. High time ye went. But you's taking wur daughters with ye. The flowers o' Scotland, wur bonny women, away tae Poland to be your Polish wives. In a fuckan Communist country. Mister, I had a few drinks, right, so nae hard feelings. Excuse me. But I'm telling you: Helen Houston will be greetan bitter tears, day and night, in thon dreich land of yours. And I hate that. I truly hate it.'

When he put on his cap and swayed towards the street door, I stayed in my corner. I wanted to get Dougie out of my head. But instead, as I stood up to buy myself a whisky, his words were replaced by all the warning words that le Gallois and Wisia and Helen had used about me. Passive, wary of human contact, aimless.

So was this not, in fact, the first positive decision I had ever taken in my life? To marry Helen, if that obstinate creature would consent, and remove with her and the baby to a new life in a new Poland?

Easy to say: no choice. That faced with destruction in either a French or British prison, Poland was my only chance. So was this just another flight, another escape? The only decisions I had made before were negative ones: fleeing from school, fleeing from home, fleeing from Wisia's love. But this was different, I told myself. Surely this was positive. Surely I was seizing command of my life at last.

But why, then, had I lied to Helen? Those welcoming neighbours, those nice clean houses waiting for us? Well, not quite lies. I wanted to believe that a new, democratic Poland might soon be like that. It was a picture framed by some of the new government's publicity. But by now I had also been told about the trains, trucks and carts crammed with families expelled from their eastern homes, already pouring into the Recovered Territories. What would be left for us?

And I wanted to dispel the conversation with the two gentlemen in the bungalow. Easy! I would simply play along with their 'gentlemen's agreement' in order to get clear of Britain and France, and then I would ignore it. And they hadn't precisely asked me to be a spy. Merely to let a certain somebody know when I had a permanent address. Then nothing. Just wait until you are contacted again. No more. But I still felt dirty. And uneasy about questions which I could neither avoid nor answer.

What had happened to Tadek? Were there still boys fighting 'in the forest', and were the British still secretly helping them? I forced myself to hope that, as returning soldiers, we would be welcomed by the new coalition government, but I wasn't so sure about how the Communists would react to us.

Le Gallois had told me that one's decisions had to be authentic, like a painting. I admitted that my act of will still had some suspect brush strokes. These were my feelings about the 'gentlemen's agreement', about my own politics, about marrying Helen, about the meaning of 'home'.

I saw that I was diving down into a darkness. But I would make that dive. There had to be a place of light beyond.

'Hughie, speak English when you talk to Mama!'

He was a sturdy child. So he should be: a Scots-Canadian by blood. And yet when he stood before me in the kitchen, legs planted apart, I thought that he already looked like a native. With his blond hair and greenish-grey eyes, he could be Polish, apart from the Fair Isle jersey Mrs M had knitted for him before we left.

'Why doesn't she learn to talk like me?'

'What's he saying, Mike?'

I translated. Helen finished loading coal briquettes into the stove, and sat down at the table.

'He's aye asking that. And he understands English fine. Well, but for how long? He'll lose it altogether if you go on learning him Polish.'

'The boy just wants to be like the other children. And he's going to be clever, the way he's picking the language up.'

'What else is he picking up, for God's sake? I've no way of knowing. And when will the Embassy in Warsaw answer your letter? It's two months now.'

Mrs Papadakis came into the kitchen, followed by her thin, wordless daughter. Refugees from the Greek civil war, the family shared the house with us and a Polish widow with two small boys. Each family had one room for sleeping and living. We shared the kitchen and the vandalised bathroom.

Like many German houses, this one had a washroom cellar underneath, with a separate entrance in the overgrown garden. Who might be hiding there overnight – migrating families on the road from the east, Czech smugglers with black-market chewing gum, even terrified Germans who had missed the deportation trains? We could never be sure.

The house first assigned to me in this small town had turned out to be occupied. Refugees from what was now Soviet Lithuania crowded out on to the steps as we arrived and shouted abuse. For several bad moments, they thought Helen was a German trying to reclaim her home, and a man still wearing tattered uniform brought out a revolver. In the end a room was found for us elsewhere, in what had once been a handsome villa before its owners were chased out and its contents looted.

The bath tub had been wrenched out and lay on its side in the garden; the locks and handles on all the doors had been cut away and replaced by loops of twine threaded through the holes. There were no beds. But I surprised myself – never 'good with my hands' – by buying a collapsed cart from a neighbour and sawing it up into planks which I nailed together into a bed frame. Why didn't I buy the horse too? The neighbour was puzzled; the little mare had pulled him and his wife and furniture all the way from Ukraine.

Helen had been merry on board the old liner which took

returning ex-soldiers back to Poland. We had secured a new birth certificate for Helen without too many lies, and we were married on a wet spring morning in Glasgow. Knowing what they knew about Helen's marriages, we did not embarrass Jackie or Mrs M by inviting them, and a hotel porter served as witness.

On the ship, there was a crowd of young Scottish women, several of them mill girls from Pitnechtan, all war brides steaming towards an unreadable future. At thirty-four, Helen was the oldest, but by the time we docked at Gdynia she had merged into their happy, raucous gang. Before we filed ashore, the girls all swore that they would keep in touch, that they would never forget one another.

When we reached the small once-German town where we were to live, it was late summer. Helen was not laughing now. She had seen what remained of Danzig, now Gdańsk, after British bombs and Soviet arson had done their work, and with Hughie on her knee she was silent on the long lorry journey to the west. Our town was 'recovering'. Many buildings round the market square were still fire-blackened shells, but trains were running and the German street names had been torn down and replaced. At the corner by our scarred suburban villa, Nazi 'Schlageterstrasse' had become Communist 'Dzierzyńskiego', named for the Bolsheviks' first head of police terror.

'Both shameless murderers,' said the Polish widow from upstairs, when I met her one day on the corner. I looked around to see who might have overheard. I think it was the first time I did that, and it made me angry with myself.

I found a job in the town's finance office. As almost nobody was registered yet, and none of the incomers had any intention of paying tax, there was not much to do but look out of the window at the faded red-white banner over the market square. It read 'Long Live the July Manifesto' – the first proclamation of the pro-Soviet government.

Helen worked fiercely to clean the villa, carry water in pails when the pipes choked, and clear a space in the garden's underbrush for a back green where clothes and sheets could be dried. I went with her to the market where, as well as looted German cutlery and old uniforms, it was often possible to buy ham or smoked sausage in those first years before the shortages set in. But most of the cooking was done by exuberant Mrs Papadakis. She knew other Greeks who had a way of getting rice.

Mrs Papadakis adored Hughie. He took her fondling placidly, but he preferred the company of the two Polish lads, who were older and soon appropriated the Dinky Toy cars he had brought with him. In our first month, I arranged for him to join a playgroup organised by nuns. A community resettled from some Ukrainian convent, they had set themselves up in a red-brick Protestant church previously used as a Soviet officers' club. The Sisters smiled at Helen when she brought Hughie round, and one old nun tried speaking French to her. 'Double Dutch to me,' said Helen afterwards. 'And how do they all drink tea out of glasses, with no milk?'

I soon knew it was not going to work. Helen took longer. I realised for the first time how naturally gregarious she was, thriving among the kids in the Hope Street close, the typing pool at Kincaid's, the boys on the base in Manitoba, the young wives on the ship. Helen did not really understand the brutality of the political upheaval around us; she still assumed it was vaguely the same as what the British called 'socialism'. But she couldn't learn the language and she hated the food – even the rare luxuries I sometimes brought back ('that cream's gone sour-like!').

The one domestic thing she did know about was poverty and the vigour needed to drive back encroaching dirt, cold and vermin. She found it baffling that Polish women envied her, treating her as if she were a millionaire visitor from a planet of luxury.

Helen was valiant in those first months. I watched her struggling to wash a blanket in the kitchen sink, and then I imagined this same woman guiding a four-engined bomber down through darkness and battering winds to a half-seen runway. When would she admit how lonely and how bored she was becoming? What had I done?

I had never been married, nor even lived with a woman for more than a few days in some small Paris hotel. But my solitude lacked integrity. I liked to feel alone but within easy reach of others, in company but not part of that company. I knew perfectly well that when Helen decided to face her own unhappiness and reached out to me for reassurance, I would fail her.

The break came one day in autumn. I came home to find Helen sitting with Hughie on her knee, while Mrs Papadakis rubbed some sort of herbal paste into eczema blisters which had spread over his chest and arms.

'It's no getting any better. And he's coughing. Mike, he needs properly seen to. And what's this the nuns sent him home with?'

It was a rosary, wrapped up in a letter which pointed out the fate awaiting an unbaptised infant if it died. The Sisters were concerned about Hughie's unsanctified presence among Christian children, but the community's priest was ready to perform the necessary sacrament as soon as possible.

'Religion? Purgatory, before he's even three years old?' Helen's eyes were full of angry tears. 'Mike, I need to get home with him. Just a wee break, maybe for Christmas with his Grannie Melville and Jackie, and a proper doctor to him. And that goes for me too, Mike. I cannae take this place any more, I'm telling you. I'm sorry for it, but Mike, I want out.'

She was crying now. Hughie, alarmed, joined in. Mrs Papadakis lifted him on to her own lap and tried to mop Helen's face with the herbal-paste cloth.

I applied for an exit visa on Helen's new Polish passport. Weeks passed: no response. I wrote to the British Embassy in Warsaw, begging them to offer Helen an entry visa and assist her on compassionate grounds, although she was no longer a British subject. But months went by, snow fell, a Polish winter began, and there was no sign that my letter had even reached Warsaw.

In November, the nuns congratulated Hughie on St Hugh's Day but suggested that he should find a different playgroup for Lutherans and Jews somewhere else in the town. On the BBC, we heard that the leader of the Opposition had been forced to escape from Poland in the boot of a diplomat's car. In November, a parade in the ruined market square carried posters celebrating the Bolshevik Revolution and Comrade Stalin.

Hughie celebrated his third birthday; neighbouring children came with cakes and admired his remaining Dinky Toys. Their mothers asked once again if Helen was German, and whether she knew where the Germans had buried their gold before they left. We stopped making love, not only because Hughie slept in the same room.

It was the week before Christmas. There had been a power cut all day, and an oil lamp was glowing in the kitchen as Helen read *Orlando the Marmalade Cat* to Hughie. Mrs M had sent him the picture book, in a parcel with two packets of tea.

'See the funny wee puss in trousers!' I heard a car outside in our street, still something unusual, and went to the window. An old pre-war Fiat with the plates of a Warsaw taxi had stopped at the kerb. A small woman in an enormous brown fur hat emerged and stood uncertainly in the snow.

She looked up and our eyes met. Running out, I took her hand and guided her up the broken steps and into the warm kitchen. I could hear cars revving their engines not far away, but there was nobody in the street to see her. I said: 'Margaret, this is Helen, my wife. And Hughie. And what – how – this is unbelievable!'

The two women studied one another. 'Remember I told you about Margaret? The castle where I broke my ankle?'

'In my castle, tea's all I have to offer,' said Helen.

Margaret accepted and sat down. She glanced round the kitchen without commenting, then turned back to me.

'Mike, I can't stay, it's all a bit mad but I'm with the Embassy in Warsaw. Have been for months. Brits who speak Polish are pretty thin on the ground.'

'Tadek – anyone know what became of him?'

'Okay, he's okay. Tell you another day.'

'So you came all this way, just about Helen's visa?'

'Well, no, not that. Sorry, but there's not much we can do. Don't even have the right to contact her, if she's not a British subject.'

'But she's here, you have just contacted her!'

'No, it's you I came to contact.'

There was a silence. Helen and I stared at her.

'Mike, don't be such a dope. Don't you remember – "somebody will contact you"? Is there another room where we can talk?'

'No! But I'll leave you to it.' Helen gathered up the book and the boy.

'Margaret, so you are the "somebody"! But then you aren't really a diplomat. You...'

We both heard another car draw up outside, and then another. The sound of running steps in the snow. Margaret had time to clutch my sleeve and say: 'Oh God, I'm so sorry, Oh God, they must have...' before the men raced up the steps and crowded into the kitchen.

I don't recall it very clearly. Leather jackets, two uniforms. The Polish woman from upstairs beginning to scream and sob. They shouted 'Where's your transmitter? Where's your gun?' Helen ran back into the kitchen as they began to hit me. I yelled in English: 'Get out, get back to our room', but she tried to kick one of the men in uniform and took a backhander across the face that flung her against the wall.

Margaret was waving her diplomatic passport as she was bundled out of the house and into a car. The other raiders began a house search, tearing out the kitchen drawers and emptying them on the floor. I saw Mrs Papadakis holding Hughie against her leg and stroking his hair; she looked back at me grimly, without compassion. As they handcuffed me and shoved me towards the door, I called to her: 'Look after her, look after the boy!'

She nodded slightly. Helen was sitting on the kitchen floor, knees drawn up, a bloody handkerchief to her nose. Our eyes did not meet as they took me out. It was many years before I saw her again.

Solitary confinement was not the worst. I hardly remember it as a place, a cell; there was nothing to remember. If I had been younger, it might have destroyed me. But at the outset I looked carefully at my single bleeding wound: fear and guilt about Helen and the small boy. I looked and, seeing that there was nothing I could do about it, made myself consider the wound as a deep slash, perhaps in my thigh, which would scab over and cease hurting if I kept my fingers off it.

Some people can command their dreams. I had a routine of exercises on the cell floor, pre-selected day-dreaming and mental gymnastics, and then self-directed sleep from which nightmares were banned. But the censorship was not completely vigilant,

I'll admit. Very often, in day-dream or night-dream, I saw a burning ship slowly twisting in pain, or a dead ship enlaced by rushing, indifferent water.

Prison was horrible and foul, but the best word is 'wretched'. The horror stopped after some time, the foulness came to seem unremarkable, but I remained for those years something less than fully human: a wretch.

The first interrogators, in the first weeks, wanted to know about Captain Tadeusz Ostrowski – Tadek. They knew we had been close, trained together to parachute into Poland. What had his mission been? What was mine now?

On the pretext of helping to liberate the country from the Germans, they assured me, his real purpose had been to set up an anti-Soviet spy and terrorist network. Equally obviously, my mission was to make contact with agent Ostrowski and his sabotage ring. When and where? Where was the transmitter I must have brought from London? Why did Lady Campbell visit me from the British Embassy in Warsaw?

They were telling me, in effect, that Tadek had escaped. In return, I tried offering a version of the truth: I had no idea where he was, I had come back in good faith to rebuild my country, Margaret was just an old friend from Scotland. They scoffed. No, they didn't torture in the classical sense – electrodes, fingernails, that stuff. But they hit me with fists and sticks, then left me naked in an unheated cell in the Polish winter. They did that several times, for a day and a night each time.

They were amateurs, really. In the years that followed, experienced fellow prisoners shook their heads and laughed: no professional would interrogate a *Figurant*, a suspect, straight after torture or the ice-box treatment. How could anything reliable be gained? But after the last 'refrigeration' I was wrapped in a blanket and hustled upstairs to the interrogation room. There some fool offered me a cigarette and I passed out on the floor in front of them before they had a chance to ask a question.

There were usually three or four of them. One, a young fair-haired officer, wore Soviet uniform with a row of medals and the others deferred to him. He never spoke in my presence, but took notes. After my last appearance, I was carried to a new cell in the prison sickbay and woke up one afternoon to find this man sitting beside me.

'I don't speak Russian.'

'No problem, I'm as Polish as you are. Why this uniform? Very complicated story, which began long ago in Moscow. But I have something to show you.'

It was a bedraggled little document, clearly German. A sheet of paper enclosing it seemed to be a Russian translation. Opening it, I saw that it was a Nazi soldier's *Wehrpass*, in the name of Hans Nuttgen. It was the document I had pulled out of the German tunic Johnston Melville had been wearing, one wet day in Pitnechtan. It was the paybook which I had passed on to Tadek and his fake-papers team, in the secret camp up the road so very long ago. I felt its worn texture, and couldn't speak.

'Ostrowski was carrying it when we arrested him. A Nazi identity pass.'

'Because he thought he would be fighting Germans with our partisans. It would get him through checkpoints...'

'I know that. You know that. But the old bitch who is president of the court will use it for one of her death sentences, when he's caught again. Where is he, by the way?'

I said nothing.

'Our view is that hanging and shooting for this sort of thing has become counter-productive. Some of the Polish comrades don't agree. We'll have to deal with them, but it's delicate.'

He pulled the *Wehrpass* out of my fingers and slipped it carefully into his briefcase. 'I wonder if we could arrange to lose this. Returned to Moscow, retained for analysis ... something like that. What do you say?'

'Why ask me?'

He looked at me. I must have been a repellent sight: bruised and leaking eyes, missing some teeth, bald-shaven. But his look was calm.

'You'll get life, not death – I can see to that, because of the uniform I'm wearing. It'll mean a few bad years. I know the real reason you came back to Poland: not to be a capitalist saboteur, but because of that nonsense about the French ship. But I think there was something else, too. Something you and I share, Szczucki. I'm talking to you about hope for our *ojczyzna* – our country. And I don't mean Russia.'

He lowered his eyes. 'There are terrible years ahead. The people who are taking absolute power now are scoundrels, who get their orders from ... somewhere else. But even in the Party, there are still many of us who think differently. And our day will come.'

He rose to go. 'I don't need to say this. One word to anyone about this conversation, and I will see that the Moscow friends

– not the Polish comrades – transfer you to a place beyond the Arctic Circle.'

'My wife? Can you help her?'

But he left the cell without turning round.

I am still not sure of his real name. But much later I met other convicts who had been in the Home Army and were interrogated in the same prison. They talked about a man they nicknamed 'Fox', a Pole in Soviet NKVD uniform.

'They say he turned informer against other Polish prisoners, in one of the Pechora camps in the Soviet Union. So they made him an NKVD captain and Soviet citizen, the son of a bitch. Guess what I'll do with those medals, if I ever see him again...'

I did see him again. It was after the terrible years. They came, but there were not so many of them and their weight – police terror, lies, hunger – fell mostly on people outside. I was inside. After receiving my life sentence for plotting anti-state activities, there was time spent in a filthy but adequately heated prison built in the Tsarist years. Then forced labour in coal mines, the construction of a sulphur works, building a dam in the Tatra foothills. At my age, in my forties with a limp, I usually ended up doing storeman's work, with a stove in the background, rather than outdoor manual labour.

When I saw him again, Stalin was long dead. A year after that happy event, somebody put me on a list for revision of political sentences. A year later still, pallid but free, I was allocated a tiny room in Warsaw and a job translating articles for a foreign-language magazine. In the office, I drank vodka with rowdy young journalists who jeered at Soviet art and listened to American jazz on Radio Free Europe.

Everybody was angry. Everything was coming apart. Men and women long given up for dead came walking from the east with tiny rucksacks, staring at the new buildings.

Everything forbidden had meaning. One evening I went to a cellar-club where a boy was reading Spinoza aloud to the music of a saxophone, while a girl student stood on a table and gravely stripped her clothes off. Upstairs, on the street, long queues were waiting for special editions at the newspaper kiosks. Hungary was in revolution. Soviet tanks were said to be on the move towards our own cities.

It was the next day that I saw him. Half a million people with Hungarian flags and Polish flags had come to the marble plain outside the Palace of Culture. They were singing; they wanted to attack, to burn. They cheered our new Party leader as he shouted in his shrill old voice that all our internal affairs would now be decided only by ourselves, and that Comrade Khrushchev had agreed. They cheered, but then chanted 'Budapest! Budapest!' As they chanted, I suddenly saw my old interrogator.

His blond hair was parted in the middle now, and he wore a patriotic red-white armband. Standing on the plinth beside the new leader, in a row of unfamiliar faces, he seemed to be laughing with joy and excitement.

I asked a journalist: 'Who's that?'

'That's Witold Kaniewski. Incredible man! He took over the press section of the Central Committee today. He's going to abolish all censorship tomorrow. Witek, Witek!'

He glanced towards us, but I don't suppose he saw me. The October evening was growing dark. The newspapers did indeed print what they pleased for about a year. But then the new leader brought back censorship, and the security police resumed their duties. Kaniewski, if that was his true name, lost his job and was expelled from the Party. He hung around the Warsaw cafés for a few months, then vanished for ever.

A few years ago, I met a visiting Warsaw editor who had worked under him during that 'Polish October', and I mentioned my own memories. He became furious: it was inconceivable that Witek could ever have been a Soviet intelligence officer. But just the other day I told the story to the young Pole who runs Greenock's best sports shop. 'So what? Who gives a fuck? All those Communists were Russian agents anyway.'

When it seemed safe, I went to the British Embassy. For a time, after that October, it was not too hard to get a passport to go to the West, so I applied for a British visa. But I had other questions to which the Embassy might have answers and, although the Consulate staff grew impatient with me, a very young, pink-faced diplomat eventually trotted downstairs to see what I wanted.

He had never heard of a Margaret Beaton-Campbell on the Embassy staff. I said that perhaps she hadn't been exactly a diplomat. He gave me a helpful smile but said that he wasn't sure what I meant. Anyway, nobody of that name had been around in his time.

I asked about British war brides. Instantly, he brightened up (he was a nice boy, really). What a story that had been! As years of police terror set in, soldiers who had returned from the West had been arrested, leaving their young Scottish and English wives abandoned in distant villages – often pregnant or with tiny children, not speaking Polish, penniless and treated as spies by local Party officials. But because they had given up their British citizenship in order to marry foreigners, the Embassy had no right to help or even to contact them.

'So the Embassy raised hell back home, we really did – got a lot of MPs on our side. The girls' families were often their constituents, after all. Anyway, the Labour government rushed through a new Nationality Act making the wives British subjects again, so we could get out there and help them. And our chaps went whizzing about those frightful roads in Embassy cars, clutching wads of new British passports. Wish I'd seen that, but it was all before my time.'

Yes, he could probably find out about Helen, if nobody had thrown the papers away yet. Take a day or so.

But the truth was that I knew already what had happened to Helen. When I was released, I had written to Mabel Melville in Greenock, and after several months a letter from her told me that Jackie was at Glasgow University but that Helen and Hughie were in Canada. I wrote to the Ontario address she gave me, and eventually an oversize postcard of Niagara Falls came back to Warsaw.

She was working as manageress in a Toronto hotel. Hughie was big and a fair devil at the hockey. I couldn't imagine the 'fun and games in that town of yours before my exit', but that must wait till she saw me. But she didn't say when or where that might be, and she answered my long next letter only with a musical Christmas card which hoped I was keeping well and warm. Somebody had damaged the card when opening the envelope to see if it contained dollars, and its music was only a rusty yelp which reminded me of Helen's laugh.

So I knew the basics: Helen had gone, from this country and from me. But I somehow needed to see her footprint, the paperwork of her departure, all that remained to prove that we had really been here together.

When I went back to the Embassy, it was a different, middle-aged man who was waiting for me. He was civil rather than friendly. But the papers he showed me said that Helen Szczucka-Douglas, aged thirty-eight, had been issued with a British passport for herself and her son in February 1949 and had been assisted by the Consulate with a train fare later that month.

I thanked him. 'No, don't go just yet. I hear you were asking for a Margaret Beaton-Campbell. Can you tell me why you are interested in her?'

'An old friend. From my time in Scotland in the war.'

'Oh, but didn't you run into her later? In this country, for instance?'

I knew now what was coming, and what he was. I said: 'Once. It was in 1947.'

'Yes, well. But now you want to leave, go back to the UK. Are you quite sure about that? I think we could find you some interesting work here, not badly paid either.'

'I am absolutely sure. I don't want to stay.'

'Well, understandable after what you have been through. Still . . . look, here's a telephone number. Just in case you change your mind, eh?'

Some anxious weeks followed. But the visa was granted, I heard nothing more of the middle-aged man, and on a lovely May morning the train growled reluctantly across the girders of the Spree bridge into West Berlin. In the station, the *Bahnhof Zoo*, I jumped out and ran to a stall and bought a real banana. Everything smelled different. I felt weightless, child-like.

Edinburgh? From the Waverley steps I saw it hadn't changed much. The trams were gone from Princes Street and a few shops had grown fragile glass walls. But the scent of breweries still came on the west wind, past the black fang of the Castle and its rock. And on the pavements, the usual dignified crazies were performing.

I noticed a perfectly well-dressed man crying and shouting to himself and waving his arms. Further off was a grave fellow equipped for the Flanders trenches in tin hat, gas cape and puttees: his khaki pack and water bottle dangling. I remembered him well.

To cross Princes Street I had to pass close to the noisy, weeping man. He snatched at my sleeve. I freed myself, but as I glanced into this face ugly with tears, I realised that it was me that he had been shouting at so madly, for so long. 'You dear idiot, are you deaf or blind? Is it really you, Maurycy?'

Tadek had grown a big brown moustache and wore a brown

felt hat; he looked like a British country gent. I wept too. We held each other.

'Come on now, what will the Morningside ladies think we are? Meg is over there, in Fuller's. We both saw you as you came out of the station.'

Margaret's embrace smelled like Elysium, or Harrods in London. 'God, darling, your clothes – you look like an east European refugee. Well, of course you are one.' She hadn't changed: still slim, maybe redder in those healthy cheeks.

They told me Tadek's story, as we sat at the back of Fuller's. All around us, ladies had draped their fur coats over chairs. The Edinburgh coffee tasted expensive but weak. Margaret ordered dry little rock cakes which made me cough, but I reached for more of them. I hadn't eaten that day.

Tadek had been freed by those guerrilla 'locals' Margaret had told me about. They ambushed the police convoy taking him to Warsaw, blew up a road bridge to slow pursuers and gave him a pouch of gold coins. With the money ('they had a bloody sack of Swiss twenty-franc pieces!') Tadek had paid to be smuggled over the mountains into Czechoslovakia, where the British consul in Pilsen helped him into the American zone of Germany. All arranged by Margaret and her underground contacts from Warsaw, where she had been not really a diplomat.

'Still a bit hush, even after all this time.'

Next came a plate of sugar-dusted shortbread fingers.

'What then?'

'Well, as soon as Tadzio was out, I mean in London, I resigned. They didn't like that a bit, but ... anyway, we rushed back here and got married in Forfar, and now Tadzio is the laird of Balbrudie. All done up now, that floor mended, even some heating. Tadzio is so good at finding plumbers . . . But now you have to come and stay. Helen in Canada? But that boy wasn't yours, right?'

Then Tadek wanted my own story. So I told it. Afterwards they looked at one another. She took his hand – not mine.

'Tadzio, I was only doing my job, you know. I just wasn't good at that side of it. If I'd seen we were being followed, I would have turned back. If I had known . . .'

'Time for lunch,' said Tadek. We walked in silence to Frederick Street. 'The Apéritif is the only place these days. And there's another surprise waiting for you.'

When we entered, the white-haired and magnificent head waiter slapped the menu against a table with a crack which made the diners start and glance up at him. He advanced on me as if I were an apprentice advocate daring to challenge his judgement.

'At ease, Szczucki.'

'Colonel!'

We arranged to meet each other in the restaurant next morning, before the first clients arrived. 'He's not the only one,' said Tadek, as we waited for our fresh River Add salmon. 'Our old *Baca* – our "shepherd" – yes, General Maczek himself. He's working as barman in a hotel near the Dean Bridge. No pension, and he's declared a traitor in Poland. But you should see the old warriors who visit him at the Learmonth – Brits, Canadians, Americans as well as our own lot. They salute him before they order a whisky.'

When Tadek went off to find my Colonel and pay the bill, I had to ask Margaret a question. Were her old employers still interested in me?

'God, no! The idea was to fit you into a network out there. But when you were arrested, obviously they dropped you like a hot brick. That's how it goes, I'm afraid.'

'They were going to hand me over to the French, if I didn't do what they wanted.'

'Oh Maurycy, honestly! All that was just to get you to go back to Poland. They didn't mean a word of it. All forgotten now, anyway.'

In the afternoon, I went to see a lady at a Polish charity and asked how to apply for political asylum. She gave me a typed sheet of instructions, and the address of a chapel where a Father Wiśniewski kept bunks for Polish vagrants.

I fancied this idea of becoming a barman. But it's not easy to impress a pub-keeper if you don't have enough money to buy yourself a drink. Still, I did make my way to the Learmonth.

'Sir! Szczucki, Maurycy, intelligence officer Headquarters Squadron!'

'No need for all that. I remember you.'

He smiled. 'We missed you at Falaise. But you made up for it in the Netherlands. Didn't you go back to Poland afterwards? Into big trouble, so I've heard?'

'Yes, sir.'

'Was it worth it? Going back?'

'No, and yet I don't regret it.'

His smile broadened as he noticed my embarrassment at ordering a drink from him. But he measured out a whisky in silence and set it on the bar, and when I reached into my pocket made a little dismissive flick of his hand. As I set the glass to my lips, a big man in a British Railways donkey jacket stamped to attention beside me.

'Sir! Krotowski, Jacek, Corporal, 24th Uhlans!'

'No need for all that, corporal. I remember you...'

The Colonel and I sat in a corner of the empty restaurant while the tables were being laid. I admired the sprightly nudes traced on the green walls. One of the waitresses timidly brought the Colonel a glass of black tea in a silver holder. He didn't thank her but lit a cigarette, cocked in his old way.

'I told you to make for Canada, didn't I? But you went back to Poland instead. And you from the Borderlands, too. What the hell were you thinking of?'

'Well, there were ugly, complicated reasons why I had to get out of Britain. You knew a bit about them. But even in the war – can you understand this, Colonel? – I never lost a feeling that it would be wrong not to stand on that soil of ours again. Even after Yalta, even in that unfree Poland.'

'Wrong? Are we all wrong, these hundreds of thousands of us living stateless in the West? Poland is where Poles are.'

'Yes but, Colonel, that means that our *ojczyzna* isn't just a country. It's a duty. A duty that hurts, but it's for life and we can't turn our backs on it wherever we are. I am glad to be here again, but I also did right in going back.'

'Szczucki, I cannot allow you to tell me about duty and patriotism.'

A short man with red curly hair came to the table. 'Who's your pal, Marek?'

The Colonel, after taking a heavy breath, introduced us.

'This is Mr Ross, the owner. My employer, so to say.'

'Another Pole? Jolly good. Wanting a job, I'd guess.'

I explained that I had to go back to Greenock, where a friend was putting me up.

'I've got a boat there, waiting on an overhaul. Know anything about engines?'

'Tank engines?'

'Well, one diesel's much like another – just a matter of size, really. My man down there needs help. Say Donald sent you.'

The Colonel rose to his feet when I left. But he did not shake my hand.

When the first letter arrived from Warsaw, Mrs Melville had telephoned Jackie. 'You'll never guess . . .'

Jackie took the call in her Glasgow office. The new School of Pelagic Studies was a concrete bunker, halfway down the slope between the university and Byres Road. 'See, Grannie, I've a lecture to give later this morning and then a student wanting her grant application checked. Aye, busy-busy! But I'll look in on the way home.'

She parked the little Ford in Union Street and ran up the steps. (That key, into that door... never done without telling memory to crouch and cover its eyes.) Inside, the greenish scent of gas still clung to the walls, years after the electricity had been wired in, and today everything was darker than usual – the dead bulb in the hall still not replaced. If only there was somebody younger to stay with Mrs M.

They took the letter into the kitchen, where the light was better. 'I'll send him the last address I have for Helen. But he's wanting to come here, back to Scotland. And he needs some sort of written invitation from us, before he can get a passport and a British visa.'

'I can do that, Grannie. Better coming from me, with Assistant Lecturer across the top and a big rubber stamp from the Department.'

'Well, but do we really... after all that time? Bringing things up again? And then there's your mother.'

'Mum would say yes if she was here, I know she would. C'mon, Grannie, it's our Mike; see what he's been through.'

'Nevertheless, it's just for a short visit. That's all he's allowed if he gets a Polish passport, then away home again. That's assuming he means to go home at all.'

Jackie recognised him before he recognised her. Who else could it be, coming off the train dressed like that? A foreign-looking green raincoat, a brown beret, a rucksack and an old suitcase with straps.

'Is it really Jackie? This beautiful girl?' His hair was grey. And there was something odd about his face, like a tiny delay mechanism before he smiled.

'No girl, Mike. I'm a married lady, past my prime at twenty-six.'

'Married? Who on earth with?'

'He's called Malcolm. You'll like him fine: he builds boats, writes poems, has daft views about politics. We met when he was a diver and I was at St Columba's. Mike, d'ye know something?'

'Do I know what?'

'You still have a wee Scottish accent!'

He seemed to settle in. He kept very quiet, replaced light bulbs, dug the garden, and sat with Mrs Melville to watch news on the television set Jackie had rented for her. Every morning, he went for a walk along the Esplanade. Every weekday afternoon, he went down to the yacht basin and on Friday came back with money for working on Donald Ross's launch. He often got up in the middle of the night, sitting alone at the kitchen table with his cigarettes and writing in notebooks.

Jackie and Malcolm Greig lived near the seafront at Largs, in an apartment they had rented when she still worked at the Millport research station. One weekend, she picked up Mike in the Ford Pop and took him down to Largs where he and Malcolm marched along the beach talking, heads down against the wind.

'In the end, when we're rid of this crumbling Empire, it's got to be an independent Scottish republic!'

'What's kept you? Why didn't you go for it a hundred years ago?'

They liked each other, and kept laughing and shouting over lunch. Jackie watched Mike, who could almost have been Malcolm's father, and wondered where his quietness had gone. They were like two schoolboys on a coach outing.

When they were back in the lounge stirring coffees, Jackie asked: 'What's your plan, Mike? You're getting asylum in Britain, but could you ever go home again?'

'What do you mean, home?'

'I mean Poland.'

'This is home now. Scotland is home. Poland is my... you don't have a word for it in English. More complicated than home; not just a place but a duty, an obligation. Something you judge yourself by, wherever you are.'

'I wouldn't know about that. Just a place is all a country is.'

'You do so know about all that,' said Malcolm. 'Go on and tell him what you used to tell me: where do you feel at home?'

'Underwater,' said Jackie absently. She looked away from the two men, towards the sea in a gap between the houses opposite. 'Down there, I'm doing no harm to anybody. I trust it all, and it trusts me – the creatures, the wrecks, the boulders that never see the sun. Sure, I'll take specimens. But to me that feels like adding, not taking away. Am I making sense?'

'I wouldn't say you were making nonsense,' said Malcolm.

'Oh my, thanks! But listen: up here – yes, up here with you – there's not a moment I don't feel anxious. If I go out the door, that's me treading on some tiny wee beetle or slater. If there's a cyclist falls off on the ice in University Avenue, I should have warned him before he started downhill. If I read about a train crash in London, I'm thinking: what did I do wrong?'

Malcolm clutched fingers into his black hair. 'See, Mike, I married a mermaid. A Hans Andersen mermaid who walks on jaggy things when she's ashore. But when she talks this way, I think: what entitles her to carry the suffering world on her shoulders?'

Mike said: 'She turned a key in a lock once, and the world blew up.'

'She told me about that. But, ach, she's an educated woman, she should have put that bairn's fancy behind her. I've spent as much time on the seabed as you, Jackie, and that place is nobody's home unless you're a spootie-shell in a burrow. Your country and my country is Scotland. You're getting to be like your mother, who spends her life running away from it.'

'The world's bigger than wee Scotland, and it's full of horrors. Do you never feel you could have prevented things?'

'Jackie, everything that happens was bound to happen. You're a scientist, no Jesus Christ, nor God the bloody father either.'

'Ach, that's enough of it!' Jackie jumped up and disappeared into the kitchen, returning with a bottle. 'See what I found at the back of Grannie's cupboard. All over dust, and never opened. Away and get glasses, Malcolm.'

Mike saw the same bottle of cherry brandy which Eric Kent had once offered to a young, disdainful Helen. He said loudly: 'Exotic!' The other two gave him a puzzled glance and set about loosening the cork.

It was two years later. Jackie told Malcolm to stay out of this. Malcolm, now a bit old for the jeans he wore, had gone into building wooden beach-huts after his boatyard had failed.

He said he didn't want to know anyway. It was bad enough being told only the day before the wedding that he was marrying his old boss's daughter – that fat ginger sod. He wasn't going to keep any more of that bastard's secrets, even if he had been some sort of deserter in the war.

'That's your father's ain stinky problem, no mine and no yours either. Swim clear, mermaid!' He kissed Jackie hard, grabbed his safety helmet off the peg and left the house.

At Union Street, Mabel Melville said it was none of Mike's business; she didn't want some foreigner, not even Mike, poking his nose in. Come to that, she would thank everyone to let her settle this her own way. And that included Jackie. This was for a mother to deal with, not for some sort of family doon-the-watter outing.

Jackie said that of course Mike has to come too, will you just listen, Grannie? Of course he needs to be there, it's just screaming obvious he must have known about the strongbox and the message in it all along.

She didn't explain that she had put through a long telephone call from Largs to the Duchal Hydro at Kilmacolm. There, on the crest of a misty hill, the quiet Pole known as Major Mike presided over the temperance bar and the guest bookings for the golf course. 'I see. Yes, I did know. A box – was there a box with it?'

Jackie now told Mrs M that a daughter had as good a right to confront her father as a mother. Anyway, how did Grannie propose to get herself to Faslane without a car?

They wondered what to do about Helen in Canada. 'She's about the last person we need. And she'd never keep her mouth shut.'

'She's got a right to know, Grannie. Well, she may even know about it already. And she does so know how to keep secrets.'

There was no key with it, the man had said. His clothes fairly reeked of cigarettes. With no key, he had never got round to forcing the lock and it dropped out of mind. Then it was just last month he was clearing out the howff on the back green and there was this box, see it's like a wee strongbox from the bank.

Mrs Melville said she couldn't imagine what all this had to do with her. She had kept the man standing in the kitchen, clutching his stained cloth bunnet in one hand and the box in the other.

'See, I took a wrench to it. It came away easy, and there was thon paper, the water didnae dae it any good but I could read just the end of it. And one of the names – I thought surely is that not the name of the laddie from Union Street wha got killed. Johnston Melville. Am I no right?'

Mrs Melville took the sheet of paper and read it carefully, twice. Then she looked up. The man backed away from her. He explained that he had found the box in the *Fronsac* wreck, many years back. He was working on the salvage team for Alex Ketling. 'Him that has the Faslane shipbreaking yard.

Him that's convener of the Development Agency and up for a Parliament seat.'

'Does he know you took this?'

'Mr Ketling? Ach, no. He wouldnae bother with a wee thing like that.'

Mrs Melville asked what else he had stolen. The man said that folk like her aye thought the worst of people. Mrs Melville gave him one minute to answer before she called the police.

'It's never stealing, it's the custom. It was another lad took most of the binoculars; I had only the one pair, beauties from a U-boat. Okay, two silver cigarette boxes in the wardroom, French coins. A few gold ones, right enough. But that's the custom, it's aye been.'

He had thought a mother would be glad to have a message from the dead, the man went on. In a manner of speaking, was he not bringing her words from a Loved One on the Other Side? He found himself outside on the steps, holding a ten-shilling note. 'Ya auld bitch ya.'

Alone, she fetched a box of matches from the stove and struck one. She lifted the letter with her other hand, and hesitated.

The document, typed, was water-stained but still just readable. 'We, the undersigned, declare that in the interests of European peace and Western civilisation we are taking a symbolic action against this war, by disabling a torpedo tube on this warship. It is not too late to end this pointless aggression against Germany and its farsighted, peace-loving Leader, which can only benefit the Jewish–Bolshevik world conspiracy which . . .'

The match burned Mrs Melville's fingers. She shook it out and put the letter down again. She went to the telephone instead.

Mr Ketling was away in Italy at a conference on the Law of the Sea. But the secretary could offer Mrs Melville a short appointment with him on Tuesday week, eleven thirty. She was sorry but it would need to be down at the yard at Faslane, not at the Glasgow office.

This left Union Street with time for arguments. Jackie wasn't allowed to take the letter away, but she could remember it accurately enough to mail a version to Canada.

'Jackie, just put it on the fire,' said Helen on the phone from Toronto. Her voice warbled with distance, as if she was talking through a tin can of water. 'No good will come of it.'

'Did you know, then?'

'Sure, he was in some daft Fascist thing when I first met him. I mind telling him to stick to the BB – the Boys' Brigade – and that's the last I heard of it.'

'But how did you not say something? How did you never tell me?'

'How was I to know he'd write this stuff years later, and him a father and a reserve officer? The other guy must have put it in his head. He's no very bright, your dad.'

'He rates as pretty bright these days. Big shot in Scottish industry, great at his job.'

'So let him get on with it.'

'But the other man – Mike says he saw this in a secret report – the other fellow told the French that it was Dad who went on and made the torpedo launch itself. So he's a mass murderer. So he needs to face up to it.'

'Daughter mine, you're awful young yet! Men don't face up to things like that. Aye leaving the lavvy seat up – you'll get an apology there, though it'll count against you. But assisting the enemy in time of war – he'll just tell you to away and boil your heid. You cannae prove a thing, anyhow. Burn the letter – I'm having nothing to do with this, and no more should you.'

'We're going to take him the letter next week and ask him if he did it. Mum, you should be there.'

'Och for God's sake! Well, off you go and make bad worse, but I'm taking Hughie to the CNE – the Canadian National Exhibition. We'll eat Beaver Tail pastries and see all the new gadgets. Could you not get your head out of the deep sea and look to the future?'

'My God!' said Jackie. 'Oh my God, see that!'

She brought the car to a halt at the side of the road. They had turned the high corner before Faslane, and the length of the Gare Loch lay open below them.

Down there, in line ahead, lay the empty battleships of the Royal Navy. Their greatness seemed to fill the fjord. Their black masts, encrusted with aerials and radar discs, reached up towards the pines on the slopes above them. No smoke blurred the craters of their funnels; no ensigns, white or signal-coloured, flew from their bare flagstaffs. The buoys to which the dead ships were chained were already bright with rust.

Jackie turned the engine off. Mrs Melville said she'd stay in the car. But Jackie and Mike climbed out and walked to the edge of the road, to a bank where they could see out over the frost-yellowed grass, the red bracken, the green tips of the pines below.

Mike said: 'They are waiting for your father.'

'Waiting for the breaker's yard. Yes.'

She shaded her eyes with a gloved hand. 'I remember these ships in the war. Do you not remember them? We could see them from the windows.'

'What were their names?'

'That's the *Duke of York*. How could I not know her, when I was looking each one up in *Jane's Fighting Ships*? She sank the *Scharnhorst*, she took Churchill to America. And the next ahead, she'll be *Anson*: the Arctic convoys to Russia, the Sicily landings. And the far one: hard to see, but I think it'll be the *Howe*. Displacement forty-two thousand tons, ten fourteen-inch guns in three turrets – see, it's all in my head yet.'

'Poor Britain. No more Great. A quiet little island with no battleships.'

'They were like the hills of home. And now they just sink down into wee piles of rust.'

Jackie rubbed her hands together. Her lips moved, as if she were counting the fleet below. Then she said: 'If that's the *Howe*, she gave me a moment. We got a day off school. They took us in a coach up to Erskine; we were to watch her come down the Clyde after her launch at Govan. The biggest thing I ever saw in my life, towering up there with the earth shaking as she passed. Crowds lining both sides of the river; I mind them jumping back as the water came up over the bank. Our own big ship, going out to the war.'

'Not death or glory. More like death of glory.'

'Don't you sneer, Mike. You're like Malcolm, saying: "Navy scrapped, Empire on its way to the breakers, Queen and her United Kingdom next for the hammer". He's happy. I'm sorry for it.'

The car tooted. 'Grannie's getting cold. C'mon, let's get this dirty business done.'

'He's saying he'll only see his mother. He's saying he'll not come ashore till the other two of you have left. Oh dear, I'm awful sorry about this. But Mr Ketling is just absolutely definite.'

The secretary in the quayside office chewed her pencil and glanced at one face after another.

'Where is he?'

'He's on board with the surveyors. No, where are you going, sir, no . . .'

Mike went out of the hut, slamming its flimsy door, and crossed the quay. The black carcase of a cruiser rose above him, with a gangway leading into its innards.

It was dark and chill in there. Mike stumbled down steel corridors until he saw the gleam of an inspection lamp, slung at the top of a hatchway stair. The noise of drilling and hammering was everywhere. He limped up the steps, now hearing voices, and pushed a door. In the captain's cabin, warm and full of light, the group standing round a table looked up at him.

How big this man had become, how small his features looked on the front of this red-fringed boulder of a head! As the surveyors rolled up their plans and backed out of the cabin, slight Maurycy Szczucki and massive Alexander Ketling, once Johnston Melville, stood facing one another across the table.

'For fuck's sake! Where did you spring from? You're one guy I was hoping I'd never see again.'

'Here's something else you hoped you'd never see again.'

Mr Ketling took the box, opened it, fingered but didn't read the paper. He nodded and nodded and a small grin appeared.

'Thank you. For the stolen property. You can go now, Mike.'

'Not before we have a talk, Johnston. You, your mother, your daughter Jackie and me.'

'Talk, who's talking? The guy who hid a deserter in wartime? The guy who faked a man's death so he could marry his wife? See, I could call the police and they'd be lifting you off your feet in twenty minutes from now. Or maybe a wee job for you? There's a dozen Poles in the yard with no English and no papers, getting a few bob for digging holes and living in a Nissen hut. Aye, just right for you.'

'Easy, Johnston. Nobody wants money. Just talk to us.'

'Off this ship. Out my yard. Five minutes, and I'm counting.'

'Johnston, you're making this hard. The papers say you are after the Labour nomination for where? Glasgow something?'

'Glasgow-Molendinar. Do I guess what you are saying next?'

'You do so. Who's next on the Molendinar list when you go on trial for treason and murder, Johnston?'

'Stop calling me that, fuck's sake, Mike. Next runner is a daft Fifer woman, raving Communist till two years ago. Why?'

'Her name?'

'What the hell's it to you? Councillor Fowler. She sings at the selection meetings. Ach, she's a joke.'

'Well! A joke to you, but to me she's a very old friend who might just get an interesting letter.'

There was a silence. Mr Ketling sat down. He took a heavy

silver propelling pencil out of his pocket and rolled it back and forth on the table. He frowned.

'I saved your life, Johnston. I gave you your name. Talk to us.'

He didn't look up. Examining the silver pencil closely, he muttered: 'Where's Kellerman?'

'Germany, so I'm told. When the French released him, he ran to West Germany where they don't ask questions. We won't hear of him again.'

'Tell my mother and Jackie I'll have a word with them. No with you.'

'Not without me. I know much more than they do.'

'There's nothing to know. It's all fuckan fairy tales, half a lifetime past.'

'Nothing? Twenty-eight young men, Johnston. Some blown to pieces: that's the lucky ones. Twenty-one trapped below in the mess deck. The fire came towards them. They could get heads or arms out of the portholes, no more. The fire kept coming. The naval surgeon was hanging over the side jagging morphine into those arms till the deck grew red-hot under him. The lads in the rescue boats were passing razor blades up to those clawing hands. The screaming went on a long time, Johnston, till the ship began to sink. Folk who were there still hear it. Nothing to know?'

The silver pencil flew through the air, aimed like a big dart. Mike moved his head and it struck his neck, leaving a scratch. He let it lie where it had fallen on the floor.

'Right then. Have your damned way. Bring them over.'

The small metal box lay on the table top between them.

When the grey-haired man reached out to take it back, the bald man's shoulders jerked. But then he controlled his hands and sat back slowly in his chair.

Mike helped Mrs Melville across the chains and timbers scattered on the quayside. They waited for a boiler-suited man and a boy edging down the sloping gangway from the cruiser's hull, bearing a handsome mahogany desk between them. There was a raw red split where it had been wrenched from a cabin wall.

'I believe we've met,' said Mabel Melville, more to Jackie than to the man. He gave her a vile glance, hitched the desk higher on his hands and lurched on, leaving a soaked-Woodbine reek behind him.

'See the wee maggot beasties, in and out of a dead creature.'

In the cabin, the two women found chairs and sat, while the two men stood. Mike held the box lightly in front of him.

'Some family gathering! What way have you not brought Helen too? Are we waiting on the photographer?'

'Behave yourself, Johnston. I am your mother. I have spent all these years protecting you, hiding you, lying for you to my best friends, to say nothing of the police. And I have believed in you. When others did not. I told them that it was not possible that my son, my only child, would act against his own King and country in time of war. That he would kill Allied sailors for the sake of Adolf Hitler. But now...'

'I am not taking this. Not from you, Mother, not from this

lying wee tink of a Polack that's sucking all our blood. What happened...'

Mrs Melville surged out of her chair. She stood in front of her son for a moment, frowning. Then, suddenly, she slapped him hard across the mouth. The others were too astonished to move. In a hoarse voice, she said: 'Strange, but I cannae hear a word you're saying. That dinging hammer on the deck is stopping my ears.'

He gaped at her, mouth sagging open. Then he went out. There was shouting, then silence. When he returned to the cabin, the look of bewilderment was still there. He blew his nose untidily.

'A fool I was, an idiot right enough. Young folk join things. They aye will. But never a murderer. No. An accident, I mind telling Mike all the years ago it was an accident. That daft French sailor gave the safety switch a dunt, and who was to know...?'

'You were to know. Yes, you.' The Polish accent was suddenly stronger. 'Not one switch but three. Somebody must have released all switches, one after the other, in correct order. And the launching charge: it should not have been in the tube while in harbour. But it was. And there was indicator light. To show you that charge was in tube. You knew, not possible you didn't know.'

Jackie had her hands clapped to her cheeks. The big man who was her father said in a new, quiet voice: 'So, the new torpedo expert? Was that your fat friend in the French navy learning you? Or is that you filling jotters with notes at the Greenock Library?'

'I have studied. Yes, I have read manuals.'

'Then, my wee Polish pal, I'll tell you what you didn't find in the manuals. *Fronsac* had two launch systems, not one. In the French navy, only a pair of ships was fitted that way. The primary system was compressed air. And it was only if that didnae work that you went over to the explosive, the propellant charge. I'd call it a bauchly French contraption, just designed to misfire. And misfire by accident is what it did.'

Jackie stood up suddenly. She had put on her spectacles and held herself very straight.

'Correct me if I'm wrong. The secondary system couldn't override the primary system. See what that means? It means the charge couldn't be fired unless the compressed air had already been tried and failed. So you must have tried, and you kept on trying. Till you found a system that did so fire.'

Nobody spoke.

Jackie said: 'I'm right, am I no? No accident. No mistake, and it's out of your own mouth, so it is.'

There was a knocking sound. Jackie had turned very red; she was grasping her chair and hammering it on the floor as she began to shout: 'Jesus Christ, Father, will ye say something to me? Will you tell me I'm wrong? Why did you, how could you? All those young French boys, the flames, what were you thinking of? Who are you?'

Mabel went to hold her granddaughter. Jackie shook her off. The big man sat at the table gazing at her as she spoke.

'I used to think it was my fault. When I was a wean, there I was thinking I had killed you and it was my punishment. And then when you ran away and hid and Grannie fed you like a hunted man, like Prince Charlie, I prayed for you. I dreamed of you. But now . . . all you do is destroy ships, and that poor French ship was just the first. I don't know you. Get away from me!'

He rose very slowly, even painfully, so that Mike was not prepared for the sudden hand which snatched the box. Ketling strode to the other end of the cabin, and when he turned to come back, they saw that he had used a lighter to ignite the faded paper. He dropped it across an ashtray. The flame spread round the letter's fringes, jumped so that they all felt its heat for a moment, then crawled into the centre. The black ashes convulsed before they went to smoke.

'I copied it out,' said Jackie.

'Is that so? My own wee girl, the one I missed so. And – right enough – I dreamed of you too all those years. Well, now that you're such a big clever lassie, you can stick your copy up your fud.'

He went to a scuttle, unscrewed the pane and pushed the little strongbox through it. They all heard the splash.

'Away with you all! I've work to do. I've a survey to finish, a business to run for God's sake. Will yees all just fuck off, pardon me, Mother. Away and die of cancer, the pack of ye.'

Mabel and her son looked at one another. She said: 'From now on, I'll request you to keep away from me.' Jackie, shaking and wiping silent tears off her face, helped her down the hatchway stair. That left one.

'Ya pathetic auld fuck, ya troublemaker, naebody wants ye here. What for d'ye not get back to yer ain dirty wee home country?'

'My home is any place where people tell the truth. Where's yours?'

I am too old now to walk up the Lyle Hill on my own. Not just the leg, where a few seeds of American metal still hide. More the heart, a tightening hand around my chest when I tackle a slope.

But Malcolm and Jackie came round last Sunday and took me up there in the car. I'm still at Union Street. It wasn't what I had intended when the hydro closed at Kilmacolm. I had recognised that as a chance to escape, perhaps for the last time.

In those days I feared turning into one more stone in this west Scotland landscape, with its reproachful streets and its red willow-herb deserts where fabrication halls and furnaces once stood. I thought of moving to Edinburgh, where there was a job as legal adviser to the Polish community. Or to Australia? Argentina? But I went back to Greenock, not meaning to stay, and I fell into the habit of caring for Mrs M.

She was weaker than at first she seemed, and growing wandered. She couldn't be trusted with the stove or the hot water in the kettle, and she often decided I was Eric. Yes, Eric

Kent, who used to talk to her about Brahms and Shakespeare and – but I never heard this at the time – sing *Lieder* with her at the piano.

When Mabel Melville died, the house passed to Jackie and she has allowed me to stay on. There's a lodger upstairs, a young marine biologist fellow from the department in Glasgow where Jackie's the professor. She'll be coming up for retiral pretty soon.

Last Sunday, on the Lyle Hill, it was a cold, clear afternoon. The Free French naval memorial on the brow of the hill has become a famous landmark: an anchor taller than a man, with its shank and stock forming a Cross of Lorraine. Below it, words of grief are cut in stone for the French seamen lost in the Atlantic war.

I hope the words are cut for the men of the *Fronsac*, too. Did war kill them, or carelessness, or accident, or one man's malignance? Sometimes, when I am on the hill, I see the anchor and the sky between its flukes forming the skull and tusks of a great boar's head. A war-beast carved into the grey clouds.

Jackie and Malcolm and I looked towards the Argyll hills across miles of empty estuary. The harbour where the destroyers whooped and thrashed up tawny foam, the Tail of the Bank where the battle fleets anchored, are quiet open water now. On the far shore, there's no black, broken thing marking the tide.

I was out on that water not long after the day at Faslane. Completing something. When I went back to the crematorium in Glasgow, they were kind but embarrassed. Did nobody explain to you? Well, it was wartime. Were you away in the army? They should have advised you that unclaimed ashes, after a certain interval . . .

Anyhow, they said, there was a new, very nice and reverent procedure now. Disposal by boat. The next occasion would be in a month's time. Be at Yorkhill Quay at such and such an hour.

I still had Wisia's letter. 'Corpse to be buried in a free Poland... if possible in City of Lwów after Bolsheviks removed...' But she had no corpse to bury; Poland was not free; her city was now in a different, forbidden nation.

The little rucksack with her possessions and the gold earring – I still had that. Helen brought it back with her from Poland while I was in prison, and before she went on to Canada with Hughie she left it with Jackie. 'Ach, he'll be along for it.' I imagined her saying that.

At Yorkhill Quay in the middle of Glasgow, a launch was waiting with its engine running. A 'lone piper' was trying to make his lament heard over the traffic, and a trim blonde lady in woolly gloves (it was a cold day) was lowering boxes of ashes into the launch with a pulley. Each little casket was individually wrapped in purple velvet and topped with a few rose petals.

There were thirty-five of them. There was no way to tell which was Wisia's. As the few spectators on the quay turned wordlessly away, I asked if I was allowed to go on board and 'witness the disposal'.

'That's fine, son,' said the blonde lady. 'You'll be getting a trip doon the watter with your loved one, for free.'

I liked her. I was glad that she talked and joked with me on the long voyage, all the way down to where the Clyde broadens out into the Firth. Greenock and its shipyard cranes lay beside us when the launch slowed and two men in donkey jackets began to carry the caskets to the stern.

The piper rose to his feet once more and blew. The men had their backs to me as they opened each box and, with a trowel, gently scooped the ashes into the river. At each cast of the trowel, a white mist spiralled up from the water and vanished downwind.

I walked away to the bows and faced the high hills. This landscape, this water, was so familiar to me now – the smoky towns, the Firth between mountains, a car ferry ploughing across towards Dunoon. But nothing here reminded me of Wisia. What did she have to do with the gravelly grey powder dissolving in our wake?

In my pocket I had brought the medallion of St Thérèse, the fountain pen and the single gold earring. I said some words, kissed them and slipped the medal and the pen over the side. But the earring stayed in my hand.

I'll be buried with it. So that will be Wisia's funeral, too, who never had a proper one and had nobody alive but me to care about her. I'll not mind dying so much if I know somebody will put it in my coffin. Near my lips.

Maybe Jackie will do it. Helen wouldn't, even if she came back to see me off. But only a woman would, and I couldn't imagine any other women I used to know who might be around. And I needed somebody around. In the months after giving Wisia's ashes to the sea, I had tried to find a somebody.

After that encounter at Faslane, we had driven away in silence. We headed back to Greenock the way we had come, crossing the Clyde by the old Erskine ferry. As the ferry's engine thumped and its chains rumbled, Jackie climbed out of the car and stood beside me.

'I'm done with this business,' she said. 'I'm not seeing him ever again. It's hurting me more than it's hurting him. And Grannie's hurting, too, you can see the bad colour she's taken.'

'But he knows you know.'

'So what will he do?'

'He's damaged goods now, can you not see that?'

The following week, the *Glasgow Herald* reported that Mr Alexander Ketling of Scotbreaker Metals had withdrawn his nomination for a Labour seat in Parliament. Pressures of work were cited. Six months later, a note in the business pages wished 'Big Alex' Ketling, late of Scotbreaker, good luck with his new shipyard venture in Vancouver Sound.

Miss Isabella Fowler sang her way into adoption at a happy meeting in Molendinar High School, and at the by-election two months later won the seat with a fat majority. When I heard that Tibbie MP was to speak at the Polish Combatants club in Molendinar, I ironed my best jacket and tie and went to Glasgow. But my train was late, and she was latching her guitar back into its case when I found her.

'Why I left the Party? It was Hungary that did it for me. Tanks against the workers' councils? The Party line – no way could I thole that. My God, Lenin would be birling in his tomb!'

Tibbie was glowing. Westminster was just a daft big boys' club, she told me. 'I need Robbie to hold me to the real world.'

Robbie? 'Aye, how d'ye not know Robbie Aitken? Convener

of shop stewards at Fairfields? Everybody kens Robbie. Left the Party same time as me. We'll be married in the spring.'

'You should have married me.'

Tibbie began to laugh; she grabbed my arm and shook me tenderly.

'No chance, Mike. You're lovely. You're just about the oldest friend I have left, from the war days and Balbrudie. But no the marrying kind. If you had ever asked, I would have said like we say in Fife: "Away tae Freuchie and fry mice!"'

She put on her coat.

'Get fixed up, Mike. Get yourself a home of your own, anywhere in the world, before it's too late. And somebody to bide in wi'ye.'

Tibbie's laugh was warm, an old tune. Helen's had always been a discord. It hadn't changed when she walked into the kitchen at Union Street two years later, as usual without telling anyone she was coming, and startled me into knocking my chair over.

She kept laughing as she helped me pick the chair up and stared around the room. 'So my key still works. And the old cooker's there, but did you never hear of a fitted kitchen? And no icebox, in the 1960s? Ach, for God's sake!'

She didn't give me time to reflect that we hadn't seen each other for ten years. My tall, illegal wife. She hugged me rapidly, pleasantly, then sat down across the table and studied me.

She must be fiftyish. I had long stopped writing to her, because she had stopped answering. Spectacles now on those narrow blue eyes watching me; I didn't care for their sparkly frame. That hair: not short and yellow any more but gold-tinted, down round her ears. Only a faint crease on her white neck.

'Why am I here? My old man. The flight was late into Prestwick and, well, he was in a coma by the time I got to the Infirmary. I sat with him, but he never spoke. Never woke.'

'Why did you not let me meet him?'

'Mike, we weren't close. He was hard on me and whatever I did. When I married Johnston, he took a scunner at him and we barely spoke. But you did so meet him, once.'

'How? When?'

'He saw you in the Auchmar Vaults. A night or so after the explosion. I'd talked about you, so he knew you by the Polish uniform. He was that shaken up by what he saw and heard with the rescue boats, like I never saw him. That's why he broke his auld rule against the bevvy and went for a dram at the Vaults.'

'Big man with white hair?'

'That was him. He told me after that he didn't care for the look of you. A wee foreigner in that pantomime officer get-up with the fancy boots, that was how he put it. He thought you had no business to stand there listening.'

'I'll never forgot what he said.'

Then I began to tell her about our day at Faslane and what had been said by Jackie and by Johnston, and how it ended. But I soon saw that she was losing interest. Once I could always hold her fascinated with a story, make her laugh. Now she smiled and interrupted. Her voice turned more Canadian: 'That was one king-size waste of time! I warned daughter dear, but no, she knew better. C'mon, Mike, fix me an old-time cup of tea.'

We talked. She told me about Hughie, at college studying something called cybernetics. She told me about managing her own successful hotel staff agency; I told her, reluctantly, that I sometimes did shifts as barman at the Tontine.

'But that's great,' she said seriously. 'You always had that barman's look, that tell-me-your-troubles face on you.' No, I told her, that's for American movies. This is Scotland. Those homeless foreign officers thirsting for gin and sympathy are long gone, and Greenock barmen don't hear confessions. 'It's councillors and lawyers and dentists at the Tontine now. They don't waste drinking time on me.'

'You're not old yet, Mike. Are you going to spend the rest of your life here on Union Street? Where's home for you now?'

'I have a British passport. For many years.'

'Answer me! Was it not you and I sat at this same table, all those years ago, and played words for tears? Home? You couldn't take it! You said you never needed a home.'

'Helen, I am at home in Scotland.'

'So what's Poland to you now? When we went there – the big mistake of my life – I could see you never felt: "Here I am in my own right country". And yet you knew you belonged there. I could see you trying to do what you thought you needed to do. Like trying to tell a father: "Okay, I swear I'll always be your loving son but can I go now?"'

She put her cup down, and reached across to touch my hand.

'I'm taking you back to Canada with me, Mike. If you don't like Toronto, you don't need to stay. But I'm here for four days: the funeral, then a day with Jackie and Malcolm, then the plane. I'll buy your ticket, no bother. So Prestwick! Be there at half past nine Saturday night. I'll be waiting on you at Departures.'

When I reached Prestwick that Saturday, I couldn't see her. I stood with my passport and my suitcase at Departures for a long time, peering at the queues shuffling past to the gates. The ticket desk didn't have anything for me. It became ten o'clock, then half past. The Toronto flight was called, then final called.

I rang Jackie. 'Mum? No, she went back on Friday. Aw heck, poor Mike: did you go all the way to Prestwick to see her off and get the wrong night?'

A week before Christmas, a heavy airmailed package arrived at Union Street. The postie had to help me carry it into the kitchen. It contained a block of maple sugar, a flask of maple syrup, cans of salmon caviar and Saskatoon berries and a half-bottle of Newfoundland Screech rum. Posted from Hamilton, Ontario. There was no letter with it.

In the years that followed I have often stayed with Tadek and Margaret at Balbrudie. It became a custom to have dear old Mike as guest for Christmas and Hogmanay. Every year, Tadek announces plans to turn the castle into a hotel. Every year, my breath blows a small frost-fog in the hall and I notice more damp strands of wallpaper hanging from dark corners.

We sit round big fires, we play cards with Margaret's young nephews and nieces who come over from an estate the other side of Forfar; we go for the slow walks that I can still manage in my late seventies. Tadek proudly shows me his forestry, and his vegetable business in the old walled garden.

How rarely we talk Polish these days, even when we are alone together! But one winter was different. They had taken me with them to their converted farmhouse in southern France, meaning to go on into the Alps and ski. I persuaded them to visit the address which Luc le Gallois had given me forty years before.

We found the small town near the Durance river, and a sharp-eyed lady in black who opened the door turned out to be his daughter, Françoise. I wouldn't have known her again. But, getting over her astonishment, she began to talk happily about Jackie and Union Street.

And the Commandant? She spread her hands. Then she showed me the small room which had been his study: his papers still on the desk, held down by a heavy, empty ashtray. On the wall facing his chair, there hung a long framed photograph showing *Fronsac* at full steam ahead, across a background of summery Mediterranean mountains. As I had feared, the Commandant had gone to his family tomb a few years before. So much I still wanted to ask him, to tell him. But after offering my grief to Françoise, I asked if she had heard of a certain Jean-Marie Guennec.

'Ah, ah! Him! He had come here to ask Papa to be a witness for him at his trial after the war. But when Papa saw who it was, he shut the door in his face. Not a word: just closing the door. And then – well! He ran to Algeria. When the rebellion began, he interrogated prisoners in the prefecture at Blida. But one day no Guennec, just an empty car with blood on the front seat.

Rouge-Midi, the Communist rag, wrote a story about it. How long ago that seems!'

Françoise made us stay to lunch. We were glad of the invitation; even in Provence, it was a bitter winter out of doors. Afterwards we set out to drive to Avignon, but police in white gloves were halting the traffic in the middle of the city.

Rhythmic shouts and chants in the boulevard, banners, a procession walking, stopping and walking under the bare plane trees. But the banners were red and white. I saw a girl in Kraków costume, holding up a cardboard white eagle with a crown. 'Liberty! Solidarity!'

Tadek and I went to the girl with the eagle. 'Martial law! Tanks on the streets!' The boys and girls around her, Polish students in a French crowd, all spoke at once about mass arrests, curfew, gunfire. As the parade began to move forward again, they called to us: 'Who are you?'

'We are Polish soldiers,' said Tadek.

At that, a young man with a blond pigtail turned back towards us and cried in a sonorous voice: '*Bóg! Honor! Ojczyzna!* God, Honour, Fatherland!' There was clapping. They were clapping for Tadek and me.

That night, in the cottage kitchen we quarrelled in our own language. Margaret watched us, understanding most of what we were saying but not why we were saying it.

Tadek was shouting: 'Can't you see that this is victory, not defeat? To declare war on the whole Polish people – terminal madness! The regime tries to murder Poland, which means it's committing suicide.'

'And then what sort of Poland, Tadek? Back to God, Honour,

Fatherland? If that is going to be the programme, then we have learned nothing.'

'Maurycy, you are hopeless: you can't admit it, but you are still thinking like some kind of sentimental Marxist. Listen, when this Communist corpse rolls off us in a few years, we have to return to our true roots. We have to take back Poland!'

We ended up glaring, banging the table. But next day, when they dropped me at the railway station on their way to the snow slopes, Tadek and I embraced as tightly as ever.

A year later, the Pope came to Scotland. Our Polish Pope – how could I not feel conceited about him, in spite of all my unbeliefs? How could I not go to see him at Bellahouston Park, with all Scotland's Catholics and all Scotland's Poles?

I was close when he came through the crowd. A woman was holding up a tiny girl in red-white folk dress. He stopped, and asked the child in our language: '*Gdzie Polska?* Where is Poland?'

She looked back at him bewildered. The Pope took her small fist, pressed it against her heart and said: 'Poland is here.'

I was furious to find my eyes filled with tears. Why? Such cheap sentimentality! Such shameless conflation of soul with a stretch of land, such an inoculation of that old God–Fatherland serum into the blood of a child!

But then I remembered that I had done the same to Jackie when she was not much older than this little girl. 'Poland, where is Poland?' Except that, back then, I had thumped her fist against my own chest: '*Polska tu!* Poland is here!'

'Home: a sort of honour, not a building site…' An English poet wrote that. Honour – but not God, not Fatherland? So if I have lived honourably, then I have been at home all the time without knowing it.

I am surprised to find that now, writing these last lines, I am in my eighties. And, looking back, I am not sure about the adverb to describe how I have lived. Honourably? Irresponsibly? Our Polish theologians now think that Descartes was wrong. It is not that I think, therefore I am. It is that I recognise the reality of another person, therefore I am.

Wisia, Tibbie, Tadek, many others but above all Helen? I don't think I have recognised or accepted the full humanity of any of them properly. Not sufficiently to be certain of my own existence.

I want to stop this writing now. The days and months are passing with such velocity; the slope to my end is steepening. Great and small events pass like posters glimpsed on a down escalator. Events? For example, Poland threw off Communism and returned to democracy only a few months ago.

Once, that news would have sent me running to the travel agency. To be with the crowds on the streets, to join the singing. But today I don't think about 'the nation'. Instead I think about a small, very important duty which I can now fulfil.

My Colonel died five years ago. When the Apéritif restaurant closed, he had moved to London to work as a military archivist for the Sikorski Institute. After his death, his Scottish widow told me that, in his will, he had asked that Major Szczucki –

'my loyal comrade' – should transport his ashes back for burial 'in a free Poland'.

I don't know why he chose me. Perhaps he thought I had nothing better to do. More likely, that I needed to remember how to obey orders.

So I will go to the travel agency, in my own time. It seems that it's already a common experience on flights to Poland to find yourself sitting beside an old gentleman with an urn of ashes on his lap.

It turns out that the Colonel still has relatives over there. His nephews will meet me at the airport with a car. They live in a town on what is now the eastern frontier of Poland, which is about as close as you can get these days to that city which was dear to me and Wisia. I gather that the funeral will be a big affair: a bishop at the church, speeches at the town hall, an escort of soldiers with fixed bayonets, Boy Scouts and Girl Guides lining the streets, the firemen's band playing: 'We of the First Brigade...'

Fine! But I wouldn't want anything like that for myself, even if I had a home town to go to. My life has been shaped by these Scottish waters, and by what happened to a ship here, and by what the fate of that ship did to a group of men and women who might otherwise have lived very differently.

Home. I close my eyes and I see that glass of tea steaming gently in its saucer, placed on the polished table by someone who must have loved me. I open my eyes and I see this dark, stony country of Scotland which has been kind to me. A poor, hard country but a good one, deserving to live in its own choice of freedom. A part of what I mean by home is here.

They say that wherever a Polish soldier is buried, his blood turns the soil into *polska ziemia* – Polish earth. That rhetoric is not for me. I ask for a privilege, not a miracle: that my ashes go into these cold waters until, sorted and delivered to the shore by many tides, they become part of Scottish earth. No more.

School of Pelagic Studies
University Avenue
GLASGOW G12 8QQ
November 6th, 1992.

DEAR MARIA,

I'm sure you remember how we had lunch at Howie's, when I was through in Edinburgh and you helped me track those fishery archives in the National Library.

I told you about this old Polish friend of mine, Major Szczucki, who stayed in Greenock and had been writing a long memoir, partly fiction based on fact, about wartime experiences in Scotland – his and mine. He was a sort of unofficial uncle to me. You said it was just the kind of material you were looking for, and did I think he might deposit it with the Library?

Well, I must confess I never got round to asking him. Is this what David Hume called 'the indolence of old age' setting in? Anyhow, much to my sorrow, 'Major Mike' as we called him has suddenly died.

He went to the funeral of a friend of his in Poland, although he was well into his eighties. They told us he knelt down to put a box of ashes into the grave and then couldn't get up again. He was wet through with the rain, and having chest pains when they got him back to his hotel, and they were trying to fix a hospital bed. But he set off by himself; somehow caught a train to Warsaw and then the plane. He left his bag behind in Departures, no label on it. Security told us there was nothing inside but a few nice old shirts.

When the flight was coming in to Glasgow over the Firth, he apparently undid his belt and stood up. The stewardess told him to sit down, but he was shouting something they couldn't understand in Polish and pointing down to the water below. They got him back into his seat. But when they had landed, he just 'didn't respond' as they say in hospitals. His heart, of course. Poor Mike. But I hope we all go as easily.

Malcolm and I took over. He didn't seem to own any possessions; at Union Street he lived like a backpacker. I found the memoir in the bookshelf in the kitchen, a row of spiral-back jotters.

I took a look. Maria, there's a lot of pretty shocking stuff, personal, as well as a record of wartime. Stuff I knew about, but don't ever want to go back to. Is there some form I could fill in saying it's not to be read for fifty years?

In the last pages, he seems not sure whether he wants buried or cremated. But he does mention a gold earring which was to go with him, and I found that. Anyway, we had him cremated and then Malcolm made a sort of sea-coffin out of an old metal biscuit-box. We wrapped the casket of ashes in chain to weight it, put it in the box and nailed the lid shut with copper nails.

The School's research vessel was setting off for Tarbert that week. So we travelled with it, and Malcolm put the box over the side into the deep water off Ardlamont Point, the open sea where the basking sharks used to gather. A few silver bubbles came up from under the lid as the box sank and was gone.

The earring was in my pocket. I held it tight for a moment. This tiny gold circle had journeyed from Poland to Kazakhstan to Persia to Palestine, then to Scotland and the battlefields of Normandy and after that Holland and Germany. Then Scotland again, then Poland again. And now to this final place which is no land but, to my mind, the source of all lands and all life.

Then I threw the earring into the sea. End of a story, but I will let you read it for yourself.

Yours affectionately, dear Maria, from your scholarly comrade,
JACKIE